JUDAH'S SCEPTER

AND THE SACRED STONE

D. A. BRITTAIN

First Edition Design Publishing

Sarasota, Florida USA

Judah's Scepter and the Sacred Stone

ISBN 978-1506-902-29-6 HC
ISBN 978-1506-902-30-2 PBK
ISBN 978-1506-902-31-9 EBOOK

LCCN 2016942727

July 2016

Published and Distributed by
First Edition Design Publishing, Inc.
P.O. Box 20217, Sarasota, FL 34276-3217
www.firsteditiondesignpublishing.com

Cover Design by Vanja Dimitrijevic

Author's Note: I have incorporated several word-for-word biblical quotations as part of the running text of this story, and thus they are not cited as references in most instances. For a complete list of the Scripture references I've used, please see "Appendix 2: Biblical References" at the end of this book. Thank you for your understanding.

Library of Congress Cataloging-in-Publication Data
Brittain, D. A.
Judah's Scepter and the Sacred Stone / written by D. A. Brittain.
p. cm.
ISBN 978-1506-902-30-2 pbk, 978-1506-902-31-9 digital

1. FICTION / Christian / General. 2. / Historical. 3. / Suspense.

J921

ACKNOWLEDGEMENTS

I want to thank my husband, Dennis, for all his love and support, which allowed me to pursue and fulfill my long-held dream. Much appreciation also goes to my mother, Aggie, and to all of my family and friends for cheering me on. To my sweet friend, Leah, whose love and friendship have been there through all the years, from the first to the last word written. No words can express my gratitude to her for being there for me when I shared the joy and the tears that came while writing this story. My heartfelt thanks go to the group, Hillsong UNITED, whose music became the soundtrack to my life as the words poured out of me and onto the page. Their songs continue to draw me closer to God. And to my editor, John David Kudrick. I will always be grateful for his friendship and the guiding hand that he offered to this first-time author throughout the many months of revisions and rewrites. I can't thank him enough for his sound advice and the professional skills he applied to enhance, smooth, and polish a very rough manuscript, helping turn it into a story that I am now pleased to present to you, the reader.

Every good and perfect gift is from above,

coming down from the Father of the heavenly lights,

who does not change like shifting shadows.

He chose to give us birth through the word of truth,

that we might be a kind of firstfruits of all he created.

–James 1:17-18

"I will not violate my covenant
or alter what my lips have uttered.
Once for all, I have sworn by my holiness—
and I will not lie to David—
that his line will continue forever
and his throne endure before me like the sun;
it will be established forever like the moon,
the faithful witness in the sky."

–Psalm 89:34-37

"Unless the fates have faithless grown,
And prophet's voice be vain,
Wherever is found the sacred stone,
The Wanderer's Race shall reign."

–Celtic Bard
(Translated by Sir Walter Scott)

Prologue

Scotland: Present day

The four men forged ahead, invisible in the heavy blanket of fog shrouding them and the castle that stood high above the sleeping town of Edinburgh. Sea-mist clung to hair and clothes as the men moved single file through the wet, winding streets. Their obscured figures soon crept past the guardhouse and then the long row of muzzle-loading cannons before they finally entered the upper ward, where the ascending cobblestone street led them into the castle's main square.

A soft patter of footsteps resonated for a moment, but then went silent near the east door of the Royal Palace. There, the first man in line drew a long, tarnished key from his pocket. Turning the key in the door lock, he listened for the *click* of its release before he pulled on the iron latch. The heavy wood door creaked and moaned as it opened.

The second man in line stepped into the narrow entryway and deactivated the alarm. With another key, he unlocked and opened the small interior door. While he and the first man waited outside, the last two men walked inside, crossed the threshold, and moved toward their goal.

The ancient crown room was nearly dark. The only light came from the mini bulbs illuminating the large case in the center of the room. Within that case, the Crown Jewels—the Honours of Scotland, the most treasured regalia in the land—rested in full display behind thick glass. Nestled in lush blue-velvet fabric sat the beautifully etched silver scepter and sword. A foot above them, on a gold-tasseled, red-velvet pillow, rested the solid-gold jeweled crown.

The two men moved to the back of the case, where they slipped their own keys into the locks embedded in the brass- and wood-framed door there. On a silent count of three, they each turned their keys, then watched the glass door swing slowly open. Reaching in, they lifted out the object they sought: a large, cracked block of sandstone.

They carried the battered stone outside and lowered it into a cushioned chest that had been brought to the door by the two men who awaited their return. After resetting the alarm and securing all the locks and doors, the four men hoisted the heavy chest. As they crossed the courtyard, five chimes rang out from the palace tower's clock—perfect timing thus far.

The finely bedecked commissioner of Scotland soon greeted the men as they carried the chest into the castle's Great Hall: "Thank you for bringing the stone here at this early hour," he said. "There is still much to be done before the ceremony begins." Then the commissioner paused and finally offered a wan smile. "It is a sad day for some of us to see the most ancient symbol of Scottish kingship leave the castle. I wonder if we will ever get it back."

By 9:00 a.m., dozens of distinguished guests had arrived in the castle's main square and entered the Great Hall to view the stone. Twenty-two inches long, thirteen inches wide, and eleven inches thick, the ancient artifact sat on a dais of red velvet in the center of the hall. Later, His Royal Highness William, the Duke of Cambridge, opened the formal transfer ceremony with a short speech soon followed by a twelve-gun salute fired from the castle.

At exactly 10:00 a.m., six bearers of the Royal Banner of Scotland—"The Lion Rampant"—walked in their bright red-and-gold uniforms ahead of the stone that now sat in its uniquely modified glass-roofed vehicle. The bulletproof Bentley inched along from the castle's upper, middle, and lower wards before it proceeded across the esplanade in public view, then down to the bottom of Castle Hill.

Large crowds lined the streets of Edinburgh. Many had waited hours; some had even camped out overnight. All sought to secure a good spot to watch the royal procession that began with fifty-five members of the Royal Scots Dragoon Guards, who received rousing cheers and applause as they played "Scotland the Brave" on bagpipes and drums while marching in their red tartan kilts in front of the stone's motorcade.

The morning was cold but sunny and bright for those who had turned out to see the pageantry. The British monarch's bodyguards, the Royal Company of Archers, walked behind the stone in their dark-green uniforms and peacock-feathered hats, followed by eighty members of His Majesty's Royal Marines Band, who kept up the revelry by playing a rousing melody.

The crowd's excitement swelled when they saw William and Kate, the Duke and Duchess of Cambridge. Cheers grew loud as they waved to the royal couple—as well as to a host of other nobility that included the Duchess of Kent, the Secretary of State for Scotland, the Lord Lyon King of Arms, the Lord High Constable of Scotland, and other members of royalty that followed in a procession of eight vehicles.

The motorcade stopped when it reached the front of St. Giles' Cathedral. Members of British royalty were first to walk into the magnificent house of worship, as a fanfare was sounded by twelve trumpeters. The rich musical sounds of the slim brass horns announced their arrival as they walked toward the cathedral's front row.

Once seated, all inside watched the stone being carried up the center aisle by a bearer party comprising senior officers of the Royal Company of Archers. Once at the front of the sanctuary, the officers placed the artifact on a table covered in white linen.

The cathedral was filled to capacity with a broad religious, political, and royal representation of the British Isles. A hush fell over the entire congregation as the first reading began from the Old Testament—Genesis 28:10-22, read in Gaelic, with translation in English, recalling the legend of Jacob and his pillow of stone:

> *"Jacob left Beersheba and set out for Haran. When he reached a certain place, he stopped for the night because the sun had set. Taking one of the stones there, he put it under his head and lay down to sleep. He had a dream in which he saw a stairway resting on the earth, with its top reaching to heaven, and the angels of God were ascending and descending on it. There above it stood the Lord, and he said: 'I am the Lord, the God of your father Abraham and the God of Isaac. I will give you and your descendants the land on which you are lying. Your descendants will be like the dust of the earth, and you will spread out to the west and to the east, to the north and to the south. All peoples on earth will be blessed through you and your offspring. I am with you and will watch over you wherever you go, and I will bring you back to this land. I will not leave you until I have done what I have promised you.'*

> *"When Jacob awoke from his sleep, he thought, 'Surely the Lord is in this place, and I was not aware of it.' He was afraid and said, 'How awesome is this place! This is none other than the house of God; this is the gate of heaven.'*
>
> *"Early the next morning Jacob took the stone he had placed under his head and set it up as a pillar and poured oil on top of it. He called that place Bethel, though the city used to be called Luz.*
>
> *"Then Jacob made a vow, saying, 'If God will be with me and will watch over me on this journey I am taking and will give me food to eat and clothes to wear so that I return safely to my father's household, then the Lord will be my God and this stone that I have set up as a pillar will be God's house, and of all that you give me I will give you a tenth.'"*

A throng of people crowded around outside the cathedral during the service, including many from the local and international press. Most had no interest in the stone. The majority were drawn only by the chance to cheer and take pictures of the famous royal dignitaries.

Some in the crowd of Scottish heritage, though, remained quiet as they watched the stone being readied to leave their homeland. They remembered their history. They believed the stone belonged to the Scots and should not have been merely on loan to them while England's Elizabeth II remained queen.

Two elderly men standing next to each other in the crowd waited patiently to see the stone leave the cathedral. They understood the true significance of the age-old object. They didn't have to ask why *this* stone had to be present during the British king's upcoming coronation ceremony. They knew the ancient prophecies. They believed that soon they would see them come true.

Chapter 1

Jerusalem: The Ninth of Av, 586 BC

As the first rays of dawn lit the sky, Teia rested her slender frame against the rampart's wall and looked west beyond the city, to the valley below. What was once green, covered with vineyards and fragrant fruit trees, now looked like a blackened wasteland where only the smell of smoke drifted through the air from the vast camp of the enemy. As far as Teia could see, the tents of their foes covered the land.

The eyes of the young princess were drawn upward as she watched a flock of birds fly toward her, circle above, then soar off behind the palace and settle in the olive trees that covered the hills. Their flight reminded her of the freedom she'd had when she could walk outside the city's walls. On her fingers, she counted the number of months it had been since then—and stopped at eighteen.

Teia was alone, except for the watchmen and guards stationed in the towers above her. Since the day she had been forbidden to leave the palace, the teenage princess came to its rooftop, where she could stand under an open sky and take in the endless views. She found that it was also a good place to evade her attendants and tutors.

She now stood in her favorite place of retreat, this time to escape her bedroom, where she had tossed and turned through another hungry and sleepless night. For days, the thudding drumbeat of the battering ram never ceased. The city's steep cliffs and thick walls had managed to withstand the enemy's attacks, but the Babylonian siege had choked off Jerusalem's ability to receive food and basic supplies long ago.

"Get inside!" one of the guards shouted to Teia from above.

The princess heard the soldier's call even as the ground shuddered beneath her feet. She turned and ran toward the palace door, then down two flights of stairs as she heard several shrill blasts of the ram's horn blow the call to battle.

All appeared to be chaos when she entered the palace. Soldiers, servants, and members of the royal staff fled through the halls. Teia's sandaled feet slapped against the polished stone as she ran down the long corridor toward the royal family's residence, where she found one room after the other open and empty. She stopped when she saw her sister's nightclothes strewn across the floor of the bedroom they shared.

"Princess Teia!" shouted her tutor, Ebed, as he burst into the room right after her. "Your father and most of the royal family have left the palace. We couldn't find you, and now it's too late to get you out. The Babylonians have broken down the northern wall and are flooding into the city. Soon they will be here! I have to hide you—now!

Teia's eyes widened and she swallowed hard. "Where's Hannah?"

"She left with the king. Here, put this on!"

Teia grabbed the robe from the Ethiopian eunuch's hands and put it on. With her dress now hidden, Ebed pulled the hood over her head.

"Keep your hair covered and your head down until we get across the temple grounds."

Outside, the early morning sun glinted off tens of thousands of swords, shields, and spears. Horses trampled the ground beneath their hoofs as they poured through Jerusalem's now broken-down wall. As Ebed guided Teia out of the palace and across the temple's outer courtyard, anguished screams and the clash of metal resounded from the streets below. The Judean soldiers, weakened by famine and pestilence, were in no condition to defend the city against an invading army, Teia knew. Jerusalem's streets were soon clogged with the bodies of men, women, and children who lay dying after being trampled by Babylonian horsemen or cut down by their swords.

Leaving the horrid sights and sounds behind, Ebed rushed Teia into a room stocked with wood used for the temple's daily sacrifices. No one had entered the room in months. The last few animals in the city, which should have been sacrificed to God, had instead been killed at the king's orders for his own consumption. Even the temple's grain offerings had ceased as food became scarce.

Ebed tossed large chunks of wood aside as he rushed to clear a small pathway across the room. Teia watched the tall Ethiopian kneel down and run his fingers along the floor. With one quick jerk, he lifted a large slab of rock.

"Come over here!" Ebed stood up in front of the hole in the floor. "Princess Teia, you will be safe here."

He reached down and removed the hood from Teia's head. Her light-brown hair spilled down to her waist.

"May the Lord God bless and keep you in his care," Ebed said.

She nodded and drew in a shaking breath.

Ebed slid his large hands under Teia's arms, then gently lowered her down into the hidden chamber before finally letting go of her.

Teia looked up. She stood still as Ebed dropped a bloated goat-skin bag through the hole.

"The water will have to sustain you, Princess. Tie it to your belt. There's an entrance to a tunnel off to your left that leads under the temple and out of the city. The exit is sealed, though. So just stay put, and I'll come back and get you out of here as soon as I'm able."

With shaking hands, the princess reached down and grabbed the skin of water that lay at her feet. She wound its leather ties to the sash around her waist as Ebed pushed the stone back into place. In total darkness, the princess listened to the muffled thump of wood hit the floor above her—sealing the fourteen-year-old in the underground cave.

Teia reached back for the wall and slid to the ground, her legs crumpling beneath her. Fear raced through her mind as she realized she was alone; her family was gone, and the enemy was near. With long, slow breaths, she tried to calm the beat of her heart as it pounded in her chest.

Why did no one plan for this? she wondered. *The city's been surrounded for almost two years! What did Father think would happen? Why didn't he listen to Jeremiah's warnings?* She sucked in a sharp breath. *How could they have left without me?* Teia's final thought brought a well of tears to her eyes that spilled down her cheeks.

She fought off the tears and forced her mind to move away from panic and from the darkness that engulfed her. She wiped her face and ran her wet hands over the soft fabric of her dress and wondered when, or if, she would be able to return to the palace—to her room … to her pretty clothes. She recalled the words of her grandmother: *"You are a princess, Teia Tamar, descended from the royal line of David. You are not like other girls; you are special! Hold your head high when you walk in these fine gowns. You will be a—"*

Teia's thoughts froze. She lifted her head and listened to a low rumbling sound. Soon, bits of dirt began to rain down on her as the thunderous noise grew and the walls shook—her mind imagining the hundreds of soldiers now charging across the temple grounds. She could hear men shout over the crashing noise as the Babylonian soldiers wrought destruction above her. The young princess covered her ears with her hands, then bowed her head.

Please, Lord, don't let them find me ... don't let them find me. Please ... Please ... I don't want to die!

Teia prayed until she realized all had become quiet and still. She lowered her hands and listened; only a few faint voices could be heard.

"They're leaving," she said and then sighed.

Her shoulders dropped as the tension fell. She took a deep breath and rested her head back against the wall. But then her body stiffened. She smelled smoke!

After raiding the palace of the treasures of the king and his family, the Babylonians desecrated the holy temple. They stripped the gold-covered walls and looted stacks of gold and silver basins and bowls, along with any other sacred vessels and objects they found. They knocked down the nearly thirty-foot bronze pillars King Solomon had named "Jachin" and "Boaz," which had stood for almost four centuries on the front porch of the temple. The Babylonian troops hacked the pillars into portable pieces, then took the crushed metal and everything else they could carry away before leaving the temple mount. As they withdrew, a few remaining soldiers set numerous torches afire before they tossed them into the temple and its surrounding buildings. Sheets of flames reached for the heavens as the house of God burned.

Fire soon engulfed the room above Teia. She began to choke and cough as she breathed in the smoky air. Her fingers groped in the dark for the opening to the water skin. Grabbing the hem of her dress, she soaked the linen cloth before pressing it over her face and raising herself off the floor.

With her free hand, Teia reached out for the wall. When her fingers found the rough rock surface, she guided herself forward until her hand pushed out into the empty space of the tunnel's entrance. The princess moved through the opening just as deafening cash came from behind her. Ash and burning shards of wood shot through the air as mounds of flaming timber hit the ground.

The raging fire cast an eerie golden light down the tunnel. Tears streamed from Teia's eyes as she ran forward until darkness filled the narrow passageway. With her lungs straining to breath, she leaned against the wall and dragged herself onward, until finally, disoriented and too weak to continue, she collapsed on the ground.

Except for a few small groups who managed to escape, most of Jerusalem's citizens were dead or captive and bound for Babylon. Enemy soldiers rummaged through their homes and took what they found valuable. What they didn't take, they burned. What they couldn't burn, they tore down. In a matter of hours, the battle was over.

Jerusalem had fallen.

CHAPTER 2

The tall, heavily armored soldier walked into the dining hall and approached the only man sitting at the polished wood tables.

"Jeremiah," the soldier said, "I am Bashaa, second in command of King Nebuchadnezzar's imperial guards."

The middle-aged man, who sat there picking at his food, now pushed his plate aside and looked up at the towering warrior who addressed him.

"Our king asked me to express his regret that you were brought in chains here to Riblah. Now that you've been given a change of clothes and some food, our king makes you an offer to ride with us to Babylon. You will be free and safe in our great city. Our king has commanded all those under him to do no harm to you. If you choose otherwise, all the land is before you to go freely wherever you wish. I do advise, though, that you avoid Jerusalem. There will be nothing left for you there."

"Nothing … left?" Jeremiah asked. Holding back tears, he swallowed hard on the painful lump in his throat.

"The city is burning. You warned King Zedekiah of the annihilation that was to come upon his kingdom if he didn't acquiesce to our king's leadership. You are well known and admired by your people, yet your king refused to heed your warnings. Because of his stubbornness, his reign as Judah's king is over."

Jeremiah held his composure as he scooted back his chair and stood. "I am not as well liked as you may think. I am actually hated by many of my people. They, along with our king, did not want to hear about the consequences of worshipping false idols. They didn't want to hear what would happen to them if they didn't turn back to Yahweh, the one true God of Israel. King Zedekiah also refused to follow Yahweh's command to give Babylon control of his kingdom. He didn't understand why Almighty God would ask this of him. He lacked faith, so he failed to obey. So … what will now be the fate of Jerusalem's king?"

"If he is captured alive, he will be imprisoned."

"Then who will rule the people of Judah?"

"King Nebuchadnezzar is appointing a governor," the soldier said. He lifted the bronze helmet off his head and set it on the table. "I have heard that he favors Gedaliah, the son of Ahikam, the son of Shaphan. Do you know of him?"

"Yes, I know Gedaliah. He was an adviser to King Josiah. I remember him as a strong diplomat and administrator."

Bashaa gave an approving nod. "If he's chosen, he will govern from Mizpah. It's a decent-sized city, and it will not suffer the same destruction today as Jerusalem. If you decide you don't want to join us in Babylon, go to Mizpah. You will be safe there. Ample supplies will be provided for your journey. Just be assured, Jeremiah, that you will travel safely wherever you go, as you have found favor with our king."

Jeremiah shoved his chair back toward the table, then looked up into the face of the soldier. "I am merely God's oracle. Thank King Nebuchadnezzar for giving me my freedom. I am also grateful to your chief commander, Nebuzaradan, for taking off the chains that bound my hands and feet, for the meal, the clothes, and for his and your offer to travel to Babylon. Instead, I will leave for Mizpah, and it will be there that I will wait upon the word of the Lord for what he chooses to do with his servant."

The soldier reached down for his helmet. "If that's your decision, then your friend—I believe he said he name was Ebed-Melech—he can accompany you. He's been released. He is a brave man. He remained near the palace and took it upon himself to inform us that you were locked in the court of the guards where King Zedekiah had chained you. If it were not for this man, you would most likely be dead. Because Ebed-Melech saved you, we spared him."

"That is the second time Ebed has interceded and saved my life. He is a good man who God foretold would live through the destruction of Jerusalem. I will be fortunate to have him again in my company."

When Jeremiah left the palace, he was given a donkey, two skins of water, and a couple of cloth satchels filled with bread and fruit. Lastly, he was handed a small but heavy pouch. Jeremiah untied its leather cords and peeked inside. Shiny gold coins lay piled on top of each other, a generous gift from the king of Babylon. He slipped the pouch into the pocket of his robe, then tied the large satchels to the sides of the donkey as he thought about the destruction that had swept through Jerusalem. For twenty-three years, he'd warned the people of the house of Judah that they would go into captivity.

From the top of the hill, Jeremiah looked down at the thread-like path that wound its way across the valley. He turned east and looked toward Mount Nebo. Silently, he thanked God for allowing him the opportunity to remove and hide the most precious items from the temple before he had been imprisoned. Tears filled the eyes of the prophet as he recalled the words that the Lord had given him, which warned of this day:

> *"Listen to the terms of this covenant and tell them to the people of Judah and to those who live in Jerusalem. Tell them that this is what the Lord, the God of Israel, says: 'Cursed is the man who does not obey the terms of this covenant—the terms I commanded your forefathers when I brought them out of Egypt, out of the iron-smelting furnace.' I said, 'Obey me and do everything I command you, and you will be my people and I will be your God. Then I will fulfill the oath I swore to your forefathers, to give them a land flowing with milk and honey'—the land you possess today.*
>
> *"Proclaim all these words in the towns of Judah and in the streets of Jerusalem: I warned them again and again, saying, 'Obey me.' But they did not listen or pay attention; instead, they followed the stubbornness of their evil hearts.*
>
> *"They have returned to the sins of their forefathers, who refused to listen to my words. They have followed other gods to serve them. Both the house of Israel and the house of Judah have broken the covenant I made with their forefathers.*
>
> *"I will bring on them a disaster they cannot escape. Although they cry out to me, I will not listen to them. The towns of Judah and the people of Jerusalem will go and cry out to the gods to whom they burn incense, but they will not help them at all when disaster strikes."*

Just then, a tall, dark man startled Jeremiah from his brooding as the giant stepped from behind him.

"Ebed!" Jeremiah said. A broad smiled spread across the prophet's face.

Ebed embraced Jeremiah, then stepped back. "You look like royalty!"

Jeremiah spread his arms and looked down at his attire. "Nebuchadnezzar's chief commander graciously allowed me to clean myself up, and then gave me these clothes and this robe. Then the captain of the king's guards offered to take me with him to Babylon. Perhaps he didn't want to travel with an old man in filthy rags." Jeremiah stepped forward and took hold of Ebed's arms. "Thank you, my dear friend, for risking your life for my rescue."

Ebed gave a slight bow. "Jeremiah, I am faithful to you and I am only alive by God's protection as you foretold, and by his power to free you and protect Princess Teia.

Jeremiah's eyebrows shot up. "Princess Teia?"

Ebed glanced around, then nodded and leaned in closer. "King Zedekiah and the royal family fled in darkness before Jerusalem's walls were breached. The princess, though, had been left behind. As the Babylonians approached the palace, I only had time to hide her in the chamber under the temple before I came back to find you. The soldiers led me away from the prison yard before I could tell you."

"We must hurry!" Jeremiah said.

He gazed south toward Jerusalem, where black smoke billowed into the sky.

CHAPTER 3

"Where did the king and his family go?" the Babylonian soldier shouted.

With one hand gripping a handful of the young servant's hair, the soldier's sharp sword dragged slowly across the youth's neck until a ribbon of blood ran down its blade.

"This is the last time I will ask before this weapon cuts to the back of your throat! When did they leave and where did they go?"

"Uh … Uh … Before sunrise … I … I only saw them enter the king's garden … and then … then they were gone."

"Show me!"

The soldier loosened his hold and then shoved the terrified boy ahead of him through Jerusalem's palace until they stopped in the king's garden.

"Where did you see them?" the soldier said.

"There!" The young servant stood under the palm trees and pointed toward a wall covered with hanging vines. "They were running toward that wall."

The soldier grabbed the boy again—and plunged his sword into his chest before throwing him aside and using his bloody weapon to slash through the thick foliage. As the vines fell to the ground, an entrance between the walls revealed itself.

When the Babylonian commander discovered how the Judean king had escaped, he led dozens of soldiers out of Jerusalem. The expert horsemen pursued the king for several miles before they finally rode up behind him. The king's soldiers tried to fight off the Babylonians, but were outnumbered. The king and the other surviving fighters in his group were soon torn off their horses, then bound hand and foot to be carried captive to Riblah, the nearest city held by the Babylonians. When they arrived in the afternoon, the soldiers separated the king of Judah from the other prisoners and dragged him before Nebuchadnezzar, king of Babylon.

The Babylonian monarch waved his hand and dismissed the attendants who stood near his throne. They scattered as a disheveled man was pushed down on his knees in front of their king.

"Lift your head and look at me!" Nebuchadnezzar shouted. The skin around his mouth tightened.

The thirty-two-year-old king of Judah visibly shook as he lifted his head to look up from the floor and into the dark eyes of Nebuchadnezzar.

The Babylonian king slit his eyes at the trembling man before him. "King Zedekiah, you are a weak and pitiful ruler. You let your city fall, and then, like a coward, you fled. You are also a foolish man who lacks wisdom. You could have saved your kingdom, and your people, but you refused to submit to the authority of Babylon. Instead, you tried to make alliances with the Egyptians against me. Do you think I did not know about the messages you sent to them?"

When Zedekiah said nothing in response, Nebuchadnezzar leaned forward. "As we speak, my imperial guards are taking captive anyone found in your palace and in your temple, including your priests and whoever else is found alive. They will be brought here to face me—as you do now. All of you will receive just punishment—as traitors! Get him out of my sight!"

The king gave a quick nod of his head toward the soldiers who stood behind him, and they strode forward to where Zedekiah knelt, still shaking.

After binding Zedekiah's arms behind his back, Nebuchadnezzar's soldiers led the Judean king through the palace, then up two tiers of stone steps that ended on a balcony above an inner courtyard. Zedekiah looked down and watched as his eldest son was brought into the yard. The young prince of Judah, still dressed in his royal blue robes, was commanded to kneel and bow down. A large, stocky soldier moved toward him with a huge axe. With one swing, he cut off the boy's head.

A breath burst forth from Zedekiah's lips, then his knees buckled as a soldier dragged his son's small, now headless body across the yard. The guards, though, held up Zedekiah and forced him to watch as his second son was beheaded, then his third, and then all his remaining sons. Tears streamed from the king's eyes, blurring the horror they forced him to watch.

First his sons ... then the remainder of his family and royal court ... all slaughtered before him. It took over an hour for the killing to end. The king sobbed, his body heaving, as they eventually hauled him from the balcony, then down the stairs and into the bloody yard.

The Babylonian soldier who killed his family walked toward Zedekiah through puddles of their blood. Instead of an axe, his thick fingers now clutched a dagger.

"The events of this day will remain in your memory. Your kingdom is destroyed; your sons are dead. No descendant of yours will again reign."

The soldier spit in Zedekiah's face, then took hold of the king's head while two other soldiers from behind held him in place. Then the solider with the dagger gouged out Zedekiah's right eye, followed by his left. Shrieking throughout the ordeal, Zedekiah now screamed in anguish as blood oozed down his face. Writhing in pain, he barely felt the bronze shackles that the soldiers clamped around his legs.

"And now a gift for our king," the soldier said.

He pulled Zedekiah's official signet ring off his finger, and then he led the broken king of Judah away to join tens of thousands of other Jewish captives bound for Babylon.

CHAPTER 4

Teia's body hung limp as Jeremiah scooped her off the ground. He carried her frail form out of the tunnel and eased her to the ground. A burnt odor wafted into the prophet's nostrils from Teia's smoke-saturated clothes and hair. Jeremiah cradled her head in his lap and brought the mouth of his water skin toward her.

"Drink, Teia. Please drink, sweet child," Jeremiah said.

He poured a small stream of liquid through her barely parted lips. He felt Teia's body stir weakly, then watched her swallow as the water filled her mouth. With fits of coughing and gasping breaths, she leaned forward.

"Princess Teia?"

Teia tried to open her swollen eyes at the sound of the familiar voice. "Jeremiah?" she mouthed more than said.

"Yes, Princess, it's me—it's over. You are safe," he whispered. He kissed her forehead and pulled her close, then turned his head. "Seal it up," he called out over his shoulder.

Ebed and the other men who stood behind Jeremiah proceeded to replace the large pile of rocks and brush that normally concealed the tunnel. Satisfied, Jeremiah lifted Teia into his arms and stood to move on.

"Where … are we?" Teia asked.

"We are outside Jerusalem. You have been in the tunnel since yesterday morning. Ebed and Baruch are here with me, and a few others you will know. We are traveling with a small group we met on the road this evening, those who managed to flee and hide before the destruction of the city. I also received word that your sister Hannah has been found unharmed. In a few days, we will meet up with her and some others who escaped."

"And … Mother? Father?"

Jeremiah paused, then looked down at her. "Teia, not long after your family fled the palace, the Babylonians pursed them. Some broke away from the group and rode off; the rest were taken captive. Your sister was with a group that escaped. I'm sorry, Princess, but I do not know the fate of your parents or brothers or other sisters."

Teia fell silent. She dropped her head against the prophet's shoulder and closed her eyes as he carried her down the hill through thick brush toward the waiting caravan. When Jeremiah reached the road, he turned and looked back toward Jerusalem.

On this day, with the temple in ruins, there have been twenty-one kings over Israel. David was our first king; Zedekiah will be the last over Judah, until all things should be fulfilled. Jeremiah pursed his lips, determined to fight the tears forming in his eyes. *I was God's voice and messenger to five kings who wore the royal crown. Now I will be the guardian and messenger for this tender sprig I hold, who someday will help fulfill the Lord our God's promise.*

Jeremiah turned from his thoughts, slowed his steps, and closed his eyes for just a moment. In a soft voice, he prayed, "O Jerusalem, the scepter has passed from your keeping, till the blast of the silver trumpet shall call your scattered remnant back home, to witness the fulfillment of all the laws and prophets concerning Israel. I pray that the God of our fathers—Abraham, Isaac, and Jacob—will sustain you until that day."

After walking several more paces, Jeremiah stopped and lifted Teia into the back of a cart where a young woman sat.

"Teia," Jeremiah said. He waited until she looked up at him. "This is Miriam. She will attend to you while we journey. I'm sorry, Princess, but she must remove your robe and dress, and replace it with servant's clothes. Even though you are covered in soot, if we are stopped, you must look like a peasant, not a dirty princess. It is still dangerous for you, as the Babylonians seek to destroy all of the king's heirs. I cannot hide who I am. I must be God's word to the people wherever I go, but for now, you must stay hidden. As far as I know, you and your sister may be all that is left of the royal family."

The band of refugees traveled for hours before Teia awoke to darkness. She wiped her fingers across a dirty layer of dried tears that had crusted on her cheeks. Pushing herself up against the side of the swaying cart, the princess rocked gently back and forth as she listened to the steady clump of the oxen's hoofs.

Teia peered through the slits of swollen eyelids at the stars that sparkled above her in an ink-black sky. With small breaths, she drank in the cool night air, careful not to start another spasm of coughs. Now if she could only find some way to stop the horrific memories of the previous day. The princess pulled her blanket close and wondered again what had happened to her family. *Who is still alive … and who is dead?* She looked to the stars again. *Where is Yahweh? Isn't he supposed to take care of those who love him?*

Teia had never asked Yahweh for anything for herself … until yesterday. She had been taught early in life not to have any dreams or desires of her own. She remembered what her mother had recently told her: *"What you want does not matter. Your father will decide your future. He is king, and what he wants for you is what you will have: nothing more—nothing less. When the time comes, your father will give you away … for a price. With your beauty, it will be a high price. You will be a gift to the man he chooses. And I have heard that he already has someone in mind."*

Teia pursed her lips. *A gift to be given … Is that all I was in Father's eyes? I wonder who father had chosen for me. Was he handsome … gentle … caring? Would he have loved me? He would be older—that is certain. Young princesses are always wed to older men. But … now that the palace and city are destroyed, what will become of me?*

The hopelessness of her future left Teia tired. The princess closed her eyes and said a silent prayer that Yahweh would not forget her.

As daylight approached, the small caravan turned from the road and traveled some distance toward the foothills before they stopped to settle in between a large patch of sycamores. A narrow stream poured down from the rocky slope above them and wound its way between clusters of trees and tall grass. Skins were refilled as the handlers led the oxen and donkeys to drink from the cool water.

Jeremiah directed several men to stand guard at the top of the hill and at the entrance to their camp. He then checked on Teia, who was already fast asleep in her tent. After posting a guard outside, and making certain that their camp was secured, Jeremiah looked for Ebed and found him after only after a few moments of searching.

"I need you and Baruch to come with me," Jeremiah said. "We must travel to Mount Nebo today. Prepare a cart. Load it with as much of this dried grass as you are able. Then cover the grass with any blankets that can be spared. Wait for me and Baruch at the entrance to our camp."

After Ebed nodded his assent, Jeremiah turned from him and walked to a tent being erected next to Teia's.

"Baruch," Jeremiah said, "when you finish with the tent, I need you to come with me and Ebed. We're traveling to Mount Nebo. I will gather some water skins and will also see if anyone has a small amount of food they can spare."

"Of course," Baruch said.

Soon enough, under Jeremiah's instructions, Ebed prepared one of the smaller carts, then hitched it to a pair of oxen and waited by the edge of the camp. Within a few minutes, Jeremiah and Baruch arrived.

As Jeremiah stepped up into the front seat of the cart, he said, "We will travel from here to Jericho, and then after crossing the Jordan River, we'll find a place to rest for the night. At dawn tomorrow, we'll resume our journey across the plains of Gilead and up Mount Nebo's slopes to retrieve some precious items hidden in a cave. Since we are starting our journey during daylight, we will stay off the main roads. I know a few paths we can follow where we will be hidden behind low hills and several other areas where we can move across the paths that lay between the barley and wheat fields. God willing, we will be back in two days."

After traveling without incident throughout the day, the three men reached the east bank of the Jordan River just after sunset. There, they made their camp and rested for the night. Rising at dawn, they traveled for over three hours before they stood at the base of Mount Nebo. With their cart secured among a grove of trees, they began their ascent up the gentle incline, through low mounds of scrub brush, and under small groups of carob trees.

Jeremiah stopped about halfway up the slope. Shielding his eyes from the afternoon sun, he surveyed the area around him.

"This way," he said.

He lowered his hands and led the two men up toward the southern side of the mount. After walking for over a mile, the prophet stopped near a group of trees that grew in front of a large outcropping of rocks.

"Wait here," Jeremiah said. He disappeared behind the trees and then called out, "This is the place! Help me remove these rocks."

One by one, the men lifted the white boulders and piled them up against the tree trunks until the entrance to the cave was open. Jeremiah bent down and entered the cavern. He turned toward Baruch and Ebed.

"Do not go into any room beyond where I walk. There are things hidden here that should not be touched. What I seek is a chest. It will be found on the left side of the cave hidden under a pile of rocks."

A shaft of sunlight filtered through the treetops and streamed down into the cave as the men moved into the shadows and came to a stop. They began to shift aside the large stones that lay stacked against the cave's wall.

Jeremiah ran his hands across a flat dirty surface. "It's here," he said.

When they had the chest uncovered, Jeremiah unlatched the leather straps and opened the lid. Reaching into the chest, he pushed aside a yellowed linen cloth. Baruch and Ebed stared down at a large pillow-shaped stone.

"What is it?" Baruch whispered.

"This is the Bethel Stone—the 'House of God' that followed our people throughout their wanderings. You must handle this item with great care."

Both Baruch and Ebed nodded, then Jeremiah replaced the cloth and secured the lid.

"Before you raise this treasure out of its hiding place, wait here for me," Jeremiah said.

He turned and walked around a bend in the cave, and remained out of sight for several minutes before he finally reappeared, laden with several large satchels that hung on his shoulders.

"I carry many of the temple scrolls—the parchments that contain the precious word of God. When we return to our cart, I will place these in the chest on top of the stone. You can take the chest out now." Jeremiah nodded toward the opening in the cave. "I'll follow you out."

With the cave resealed, the weary men passed around a skin of water and some dried fruit as they settled in to rest under the trees.

"We will stay here until night falls and then begin our journey back to our camp," Jeremiah said. "We must travel as quickly as we are able, so no harm comes to the items we carry. There are enemy soldiers still on our roads, as well as many of our own people left homeless, starving, and desperate. It will be only by God's protection that we arrive at our camp unharmed before we see the sun rise."

A few hours after their short meal, the silver light of a full moon cast shadows of the men as they moved down the hill. Jeremiah led Ebed and Baruch along the smoothest path he could find. He silently prayed that the men behind him would not lose their footing while carrying the heavy chest.

Staying out of the dark shadows under the trees, the three men inched down the mountain slope. When they reached their cart, Jeremiah opened the chest and placed the satchels of scrolls on top of the stone. After the chest had been secured in the cart, Baruch covered it with blankets, and then he and Ebed scattered mounds of dried grass on top.

"This precious cargo is now in our care," Jeremiah said. He grabbed the oxen's reins. "Now let us hope and pray that our journey back to our camp is a safe one."

CHAPTER 5

"Princess Teia? Princess?"

Teia stirred under her blanket as she woke to the sound of someone calling her name.

"Forgive me for disturbing you, but you have slept through the day," Miriam said.

As Teia struggled to open her eyes and focus, Miriam stood over her, holding out a small cup to her.

"It's nearly sundown," Miriam said. "Please … drink this."

Teia took the cup and nodded. "Thank you." She pushed herself up and drank the refreshing water before handing the empty cup back to Miriam.

"There's plenty more if you're still thirsty. A stream flows next to our camp—and I can show you. But first, here, I have a piece of bread for you."

Miriam unfolded a small cloth bundle and handed it to Teia, who eagerly took the food.

"While you slept, our guards spotted another group of refugees on the road, and then escorted them into our camp. They have food and said that they will prepare a meal for all of us tonight."

Teia swallowed a bite of flatbread, then asked, "Are they from Jerusalem?"

"I heard that they lived outside of the city, on farms.

"How big is the group?"

"Umm … I guess maybe about thirty. Mostly adults and then some small children."

Teia pushed her blanket aside. "Miriam, before the evening meal, I'd like to go to the stream to clean up a little. I've never felt so dirty."

Miriam nodded and offered a little smile. "I have a small cloth," she said. "We could also rinse out your hair, and then if you want, I will braid it for you."

Now Teia smiled back. "Yes, I'd like that. Thank you, Miriam. Thank you for being so kind to me. Please, sit with me for a bit."

Miriam sat down and crossed her legs in front of her. "Do you mind if I ask how old you are?"

"I'm fourteen … but I'll be fifteen after the next two full moons," Teia said.

"You're only three years younger than me, then. How old were your palace attendants?"

"Most were older women. And then there were the men—the eunuchs. But they were my teachers. Someone always took care of me … and my sister—Hannah. We were almost always together." Teia felt a well of tears forming in her eyes. "I … I miss her so much. Jeremiah … he said she escaped and that I will see her soon."

"I've heard of the many princes of Judah … your brothers. Is Hannah your only sister?" Miriam asked.

"No, but she is the only sister I have with the same mother. My father had children with other wives and women who lived in the palace besides my mother. I rarely saw my brothers. They were always training as soldiers or studying Yahweh's Law in school." Teia paused, then pursed her lips before saying, "My brothers were my father's joy. He didn't pay too much attention to his daughters."

Miriam gave a nod, but said nothing.

Teia ate the last of her bread, then asked, "Where is your family?"

For a moment, Miriam gave no reply, but then she looked at Teia and said, "It's … It's been almost four years since I've seen my family. I have two younger sisters and one older brother. My family needed money, needed food, so I was … sold … to an older man." Miriam cast her eyes down. "When he found out I was barren, he married another girl. I became their housekeeper—their servant."

"I'm sorry," Teia said. "I didn't mean to … You don't need to talk about it if you don't want to. But can I ask how you ended up traveling with Jeremiah?"

"When we heard the shofar blow the call to war, he—my master, I mean—he grabbed his sword and left me and his wife alone in our house. As soon as he left, I ran out of there and through the city as fast as I could. I hid up high in one of those big trees at the west end until it was dark. That's when I snuck out. I couldn't believe it—the gates were wide open! I guess they figured everything worth anything was gone, and the people were either captured or dead. And … there were dead bodies all over the streets."

Miriam looked down. She tucked her dark, shoulder-length hair behind her ears. "So I made my way back to the village where my family lived. When I arrived, there was nothing left. Everything was burned to the ground. I walked for hours from there and had just come out of a wheat field when I heard some noise on the road. I hid in the stalks and watched the group pass by until I heard someone call the name 'Jeremiah.'

"When he spoke in return, I recognized his voice. And then I saw him. He had been in our village many times pleading with everyone to worship Yahweh and not the idols of Baal and Ashtoreth. So I just waited and then came out on the road behind everyone as if I belonged with them. Pretty soon, someone noticed me and brought me to Jeremiah. I told him where I had been. He gave me the warmest hug I have had since the day I left my family."

Teia smiled. "I've known Jeremiah as long as I can remember. He came to the palace often to see Father. Sometimes after they met, he would watch us children in the courtyard when we were brought together in the afternoons to be taught about Yahweh. A few times, he even questioned us to see what we had learned. I'm so glad he's here."

"Would you like me to get you anything more to eat?" Miriam asked.

"No, not right now."

Teia stood and smoothed the wrinkles on her thin wool tunic. Miriam also rose next to her.

"I'd rather go and get cleaned up," Teia said.

When they reached the stream, Teia sat down on its edge and dipped a thin linen cloth into the flowing water. She rubbed it down each of her arms and removed a light layer of gray ash that covered her skin. After rinsing out the cloth, she ran it across her forehead and then her cheeks.

"Here, let me help you," Miriam said.

She reached for the hand towel, which Teia gave to her. Miriam soaked and squeezed it out several times until the dirty liquid ran clear before she brought it toward Teia.

"You have such long, thick lashes." Miriam wiped gently under Teia's almond-shaped hazel eyes. "After Jeremiah told me what he saw inside the tunnel … where he found you, it's a wonder that your lashes and the rest of your hair were not singed."

Teia said nothing while recalling her escape from the fire as Miriam continued to wipe the soot off her chin and neck.

"There!" Miriam said. "That looks much better. Now let's do something with your hair. I brought a small comb. Do you usually wear your hair down?"

"Most of the time; sometimes I braid it. I have even wrapped it up fancy on top of my head on special occasions."

Teia bent over and dipped her head in the water, swishing her long hair around before finally throwing her head back and then ringing the water out with her hands. She leaned back on her arms as Miriam worked her comb slowly through the golden-brown hair. When it was tangle free, Miriam swept it over the princess's left shoulder and began to weave three thick ribbons of hair into one long braid that reached almost to Teia's waist.

"You are so beautiful," Miriam said. "You have uncommon beauty. If … If I may speak more boldly?"

"Yes, please … speak freely with me."

"You, a princess … at your age … being so pretty, I wonder why the king … why had he not already made you a bride for some nobleman. Most girls in your position, at your age or even younger, would already have been married, or at least betrothed."

Teia shivered at Miriam's words. "I often hoped and dreamed of a good and kind husband, maybe even a handsome one. But I saw the men my father befriended and entertained. Before the siege, sometimes I hid in the large curtains at the entrance to the banquet hall. The men my father usually favored would drink themselves into such a state that their large, bloated bodies would lay lifeless with dribble running from their mouths after they had gorged themselves on meat and wine. I would sneak back to my room and try to forget what I saw. I always feared that one day my life would be placed under the control of such a man."

Teia stared off into the distance as she continued. "When the siege began, I feared that I might become someone that my father would use for trade—that I might be bartered for anything: food, weapons, or even wine. I overheard some of his generals talk about using me and my sister, as well as some of my father's wives, for gaining supplies. But it never happened. Why, I'm not sure … Maybe Yahweh was protecting me. Mother once told me that father had chosen someone for me. But now I guess I will never know who he was."

Teia sighed and reached out for Miriam's hand. "Thank you. Thank you for listening to me and for helping me. I actually feel somewhat clean again."

"I am pleased and honored to help you in any way I can." Miriam squeezed Teia's fingers. "You have been kinder to me than the others I served."

"Please think of me as your friend, not someone you serve," Teia said. She stood and dusted the slivers of dried grass off her tunic. "The sun is almost down, so we better get back. I also want to get a quick look at the strangers that have joined our camp."

A loud chorus of crickets chirped their mating songs into the night while pots of thick lentil and vegetable stew brewed on a few fires around the refugee camp. Sitting next to Miriam, Teia savored her small portion of the warm cumin-spiced food. She picked out the little chunks of carrot and ate them slowly, relishing each bite of their sweet flavor. The princess tried to recall the last time she'd had something so good to eat. She knew each mouthful she now tasted was better than anything she had consumed over the past few months.

Teia wiped her bowl clean with a small piece of bread. As she swallowed the last of her meal, she looked across the campfire at all the young and old gaunt faces framed by straggly hair. Their vacant eyes seemed huge on their thin faces as they stared into the fire while they ate.

What horrors did they see? What family members have they lost?

As she scanned the faces, Teia's eyes locked onto someone who looked familiar. She grabbed Miriam's hand.

"Oh my! Miriam … My sister … I see my sister!" Teia whispered.

"Where?"

"Over there." Teia turned her head to the right. "The three girls facing us on the other side of the fire. My sister … She's the one in the middle. Oh, I wish Jeremiah was here to counsel me! Should I go to her … go to their side of the camp? Do you think it would be okay? Do you know if they have a leader in their group?"

"I'm sorry, I don't know the answers to your questions. And I think it would be best if you waited for Jeremiah to return. I'm sure he will find a way to reunite you and your sister. But don't risk revealing who you are. We don't know who these people are and what they might do if they thought they might receive a reward for turning you or your sister over to the Babylonians. For now, wait and be thankful that you see that your sister is alive and well."

Teia nodded and gave tight-lipped smile. "Jeremiah said Hannah had escaped, but to see her now! You cannot imagine how wonderful it feels. She is all that I have left of my family. It's unbearable that I cannot run and embrace her."

Teia gazed at her sister. How she resembled their father, Teia thought, with her dark, wavy hair, full lips, and round face, so different from Teia, who bore the high cheek bones and fine features of their mother.

"My little cherub ..." Teia recalled the favorite pet name she had given to her sister when they were little.

Now Teia felt warm tears roll down her cheeks. She rubbed her wet lashes to clear her vision as she watched her sister's face fade in and out of the dancing firelight.

Chapter 6

The roads leading in and out of Jerusalem remained clogged for days with Nebuchadnezzar's troops, who guarded long caravans of carts laden with the spoils of war bound for Babylon. Above them, high in the hills of Judah, small remnants of Jerusalem's soldiers watched from the safety of their hidden positions, gazing at the exodus of goods leaving their conquered city. When the roads finally emptied, a few dozen soldiers led by one of Jerusalem's chief captains moved out toward Mizpah. Upon their arrival there, they rode directly to the estate of Governor Gedaliah.

"Lord Governor, may I enter?" asked a soldier as he stood at attention in the open door of his commander's work quarters.

"What is it?" the governor said. He didn't look up from the scrolls spread out on the table he stood over.

"Johanan, son of Kareah, desires to have a private hearing with you."

Now Gedaliah looked up. "The captain of King Zedekiah's elite guards is here?"

"Yes, Lord Governor."

"What does he want?"

"He told me only that it was urgent that he meet with you in private."

Gedaliah paused. "Go ahead, send him in. But stay close by, should I need you."

A moment later, the tall Judean captain strode into the room in full battle dress. With his right hand, he held his helmet against his waist as he bowed his head.

"Thank you for seeing me, Lord Governor."

"State your business," Gedaliah replied, only glancing up from the scrolls.

"I come to you with a warning," Johanan said. "I have received news that Baalis, king of the Ammonites, has made an alliance with Ishmael, son of Nethaniah. He plans to send Ishmael here, to take your life."

"Yes, yes, I've heard these rumors," Gedaliah replied. Without looking up, he continued. "This is the reason you interrupt me? You come to me with rumors? I haven't the time to worry about Baalis or Ishmael; I concern myself only with what pleases the king of Babylon. Nebuchadnezzar sent me here, to Mizpah, to restore some semblance of order and life to what's left of the people of Judah."

Finally, Gedaliah moved out with slow steps from behind the table and toward Johanan. "I need to coordinate the people to sow their seed, plow their fields, and gather wine, summer fruits, and oil from the olives to store in their vessels—much of which is expected to be sent to Babylon. What is left and sold throughout Judah must be taxed. These higher taxes are also expected in Babylon. If I don't please Nebuchadnezzar, it will be *he* who has my head, not Baalis, or some renegade captain like Ishmael."

When Johanan said nothing, Gedaliah clasped his hands behind his back and paced back and forth, then stopped in front of the captain. "Did you see the refugees flooding into this city? Each day, they come from Moab, Ammon, and Edom, as well as those who escaped Jerusalem. Housing and food are needed for all of these. If you want to help me, then you—and whatever number of soldiers you have left in your service—provide security for the people of Judah, instead of being troubled about Ishmael. I'm sure you know, most of our villages are in ruins. Why don't you refocus your attention on stopping the looting and provide protection in these places? That would be of help to me!"

"Governor, whether rumors or not, Ishmael is a dangerous man. He has united with the Ammonites and desires to take control of Judah. If some evil should fall upon you at the hands of Ishmael, then what is to become of the remnant of Judah? Are the people left in this land to then scatter and perish? Give me your consent: let me and my men go after Ishmael, and I will kill him. Then there will be no need for you or any of us to concern ourselves with his threats."

"No! You speak falsely against Ishmael. I have already met with him. He showed no threat to my life. Instead, on my orders, he and his men are now guarding some of the roads leading to Mizpah. You will not harm him; instead, you will serve me as I have asked. Now get out!" Gedaliah ordered.

"As you wish, Lord Governor."

Johanan made a slight bow, then turned and walked out of the room.

CHAPTER 7

Teia woke before dawn and waited among the trees at the edge of the camp. The princess stood in the semi-darkness near the tent that she had seen her sister enter last night. She peeked through the low branches as the camp slowly came to life. She caught her breath when she saw her sister finally exit the tent only twenty feet away from her.

"Hannah!" Teia called softly.

The young girl froze.

"Hannah! It's Teia!"

Now Hannah turned toward the sound of the voice. When she saw Teia's face peek out from behind the tree, her eyes grew wide and she ran to her.

"Teia! Oh … I never thought … I never thought I would see you again!"

Hannah fell into Teia's arms and sobbed as she clung to her older sister.

How thin and frail Hannah felt in her arms, Teia thought as she leaned back to gaze at her sister's face. She looked into the sunken eyes that flowed with tears. She supposed she also looked different. Much had happened to both of them since the siege and since their last days together in the palace.

"Shhh … It's alright, Hannah. We're together again! I'll take care of you now," Teia said as she ran her hands over Hannah's head.

"I … I was scared when I saw your empty bed … when Mother woke me and told me to hurry and dress. Then we left. Where were you? How did you get here?"

"Jeremiah brought me here."

"Jeremiah?"

"Yes. You will see him."

"Oh, Teia, how I was afraid for you." Hannah held tight to her sister. "It was so frightening. I thought—"

"There is much to say," Teia interrupted. "But first, can you tell me what happened to Mother? When did you last see her?"

"It was just before the Babylonian warriors came up behind us. I was riding with a soldier on a horse near Mother … then the soldier lashed at his horse when he heard the fighting start and we sped away. I don't know what happened with Mother or anyone who was behind us. She may have rode away … I … I don't know."

"Does anyone know that you are the king's daughter?"

Hannah shook her head. "No. I don't think so. When we escaped near Jericho, I rode with one of Father's guards to the village of Geba. With the way I was dressed, I guess he thought I was someone important. I don't know why he saved me. We rode to a farm that his family owned. He left me with them. They are the ones I have been traveling with."

"Tell no one who you are. Pretend that you ran away, out of Jerusalem. Only Jeremiah, Baruch, and Ebed will know who we really are."

"Ebed and Baruch are here?"

"Yes, they helped rescue me. And you will meet Miriam. She is wonderful. I will tell you everything, but now is not the time. Go back to your camp so we don't draw any attention to ourselves. When Jeremiah returns, I'll talk to him and see if there is a way we can spend time together. Oh, sweet Hannah! How God has answered my prayers." Teia kissed each of her sister's wet cheeks. "Now go!"

Hannah hesitated, then finally slipped out from behind the trees and joined the others on her side of the camp.

It was near midnight when, under the light of a full moon, three men turned off the road. Other than the guards posted nearby or up on the hill, none saw them enter the camp. Jeremiah guided the cart under the trees near his tent. After clearing the blankets and grass away, Ebed and Baruch took hold of the chest and carried it into Jeremiah's tent, where the prophet led them in a prayer of thanks to Yahweh for their safe return. The three men then spread a couple of blankets next to each other over the thick grass and slept late into the following morning.

After Jeremiah awoke, he immediately went to meet those who had entered their camp while he was gone. Some were happy to see the prophet; many were not. They believed Jeremiah to be a traitor, as it was well known that he had befriended the king of Babylon. When he came to see the people in the last tent, though, he saw a familiar—and welcome—face sitting outside.

"Well, little one, how good it is to see you!" Jeremiah moved toward the small eleven-year-old girl and wrapped his arms around her. "I'm so happy to see you."

"And I'm so happy to see you!" Hannah said with a broad smile when Jeremiah released her.

"I met a girl in our camp …" Hannah looked around to see if anyone was close enough to hear. "She's a little older than me. Could I please spend some time with her?"

Jeremiah gave her a little smile. "Yes. I'm sure you can. Come see me after you have had your breakfast and I will introduce her to you." Jeremiah gave her a wink, then said good-bye.

—

Over the next few days, Teia and Hannah spent most of their time together with Miriam and the other girls in their camp. It became common to see the two girls together and eventually share the same tent where they were now busy packing.

Everyone was packing because the small amount of food and supplies initially brought into the encampment were almost gone. The refugees would be forced to leave this site and travel to the nearest city—or stay hidden and starve to death. They hoped that they would find food and shelter when they arrived. They prayed that they would arrive safely.

Chapter 8

By sunset, any trace of their camp had disappeared. Traveling by night and hiding by day, the Judeans continued to move northwest toward Mizpah. Upon their arrival, the people of Mizpah welcomed the weary band of exiles. Everyone shared what little they had left after the Babylonian invasion. The refugees finally felt secure as they settled in and set up their tents at the far end of the overcrowded village.

A few peaceful weeks had passed before everyone woke to a thundering sound that grew even as anguished cries rose from the village square. Teia peeked out the front of her tent and watched through the early morning haze.

Dozens of horses charged into the center of the village. Swords slashed through tents. Many Judeans roused themselves from sleep and streamed into the town square, shoving each other as they screamed their way out of the path of the stampeding horses. The riders, though, wielded their swords for more than hacking at tents—now cutting down villagers as they ran in every direction. Some of the horsemen began driving their mounts into the tents to charge back and forth, crushing those who remained inside.

"We have to get out of here!" Teia shrieked.

She turned around and grabbed Hannah's hand.

"What?" Hannah said. "What's happening?"

Teia said nothing, but pulled her sister up, then dragged her out of their tent and down the nearest backstreet.

"Hide under here," Teia said.

She pushed Hannah under an empty cart just as she heard galloping hoofs come from behind her. Teia ran down the narrow alleyway. She glanced back to see a mounted soldier speed toward her and then heard him shout.

"Get the girl behind me under the cart. Leave the one running for me!" he ordered.

A second horseman rode up the alley toward Teia, blocking her way of escape. The soldier lashed at his horse, then rode past Teia toward Hannah.

Teia hesitated, looking back toward her sister before running again as the first horsemen was almost upon her. Within seconds, the princess felt the breath and spray of the snorting horse as it rode up close behind her. She screamed as she tried to fight off the soldier, clawing at the large arms that leaned toward her over the saddle. With little effort, the soldier reached down, grabbed the slender princess with one arm, and then threw her face-down across his horse.

The soldiers gathered in the center of the town with their captives, whose hands they bound before separating them into groups of males and females. A heavy man, with bulbous eyes and long, wiry black hair and matching beard, sat on a horse and surveyed the male hostages that were paraded before him first. His ugly face and cold, dark eyes watched the long line of bloody and battered men who shuffled forward in front of him.

"Stop!" he ordered.

The captives stood in place as he rode toward a man with a dark gray beard and dressed in Babylonian robes.

"Whom do we have here?" the man said. "Am I looking at the great prophet Jeremiah? I thought you were imprisoned in Jerusalem—and most likely dead! Step forward, Prophet of God, and tell me how you have come to be here."

Jeremiah took a few steps forward. "King Nebuchadnezzar released me and gave me leave to go where I choose! Who are you?"

"Yes, I've heard that the king of Babylon favors you. It seems we are both fortunate that you were not killed today. As for me, I am Ishmael, son of Nethaniah. I was an army captain for the king of Judah—but now I fight for the king of Ammon. I'm surprised, Prophet, that your fellow Judeans would want you around, since it was your friend, Nebuchadnezzar, who starved our people or had them slaughtered or taken away as slaves."

Jeremiah said nothing, but only looked up at Ishmael.

"Unbind his hands and pull him aside!" Ishmael ordered.

At his command, several soldiers came forward. As they cut the straps on Jeremiah's wrists, the prophet called out, "There are others, Ishmael. My companions are here with me. You must not—"

"Must not what? Kill them?" Ishmael turned his horse away. He laughed. "Don't worry, Prophet, we won't let any harm come to you—or those you seek to protect … *if* they are still alive. It seems it would be in my interest to keep the puppet of the king of Babylon content. I must also remain in your favor, as I don't want you sending the wrath of God down on me as you did on Jerusalem!"

Ishmael laughed again, and Jeremiah once more gave no reply.

"Pull out the strong ones," Ishmael said. "They will make good slaves. Kill the rest of them and show me the women. And hold Jeremiah over with the strong men until I finish viewing the females."

As the men were led away, Ishmael dismounted his horse and approached the line of female captives. He walked slowly back and forth, closely eyeing the faces and bodies of his prisoners.

"Hmm … You're a pretty one," Ishmael said. He dragged his pointer finger down the face and neck of one of the teenage girls. "Untie this one!"

As the soldiers did so, Ishmael continued down the long line of young girls and older women.

"You! Lift up your head and look at me." Ishmael stopped in front of a young woman.

When she refused the command, Ishmael reached out and grabbed her jaw in his fingers.

"Let me see you, girl."

He tightened his grip and forced her face up, then withdrew his hand. He threw his head back, laughing and exposing missing teeth usually hidden by his thick mustache.

"You may be wearing a dirty tunic, but you are no servant girl. Step forward so all can see you."

When she didn't move this time, Ishmael grabbed her arm and yanked her toward him.

"Ha! This is Princess Teia! Daughter of our beloved and now imprisoned King Zedekiah," Ishmael shouted.

Teia stood silent, feeling both scared and angry as her chin burned where the red imprint of Ishmael's fingers now swelled.

"How fortunate that we rescued you." Ishmael leaned in close to Teia. "My eyes were on you many times when I visited your father. Even dressed like this … mmm, you are a beauty." Ishmael drew his tongue back and forth over his lips.

A swell of nausea turned in Teia's stomach.

"Were you aware, Princess, that after the last battle I fought for your father, he made me a promise? He told me that I would have you as my bride!"

Ishmael grabbed Teia around the waist and pulled her hard against his chest. Teia struggled to free herself, but the more she pushed, the tighter Ishmael held her.

"Let me go!" Teia shouted.

"Come now, Princess. It's time you learned to act with respect toward your future husband."

"No!" Teia spat. "I won't marry you! You can't make me! Gedaliah now rules Judah. He won't award you my hand in marriage."

Ishmael slit his eyes at her. "Gedaliah is dead."

"What?" Teia whispered as she gazed into Ishmael's dark eyes.

"Yes, Princess. To you and everyone else who can hear me," Ishmael shouted, "Gedaliah is dead, along with all his men here in Mizpah. He was easy to deceive and foolish to invite me and my men here last night to feast and revel with him through the early hours of this morning. Now no one rules the land of Judah!"

Teia could hear gasps and murmurs of disbelief among the captives.

"Don't worry. I'll take care of you, Princess," Ishmael said. He leered at Teia, then turned and shouted to his soldiers, "Select the finest of the females to take with us. Kill the rest. We leave immediately for Ammon."

"Wait!" Teia said, her mind racing. "My sister ..."

Ishmael looked at her. "Your sister?"

"Hannah ... she is here," Teia said. She turned around and looked up and down the line of females.

"Two princesses—how pleasant for me," Ishmael said. "You and your sister will be well taken care of. I wouldn't want to do anything to anger my future wife."

Ishmael smiled at her, then turned and walked toward his horse.

"And my friend ... Miriam," Teia said. "Please spare my friend—"

"Don't ask any more favors of me, Princess!" Ishmael mounted his horse. "Your friend's appearance will either spare or condemn her."

Teia's teeth clenched even as she felt her stomach roil with fear.

"Prepare the younger princess, Jeremiah, and his men for our departure. Put Jeremiah and his men together in the carts scattered around here. Princess Teia will ride with me."

Chilling screams and loud cries from men, women, and children resounded as Ishmael's captives rode out of the gates of Mizpah.

Hour after hour, Teia pitched back and forth on Ishmael's horse. The steady pounding of its hoofs kicked up waves of dry earth that covered their riders with dust. Teia's lashes became caked with grit that scraped across her eyes each time she blinked. The princess shut her eyelids and coughed on the dirt particles she breathed in as a wave of despair engulfed her.

I thought I was free. I thought I would never again have to fear ... to fear this. A hideous savage ... That's the man my father promised my hand in marriage? I would rather have died under the temple.

"The Israelites!" one of Ishmael's soldiers shouted. He rode up alongside Teia and her captor. "Johanan and his men have followed us!"

Ishmael slowed his horse and turned in his saddle. He looked up to where his soldier pointed. Ishmael squinted and saw a dark mass moving along a nearby ridge.

"Hmm ... They are still some distance away," Ishmael said. "We won't stop now until after we pass far beyond Gibeon. By then, the sun will have set and we can lose them. We need to increase our speed and put as much distance between us as possible. Johanan and his men are mighty warriors. Tell the rest of the men to be prepared for battle if they should come upon us."

Ishmael tightened his left arm around Teia's waist as he held onto the horse's reins with that same hand. With his right hand, he grabbed his whip and lashed the stallion. Billowing dust veiled the long line of horses as they sped away. After riding for miles, they neared the border of Gibeon. That was when Teia heard the clash of metal behind them.

Ishmael released his grip on Teia, then pulled the reins on his horse and turned toward the noise. He looked away from the princess and reached for his sword.

Teia saw her chance for escape and flung herself off the horse. As Ishmael shouted a curse, she ran through clouds of dust and up the nearest hillside. Without looking back, she dropped to the ground behind some low brush.

From her hiding place, Teia heard the violent sounds of metal clanging, mixed with the groans and cries of men as the opposing soldiers fought for their lives.

When the battle finally quieted, a deep voice shouted, "Find the princess!"

Teia's heart quickened when she heard the order. She parted some of the brush to see who had given the command. In the waning light on the road below, Teia saw the dead bodies of many men scattered on the ground. In the midst of them, sitting on his stallion, was a man she thought she recognized from his past visits to the palace.

"Princess Teia!" the man shouted. "It's Johanan, captain of your father's army. Ishmael is gone."

"Johanan?" Teia called out.

She emerged from her hiding spot, then ran down the hill toward the tall, burly soldier.

As soon as he saw the princess, Johanan dismounted his horse. He waited on the road, and Teia soon threw her arms around him and cried into his chest.

"I'm sorry, Princess, that we didn't arrive sooner," Johanan said. He gently pulled Teia off his body and held her out in front of him. "We will now guard you and the rest of Ishmael's captives."

"Is ... Is he dead?" Teia asked.

Johanan looked down the road, then shook his head. "Ishmael's gone. The coward sped off. He won't get far before my men find him and kill him."

"Oh, Teia!" came a shout from behind. "Are you alright?"

Teia turned to see Hannah running toward them, followed by Miriam and Jeremiah.

Taking Hannah into her arms, Teia said, "I'm alright ... just a bit shaken."

Then Teia wrapped both herself and Hannah into Jeremiah's open arms. Jeremiah reached out and stroked Teia's hair.

"We have protection now," the prophet said. "Johanan and his men will guard us."

Teia cast a glance at the captain, then nodded.

"Princess Teia," Johanan said, "you will ride with me until we arrive safely in Geruth Kimham. There is no reason for any of you to return to Mizpah. We found only a few people left there alive who had escaped into the fields outside the city. They hid there while everyone else was captured or killed. They returned only after they saw Ishmael and his soldiers ride out of the city with you."

"But I must return to Mizpah for … for my scrolls," Jeremiah said. "They are in a large chest. It was in my tent."

"Prophet, I doubt there is anything of value left there. When we rode through the city square, it had been destroyed. We found piles of bodies in the main cistern. That's where Ishmael's men disposed of the badly injured, and the dead."

"No, I must go back!" Jeremiah said.

"Prophet, there is nothing left!"

"If none of your men will take me, I will walk."

"Alright! Enough!" Johanan said, then sighed. "Very well. I will send a few of my men back to look for your scrolls, but you stay with me."

Jeremiah nodded. "Baruch—my scribe—he knows what the chest looks like. He can go with your men and show them where to find it. It's heavy, so you may need a cart to bring it back."

At that, Johanan raised an eyebrow at the prophet. "Jeremiah, we will be lucky enough to find your chest, let alone a cart that is still in one piece to carry it."

Chapter 9

Between gulps from his water skin, Johanan relayed the story of the recent battle with Ishmael's soldiers to the gathering crowd who began surrounding him and his men when they arrived in Geruth Kimham.

To the surprise of Jeremiah, who stood nearby, Johanan told the large crowd that they should prepare to leave in a few days.

"What's this you say?" the prophet asked. "Are we not safe here with you and your men?"

"Ishmael killed Gedaliah and most of his guards," Johanan said. "We now not only have the Babylonians to fear, but also Ishmael and the Ammonites. My men never found him. Ishmael got away and will not forget that we killed many of his best soldiers." Johanan paused. "Jeremiah, Ishmael will also remember what we took from him. Until we have word that he is dead, none of us are safe. Ishmael will seek us out with an army of men provided by the king of Ammon, and they will far outnumber us. We can't stay here. We are not safe in Judah. I advise we leave as soon as possible."

"Leave for where?" Jeremiah asked.

"For Egypt."

"Yes! To Egypt! To Egypt!" some in the crowd began to chant.

"Wait!" an old man shouted. "Shouldn't we ask the prophet? Let's not decide without asking Jeremiah. If the king would have listened to him … if we would have listened to him … to Yahweh, Jerusalem would still be our home!"

Johanan turned to Jeremiah. "Prophet, will you seek the Lord's will in what he wants for his people?"

Jeremiah stroked his beard as he studied Johanan's face, then answered, "I will pray to the Lord our God and ask for his guidance. Let no one disturb me but my scribe, Baruch. Send him to me as soon as he returns from Mizpah."

With that, Jeremiah walked through the crowd toward his tent, which had been set up near the center of the town square.

As the time passed by, the refugees gathered nearby and waited for the prophet to instruct them. Day after day, though, Jeremiah remained inside his tent as he fasted and prayed to the Lord.

The town soon overflowed with new travelers that continued to stream into the village. After Gedaliah's death, news of Johanan's victory over Ishmael's soldiers spread across Judah. Others flocked to Geruth Kimham to be near Jeremiah, whom they believed to be God's prophet. Groups of families and some entire small villages sought security or direction from both the captain and the prophet. Soon, a multitude filled the town as they continued to wait day after day for Jeremiah to emerge from his tent and give them God's word.

"Jeremiah, come out!" one man shouted on the ninth day of waiting. "Let the Lord show us where we should go."

But only silence greeted the crowd in reply.

On the eleventh day, Jeremiah finally opened the flap of his tent and slowly walked out, ready to address the people. "Bring Johanan and his army of men before all of our people in this town. Then, when they are gathered here, I will give you the word of the Lord."

Crowds filled the streets and gathered on rooftops to hear the prophet speak. Jeremiah stood and held up his hands to quiet the murmur of the people before he spoke.

"This is what the Lord, the God of Israel, to whom you sent me to present your petition, says: 'If you stay in this land, I will build you up and not tear you down; I will plant you and not uproot you, for I am grieved over the disaster I have inflicted on you. Do not be afraid of the king of Babylon, whom you now fear, for I am with you and will save you and deliver you from his hands. I will show you compassion so that he will have compassion on you and restore you to your land.'

"However," Jeremiah continued, "if you say, 'We will not stay in this land,' and so disobey the Lord your God, and if you say, 'No, we will go and live in Egypt, where we will not see war or hear the trumpet or be hungry for bread,' then hear the word of the Lord, O remnant of Judah. This is what the Lord Almighty, the God of Israel, says: 'If you are determined to go to Egypt and you do go to settle there, then the sword you fear will overtake you there, and the famine you dread will follow you into Egypt, and there you will die.'"

Jeremiah looked at the crowd and shouted, "Remnant of Judah, Yahweh has told you, 'Do not go to Egypt.' Be sure of this: I warn you today!"

Scattered cries broke out amidst the crowd:

"Silence the traitor!"

"He's a false prophet."

"Silence him! He is Nebuchadnezzar's puppet."

"He betrayed us and our king."

"Don't listen to him!"

"To Egypt! To Egypt!" The chants rose from the angry crowd.

Those loyal to Jeremiah formed a shield in front of the prophet as the mob surged forward.

"Stand back!" Johanan yelled.

His voice boomed over the crowd as he held up his sword and then moved through the crowd toward Jeremiah.

When he stood before the prophet, Johanan said, "The people are in fear, Jeremiah. They believe that as long as they live anywhere in Judah, they will be hunted by the Ammonites or the Babylonians. They want to go to Egypt and settle there. And they want to leave soon. While you have been hidden away in your tent, the people have grown restless and afraid. I don't have enough men to protect the number of people that are here now. We can't stay here!"

Jeremiah didn't respond but only glared at the captain.

Johanan frowned and turned to face the crowd. "The prophet has spoken, and the people have spoken!" Johanan shouted. "I believe we are not safe here! My men and I cannot protect all of you. We are few in number compared to our enemies. I say we prepare to leave for Egypt!"

Baruch came forward and stood in front of Johanan. "What you say means death to those who ignore the word of the Lord. How can you deny the words of God's prophet? Did you not learn anything from the destruction of Jerusalem? Was your faith in the power of the word of God not strengthened?"

Johanan cut his eyes at the scribe. "Don't question my faith! I don't think you understand what we face here. I can't provide protection for all these people. Even if I could, the people of Judah don't want Babylonian masters. I don't see a good life for our people anymore in this land. Why should we remain here where there are only the bonds of slavery and a slow starvation from the higher rate of tax now demanded by Nebuchadnezzar on this season's already lean crops? There will be plenty of food for all of us in the land of the Nile! Egypt is our friend. There are already many Hebrew colonies established there."

Baruch shook his head and looked at the ground.

Johanan turned to Jeremiah. "You and the princesses will come with us willingly—or we will lead you by the sword."

"There will be no need for threats, Captain," the prophet said.

Turning away again, Johanan shouted to the crowd, "We are going to Egypt! The decision is final!"

The anger of the crowd vanished even as a spontaneous cheer went up, and again they chanted, "To Egypt! To Egypt!"

The people in the village immediately began to pack their belongings, and by sundown, they were ready to begin their journey. Johanan and his soldiers led the people from Geruth Kimham to the village of Beersheba, where they rested overnight before making their way to the trade route along the Judean coast.

The long line of refugees crawled along the dirt path with their overflowing carts laden with children, tools, and household goods. The farmers and their wives, meanwhile, trudged behind their covered push carts, in which fruits, vegetables, and grains from their last harvests were piled high.

A trailing wake of dust followed the caravan for several days as it moved south past Gaza. The noise of jangling harnesses and creaking carts carried through the desert heat above the muffled sound of human voices.

Teia spoke little as she thought about her mother and her home in Jerusalem. She silently prayed that someday she would return. But the farther she traveled, and the more unfamiliar the terrain became, the more she felt her hope fade away.

The princess sat next to her sister and Miriam as they bounced along the uneven roads in a cart led by Jeremiah, Baruch, and Ebed. The girls rode on a pillow of hay that covered a large chest. Their caravan passed by fields of golden wheat and barley, where some of the people paused in their walk to harvest what they could from the side of the road.

Seven days after starting their journey, the weary travelers reached the Egyptian coast late at night and they set up camp. Once inside her tent, wrapped in a blanket on a reed mat with Hannah at her side, Teia fell fast asleep.

Chapter 10

A light ocean breeze greeted Teia as she pushed open the flap of her tent. Her eyes scanned over the scattered camp of the refugees, then across the sand to the sea, where small waves rose then broke into a frothy foam as they washed ashore. *It's beautiful here,* Teia thought as she took in a deep breath of fresh morning air. After the long journey over many dusty roads, she was glad their caravan had chosen this place to set up their camp when they'd arrived four days ago.

Teia let the tent flap slip back into place and then padded over to where Hannah lay.

"Wake up, Hannah," Teia said as she gently shook her sister's shoulder.

"Hmm? What?" Hannah pulled her blanket toward her face.

"Come on, let's get dressed. I want to go exploring today … by ourselves. We've stayed in camp since we got here, and I overheard Jeremiah say last night that we are leaving soon."

Hannah yawned. "Where … Where do you want to go?" she asked.

"Down by the water."

Another yawn. "Mmm, I don't know, Teia. You better ask Jeremiah first."

"I don't want to bother him. Besides, we're not going that far."

"Alright, I'll go with you, but can we get something to eat first?" Hannah tossed her blanket aside. "And what about Miriam and Tirzah? Should we see if they want to go with us?"

"Umm … let's just you and I go. We'll see them when we get back, okay?"

After getting dressed, the sisters walked to the center of the camp, where several older women sat outside their tents, kneading and stretching dough into thin sheets. Then they slapped the irregular oval shapes against the inside of large clay pots filled with burning shards of wood. There, the dough bubbled and turned golden brown as it heated. When the flat bread finished baking, the women stacked the warm pieces on a blanket already laden with mounds of dates and figs. The princesses helped themselves to their morning portion: one piece of bread wrapped around several chunks of the sweet dried fruit.

They moved on to the next tent, where two women sat in front of clay urns filled with barley water. The sisters filled a couple of gourd ladles and drank the nutritious honey-sweetened water. It quenched their thirst as they munched on their breakfast and wandered through the camp.

When they reached the last tent, Teia grabbed Hannah's hand. "Now!" she said.

Teia pulled Hannah behind the tent. Their feet sank deep into the soft sand as they ran up and down the small dunes toward the shore.

"Let's get our feet wet," Teia said.

She plopped down onto the edge of the shore and untied her sandals. When Hannah had hers off, Teia took her sister's hand and pulled her toward the water.

"Doesn't it feel wonderful?" Teia said.

The sisters held hands and walked across the cool, wet sand that squished between their toes. Teia laughed and gave her sister's hand a tug forward when she found Hannah looking back toward their camp.

"Don't worry," Teia said. "Everyone is too busy to notice us missing. Let's just enjoy our freedom for a little while."

She pulled Hannah along into the soft foam that swept over their ankles.

"It's cold!" Hannah shrieked.

"You'll get used to it. Come on! Let's go out a little farther," Teia said.

She began to wade deeper into the sea, careful to lift her dress above the water.

"No, Teia! I don't want to go!" Hannah pulled free of Teia's hand. "You're going to get all wet."

"I don't care."

Teia moved into deeper water and savored the freedom that flooded through her. She giggled and danced with joy, swaying back and forth and twirling around and around. When she turned to look back at Hannah, her laughter fell silent.

"Oh no!" she whispered to herself.

Two unfamiliar men strode toward Hannah, who was still facing the sea and smiling at Teia. Not wanting to alarm Hannah, Teia pushed through the small surf back to shore.

"Teia? What's wrong?" Hannah said. "You look so—"

As Teia put herself between her sister and the two men, Hannah turned and sucked in a sharp breath.

"Oh, Teia!" Hannah said.

Teia froze in place, arms back just a bit to keep Hannah behind her. If Teia had been alone, she would have tried to run away, but not with her young sister. Teia glanced across the sand and realized that most of their camp lay hidden behind the dunes. No one could see the encounter that would soon take place.

The taller of the two men moved forward. He wore a dark green tunic and ornate gold arm and wrist bands. He spoke to them in a language Teia didn't understand. She forced a smile as she looked at the young man's finely chiseled features. In an instant—without a thought—she felt drawn and attracted to him.

Teia fumbled in her mind for words. "If … If you would excuse us, we … we really should get back to our camp," she said.

"Oh, you don't speak Egyptian. My apologies," the young man responded in Hebrew. "I am sorry if we startled you. Please, go on and enjoy yourself. Although, I do find it is quite unusual and daring for beautiful girls to be alone without an escort. There are many men here who have been long at sea, and the sight of you might cause them to be … less than respectful."

Teia had to force herself to focus, as she had been prepared for the worst possible scenario to unfold. "Uh … Thank you … Thank you for your concern, but our elders … uh, they know that we are here and are watching us now."

"Is that so?" the young man said. With a slight smile, he looked around. "Where are they? Point them out to me."

The stranger held his gaze on Teia, then his eyes swept over her.

"Um … I'm sorry. My sister and I must be going. Our family will be waiting for us," Teia said. She turned away and grabbed Hannah's hand.

"Wait!" The young man stepped forward and reached a hand toward Teia. "I do not intend to detain you. I only ask your name?"

Teia hesitated as she looked up into the soft blue eyes of the stranger, who had an unsettling way of looking at her—pleasantly unsettling, actually.

Finally, Teia shook her head. "I'm … I'm sorry … We must go." Then she pulled her sister away from the shore.

"Teia … our sandals!" Hannah whispered.

"We'll get them later."

Teia led Hannah back over the dunes. She was out of breath when she pulled Hannah past the first tent that led into their camp.

"Wait here," Teia said.

She peeked around the back of the tent. Her eyes searched up and down the visible shore. The two men were not anywhere in sight. Teia turned back to her sister.

"Hannah, please don't say anything to anyone about what just happened!"

"And what will you give me if I stay quiet?"

"Hannah, you bribe me?"

"I'm teasing! But maybe … maybe I should think of something to make it worth keeping my silence." Hannah smiled, then strutted away.

Teia lay awake all that night. The rhythmic sounds of the waves that usually lulled her to sleep now only brought back memories of her encounter with the handsome youth. *Why do I still see his face and hear his voice?* Teia wondered as she turned back and forth on her mat until the faint light of morning filtered into her tent.

Certain that Hannah was still asleep, Teia grabbed her shawl and slipped out into the cool morning air. She walked across the sand to one of the tallest dunes near her camp, then chose a place to sit where she could watch the ships in the distance as they came and went in the harbor. After a few minutes, she noticed a familiar figure walking along the shore. Teia sprang up and hurried across the sand toward him.

"Good morning, Jeremiah."

"Good morning, Princess." Jeremiah turned, then opened his arms to give Teia a warm hug. "You're up early. Can't sleep?"

"Uhh … Oh, I slept a little. It's just so … so different here." She tried to push the thoughts of yesterday morning out of her mind as they walked toward the seaport. "Where do all the ships come from?" she asked.

"From all over the world. You can tell where they are from by the flags and standards they fly. You see this first ship—the one that has a blue flag with a red star?" Jeremiah lifted his hand. "They sail from the island of Crete. And the one next to them, with the flag of a cedar tree, they're Phoenician."

"Where do you think that big ship is from, the one farthest away with the flag that has a red hand?"

Jeremiah's eyes followed to where Teia's finger pointed.

Teia heard Jeremiah's breath catch. "No. It can't be," the prophet whispered.

"What?"

"That flag … that design of the red hand … that belongs to one of our ancestors—the sign of Zerah-Judah."

"Who?"

Now Jeremiah looked at Teia. "Surely you were taught about the birth of the twin sons to Jacob's son, Judah. The births of a great many people are recorded in God's word, yet none but the birth of the twins Zerah and Perez was recorded in such detail to be singled out for all to understand its significance. Hmm … When we return to camp, we will have to study the scrolls together that tell this story. But for now, come with me. I must see if there is someone on that vessel who will tell me from what land they sailed."

As Teia and Jeremiah approached the ship, the princess noticed a very familiar-looking young man standing on the top deck.

"Oh … I … I think I'll go back to camp," Teia said. Then she started to turn away from Jeremiah.

"Nonsense, child! You'll follow me. If this ship belongs to one of our ancestors, you as a member of the royal family should meet them."

Teia gave the prophet a little smile and fell in behind him. As they drew closer to the ship, the young man on deck appeared to be giving orders to the crew. Soon, he turned toward the shore and his eyes fell on Jeremiah and Teia. The princess looked down at the ground.

"Well, hello there!" the young man called down in Hebrew. "I didn't expect to see you again after you ran off yesterday."

Jeremiah stopped and raised his eyebrows at Teia. "You … You two have met?"

The young man laughed. "It seems the young lady likes to frolic in the sea with her sister. I came upon them yesterday morning. I was quite surprised to find them there alone," he said. "I am glad to see you made it safely back to your camp." The young man smiled at Teia.

She gave a quick smile back and then returned her attention to the ground.

"Yes, that makes two of us," Jeremiah said, taking a sharp sideways glance at Teia. "We will speak of this later, Princess." The prophet turned back to the young man and said, "You speak our language."

"Yes, and several others. It is useful to speak the language of the people who reside in the lands where we set our anchor. We travel to many different nations."

"It is your flag that drew us to your ship," Jeremiah said. The prophet's keen eyes probed every detail of the stranger's body and dress. He appeared to be no more than in his early twenties, yet he wore the insignia of royalty. Jeremiah's glance rested for a moment on the golden bands that wrapped around the young man's wrists. "May I ask who commands your ship?"

"Sir, I am in command. Forgive me … I am Eochaid Finn, prince of Meath, son of Ailill—king of the Isle of Erin. I come from a land beyond the Pillars of Hercules." The young man held up his hand. "Wait there … I'll come down."

The young monarch who approached the prophet and princess appeared to stand over six feet in height. His green knee-length tunic was attached with gold clasps over broad shoulders. The sleeveless garment exposed tanned, muscular arms and legs. Blue-gray eyes and sun-streaked blond, shoulder-length hair accentuated his handsome features.

With his head held high, the prince continued. "I am a descendant of Gallam Milesius, from the line of Heber, the Milesian prince, who conquered Iberia five centuries ago. My ancestors came from Zaragoza. After they won battles from one end of the Great Sea to the other, they lastly conquered and settled in Erin. There, my father, Ailill Finn, High-King of Erin, married the daughter of Lugaid MacLatha, my mother, Queen Noirenn."

Jeremiah closed his eyes for a few moments, then said, "Prince of Meath, the Lord God Almighty has brought our paths together today and has revealed to me that you are not only a prince of Erin, you are also a prince of Israel. There is much that I would like to speak to you about. Perhaps you and some of your crew could join our camp this evening?"

"I don't know who you are, but I am intrigued by the sincerity of your declaration of what you proclaim is my royal heritage."

"Forgive me, I am Jeremiah, prophet of Yahweh, the one and only living God. I was appointed at birth to be his voice to his people. And this young lady …" Jeremiah turned toward Teia. "… whom it seems you have already met, is Princess Teia Tamar, descendant of King David, daughter of the house of Judah, daughter of King Zedekiah."

"Princess ... Teia Tamar, I am pleased to meet you—again." The prince made a slight bow, then smiled at the princess.

Teia stared into the eyes of the prince. Her stomach fluttered. She felt her face warm as a rosy blush crept up her neck and cheeks. Teia looked away to break Eochaid's gaze as Jeremiah continued to speak.

"Are you aware, Prince Eochaid, that 'Heber' is an Israelite name and that it is recorded among us that the Milesians of Iberia were originally an Israelite colony? Now that we stand below your ship, I see you fly two flags. One with the red hand of Zerah-Judah. The other has four symbols, all of which represent various tribes of Israel. It seems clear that the people of the land you call 'Erin' are also people from the family of our father Jacob."

"Hmm ..." Eochaid said. "Our bards sing many stories of our ancient ancestors coming from far-off lands in the East. I have also heard legends of a great King David and his son Solomon. Some even say that one of our insignias of a harp came from David's harp that was brought to our shores long ago. That harp now sits in my father's throne room."

"We have much to discuss, then, Prince. Will you please join us after the sun sets this evening for a meal and for some time where you and I may talk in private?" Jeremiah asked. "We leave for the city of Tahpanhes tomorrow morning, and there is much I wish to tell you, and more that I would like to hear about you and your homeland before we go."

"I am also leaving Egypt. We sail at dawn. We stopped here only to make repairs to our ship and restock a few provisions before we resume our journey back to Erin. I am anxious to arrive home since I recently received word that my father is ill." Eochaid looked from Jeremiah to Teia. "But, yes, I would like to spend more time with you, so I would be glad to join you this evening."

CHAPTER 11

A soft orange glow lit the faces of the women sitting in the sand around a dozen fire-pits. They talked and laughed with each other as they turned long sticks of speared mullet back and forth over the heat of the fire. The fish smoked and crackled as the flaming wood cooked and charred its oily skin. Younger girls sat nearby and kneaded dough, or stirred steaming clay pots filled to the brim with chopped vegetables. But when a small group of strange men entered camp, all eyes lifted from the food and from each other.

Whiffs of aromatic smoke drifted by Eochaid and his three crewmen as they walked into the encampment and moved toward the large, torch-lit circle of tents. Johanan stood stiffly near the entrance with several of his soldiers and stared with a cold gaze at the four men who approached. He moved forward and blocked Eochaid's path.

"I am Johanan, captain of Judah's soldiers. I am in command of this camp and its people."

"I am Eochaid, prince of Erin, and these are my ships officers. Your prophet, Jeremiah, invited us to join you this evening."

"Yes, he informed me. Do you carry any weapons?" Johanan asked. He looked over the prince and his companions.

"We each carry a dagger." Eochaid pushed back his cloak to reveal the silver knife that hung from his belt.

"You must remove your weapons. They will be returned to you when you leave our camp. These are my rules."

Eochaid hesitated, then pulled the dagger from its sheath and motioned for his men to do the same.

Teia sat outside her tent and watched the prince and his encounter with Johanan. The blond hair and tanned face of the prince looked golden under the glow of the flaming torches. She thought the prince to be taller and more muscular than most young men she had met. She didn't know that it was his years of training as a warrior and many long journeys commanding at sea that had formed Eochaid's body into more man than youth.

The prince's eyes scanned the faces around the camp as he moved past the soldiers. He searched for the face of Jeremiah, but stopped when his eyes rested on Teia, whom he found studying him. When their eyes met, she looked away. Eochaid began to lead his men in Teia's direction when he heard his name called: "Prince Eochaid! Thank you for coming."

Eochaid turned around to see the prophet walking toward him. "Thank you for inviting us," the prince said. "I asked a few of my officers to join me, as the rest of my crew is preparing for our early morning departure. My officers, like me, also speak Hebrew. I have also told them that you and I would need some time tonight to talk in private."

"Well, then," Jeremiah said, "let me start the evening by introducing you and your men to my most trusted companions, Baruch and Ebed. If it meets with your approval, your men can sit with them during the evening meal. I am sure they will have much between them to talk about. When they are settled, you can join me in here." Jeremiah gestured with an open hand toward the large tent behind them.

After all the men had been introduced, Jeremiah and the prince walked back to the prophet's tent.

"Will the princesses be joining us?" Eochaid asked. He kept his eyes down as he took his turn washing his hands in the ceramic bowl of water perched on top of a few thick pieces of driftwood just inside the tent.

Jeremiah's lips curved into a smile. "Later. First we will talk, then you may speak to Princess Teia. Ah! Here is our meal."

Two women entered Jeremiah's tent, carrying several platters covered with barbequed fish, vegetables coated in olive oil, stacks of flatbread, small mounds of dates, fresh red grapes, and a jug of wine. They set the food and drink down between the prophet and the prince. The two men settled down across from each other on a thick rug that covered the earthen floor.

Eochaid looked over the variety of food. "This is quite a feast."

"Yes, Yahweh has generously provided for us, so we will first give thanks to him." Jeremiah closed his eyes, raised his hands, and said, "Blessed are you, Yahweh, O Lord our God, creator of the heavens and the earth. We give thanks to you for creating all that is needed to sustain us. We give thanks to you, O Lord, for this meal, gathered from the bounty of your land and sea. We pray that it will strengthen us so that we may go forth to do your will. Amen."

Jeremiah opened his eyes and reached his right hand down toward the food. "The natural calming effect of the sea has lifted our spirits since we arrived here. The sea's inlet has also supplied us with a daily source of fresh fish. Some of our men are good fishermen who brought their nets."

The prophet used his fingers to peel a moist piece of mullet off its needle-thin bones. After eating the fish, Jeremiah poured some wine into a cup, then continued. "Many of our people who lived within the walls of Jerusalem during the Babylonian siege died of starvation. But those living far outside the city, like the farmers, they still tended their crops, their vineyards and orchards. They brought what they could harvest with them when they left Judah. We are blessed tonight to eat their food and drink their wine."

Jeremiah reached for the small pitcher and poured some of the dark, crimson liquid into Eochaid's cup. The prince nodded, then wrapped a chunk of fish in a small piece of flatbread before taking a couple of bites. After finishing the fish roll, he sipped the wine.

"Is that your royal emblem … the lion? The one sewn on the flag outside your tent?" Eochaid asked.

"Yes. That, my Prince, is the banner and insignia of our tribe: the Lion of Judah—the tribe of our father David and of Solomon, his son. It has been our standard since a man named Jacob blessed one of his twelve his sons named Judah. What he said was this:

"'Judah, your brothers will praise you; your hand will be on the neck of your enemies; your father's sons will bow down to you. You are a lion's cub, O Judah; you return from the prey, my son. Like a lion he crouches and lies down, like a lioness—who dares to rouse him? The scepter will not depart from Judah, nor the ruler's staff from between his feet, until he comes to whom it belongs and the obedience of the nations is his.'

"That last line is the important one," Jeremiah said. "That is the one to remember!"

Nodding, Eochaid picked up a small handful of grapes. "When I was very young, my mother would tell me many stories. One legend I recall was that long ago, there were two great kings, a father and his son. She said that they were our ancient ancestors. But the details of this story were lost over time. I never knew if the fables were true or false. As I mentioned to you this morning, our bards still sing occasionally of David, a shepherd lad who rose to be a mighty king of a great people."

"What you mother spoke was true. David and his son Solomon were great kings." Jeremiah brushed off his hands and grabbed a piece of flatbread. "David was a shepherd who kept his father's flocks in the days of Saul, the first king of Israel. David was a great king, yes, but he was also a great warrior and poet. In his life, he knew happiness and tragedy; he had to flee from a jealous and mad king; he lost his best friend in battle. He also lost a seven-day-old son.

"David rose from humble beginnings to become the absolute ruler of his people. He was passionate in his love of and belief in the one true God, to whom he ascribed all his successes, and to whom he wrote and sang songs that we still sing today. But, like all of us, David had his human faults and at times was weak in spirit and gave into the temptations of the flesh. But none loved Yahweh like David. I have many scrolls that contain the words of his songs, his prayers and praises to our God."

Jeremiah paused, then took his eyes off the prince as he tore the large piece of bread in his hands into smaller pieces. He used the folded irregular shapes to scoop up a few mouthfuls of cooked vegetables.

Eochaid swallowed the last bite of his grapes, then waited for the prophet to finish eating before he spoke: "I would like to hear more of your God, but may I first ask how you became what you call … a prophet?"

"The call to be a prophet was not of my choosing. When I was a very young, living in a little town called Anathoth, not far from Jerusalem, the Lord came to me in a vision. He touched my mouth and said to me, 'I have put my words in your mouth. See, today I appoint you over nations and kingdoms to uproot and tear down, to destroy and overthrow, to build and to plant.'

"The Lord chose me to be his voice. He speaks to me so that I may speak his words to his people. In his words, the invisible God, the creator, the great mystery becomes … evident. He becomes known. The prophet helps God's people to hear. He helps them to see. But God leaves it up to those who hear his words … to believe.

"Many times in the past, I thought I should have been a priest like my father and brothers. As a prophet of the Holy One of Israel, I have been despised by my people. I have even been starved and imprisoned by my own king for speaking the truth." Jeremiah paused. "It has not been an easy life. But now, as I approach the age of sixty, I am fully content. Yahweh's laws, his words, now fill my senses. I live for him, the Creator of all that we see … and all that remains hidden."

"Are you the only one called prophet?"

"No … There have been many before me, and I am certain that there will be more to follow. As we speak, a man named Daniel and another named Ezekiel are God's voice in Babylon to the captured people of Judah. God's prophets do not ask for his illumination—we do not call for it; we are called upon.

"You see, Prince Eochaid, Yahweh has always communicated with his people since the beginning of time. He initially spoke directly to those he created. At least, he spoke to those who followed his ways and chose to put their faith in him." Jeremiah fell silent. His eyes looked distant.

"Please go on," Eochaid said. "I would like to hear more."

Jeremiah smiled, took in a deep breath, then continued. "Long ago, Yahweh made an everlasting covenant with his people. Our great ancestors, the fathers of our nation, were Abraham, Isaac, and Jacob. They lived up to their side of the covenant, and so God is bound to keep his promise, even though many descendants of these great men were and still are not worthy. But our God does not lie. He never fails. He fulfills his promises.

"Yahweh promised Abraham that he would be a father of many nations and kings. He said, 'Your name will be Abraham, for I have made you a father of many nations. I will make you very fruitful; I will make nations of you, and kings will come from you. I will establish my covenant as an everlasting covenant between me and you and your descendants after you for the generations to come.'

"From Abraham came his son Isaac; from Isaac came his son Jacob … the same Jacob that I mentioned before." Jeremiah lifted the wine jug and refilled his cup. "God changed Jacob's name to Israel, which means 'prince with God.' Jacob then fathered twelve sons who eventually became the tribes of Israel. Over time, our tribes divided into two kingdoms. One was called the House of Israel, the Northern Kingdom. The second was the House of Judah, it is … was, the Southern Kingdom. Its center was in Jerusalem—before the Babylonians destroyed it.

"Prince of Erin, what I tell you is very important. No one can understand Yahweh's word, his plans and prophecies, if they do not understand the division and the destiny of these two *separate* nations. The kingship, the scepter of God's people, and the Promised One—blessed be he whom we wait for—will come from the House of Judah. The birthright, an inheritance of great nations, will come from the House of Israel, whose tribes have been scattered across the earth."

"You sound like a man of great wisdom. I have never heard anyone speak as you do," Eochaid said.

"God has revealed much to me. But he also reveals himself to all those who seek to know him. His word says, 'I love those who love me, and those who seek me find me.' Many do not seek him. Instead, they remain blind to the truth of his word and his plans for his people. Some believe that what was written was only for a time long ago. Nothing can be further from the truth. Every word from Yahweh breaths; it lives for all time: for the past, the present, and for the future!

"Forgive me, Prince Eochaid. It is easy for me to get carried away in speech with someone who is willing to listen. But tonight, you and I have little time together. So now, I would ask you to tell me about yourself and your family."

Eochaid cleared his throat, sat up straight, then crossed his legs in front of him. "I am the oldest son of my father. I am twenty-one and have one brother, Collin, who is three years younger. There were three of us ... but my youngest sister died not long after she was born. After that happened, my mother didn't have any more children. I know she loves me and my brother, but I think there will always be something missing for her since she lost a daughter.

"Even though I was born a prince, when I was very young, my father would have me work alongside some of the stable boys, cleaning stalls and feeding his horses. At the same time, I began lessons to learn to read and write. I was taught the basic skills of a warrior, and by the time I was thirteen, I became skilled with the use of swords and daggers. I rode horses and learned to hunt with the bow. In Erin, most boys brought up in homes of royalty start their training at age seven and they are fighting at fourteen or fifteen ... many are dead before they reach my age."

Eochaid tilted his cup and drank the last of his wine. "When I turned fifteen, I would ride into battle with my father, tending to his weapons and armor off to the side, away from the fighting. That's where I watched and learned the strategies of war.

"My father also took me to sea with him as often as he could since I was about seven. Traveling with him across the seas is how I acquired my skills in speaking several languages. When we sailed to distant lands, my father brought a tutor with us, and before we would set our anchor in a foreign port, he would test me on the language spoken by the people who lived there. All these skills have saved my life many times since I was given command of my father's ships.

"My father is a good man and a great king. His castle, my home, is in the region of Ulster, in the county Meath, in a village called Cathair Crofinn. My father is known to our people in our language as the 'ard-righ,' which means the 'high-king.' He is a king of kings. He reigns over four kings that rule the other four regions that cover our island. My father has many ships and an immense land army. He is a great man, but he has grown tired. He said one of the reasons he was sending me out on this journey, on my own, was to prepare me to take his place. I am not anxious for his throne, but am most eager to return home to see him."

Jeremiah gave a small nod. "I can tell that you love your father by the way you speak of him. I can also see that he has raised a good and wise son."

"Thank you."

"May I ask what you believe in, Prince Eochaid? Whom, if anyone, do you worship?"

"As I said, my mother told me stories at a young age of a great God and his kings. But our Druid masters have taught me to worship in the forest and on our hills at the temples of Baal."

"Baal! Baal is from the bottomless pit!" Jeremiah spat out in a loud voice. He sat up and glared at the prince. "Fear the Lord, the One God, Prince Eochaid, and take leave of the temples of Baal. You will come to no good worshipping at the foot of evil!"

Eochaid sat still, stunned at Jeremiah's rebuke.

Jeremiah continued in a softer voice: "Prince Eochaid, the Lord has revealed much to me about you. You are as God has predestined this day a prince of Erin … and a prince of Israel. You and your people are from the family of our father Jacob. We spoke earlier of King David. What is important for you to know and understand about David is that Yahweh promised him an everlasting kingdom. Gods words about David's were these: 'I have made a covenant with my chosen one, I have sworn to David my servant, I will establish your line forever and make your throne firm through all generations.'

“The rule and kingship of the house of David, the House of Judah, will prevail, just as the prophet Nathan spoke and said to David, ‘Your throne will be established forever.’

“Prince Eochaid, the Lord has revealed to me that this prophecy is a part of *your* destiny. When you return home, I ask that you turn away from Baal and—”

Jeremiah stopped his plea to the prince when he heard the sound of music.

“If you are finished with your meal, would you join me outside?” Jeremiah reached for a small bowl that held two damp cloths. “Some of our people will be dancing and playing music for us. Teia and her sister Hannah will be singing.” As Jeremiah cleaned his hands, he watched for Eochaid’s reaction, then passed the bowl with the remaining cloth to the prince. “After they finish their song, I would like to introduce you to our people and then give you a blessing. Would you allow me that?” Jeremiah asked.

As the prophet stood up, Eochaid also rose off the carpet. “Yes, if you desire to do so.”

Hmm … give me a blessing? the prince thought. *I hope he won’t do anything unusual … or ask me to sing or do something to embarrass me in front of my men … or Princess Teia.*

Chapter 12

A light breeze swept in from the ocean and over the refugees who gathered on blankets and mats outside their tents. They sat in a circle around a large open area where several men tapped their fingers on drum skins, while others strummed small lyres and harps. The men sat near a deep pit in the sand where a huge pile of driftwood crackled and lit up their faces. Small sparks flew high in the air as the amateur musicians played. At the same time, a group of young girls shook tambourines while they danced in the sand around the ring of spectators.

Teia sat cross-legged on a blanket and watched the girls smile and giggle as they dipped and swayed to the music. The princess moved in rhythm to the music until she realized that someone had walked up beside her. Turning her head, she looked up into the face of the prince.

"May I sit beside you?" Eochaid asked.

"Yes. Yes … please do," Teia said as she scooted over.

The prince sat down and stretched his legs out on the sand in front of him. Teia stared straight ahead as her heart began to race. *Take a deep breath. Breathe slow … Breathe slow …*

"I noticed you smiling as you watched the dancers," Eochaid said, "the same way you looked when you danced in the sea. Is this a common and favored activity for you and your people?"

Teia focused her eyes on the bonfire as she spoke. "When I was very young, my sister and I would hide in the thick curtains at the entrance to my father's banquet hall and watch the dancers entertain my father and his guests. When times were good, there were many parties and celebrations, and always dancing. When we were not able to watch, Hannah and I would dance in our room where we could still hear the music.

"As members of the royal family, we were also taught to dance for our father and for other noblemen who visited our palace. So, yes, watching the dancers and hearing the music reminds me of home and makes me smile. It brings back happy memories. It has been a long time since I've heard cheerful music and seen those around me happy."

Eochaid nodded. "I guess no matter what happens to us, where we go or how far we travel, we bring our treasured memories with us. No one can ever take them away," he said. He leaned back on his arms and looked up into the night's sky.

Teia looked at the prince as he gazed above. She had never felt completely captivated by anyone like she was now with this stranger. She forced herself to turn away before the prince caught her staring at him. She looked back only when he began to speak.

"Your prophet, Jeremiah, told me about some of your kings and the founding fathers of your nation. I have been to the coast of Judah. A few months ago, my ship anchored off both Joppa and Dor for several days, where we traded some of our tin for food and other supplies."

Teia began to relax. "I hope someday I will be able to return home. But I wonder what or who I will find there. Jerusalem, my home, was still burning when we left." She paused, then asked, "Where is your home?"

"My home is far away." Eochaid sat up and leaned in close to Teia as he smoothed the sand in front of them with his hands. "Here, I will draw a map for you." Eochaid dragged his finger through the sand in a large oval circle. "This area is the Great Sea. And here we are on the coast of Egypt." Eochaid marked an *X* in the sand in front of Teia. "This is the route I will follow home: west all along the coast. Then I will turn north here, and then cross through the Pillars of Hercules way over here in the northwest." Eochaid drew a short horizontal line, then an outline in the shape of a closed fist. "I will sail here, up the coast of Iberia, and then across the North Sea past the coast of Britannia." Eochaid drew an irregular circle. "Before we finally set sail for home—here … the Isle of Erin." The prince drew a smaller oblong shape to the upper left of Britannia, then turned his eyes from his map to Teia.

The princess shook her head. "You know so much about other lands. Your home *is* far away." Teia's voice was soft as she looked at Eochaid before she broke his gaze and looked back down at his drawing.

"Yes, Princess Teia." Eochaid stuck his finger deep through the *X* in the sand. "You are here. And I will be way over there." Eochaid pulled his finger from the sand and sat back. "Egypt is very different from Judah. I wonder if you will like living here."

"I don't know. But I don't think we will stay here … forever."

"Why is that?"

"Because Yahweh told Jeremiah that our people should not come here."

"Then why are you here?"

Teia looked around to see who could hear their conversation, then answered the prince in a low voice: "We were forced. After we fled Jerusalem, the village where were settled was attacked by rebel soldiers. They killed most of the people there, but took some of us from the village captive. Johanan, the man you spoke to when you entered our camp, he and some of his soldiers rescued us and then decided that we should all travel to Egypt. Johanan and most of the people ignored the warnings of Jeremiah to stay in Judah. They thought we would have a good life in Egypt, and we would be safe and no longer have to worry about being attacked by the Babylonians."

"Do you feel safe now?"

"I do in some ways, but I am worried because our people have disobeyed Yahweh. Nothing good ever comes from that."

"Teia. It's time!" Jeremiah called from behind her as he walked with Hannah toward them.

The prince stood. "Hello, Princess Hannah. It is nice to see you again." Eochaid looked down at Teia and lowered a hand to her. "Here, let me help you."

Teia placed her slender fingers into the prince's warm hand, then slowly withdrew it when she stood. "Thank you, Prince Eochaid." Teia looked up at the prince with a little smile before she turned and walked with Hannah toward the musicians.

The sisters' years of training in the palace kept them poised as they turned and graciously made a small bow to their audience. Teia glanced at Eochaid, whose eyes did not stray away from her. She was thankful that she had borrowed a nice dress to wear tonight.

One of the musicians handed Teia a small harp. She started the performance by softly strumming the instrument. As she plucked the strings individually, a pleasing melody emerged, and then the sisters began to sing:

"The Lord is my shepherd, I shall not be in want.
He makes me lie down in green pastures,
he leads me beside quiet waters,
he restores my soul …"

Eochaid felt captivated by Teia as he watched and listened to her sing. The sisters' voices complemented each other, but it was Teia's sweet and tender tone that touched the heart of the prince. The words to their song seemed vaguely familiar to him as he listened to the princesses sing to the crowd and into the heavens as their voices ascended in praise to their God. Silent tears fell from many in the camp. The song ended with soft clapping, then only sniffles and the crackling of the fire was heard.

The quiet spell was broken when Jeremiah walked to the center of the circle. After giving the princesses each a kiss on their cheeks, he turned and addressed the crowd. "People of Judah, hear me. I would like you to meet a special guest that I invited here this evening. He commands a great ship that it seems has not by chance anchored off this shore, at the very same time we are here. He has joined us tonight with a few of his men who sailed with him from an island far away in the west.

"The island he hails from is one where long ago the prince's ancestors, our ancestors, from the tribes of Judah and Dan landed after they escaped from Israel and were scattered across land and sea during the Assyrian captivity. The Lord our God has told me many things about this young man, whom I would now like to bless."

Jeremiah stretched out his arms. "Prince Eochaid, would you come forward?"

The prophet stood with Eochaid in the center of the camp. The prophet clapped his hands a few times until the murmur of voices subsided and all eyes were turned his way. Eochaid knelt in the sand as Jeremiah gently placed his hands on the prince's head. The prophet paused, then raised his eyes toward heaven and prayed:

"Behold, Yahweh blesses you, descendant of Jacob, descendant of Judah.

You are now prince of your people but soon you shall be their judge and leader.

And in the days of your greatness, you shall have a throne of stone.

You shall hold a scepter, and will have a queen fair to see from the branch of David.

I pray that your seed shall grow across the earth, as will your faith in the one true God.

I pray that your faith not fail you in the days of trouble;

I pray that the help of the Almighty will always accompany you.

Return home, Prince of Erin, and forget not that you are also a prince of Yahweh.

Remain away from the shrines of Baal.

Know that there is one God, the One and only Holy God of Israel.

Know that the ancient stone circles of your people are too narrow for him who dwells above."

Jeremiah stopped and pulled his shawl over his head, then raised both of his hands shoulder height as he continued to pray:

> *"The Lord bless you and keep you!*
> *The Lord deal kindly and graciously with you!*
> *The Lord bestow his favor upon you and grant you peace!"*

Jeremiah pulled back his shawl. "You may rise up, Prince of Israel." Jeremiah motioned for the musicians to resume the entertainment as he spoke privately with the prince. Eochaid noticed that Johanan's frigid gaze remained fixed on him as he talked with Jeremiah, and then when he walked over to his ship's officers, whom he spoke to briefly before leaving them.

Chapter 13

Teia stood looking down at Eochaid's map when a long shadow fell across the sand as someone approached.

"I enjoyed your song," the prince said.

"Oh … thank you."

After a few awkward moments of silence, Eochaid pointed down at his drawing. "So what should we do about this?

Teia looked confused. "What do you mean?"

"Well, the fact that you are here in Egypt, and I am leaving for Erin."

Teia's eyes grew wide. Her mouth started to open, but she remained speechless.

Eochaid smiled. "After Jeremiah gave me his blessing, I asked my men to retrieve our weapons from Johanan and then return to our ship to prepare for tomorrow's journey. I also asked Jeremiah … I asked him if he would allow you to walk with me around your camp. He gave me his consent. So, Princess Teia, will you give me the chance to get to know you a little better before I leave tonight?"

Teia looked up into the eyes of the prince, then answered softly, "Yes, I would like that."

The prince had met many beautiful young women on his voyages and at home across the Isle of Erin. But it was only Teia's beauty that he found breathtaking. The natural charm and grace of this princess also intrigued him. He noticed that all eyes were on them as they strolled by those who sat outside their tents and around the campfire.

When they reached the far end of the campsite, Eochaid stopped. "Would you walk a bit farther with me … away from all the prying eyes?"

"I … I should ask Jeremiah first." Teia turned around and her eyes searched across the camp for the prophet. "He is my guardian and—" Teia's voice went silent when she saw the face of Jeremiah looking directly at her. As their eyes met, Jeremiah gave her a nod.

Did he already know the prince would ask this of me?

The beat of Teia's heart quickened when she spoke again, "Yes, I'll go with you."

The prince led Teia behind the tents and across the sand away from her camp. Teia and Eochaid were silent when they stopped and looked across the sand that stretched to the sea, where a three-quarter moon gave the approaching fog a soft glow as it moved ashore.

"Princess Teia, maybe it is not by chance that we met." Eochaid turned and faced Teia. "Your prophet told me much about you and your ancestors, and of my ancient ancestors. It seems they are the same.

"This might sound … impossible. Even so, I will tell you. I feel that …" Eochaid swallowed. "I feel as if I already know you, even though I am certain that we have never met. But someone … someone just like you has come to me in my dreams. That is the reason I asked your name … when I first saw you."

Teia looked at the prince but said nothing.

Eochaid turned away. "I shouldn't have told you. I now feel foolish."

"My grandmother used to tell me that a dream is what your heart makes when you are fast asleep," Teia said softly.

"So what does your heart dream of?" Eochaid stepped a little closer to Teia.

"I guess the same thing as most young women my age," Teia said, afraid to say what was really in her heart.

"Here I stand, right next to you, not dreaming this time," Eochaid said. "But after tonight, we will probably never see each other again. It's not likely to happen, but would you ever want to come to Erin?"

Teia looked out at the surf, then at Eochaid. "There are many things that I would wish for, but it seems my life, my future, is not for me to choose. It seems I was born to serve my God. Jeremiah has made it very clear to me that I was born for a special purpose. So I am trying to learn to set my dreams … and my desires, aside."

"In many ways, our lives will be the same. My father has groomed me all my life to take his throne." Eochaid paused and looked out across the water. "I would be content to do nothing but sail the seas, but it looks like I am destined to govern the land of Erin." Eochaid lowered his head and looked into Teia's eyes. "So what should we do with our dreams and our desires?"

Unable to answer, Teia gazed back at the prince. Her heart melted at his tender look. She felt the warm blood rush up her neck and face, and was glad the night hid her blush. With their eyes locked together, the princess was vaguely aware of Eochaid's movement before warm fingers took her hand. She jolted from the sensation racing up her arm. They were now standing so close that Teia could feel Eochaid's warm breath on her face. Teia's heart began to race as the prince lifted her hand and pressed his lips to her fingers.

"A gift for a beautiful princess," Eochaid said.

Teia saw that the prince held a gold band in his free hand. He slid the bracelet over Teia's fingers and onto her arm. Her skin quivered as the prince reached up under her sleeve, stopping just below her elbow, where he squeezed the band lightly into place.

"This torque is one of a pair that has been in my family for many generations. I wear one on my right arm; you now wear the other on your left. They belonged to my father. He gave them to me on the night before I left Erin. I've worn them every day since then. My father wore them since the day his mother and father presented them to him."

"It's beautiful." Teia lifted her sleeve to see the stunning, slender gold band with a lion's head on each end. "But ... it's too precious. I cannot accept such a gift." Teia started to loosen the bracelet and slide it down her arm.

"No. It is mine to give. I want you to have it. Keep it, please." Eochaid wrapped his hand around Teia's fingers and slipped the band back in place. "Promise me you'll wear it ... Promise that you will think of me when you do."

She nodded. "Yes ... I promise."

Teia watched Eochaid raise her hand and begin to kiss her fingers. She closed her eyes at his touch and, in a moment, felt his soft lips on hers. It was Teia's first kiss, a gentle kiss, exquisite and chaste. Her stomach quivered as a soft passion awoke a sleeping hunger inside her. Their lips parted and she opened her eyes, then rested her head against Eochaid's chest as he enfolded her into his arms. Teia felt the warmth of his body as it blocked the moist air that blew in from the sea. She completely surrendered to the moment. For the first time, she felt safe—and something more that stirred inside, which she had never felt before.

Eochaid lifted his head and turned toward the sound of voices that drifted in from the harbor. "It's not what I want, but I must go," he whispered. "I still have much to attend to with my crew before we sail. They will be waiting for me. Let me walk you back to your camp. Then I must go." Eochaid opened his arms from around the princess.

Teia stood silent for a few moments as she looked at Eochaid and wrestled with her feelings. Caution against impulse, desire against restraint. Stretching up on her toes, she placed a lingering kiss on Eochaid's lips before she drew away and, without a word, turned and ran back across the sand.

Teia rose before dawn and left her tent. She sat alone on top of the dunes and watched the harbor. Just as the sun began to rise, she saw the prince's ship move out to sea. Her eyes locked on the vessel until it became a small speck that disappeared. Teia stared blankly at the sea until she heard her name called.

"Teia … Teia? It's time to go," Jeremiah said. He laid a gentle hand on her shoulder.

Teia stood and held the prophet's hand as they walked in silence back to their camp. When they arrived, the refugees were busy packing. Puffs of smoke rose from fires that had recently been extinguished. Poles clattered as tents were taken down, then folded and loaded back into carts and onto the backs of donkeys, and camels sent by Pharaoh of Egypt. Soon, their caravan would depart for Tahpanhes, where accommodations were being prepared for them in Pharaoh Hophra's palace.

Eochaid stood at the stern of his ship and looked back on the coast of Egypt.

Eochaid's first captain, his best friend Aric, walked up next to him. He put his hands on the ship's rail. "What do you see?" Aric asked. "Do you see a fair maiden dancing in the water? Or do you hear her singing?"

"You are in a waggish mood this morning," Eochaid responded.

"I'm just my usual witty self." Aric brushed back strands of his red, wavy hair that a gust of wind had blown across his face.

"She was a fair maiden, wasn't she?" Eochaid said. He spoke his words quietly, as if to himself.

"The fairest we've seen in all our travels," Aric answered.

Eochaid stood silent, then took a deep breath and turned toward his friend. "Come on, it's time we take another look at the maps in my cabin. We may need to change our route and sail farther out to sea than we initially planned after the Phoenician captain warned us of the pirate ships he evaded along the coast. It appears we will face either a battle with the sea or a battle with men, depending on which route we follow."

CHAPTER 14

Johanan, with his twenty-two soldiers, two Egyptian guides, and a half-dozen of Pharaoh's soldiers, led the Judeans all day along a road adjacent to one of the small Nile River tributaries. The refugees had departed in the early morning, using midday to rest and shelter in their tents from the scorching summer sun. Their progress was slow as they traveled over the sometimes muddy path.

The refugees, though, traveled without fear of bandits or attack, as the Egyptian soldiers rode in front and behind the long line of refugees. The Egyptians' presence delivered a clear message to those they passed: this group would travel unharmed.

On the second day of their journey, the road became firm as it wound past one small village after another. Most looked the same with their tightly clustered mud-brick homes built not far from the river that flowed north to the sea. The strong smell of fish filled the air as Teia watched ferries and small reed boats steer up and down the Nile. Some would draw their vessels near to shore and call out to the travelers in an attempt to sell their goods.

Hannah chattered on while sitting next to Teia as they rode in a cart that bounced along the road.

"Teia? Teia?"

The voice grew louder, bringing Teia's thoughts back to the present.

"Are you listening to me?" Hannah asked.

"Oh. No … I'm sorry. What did you say?"

"Teia, what's the matter? You seem so … I don't know, kind of like you're far away. You've been so quiet. Is something wrong? Do you miss being by the sea? You seemed happy there."

"Yes … I miss the sea."

"Mmm, it's more than that. What is it? I know you better than anyone. I know something's bothering you. I see it in your face … in your eyes. You've barely eaten anything over the past couple days." Hannah softened her tone: "Is it Mother and our home you miss?"

Teia offered a sad smile. "Yes, I miss Mother, our family … our friends. I wonder sometimes if anyone we knew and loved survived. I wonder if we will ever return home."

"Is that why you seem so sad? I have been watching you and—"

"Hannah, please, stop asking. I'm fine."

"Teia … tell me."

"Please. Not now. When we arrive in Pharaoh's palace, we'll talk then."

"Alright. I won't forget."

"I know you won't." Teia smiled and slid her arm around Hannah's waist and gave her a little hug as she remained silent. *How can I tell my little sister what pulls at my heart … what consumes me?*

The Egyptian guides turned from the road and led the refugees over a wide bridge that crossed the river. They led the caravan into a shady area under an umbrella of large palm trees where they would make their afternoon camp. As the thirsty animals were being led to the side of the river, the hot and weary travelers settled in for their midday meal and period of rest.

Teia jumped off the cart and stretched her back. "I'm going over to the river. Do you want to come with me?"

"You're not going in the water, are you?"

"No." Teia smiled. "I might sit on the edge and cool my feet … that's all."

"I think I'll stay here. I want to get out of the sun. I'll tell Jeremiah where you are."

Teia followed the trail of animals through the tall papyrus stalks toward the Nile. The princess found a quiet place where she pulled some of the tall fronds down across the firm mud bank before she sat down. After sliding off her sandals, she dropped her dust-covered feet into the river. She reached down into the water and splashed some onto her legs and under her tunic. She wiped her wet hands down her arms to cool them.

As her fingers brushed over the gold band, tears formed and spilled down her cheeks. *What's happening to me? Day and night, I hear the words he spoke. I see his face … his eyes … his smile. I crave the taste of his kiss.* Teia bit down on her lip and closed her eyes. *I can't go on like this. Lord, please … bring the prince back to me … or please … please take away these feelings. Take away this aching inside … for more of him.*

Teia scooped up a handful of water and splashed it on her face. As her tears washed away, she continued to pray. She leaned back on her arms and lifted her face to the sun until its heat dried the water droplets that sparkled on her skin. The sound of men's voices and the snapping of reeds alerted her that the animals nearby were being led away from the river. Teia pulled her feet from the water and grabbed her sandals. She felt hopeless as her thoughts returned to Eochaid.

—

Teia found a place in the shade to sit behind her group, which was reclining on mats or blankets. One of the Egyptian guides held everyone's attention as he strode back and forth, making faces at the children as he told stories.

"Just above the water, that is where you will see the creature's eyes bulge out of the top of a thick scaly head. Hidden below the surface, hanging from his mouth are two rows of large, pointed teeth. He will move fast from the river to shore using short legs that end in sharp claws. When he swims, he is blind, but on land, he can see all the hairs on your head. We call them 'crocodiles.' Do not stray near the river water on your own … or you may become their next meal."

Goodness! I won't be putting my feet in the river again, Teia thought as she watched the children's mouths gape open and eyes grow wide as they listened to the fantastic tales.

"We also have sacred serpents, not at all harmful to men, which are small in size and have two horns that grow from the top of their head: when these die, we bury in the temple of Osiris, for to this god they are sacred.

"Tell us more!" one of the young boys said when the guide paused in his storytelling.

"We have a legend that says at the beginning of each spring, winged poisonous snakes fly from the east toward Egypt, where long-legged birds called 'ibises' gather and wait for them near our border. They do not let the serpents fly by, but instead they attack and kill them! Because of this good deed, the ibis is greatly honored by our people."

A breeze rustled the palms high above the Judeans as they passed around a few baskets of dried fish, dates, and flatbread that they nibbled on while they listened to the stories of unfamiliar creatures and customs of the land in which they would soon dwell.

Teia looked up when she heard the chatter of birds. She watched the small black bodies fly back and forth, and peck at large clusters of dates that hung down from the trees. The sound of their chirping reminded her of the many times she'd played or read under the palm trees that lined the palace courtyards in Jerusalem. The birds' soothing serenade, though, was soon interrupted by the loud voice of Johanan, who stood behind the group with his soldiers.

"This fish is good!" the captain said. "I could eat a basket of these!" After sucking every morsel off the small skeleton, Johanan tossed it to the ground and asked, "What other foods do you have in Egypt?"

"Quail … and other birds, when we can catch them in our nets above the Nile's water. If we are lucky, we catch ducks. And each year when the river overflows and the plains flood, a large amount of lotus flowers grow. Our women cut and dry the flowers in the sun before they pound their centers into fine crumbs. They add water to the crumbs and make loaves that are baked. We also eat the root of the lotus plant, which tastes like a fruit. You will taste all these flavorful foods. Before the sun sets today, you will enter our magnificent city of Tahpanhes."

Chapter 15

Huge stone structures and statues seemed to rise magically out of the desert sand as the refugees approached one of the most beautiful cities in the world. The massive pillars and grand buildings shimmered in the heat as they reached into the sky alongside looming statues of men.

What the people of Judah were used to seeing across the skyline on the highest hill in Jerusalem was Yahweh's temple: God's house, where heaven met earth. Before it had been destroyed, the temple's white limestone walls shone bright each day above their city. Now they gazed upon the giant temples of Egyptian gods. Their huge stone structures glowed with a golden-amber hue from the sun that set low behind them. The refugees looked around in wonder as their guides led them past enormous statues of Pharaoh that stood at the entrance to the city.

The Egyptian people stared at the ragged travelers who passed through their gate.

"There is so much to see," Hannah said.

She reached for Teia's hand as they moved through the village streets crowded with booths, stalls, men, women, children, sheep, and camels. The air was thick with the smells of exotic spices mixed with the scent of burning incense. The city seemed to be bursting at the seams with life.

The Judeans weaved their way past vendors who stood inside their booths aggressively hawking their wares: earthenware dishes and pottery, linen clothes, leather sandals, woven rugs, and beautiful alabaster drinking vessels and vases.

Fruits and vegetables were set out under the shade of awnings, where their striking contrast of color was displayed above the dusty, dirt street. White onions, garlic, and leek bulbs, with their long green tops, were fanned out alongside red radishes, green cabbages and cucumbers, orange melons, and shiny red pomegranates.

Heady aromas filled the air from crushed cumin seeds, coriander, and cinnamon spices that filled large, tightly woven baskets that sat next to canvas bags overflowing with mounds of hazelnuts and almonds.

Egyptian priests, bald, barefoot, and draped in sheaths of linen fabric, scurried through the streets on their way to and from the myriad of temples that peppered the city. There, women busied themselves sweeping the dust off the stairs that led into the temples of their gods—the uncountable number of gods that governed all aspects of Egyptian life.

Most Egyptian men they passed were bare-chested with shaved heads. They wore only linen skirts and sandals of leather or woven reeds. The women, all dark haired, wore sleeveless, thin, pleated white ankle-length gowns. Many of the men and women had kohl-painted eyes.

The Judeans—forbidden to look upon idols—found few places other than the street vendors to rest their eyes upon as they moved farther into the city, where they were soon surrounded by a multitude of foreign gods. They passed by statues of men with the heads of birds, and carved images of lions with the faces of men.

As the refugees approached Pharaoh's palace, they saw not just a building, but a whole city in itself behind towering walls and guard posts. On each side of the palace gate loomed a statue of one man, threateningly tall, even though he was seated.

Jeremiah noticed the look of wonder on Teia's face. "Yes, the statue's image is impressive, but Pharaoh himself is only a man, not a god as the Egyptians believe. You will see many fascinating things in the land of Egypt: some good … some evil."

"Stop! Wait here," Johanan called out as he rode up and down the long line of refugees.

As they waited in front of the gate, Teia noticed that the stone wall surrounding the palace was carved with pictures of Pharaoh in battle. One large carving showed him drawing back his bow to send an arrow flying toward his enemies. Dozens of dead soldiers, their bodies pierced with arrows, were engraved along the base of the wall.

When the tall bronze gate opened, the refugees entered the palace grounds. The noise and all thoughts of the marketplace quickly faded away. The Judeans now looked at Pharaoh's compound with its two massive temples.

The palace grounds in Tahpanhes had been designed and constructed on a grand scale. Pharaoh's palace and several smaller adjoining palaces were situated behind high walls on the north side of the forty-acre square. The great temple of Osiris, the god of the Nile, stood in the center of the east side of the city. On the west side stood the tall pillar-columned temple of the fertility goddess, Isis. Flanking the temples on both sides of the square were the private residences of Pharaoh's priests and officers. Several other buildings used for community festivals stood near the center of the city.

As the refugees waited together, a palace guard approached. "Which one of you is the prophet Jeremiah?" he asked.

"I am he." Jeremiah raised a hand and stepped forward.

"I will speak with you first." The guard unrolled a papyrus scroll. "Pharaoh Hophra welcomes you and has granted a portion of his palace for your use and for the two princesses who he was informed travel with you. Because King Zedekiah was an ally of Egypt, Pharaoh Hophra in return extends a warm welcome to you and the king's daughters to—"

"I am Johanan, captain of the King Zedekiah's army!" Johanna called out. He strode through the open gate and placed himself in front of the Egyptian. "I am the one who sent the messengers to Pharaoh—"

"You will remain silent and wait until I am finished speaking with this man," the Egyptian guard said, shooting a stern look at Johanan before turning back to the prophet.

"Jeremiah, this is Naketa." The guard pointed to a tall, almost charcoaled-colored Nubian man who wore large gold hoop earrings. "He will take you and the princesses to your rooms. Pharaoh has instructed his staff that they are to be at your service for whatever you may need. I was told that two men also travel with you."

"Yes," Jeremiah said. "My scribe and a teacher. They are also my friends."

"Pharaoh has provided several rooms near yours that are available for their use."

"When may I see Pharaoh Hophra to thank him personally for his generous hospitality?" Jeremiah asked.

"Once you get settled and have had some time to rest, Pharaoh Hophra will call for you. Naketa oversees a staff that is assigned to your area of the palace. If you need anything, let him know and it will be taken care of."

The dark Nubian then addressed Jeremiah in a deep voice: "If you are ready, follow me."

Jeremiah, though, hesitated. He wanted to hear what Pharaoh would offer to the rest of their people. "Give me a moment to gather the princesses and my companions together."

Jeremiah moved slowly toward the gate, but still within hearing range of the Egyptian soldier as he waved Baruch and Ebed forward.

"Now, Captain Johanan, I will speak to you." The Egyptian soldier paused as he further unrolled and read from a long piece of parchment. "Pharaoh Hophra has granted all your exiled people their own property where they can establish homes. He has granted them land near the river in the towns of Migdol and Kahn. He will also provide enough food and supplies to last through the next few months during the time when the Nile floods and replenishes the land. After that time, your people will be responsible for their own plowing and sowing. Then what food they eat will be supplied only from the harvest of their own labor."

The soldier looked up from the scroll. "There are a few empty buildings already constructed in both villages that can be used by you and your soldiers. Your men will be given enough food to last through the summer and fall months, after which you will have to depend on your people to supply you with whatever food and drink you may need."

"We are very grateful for Pharaoh's generosity," Johanan said. He gave a nod of his head down toward the foreign soldier. "How may we repay Pharaoh?"

"Pharaoh Hophra will call for you when or if he desires to seek some sort of repayment. For now, you and your people will go back through the palace gates and follow these men behind me, who will lead you to your villages. Your people can select a place to set up their tents until they are ready to construct their homes. A good number of your people already live in both villages. They can help with whatever is needed in getting all of you settled."

The soldier rolled up the parchment he had read from before raising it toward Johanan's face. "Be aware: many Egyptians will not be welcoming or friendly as they see more of their villages and their land being taken over by you … Hebrews. I would strongly advise that all of you make sure your settlements are built well within the boundaries of your allocated regions!"

Chapter 16

Teia awoke enveloped in a cloud of creamy sheets and soft cushions as the yellow glow of summer's rising sun filtered through the high palace windows. She caressed the smooth sheets against her clean skin. The bath she had taken yesterday seemed like a dream from her past. Teia pushed herself up, blinked her eyes open and surveyed her luxurious surroundings. Bronze lamp stands, woven rugs, and colored tapestries filled the large room.

"Oh good, you are awake!" Hannah said. She threw off her covers and bounced across the floor before she jumped up and sat next to Teia.

Teia stretched her arms over her head. "When did you wake up?"

"I've been up for a little while. I have been waiting for you to open your eyes. So now that you're awake, tell me."

"Tell you what?"

"Tell me your secret. You know. You promised to tell me what has been bothering you."

"I'm fine … really. Let's just forget it. Please."

"You promised."

"Oh, Hannah, why do you persist? I shouldn't speak of such things to you, but you have made it impossible!"

"What? What has happened?" Hannah scooted closer to her sister.

Teia looked down, then answered in a soft voice. "The prince … the prince of Erin is what happened."

"The prince! The one from the seashore. What did he do to you?"

Teia lifted her head and smiled at Hannah. "No, don't be upset. He did not harm me. At least not in the way you might think." Teia slowly raised the sleeve of her sleeping gown to reveal the gold band. "Look."

"Oh, Teia! It's beautiful!" Hannah traced one of the lion heads with her fingertips.

"The prince gave it to me the night before we left for Tahpanhes. Hannah, I don't know if you can understand this. The prince … he made me feel like … like I have never felt before. When he was near, my heart raced. When I think of him … which seems to be all the time, my insides feel as if they are tied in knots. That's why I don't eat."

"But you know nothing of this prince!"

"I know … it happened so fast. But we talked a lot. We shared stories of our lives and found in some ways that they were the same. It felt like we were being … pulled together. I tried hard to not speak the words that would reveal my feelings for him. But all that changed when we kissed."

"Teia! You didn't!"

"I know. I know it was wrong … even forbidden for me to do so. I can't explain how it happened, or what it felt like when I was with him. Now … every moment I'm awake, I think of him." Teia closed her eyes as tears began to form. "And every night before I sleep, I ask Yahweh to put me back … to the way I was … before we met."

"Does Jeremiah know that he gave you this gift?"

Teia opened her wet lashes, which released a few warm tears as she looked down at the gold band. "No, he doesn't know. So please … keep it our secret."

"Don't cry." Hannah leaned over and wrapped her arms around her sister just as they heard their names being called from outside their room. Two female servants came around the curtain that covered the opening to their room. Before one spoke, they bowed to the princesses.

"Our pharaoh has asked us to provide you with clothes to wear as befits the royal princesses of Judah."

Teia and Hannah watched as the servants unfolded several dresses before they laid them across their beds. The gowns were made of shimmering pale peach, blue, and cream-colored fabrics. Exquisite wide golden embroidered sashes wrapped around the waists. The peach and cream-colored dresses had square necklines with two wide embroidered shoulder straps. The fabric on the blue gown was gathered up across one side of the bodice, where it was cinched at the shoulder with a large golden clasp.

"Are they to your satisfaction?" one of the servants asked.

"Yes," Teia said. "They're beautiful. Thank you. Thank Pharaoh Hophra for us."

"Would you like us to help you dress?"

"No, that won't be necessary," Teia answered.

The servants bowed and left the room.

Hannah jumped up, ran over to her bed, and held up one of her dresses, admiring herself in the tall bronze mirror. "It's beautiful! Oh, Teia, feel it! We will look like princesses again!" Hannah twirled around while holding the peach-colored dress tightly to her waist. "I'm so glad we came to Egypt."

"Don't let Jeremiah hear you say that. Remember, Yahweh told him that we should stay in Judah."

"Well, we are here now and I want to wear this dress. Come on, Teia, try one of yours on." Hannah walked to the side of Teia's bed. "Don't be sad. We might have a new and exciting life now. Who knows who you might meet right here in Egypt. You might meet someone that you will like even better than the prince!"

Teia didn't respond as she got out of bed and picked up one of the dresses. She tried to clear her mind as she removed her nightgown, then pulled the Egyptian dress down over her head and shoulders. The fabric felt soft and smooth as it draped over her body in gentle folds. Teia cinched a golden sash around her small waist, then pulled her hair up from under the blue fabric. Her hair fell in long waves down her back and over her bare right shoulder.

"Let me help you," Teia said. She reached for Hannah's sash.

"May I enter?" the sisters heard a male's voice ask from behind their bedroom door's curtain.

Teia walked over to the thick drape that closed off their room and pulled it aside. She met Baruch's gaze.

"Don't we look beautiful?" Hannah said as she twirled around toward the entrance.

"Y-Yes … you … do," Baruch said. He swallowed hard, then looked away from Teia. "Excuse me for intruding on you, but Jeremiah wanted me to ask both of you if you would like me to escort you around the palace grounds today."

"Oh that sounds wonderful!" Hannah said.

"Princess Teia," Baruch said, "Jeremiah will be meeting with Pharaoh Hophra in a little while, but he would like to see you first. When you finish your meeting with him, your palace attendants will prepare breakfast for you and Hannah. Would you like it served here in your room or in the garden?"

"Here will be fine," Teia answered. "Can you give me a few minutes to finish getting ready, and then we can go see Jeremiah?"

"I'll wait for you outside your door."

Soon, Baruch led Teia down a long hallway. Her eyes roamed from wall to wall as she took in the exotic paintings of Egyptian temples and landscapes that covered their surface. When they reached Jeremiah's room, Baruch pulled back a thick drape and motioned for the princess to enter.

"Ah, Teia, you look lovely, my child!" Jeremiah walked across the room with outstretched arms.

"Good morning, Jeremiah." Teia fell into his warm embrace.

"How are you feeling today, my precious one?"

"Very well. I haven't slept so good and felt this clean since …"

Jeremiah nodded. "Yes, I know."

After a moment of Teia's silence, Jeremiah loosened his arms from around her and sighed as he lifted his hand and, with his fingers, gently brushed a loose curl of hair away from her cheek.

"You once again are able to look like who you are: a princess. Come. Sit." Jeremiah took Teia by the hand and led her over to a low couch. "Teia, now that we are settled here, you must begin your studies of the Torah. It is usually only our males who study the Law. But there will be a yielding in this rule, because in time, much will be expected of you. Yahweh has revealed to me that you are the one whom he will use to advance his plan for his people.

"I am going to give you my scrolls to study. To hold his words in your hands … to read of his love and his everlasting plan for his people is a wondrous thing." Jeremiah's eyes grew moist. "Read from it every day. Commit it to your head and to your heart. Yahweh already knows you, my child. You must come to know him. His word is true. He has said, 'You will seek me and find me when you seek me with all your heart.' No greater treasure on all the earth can be had than to come to know and feel the love of the Holy God of Israel.

"Wondrous things will happen to you when you seek to draw close and then fall in love with the everlasting, the ever-present God. Blessings that cannot be contained will be poured out upon you. His word does not come back void, as it is written: 'As the rain and the snow come down from heaven, and do not return to it without watering the earth and making it bud and flourish, so that it yields seed for the sower and bread for the eater, so is my word that goes out from my mouth: It will not return to me empty, but will accomplish what I desire and achieve the purpose for which

I sent it. You will go out in joy and be led forth in peace; the mountains and hills will burst into song before you, and all the trees of the field will clap their hands.'"

Jeremiah sighed deeply before he continued. "Should you have any questions—and I expect you will—Baruch and I are here to bring understanding of God's word when or where you might need it."

"Thank you," Teia said. "I will do my best to honor you and Yahweh by learning his laws. To be truthful with you, sometimes I would rather be just a student of Yahweh's teachings, instead of a princess who will have so much responsibility."

Jeremiah placed his hand under Teia's chin and gently turned her face toward his. "You can be both. The Lord calls whom he calls. Today you are a princess; one day you will be God's queen."

Teia gave a small nod.

"Before you leave, Princess, I wanted to ask you what your thoughts were about the prince of Erin. Did you enjoy Prince Eochaid's company?"

Teia looked down at the floor. "The prince? Oh … uh, yes. He … He was very nice."

"That's it? He was very nice?"

Teia felt her face grow warm, and she swallowed down hard on the pain that welled up in her throat. "Uh … yes. Yes, he was. What … Um, what is it that you would like me to say?"

Jeremiah smiled, then put his hands on the couch and pushed himself up. "Nothing more today, Teia. We will talk of the prince another time."

CHAPTER 17

Streaks of lightning flashed ahead. For several weeks, Eochaid and his crew had sailed without incident. Now everyone on deck watched dark clouds swell and cover the sky while listening to the low rumble of thunder grow louder as the stormy weather moved toward their vessel.

Eochaid ordered his crew to turn their ship south and scan the horizon for land. The prince remained calm as the tempest advanced. He had sailed many times with his father when they'd ridden over violent waves as menacing clouds overhead unleashed bolts of fire. At a young age, he'd become unafraid of booming thunder, pounding rain, and stones of ice that pelted his body. He no longer feared the power of nature, as did most.

Daylight began to fade as Eochaid's ship struggled through massive whitecaps. Cold, stinging rain now struck all on deck as ear-splitting cracks of thunder echoed above.

"Land! Land ahead!" a lone voice cried out.

Eochaid turned in the direction his crewman pointed. Through the rain, he saw a distant, dark form on the horizon. The prince nodded and ordered the vessel toward the land mass.

Soon enough, the low hills above the cove gave the ship some shelter from the gale winds that blew down and across the sea. By the time the ship had been securely anchored and assessed for damage, most of the rain clouds had blown past. The ship had managed to escape the fast-moving storm with little more than some shredding of its mainsail. After mending the sail, the exhausted crew ate their evening meal, then settled in for the night in hopes of getting some sleep before the following day's scheduled departure.

Eochaid awoke early to the screams of men and the clang of swords. They came from all sides of his ship. The prince grabbed his sword and threw open his cabin door. He stepped into a gray cloud. In the thick mantel of morning fog, he could barely see Aric, who had just exited the room next to him.

"Get a couple of men to pull up the anchor and get as many as you can down below to row away from here!"

Eochaid gave the orders after determining a quick escape to be their only option. He had no time to form a real battle plan against the swarm of dark shadows that flooded across his ship's deck.

Eochaid's men fought the best they could in a fog so thick that they could move it along with their hands. They wielded their swords against the silhouettes that attacked through the clouded air, even as the cries and wailing of the wounded echoed through the cove.

The prince crept out toward the sound of the fighting, but jerked back when he saw the faint gleam of metal. He reacted swiftly, his reflexes sharpened by years of training as a warrior. He twisted and swung his own sword down hard against the neck of the approaching adversary just as the man's face came into view. Eochaid's iron sword struck with such power that the blade sheared through flesh, muscle, and finally bone. As the unknown enemy fell, a geyser of blood spurted out and then pooled around the headless body on the deck.

From that point onward, Eochaid and his men fought a wild and terrifying battle blinded with mist and muted by the air's thick moisture. As the ship began to crawl away from shore, Eochaid defended himself against yet another attacker, but then he felt a sharp sting in his right shoulder—and realized that a rain of arrows from the top of the cove now fell across the deck. The prince reached up toward the pain and touched the narrow shaft protruding from his tunic as a wet circle of crimson began to spread across the cloth.

The prince cried aloud as he pulled out the arrow's jagged tip, which tore through his flesh. Blood poured from the open wound, and Eochaid moved toward the bow of the ship where the sound of fighting continued.

As the ship moved farther out to sea, the small number of assailants that remained alive on board were tackled by the crew and killed before their bloody bodies and severed limbs were tossed overboard.

"You're injured!" Aric yelled.

He moved with quick strides across the deck toward Eochaid.

The prince waved him off. "I'm alright. Just hit in the shoulder."

"Let's get inside your cabin and tend to your wound."

"Do you know how many we've lost?" Eochaid asked.

"At least three."

"How many wounded?"

"From what I've seen so far, about a half-dozen seriously; the rest just minor flesh wounds. By their manner of dress, I couldn't tell who attacked us. Their weapons looked crude."

"Just renegade pirates; most likely they wanted our ship. I need to see the dead and the wounded." Eochaid turned from Aric. "Where are they?"

The fog finally began to lift as the prince and his first officer walked the ship. They moved around the men, who were dipping their roped-tied buckets into the sea, hauling them back up, and then splashing the saltwater across the deck to wash away the red stains and blood puddles.

With Aric standing at his side, Eochaid knelt quietly for a few moments by the dead bodies of his crewmen. "Have them prepared for a respectful burial at sea."

Eochaid stopped to thank and complement each standing man for their skills and bravery. He then patted the shoulders or backs of those sitting or stretched out on blankets, where their pierced and torn flesh was being bandaged. Bottles of strong liquor were brought out of storage and passed among the men to ease their pain.

Once he'd made his way around topside, Eochaid went below and praised the men who had skillfully moved their ship out of the cove and away from danger. After thanking everyone on board, Eochaid finally entered his cabin and dropped down to sit on the side of his bed. With his left hand, he peeled off the blood-soaked shirt that now stuck to the skin on his right arm and shoulder. A cool wetness surrounded the burning, bloody hole. Eochaid frowned, then looked up when he heard someone enter, knowing it could only be one person.

"You know that you have to get that cleaned out," Aric said. He looked down at the prince. "It should be done soon or it might become infected."

"I know … I know. Can you hand me that map on top of the table?" Eochaid nodded as Aric lifted a large piece of yellowed parchment. "Yes, that one." Eochaid motioned with his eyes toward the bed. "Put it down here," he said.

After Aric did so, the prince lifted the map in his left hand just as the ship's medic entered his cabin.

"Can you just get the hole covered and bound up to stop the bleeding?" Eochaid asked.

"Let me take a look at it."

The physician dabbed a clean cloth on the blood that was coagulating around the open wound. Eochaid winced as the doctor pressed against his tender, raw flesh.

"It's pretty deep," the physician said. "Almost all the way through the other side. Might have just caught the side of your muscle. I need to clean it out before I wrap it."

The prince shook his head. "Just pour some of that clear liquid on it that you always use. Then bandage it up."

"I need to clean—"

"No!" Eochaid interrupted. He looked back down and touched the map with his pointer finger. "Here. We will sail to Carthage. Our ships have always been welcome there. That's less than a day's journey. We'll get help there for our wounded and for my shoulder. We can trade some of our tin or some of the goods we brought from Judah and Egypt for extra food and supplies." Eochaid then traced his finger across the map. "When we leave Carthage, we'll sail as far as we can along the coast, past Numidia, before we'll stop again to restock some of our provisions, then sail up the west coast of Iberia."

He looked up at Aric and continued. "Let's just hope we proceed without another attack. It looks like the Phoenician was right in his warnings. So, tomorrow, we will return to our plan of sailing farther out to sea. If the weather permits, we will sail through the Pillars of Hercules in a little over a month. We can stop on the coast of Iberia, or maybe once along the Bay of Biscay, before we sail past Britannia and then finally back to Erin."

Aric nodded as the physician busied himself with some of the items he'd brought along.

The prince looked at the map and then up at his first officer. "Aric, I need you to get as many able-bodied men as you can to help our oarsmen. They can split shifts. I want to arrive in Carthage as soon as possible so we—Ahh!"

Eochaid caught his breath. A sharp, burning pain emanated from his shoulder as the physician dabbed a wet cloth on his wound before starting to wrap a clean, wide strip of cotton fabric tightly under his arm and around his shoulder.

Eochaid gritted his teeth and saw Aric turn away to give him his privacy. His friend placed the map back on the table, then looked at Eochaid as he opened the cabin door.

"We've been gone a long time, my friend," Aric said. "It is good to be sailing home. I look forward to the day when we place our feet back on the shores of Erin."

The prince offered a tight smile. "I hope we receive some word of my father before then. Maybe we'll hear something in Carthage. The news we received of his illness is already months old."

"Here drink some of this." The physician handed Eochaid a bottle of amber-colored liquid.

The prince looked at the elixir. "I'll take one mouthful. No more until later. I want my mind clear just in case there is another need to fight. I will gladly indulge in drink when we are anchored safely before nightfall in Carthage's harbor."

With his ship now moored just off the coast, and he and a handful of his officers at a Carthage inn, Eochaid gave a short nod to the physician. "Alright, I'm ready for whatever you have to do. Just give me something to bite on. I don't want any of my men to hear me howl," he said.

"Alright," the physician said. "Just try to relax."

As the physician left Eochaid's room, the prince laughed. "Relax, he says." He sat there, alone, with his entire body tensed from being bound to a wooden chair with his legs, arms, and torso all strapped down.

The physician finally returned a few minutes later with Aric in tow.

"I have this piece of rope for you to bite down on," the physician said, "but first I want you to drink all of this. If it doesn't help with the pain, it will at least help in dulling your memory of what I am about to do to you."

The physician held the bottle to Eochaid's lips. The prince guzzled several mouthfuls.

"Give the rest to him," Eochaid said, nodding toward Aric. "I left you a swallow, old friend, as this will probably hurt you more than me."

"Ha. That's what you think," Aric said. "I will be holding the chair steady when you begin to kick and scream like a child."

Eochaid nodded, then bit down on the thick piece of twisted rope. He drew in his breath as the physician approached with a thin iron shaft that glowed white hot at its tip. The prince closed his eyes as the rod was lowered. Eochaid screamed through clenched teeth as the point of the rod was pushed in and out of his wound. Tears rolled from his eyes and down the side of his face before he passed out.

Morning light streamed through a small window when Eochaid opened his eyes. His shoulder and head throbbed with pain.

An unfamiliar young woman walked to the side of Eochaid's bed. "I see you are finally awake. I need to check your shoulder."

"What time is it?" Eochaid asked. His head spun as he struggled to sit up before he fell back down on the bed.

"Lie still," the woman said.

"Where's my ship's first officer?" Eochaid asked.

"Right here." Aric raised himself out of a chair near the foot of Eochaid's bed.

"When can you get the crew and ship ready to sail?" Eochaid asked.

"When you have had more rest and we are sure there is no infection in your shoulder. One or two more days of rest for you and the crew won't make a difference for the two months of sailing we still have ahead of us. You'll feel better tomorrow. Maybe we'll sail then. Now … do you want something to eat?"

Eochaid shook his head. "No. No … Not now … Maybe later."

"Then drink this." Aric poured some amber liquid out of a jug into a cup he held out to Eochaid.

"What is it?"

"It's something to help ease the pain and help you sleep."

"Did you talk to anyone in the harbor—anyone who might have heard word about my father?"

"I checked. But no one in port sailed from the west. All I spoke to came from the north or the east."

Eochaid took the large cup from Aric and gulped down the burning liquid. Soon, a warm blanket of numbness covered his body.

Aric took the empty cup from Eochaid's hand. "Get some rest, my friend. We will be back to sea soon enough."

Eochaid nodded as his eyelids became heavy. When they closed, all became silent and he drifted off to sleep. His dreams carried him to a grassy hill surrounding a castle, where Eochaid stood and wore the crown of the ard-righ—the high-king.

Then the dream shifted to a scene where Eochaid found himself sitting in a shaded forest before a large stone altar. A number of hooded priests were gathered around the backside of the altar, where they prepared a human offering to their gods. Eochaid watched the male victim arch his back and twist side to side as he struggled to free himself from the leather lashes that tied him to iron hooks embedded in the altar's flat stone.

The chief priest approached the terrified man with a large dagger just as a young woman fell weeping at Eochaid's feet: "Great and mighty King, by the glory of God Almighty, by whom all things were created, by the love of your queen, by the everlasting reign of your scepter, I implore you, in the name of the only living God, to stop this evil sacrifice. Obey the God of Israel, who abhors the shedding of blood to your heathen idols. Be merciful! Be merciful!"

Eochaid looked down—into Teia's face.

The Druid priests then began to surround him. "This is our ritual," the chief priest said. "This is our tradition. Do you deny this? Do you disregard the power of your priests? Will you listen to this woman who grovels at your feet, or to those who placed that crown on your head?"

Eochaid hesitated. He looked from Teia to the chief priest, then responded in a low voice: "Let the sacrifice proceed."

As the words fell from his lips, Teia pulled herself up. Eochaid watched as she pushed past the priests and then disappeared into the crowd of worshippers. When he turned back, he looked up into the face of the high priest and found himself lying on his back! He couldn't move. His hands and feet were bound to the altar.

Just at the priest's dagger was brought down into his chest, Eochaid awoke from the nightmare.

With rapid breaths, Eochaid opened his eyes. He lifted his head and looked around, relieved to find that he was lying in his bed at the inn.

What a … strange dream. Eochaid dropped his head down onto the pillow. *Again … I dream of you. Should I return to Egypt to make you more than just a fleeting vision in my life?*

Eochaid mentally replayed the scene of the first time he saw Teia, dancing in the sea, seeing it over and over in his mind until he finally fell off into dreamless sleep.

Chapter 18

Jeremiah and Ebed moved down the hallway and stopped in front of the two Egyptian guards who stood on each side of a polished brass screen. The golden grille stood in front of the thick embroidered curtain that covered the door to Teia and Hannah's room.

The tall, dark-skinned men bowed their heads, then opened the brazen gate. Jeremiah pulled the heavy drapery aside and entered the vast room. His feet sunk into the soft-pile rugs of various designs and colors that covered most of the attractively patterned tile floor.

Jeremiah approached the two princesses reclining on a couple of low divans. Seeing Teia dressed in one of her new Egyptian gowns, Jeremiah thought the close-fitting fabric exposed more of her curves than what would have been approved of in their Jerusalem palace.

Surrounding the princesses were two Egyptian attendants assigned to the princesses when they'd arrived in the palace. The young Egyptians had become the princesses' constant companions. One engaged in needlework; the other in such trivial duties as smoothing cushions and waving fans.

When the princesses saw Jeremiah, they rose up to greet him. Jeremiah walked directly toward Teia and placed his right hand on her head.

"May the Lord God of Israel bless and keep you, and restore through you the throne of your father."

"What about me?" Hannah asked. "It's always Teia that you bless with restoring the throne of our father. Why can't I be the instrument of Yahweh? Just because Teia is a few years older than me doesn't mean that I shouldn't also be considered as a queen someday! Teia may be a better student of the scrolls, but you know she is not tough like me. You know that I have a stronger will than she. What blessings do you have for me?"

"Hannah, you *will* be an instrument in the hand of our God. You, my little precious one, should think less of scepters and thrones and more of learning and knowledge; for the power of wisdom is a crown that none can ever take away."

Hannah put on a pouty face. "I *am* learning. Ebed will tell you that I work hard at studying the old scrolls. But I … sometimes I hate staying in this palace. I don't like sitting here day after day, week after week, reading and studying or stitching with thread. I want to be outside! Sometimes I think I would rather become a warrior like my father and brothers, than sit here!"

"Settle down, Hannah," Jeremiah said. "Truly, my child, you do have the strong spirit of your royal race—sometimes too strong. You must learn to be patient."

"Hmph." Hannah turned away. "I'm going into the garden. Baruch, would you like to come and see the new fish that swim in our pond?" she asked.

When the scribe nodded, the young princess led him out into the flower-filled courtyard.

Jeremiah watched Teia as her eyes followed her little sister. "What are you thinking, Princess? I noticed you shaking your head."

"Oh, I was just thinking about how strong willed Hannah is for one so young. I realize that I don't have the same ambition as my sister. She would take joy in the possibility of being queen. I sometimes wish that it had pleased the Lord to make her the elder and me the younger. Hannah seems created to make a place for herself in the world, while I … I'm not always sure if the path I walk is right for me. Sometimes I feel alone. I feel like Yahweh is not here, that he is still in Jerusalem. I feel like we left him behind. It's hard for me to feel his presence here in Egypt, among all these statues of foreign gods."

"Teia, you are not alone. Yahweh has never left you. It can only be you who can choose to walk away from him."

"But why has he taken so much away from me? I do try hard to understand … to accept all that has happened."

"You have endured much for one so young. But in time, you will have what you desire."

"What do you mean?" Teia asked.

"God will one day grant you the desires of your heart, but know that it will be in his time—not yours."

Teia started to speak, but Jeremiah held up his hand, then continued. "Now I must discuss the reason for my visit with you. You know the pharaoh has grown fond of you and your sister. I was surprised to see him welcome you into his home and his life, as if you were a part of his family. It also appears that a few of his sons have become quite taken with you. Have you any interest in the princes of Egypt?"

Teia's eyes widened. "They have been very kind to me. But, no, I have no … interest in them."

"Good. I am glad to hear that. But we do not want to insult Pharaoh, so I will have to find a reason to delay you spending any more time around his sons.

"Yes, please do. I don't want to be alone with them."

"You would never be alone. But allowing even the smallest appearance of interest could result in a problem. I will see what I can do. But there is another reason I came to see you and your sister today. Will you please bring Hannah in from the garden?"

Jeremiah waited for the princesses to return to the room before he began. "I know you both have been confined to the palace and its compound for several months. Would you like to walk around the city today with Oporah as your guide?"

"Oh, yes!" Hannah said. "That would wonderful." She ran to Jeremiah and gave him a hug.

"Thank you," Teia said. She also walked into Jeremiah's open arms before he closed them tight around her and her sister.

"You are both so precious to me. I hope you know that I love you like you were my own daughters. Long ago, the Lord commanded that I take no wife and have no family of my own. But how he has blessed me with the two of you." Jeremiah kissed the tops of the sisters' heads, then released them.

"Come with us … please?" Teia said. She held on to Jeremiah's hand.

Jeremiah smiled, but then shook his head. "Not now, Princess. There is a man waiting to see me, from a city called Elephantine. It's an island that sits in a wide stretch of the Nile, far south from us. I have been told that they have a temple to Yahweh built there, where they have reinstated some of the temple sacrifices. Perhaps I will have some time to join you after my meeting with him."

Chapter 19

"Listen to the music! Can we go see where it's coming from?" Hannah asked.

"Yes, but stay near me," said Oporah, the Egyptian eunuch escorting them.

He and the sisters made their way around the palace grounds, then out into the main square where they waded through a throng of people moving slowly through the streets. Exotic music filled the air as it flowed out of the open doors of several large stone structures that rose high above them.

Teia watched the people gather around dozens of stalls and open tents, where barley beer and a variety of fig and pomegranate wines were being sold. In between the drinking stalls, a number of booths displayed baskets filled with little figurines.

Nodding toward one of the baskets, Teia leaned toward her sister and whispered, "It seems that the Egyptians believe almost every living creature is sacred along with countless gods and goddesses. They even worship insects! No wonder Yahweh warned Jeremiah not to come here."

Teia's eyes scanned the unending displays of beetles, dragonflies, birds, snakes, and scorpions that had been formed from varied hues of clay and stone. At the same time, Hannah nodded, but was unable to speak as she watched a group of women walk by in almost transparent white-linen sheaths.

Then, as they passed several booths, Teia noticed that many of the people buying the small idols were Hebrews! She could easily tell her people apart from the clean-shaven Egyptian men, and from the Egyptian women, who usually wore black shoulder-length wigs.

"Come. Let's go see why everyone is gathered over there," Teia said.

She looked across the street as they were carried along with the flow of the crowd that surged toward the unending display of merchandise, food, and fermented drinks.

"Look!" Hannah said. "There's Tirzah and Elan." She pointed her finger toward the booth next to them.

Teia and Hannah snaked their way through the crowd toward their friends they'd met in Geruth Kimham before they all left for Egypt. Each time Teia saw the disheveled pair, she struggled to hold herself back from smoothing down the frizzy strands of hair that stuck out all around Tirzah's head and sad, plain face. Her older brother, Elan, looked no better with his dark matted locks dangling down the sides of his narrow face all the way to his shoulders. His name, which meant "tree," fit his long torso and tall, thin body. Even at fifteen years of age, he towered over Teia, his sister, and most of the friends they had met since leaving Jerusalem.

"Tirzah!" Hannah called out. She waved to the twelve-year-old girl and her brother.

Elan guided his sister toward Hannah and Teia. "What're you two doing here?" he asked.

"It's our first day out of the palace!" Hannah answered. "We came here to see the city, with Oporah, one of Jeremiah's attendants."

"Oh, so they let the protected little princesses out today," Elan said.

Teia ignored his comment and asked, "Are you here alone?"

Elan shrugged. "It's just us. Tirzah and I have pretty much been on our own since we left Judah. Momma spends most of her days curled up on her sleeping mat. She's been like that since we got here. She's actually been like that since before we left Judah, since my older brothers, who were soldiers, never came home. Since we've been in Egypt, Abba is usually gone before the sun rises and he doesn't return home until it begins to grow dark to eat whatever bad meal Tirzah's cooked before he falls dead asleep."

"My meals aren't bad. You always clean *your* plate, I notice!" Tirzah replied.

"Where does your abba go all day?" Teia asked.

"He's helping the other men in our village build their homes and prepare their fields. Ours was one of the first homes to go up. So Tirzah and I spend most of the day together or with friends in our village. We heard there was some kind of festival going on today. We had nothing better to do, so that's why we're here."

Tirzah craned her neck to look past Teia and Hannah. "So where's this Oporah person?" Tirzah asked.

"Oh … I don't know." Teia looked around. "I guess we lost him somewhere in the crowds." Teia stretched up onto her toes and tried to see over the heads of the moving masses. "I can't see him anywhere."

"And I'm too short … I can't see through all these people," Hannah said. She stopped looking around.

"Why don't you go up there?" Elan asked. He pointed to the top of a staircase that led into one of the large stone buildings. "You'll be able to see everyone from up there."

"I think maybe we should just go back to the palace," Teia said. She raised her hand to shield her eyes from the sun while searching for any sign of their guide.

"I'm not going back to the palace—not already!" Hannah whined. "This is the first day we've been able to do anything. We'll find Oporah, or he'll find us. I'm sure he's looking for us."

"Come on," Elan said. "Let's go up there. I'll help you look for him. Grab onto each other."

Elan took Tirzah's hand and then he began to weave his way through the crowds. Teia took one more look around, then grabbed hold of her sister's hand, as Hannah had already latched onto Tirzah.

"Alright," Teia said. "We'll go with them."

Elan led the sisters up the long stairway, where the shade under the stone colonnade made for a cool refuge from the burning heat of Egypt's midday sun. Teia and Hannah stood at the top of the covered entrance and scanned the river of people that moved below them.

While Teia and Hannah looked for Oporah with Tirzah standing nearby, Elan walked through the huge golden door that stood open behind them. Within a few minutes, he came running back out.

"Wow!" Elan said. "You should see what's inside. I never saw anything like that in Jerusalem!" he shouted to the three girls over the music that now spilled out of the structure. "I'm going back in."

"Ooo! I want to see!" Hannah turned and started to follow behind him.

"No, Hannah!" Teia said. "Get back over here!"

"Please! Just for a minute. Pleeease! Then I'll go back to the palace with you. I promise."

Tirzah stepped closer and said, "You two can go ahead. I'll stay here and look for your friend. What does the man look like? What's he wearing?"

"He looks like … He looks like every other Egyptian!" Teia said. "Just wait here for us. We'll be right back."

"Okay," Tirzah said.

"Alright, Hannah," Teia said. "We'll look inside, but just for a minute."

It took the sisters some time for their eyes to adjust to the dimly lit, torch-lined interior as they moved from the porch into a wide entrance hall where they passed colorful paintings of Pharaoh wearing his long, rounded phallus-style ceremonial beard, and a blue-and-gold striped headdress. Pictures of Egyptian men, women, and unfamiliar-looking animals covered four large columns and every inch of the surrounding walls. They followed the music into a huge room where dozens of beautifully carved stone pillars rose up from the red-carpeted floor to support the fifty-foot-high ceiling.

The sisters stopped behind the standing-room-only crowd of spectators just as a long line of young Egyptian women, in long transparent dresses, danced across an elevated stage in the front of the room. Shafts of light beamed down on their moving bodies from several square openings in the roof. A bit of the light filtered out across the dimly lit room.

The girls on stage gyrated from side to side as the music's slow tempo increased until it rose into a fast rhythmic beat, coming from the musicians who played on the far left side of the stage. The sound of their small and large drums, high-pitched reed flutes, bells, and rattle instruments echoed off the polished limestone walls.

As the loud pounding rhythm of the drums quickened, crowds of people began to press in behind the princesses, pushing them even farther into the room. Then everyone squeezed close together when some of the spectators parted to make an open aisleway for a long line of girls who came dancing into the room.

From what Teia could see, they wore wide, multicolored bead necklaces and only a thin leather belt around the waists of their naked brown-skinned bodies. The girls danced wildly to the drum beat as a heavy fragrance of incense now wafted through the air.

Teia realized as she looked around that many in the room seemed drunk. Along with the pungent scent of incense, she began to smell the sour odor of wine and beer as some in the crowd continued to pour the amber- and red-colored liquids out of animal skins into their mouths, down their chins, and sometimes over their clothes as they were pushed or knocked aside by those who danced or staggered around next to them.

Teia pulled Hannah close and shouted over the loud music, "We're leaving!"

"I can't see anything. It's too crowded!" Hannah yelled back.

Teia held tight to her sister's hand and turned to lead them out of the room just as several lines of bare-chested men blocked the entrance. The men moved through the door and into the crowd that now pressed in closer on the sisters, blocking any easy way out. Teia turned around and looked in every direction for another exit, but found only the sight of bloodshot eyes and bloated red faces as the sisters were squeezed shoulder to shoulder and back to back with others in the crowd. Fear sharpened the intake of her breath as Teia heard a chant begin, shouted from the stage by men who danced around wearing only thin, short linen skirts.

"*Ka Mut ba!*"

Everyone in the crowd repeated the chant. Louder and faster, the voices cried out as the girls and men on stage began to dance close together while the naked girls below danced wildly before they wrapped their bodies around the tall pillars like slithering serpents. Peeling themselves off the pillars, they moved into the aroused crowd as everyone began to grab at each other in an erotic frenzy.

Terror gripped Teia's heart as some of the men turned and reached for her and her sister. She wrapped her arm tightly around Hannah and pulled her close against her chest, shielding her as she pushed hard and desperately through the maze of crazed men and women whose hands grabbed and tore at her and her sister's clothes. Teia shoved her shoulders hard into the intoxicated assailants, knocking some off balance and clearing small gaps in the crowd that she worked her way through to move closer to the door. Just as she pushed through the opening, a strong grip took hold of her. She looked up.

"Jeremiah!"

"Go with Ebed," Jeremiah ordered Teia as he pulled her and her sister outside.

The Ethiopian stood well above the crowd. He easily forged a path through the crowds, past the waiting Tirzah, and down the stairs for Teia and Hannah, whose bodies shook, their eyes on the verge of tears.

"Jeremiah will be angry to have found you at that heathen ritual," Ebed said. "A festival of drunkenness, they call it!" Ebed stopped and looked at Teia when they reached the palace gates. "What made you go in there?" he asked.

Teia sniffled and shook her head. "We were separated from Oporah in the crowds when we wandered over to see what some of the booths were selling," she answered. "We went up the stairs to that building to look down and see if we could find him. That's what we were doing when we heard the music … We were just going to look inside, but … I'm sorry! I never thought we would be …" Teia reached down with her hand and pulled up the torn strap on her dress.

Ebed frowned, but gave a small nod. "Oporah rushed back to the palace to get us when he lost sight of you. We searched everywhere. That building was the last place for us to check. I don't think you will ever be allowed to go anywhere outside the palace grounds again, unless you are tied to one of us!"

Jeremiah stood inside the entrance to the hall and observed all the Hebrews whose writhing bodies danced as part of the wild orgy. He felt sickened by the sight—and, even more, feared what being here might have done to the innocent minds and spirits of the princesses. He would pray that what they saw and experienced would flee and be cleansed from their memory. He would pray that what remained would only be the revelation of the huge chasm between the actions of those who loved and followed the laws of Yahweh, and those who did not.

Jeremiah turned from his thoughts of the princesses and shouted the words of the Lord into the crowd:

"'I am determined to bring disaster on you and to destroy all Judah. I will take away the remnant of Judah who were determined to go to Egypt to settle there. They will all perish in Egypt; they will fall by the sword or die from famine. From the least to the greatest, they will die by sword or famine!'"

The prophet's words, though, were drowned out by the beating drums and screaming frenzy of the inebriated crowd.

"How much longer will the Lord hold back his hand?" Jeremiah said as he turned and walked away.

CHAPTER 20

Had it been almost two years since he sailed from home? Eochaid wondered as he recalled all the distant lands he'd traveled. His recollections always stopped with his memories of the beautiful hazel-eyed princess.

As his ship neared the bay of Drogheda, on the northeast coast of Erin, Eochaid noticed the flags on land flew at half-mast—and he felt his heart sink, hoping against hope that what he suspected was not true.

The flag of the ard-righ, his father's flag, flew from his ship's masthead, so all the people on shore knew that it was the prince of Erin who drew near to his native land. As their ship entered the harbor and prepared to dock, the flags were run all the way up their poles. Then shouts were heard from land: "The king is dead! Long live the king!"

Eochaid swallowed and took a sharp breath. He had been gone too long. His father ... was gone.

The prince stood with Aric beside him at the bow of the ship and listened to the chant that brought him news of his father's death. He forced himself to smile and wave to the crowds who welcomed him home as he walked from his ship and down the dock toward the boat that would take him upriver to his home.

Soon, hundreds of villagers flocked to the shores and banks of the waterway. The prince felt overcome with emotion at the loss of his father and, at the same time, at the love and devotion being displayed by the people who wanted to welcome home his son.

By the time the prince's boat had been tied to the dock below the road that wound up the hill to his home, the cheering throngs had gone, as the sun had long since set. With torchbearers in front and behind him, Eochaid held back his tears as he bounded up the stone steps that led from the dock toward the castle. At the sight of the approaching lights, several soldiers crossed over the moat and formed a line along each side of the lowered bridge, as a soldier on horseback had just moments before informed them of Eochaid's impending arrival.

The soldiers stood stiff and tall as the prince of Meath approached. "Welcome home, Prince Eochaid," the commander of the soldiers said when Eochaid stepped onto the bridge.

The prince acknowledged the welcome with a nod as he tried to hold his emotions back, walking past the men and toward the open gate of his home. A moment later, Eochaid spotted a barrel-shaped woman crossing the courtyard in front of the castle's main entrance.

"Deidre?" he called out.

The castle's chief cook stopped and turned when she heard her name. She squinted at the line of men who approached and then thought she saw someone in their midst who looked familiar.

"Prince Eochaid?"

"Yes, it's me. How good it is to see you." Eochaid strode forward and greeted the plump, rosy-cheeked woman. He gave his favorite cook a tight hug before he released her.

"What joy you bring back to me and to this place," the middle-aged women said. A few tears glistened in her eyes. "How we have missed you, Prince Eochaid."

"Who's 'we'?" Eochaid said, forcing a small smile.

"Everyone. Especially your mother."

Eochaid pushed down the surge of emotion he felt. "Do you know if she's awake?"

"I am told that the queen mother is in bed. She has spent many long nights and some days in bed since the death of the king. Oh ... please forgive me." Deidre drew her hand over her mouth.

"It's alright." Eochaid reached for the worn, callused hand and patted it gently.

"I'm sorry, Prince Eochaid. The words just spilled from my mouth."

"It's alright. You told me nothing that I did not already know."

The castle was quiet as Eochaid moved through the arched stone hallways, then upstairs toward his mother's room. Flickering candle light danced across the bedroom walls as Eochaid walked slowly toward the canopy bed.

"Mother?"

Noirenn stirred and turned toward the voice she had longed to hear. "Eochaid?"

The prince knelt at her bedside. "How are you, Mother?"

"Eochaid. Oh, my son … I had no word of your arrival." Tears of joy welled in the queen mother's eyes as she pulled her arms out from under her blankets and reached for the prince.

Eochaid leaned forward and let his mother embrace him as he placed a gentle kiss on her cheek. "I'm sorry that I did not arrive sooner … before …" Eochaid's words drifted off as tears spilled from his eyes.

Noirenn held tight to Eochaid, then slowly released her arms and pushed herself up. She leaned back against a mound of pillows before speaking softly.

"Eochaid, your father loved you very much. He trusted you to command his largest ship. When his illness overtook him, you were where he wanted you to be."

"Still, I wish I would have been here to …" Eochaid struggled to hold back more tears.

His mother gazed at him. "How you have grown since you left. You seemed but a youth when you departed, and now I see a man—a man who will soon be king. You smell of the sea." With a small smile, she leaned forward, then reached up and stroked her son's blond sun-bleached beard. "Do you intend to keep this?"

"No. It will be gone soon enough." Eochaid wiped the tears from his face. "I didn't want to delay in seeing you once I arrived."

"You look well my son, but tired."

"I'm fine, just a bit worn and maybe a little weak. Most of our provisions lasted up until a few days ago. We have had little to eat since then."

Noirenn took in a deep breath, then settled back against her pillows. "It's so good to see you … to have you home. You are the answer to my prayers. I want to hear all about your travels, but first go; let the pages attend to you. Then off to the dining hall where you will fill your belly with your favorite foods and drink. Eat, and then rest. We will talk of your travels in the morning."

"How's Collin?" Eochaid asked.

"Your brother's fine. He will be so glad to see you."

"I can't wait to see him. But I won't wake him tonight."

She nodded. "Welcome home, my son."

"It's good to be home." Eochaid stood, then bent down and planted a gentle kiss on his mother's forehead. "Sleep now and I will see you in the morning."

Noirenn smiled as she watched Eochaid move toward the door. "I'll see you in the morning," she whispered.

Eochaid turned back to look at his mother once more before he slipped out of her room.

Deidre was working in the kitchen when Eochaid walked through the door.

"Mother looks weak … pale," he said.

"Yes, Prince Eochaid. The death of the king has taken a heavy toll on her. But now that you're home, perhaps the pink color will return to her cheeks and we will see her once again as the strong woman she was." She stopped and looked up. "May I be of any service to you this evening before you retire? The staff has made sure that your room has remained cleaned and always ready for your return."

"I'm sorry to ask this of you at such a late hour, but I would be grateful if you could you have someone prepare or just bring some food into the dining hall for me. Or I'll just eat it in here." Eochaid felt the rumble of hunger in his empty stomach. "I'm famished. Anything … fruit, bread … whatever you have."

"Consider it done. I cooked for you when you were only up to my knees. Now look at you. You tower above me. You've grown at least a foot while you were gone, and you sound like you still have the same big appetite. Here, have some of this." Deidre grabbed a long knife and sliced a thick piece of bread off one of the half-dozen baked loaves cooling on the wood counter.

Eochaid devoured the soft, warm bread. "I've sure missed your cooking."

Deidre smiled when she heard the compliment. "Well, you go ahead and wash, and when you are ready, I'll have a table in the dining hall filled with food for you."

"One more piece before I go?" Eochaid stretched out his hand.

"I can see that I'll need to double my recipes now that you're home." With a broad smile, Deidre cut another thick slice from the loaf.

With a clean body and a full stomach, Eochaid lay down in the quiet of his room. How strange it felt to hear nothing: no whistling of the wind, no flapping of a sail, no sound of water moving against the hull of his ship. Eochaid just lay there in utter silence. His body, though, still felt the sensation of the rolling motion of the sea. In a few days, that would also disappear, he knew, as he adjusted to living on land again.

Eochaid had forgotten how soft the overstuffed, feather-bed felt as his tired body settled into the goose down. He stared through the large window that his bed faced. Outside, the night was dark. Just a sliver of moon hung in the sky. Now, all alone, Eochaid finally let his tears pour out. His chest rose and fell as he cried.

"Father …" he whispered. "Father … Father! Noooo … this can't be … this can't be. I lived to stand by your side … to make you proud. What … What is my purpose now?"

Eochaid turned and curled up on his side. His shoulders began to shake, as if something within him was breaking. *I never imagined how … how painful it could be … It is as if I am no longer whole …*

Endless tears streamed from Eochaid's eyes. His loud, aching sobs went unheard, though, his face buried deep into the pillow.

Eochaid slept late into the morning. When he made his way to the dining hall, he found his mother and brother waiting for him.

"Welcome home, brother," Collin said. He rose from the long wooden table.

Eochaid moved toward his brother with a smile and they embraced, then slapped each other on the back. Eochaid stood back and sized up his younger brother. "Look at you. You've really grown since I've been gone."

"Come sit," Noirenn said as she patted her hand on the table.

In between mouthfuls of porridge, sliced apples, and thickly buttered wheat bread, the elder prince recalled the high points of his travels in a string of stories to his mother and brother, both of whom sat across from him.

"We sailed across the Great Sea and traded our tin in many ports all the way to Judah's coast and back again. Early in our voyage, we encountered many enemies from here to Egypt's shores. The pirates and brigands we encountered were cunning and bold. But we outsailed and outfought them—and lost few of our men in the process."

"We heard sporadic news of your voyages," Collin said. "Reports came of great battles—one even of your death!"

Eochaid cocked his eyebrows. "My death! I wonder who spread that tale? I was fortunate to have suffered only a few wounds from our battles—the worst from an arrow in my shoulder." Eochaid lifted his left hand without thought and rubbed the area around his old wound. "Our last fight was months ago, off the coast of Africa. There were times when the weather was our greatest foe. We rode out several storms, including one that brought our battered ship into an Egyptian port. It was while we were there that I received word about ..." Eochaid caught the lump in his throat and forced his mind to move elsewhere. "As soon as repairs were made to our ship, we sailed for home."

"How long were you in Egypt?" Noirenn asked.

"We were there ... six days." Eochaid gazed past his mother and sighed, his mind again turning to Teia.

A smile teased the corners of Noirenn's mouth. "Mmm. Six days. And did you perchance meet anyone of interest on your voyages?"

Eochaid yanked his eyes back to his mother. "Uh ... yes," he said, then cleared his throat. "Yes, I did meet someone of interest. I met a man. He said he was a prophet. When we first met, he began to tell me of what he said were my ancient ancestors."

Noirenn and Collin both leaned forward. "What did he say?" the queen mother asked.

"He said I was from the Israelite tribe of Judah and that I was a prince of Israel, and that on our flag was a symbol of a man named Zerah. That part became a bit confusing. He told me a lot about the king named David—about how his kingdom will go on forever."

"King David!" Noirenn said. "Yes, you know of King David. Do you remember?" Eochaid's mother began to recite in a soft voice: "'The Lord is my shepherd, I shall not be in want. He makes me lie down in green pastures, he leads me beside quiet waters, he restores my soul. He guides me in paths of righteousness for his name's sake...."

Noirenn continued until she finished the ancient psalm.

"Do you not remember those words as the same ones I sang you to sleep with when you were a child?" The queen mother looked at Collin sitting next to her, then across to Eochaid. "I sang those words to both of you! You must remember?"

"Yes, I remember," Collin answered.

Eochaid nodded. "I heard the same song when I was in Egypt … with the prophet."

"Your teachers must have told you the history of King David and the ancient migrations to our land?" Noirenn said.

Eochaid pushed his empty bowl aside. "Honestly, Mother, I remember very little about our ancient ancestors other than what …" Eochaid took a deep breath. "… other than what Father once told me of his heritage. At the time, I was more interested in riding horses, improving my fighting skills, or going to sea. I have to admit that I put little effort into some of my studies."

Noirenn clicked her tongue. "You are so much like your father." A little smile crossed her lips before she continued. "As for this prophet you met, what he told you is true. Both of you should know that I was told that my lineage goes back to the ancient tribes of Jacob and his son Dan. Your father was a descendant of the Milesians, whose ancient records claim that they are the descendants of Eber, the great-grandson of Noah's son, Shem. Your father once showed me an old scroll where it was written that a line of his ancient ancestors came from Jacob's son Judah, and his twin son named Zerah, born through Tamar."

"Tamar?"

"Yes … Tamar." Noirenn paused and gave Eochaid a puzzled look, then continued. "The story that you found confusing about Zerah is as simple as this: long ago, Jacob's son Judah fathered twin sons through Tamar. As Tamar was giving birth, one of the babes put out his hand, and the midwife helping Tamar tied a scarlet thread on his wrist to show that he was the firstborn. But an unusual thing happened. The baby drew back his hand, and the second son was born first. He was named 'Perez,' which means 'breach,' or 'burst forth.' His brother with the scarlet thread was named 'Zerah,' and his symbol became the red hand.

"So even with the scarlet thread, Zerah was not the first son in line as the rightful heir to the birthright and all that comes with it. As the boys grew to manhood, they each headed their own tribe. But they continued to argue as to the question of who was really the firstborn and who was the rightful heir to the birthright.

"Eochaid, our ancestors have left traces of their tribes and their names wherever they migrated. The names of towns, villages, and rivers bear the name of Jacob's tribes across many lands all the way here to Erin. Do you recall the coat of arms for your father's original homeland of Zaragoza?"

Eochaid shook his head.

"I know," Collin said. "It was a red flag with a gold lion."

"That right! The Lion of Judah," Noirenn said.

"That was the same flag that flew outside the prophet's tent," Eochaid said.

"Judah was not the only tribe of Jacob's sons to reach this land," Noirenn continued. "The history of this land tells of a dark-eyed, dark-haired people who arrived here long ago. Legends say they were descendants of the Israelite tribe of Dan. That's the tribe of my ancestors. The Danites took their ships and planted colonies from the Black Sea all the way west to our isles. Their descendants, my family, are those who call themselves the 'Tuatha de Danann.' Some say the name means the 'Tribe of Dan,' while others interpret it as the 'People of God'!

"So now, when you both look at the red hand that flies on Ulster's flag, know that it *is* the sign of Judah and Tamar's twin boy Zerah, one of your ancestors!"

"That's what the prophet said." Eochaid's voice was just above a whisper. "I am the decedent of Zerah … and the princess … she is a descendant of Perez …"

Noirenn leaned back and stared at her oldest son. "Who is this princess you speak of? It seems there is more to tell of your travels than what you have revealed so far. You were never one good at concealing your thoughts." She smiled and reached out across the table for Eochaid's hands. "Each time you seemed to recall this princess, your heart and attention have left the room to return to her."

Eochaid pulled his hands free and sat back. "I … I don't know what you're talking about. You draw conclusions from nothing!" His words stumbled out hot and sharp. Eochaid felt angry, but not at his mother—rather, at himself, for revealing his thoughts … his feelings.

Noirenn searched her son's face. "Eochaid, do you not think that a mother knows her son? I will wait. In time, if this princess is important to you, you will tell me of her."

Eochaid remained silent. He wondered what he could say. What would he tell his mother? Would he tell her that the princess came to him in his dreams? Would he tell her how beautiful she was, how her smile quickened his heart? How he remembered her soft voice and sparkling eyes? Her golden-brown hair that flowed in waves down her shoulders, her slender curves … their tender kisses?

Why couldn't he just forget her after all this time?

Chapter 21

Muirdach, the king of Leinster, raised a jeweled finger. "I will not support the appointment of that *boy* to be the ruler of Erin. I don't care if he is the son of Ailill Finn! His right to the throne by blood does not apply to the position of high-king. Give him the throne of Meath, yes—but not the throne of the king of kings! Will you stand with me on this?" Muirdach asked.

The other three kings sitting around the table sat in silence for a moment.

Finally, Ugaine, the king of Munster, spoke up: "Muirdach, we know you to be a man of great wisdom. We also recognize the power of your position as one of the greatest rulers in all of Erin. I agree with you. The boy is young and inexperienced. But we can accomplish nothing just among ourselves. You heard of how the people rejoiced at Eochaid's homecoming; how they proclaimed his return with shouts of adoration to him as their king. They love the son as they loved the father." Ugaine turned toward the other two kings. "Lugaid, Cormac, what are your opinions?"

"I think we must decide this in a way that will not cause uproar among the people," said Lugaid, the king of Connacht. "We should select our high-king in a way the people will support and accept. I propose that we take a vote: one vote for each king of each region in Erin. There are five of us, including Eochaid himself. That is the fair way to decide this matter. Otherwise—"

"You are all aware of the strength of my army, and the riches of my land," Muirdach said. "It is greater than some of yours combined. It would be wise for you to consider who will receive your vote."

"We understand you clearly," replied Cormac, the king of Ulster. "I agree that we should each cast a vote. So if we can all come to an agreement on that, I will call upon Eochaid tomorrow and see if he is willing to see things our way. Then, we can select our high-king in solidarity."

Eochaid received the news almost immediately after arriving home that his claims to succeed his father to the coveted throne based on heredity had been rejected. He was also told by his father's most trusted advisor that the kings of Leinster and Munster were planning to secure their counties' complete independence from the authority of the high-king.

But the kingship was not on Eochaid's mind as he now ascended the highest hill in Meath. Morning dew clung to his leather boots as he made his way alone through the tall grass. He opened a small wood door, framed with standing stones, that led under the top of the dome-shaped hill. The prince bent down and moved through the low entrance. A shaft of light from the rising sun followed Eochaid down the short passageway, then spilled out across the circular cave when Eochaid moved farther inside.

The prince stood in front of a large stone box. Two silver swords lay crossed over each other on top of the green-and-gold embroidered cloth covering the coffin. Eochaid knelt and placed both of his arms across the cover.

"I am home, Father. I'm … sorry. I …"

Eochaid's body convulsed as he wept. Loud, painful sobs poured out until, completely drained, he rested his head down on the coffin.

"I … can't bear the thought of not seeing you again," he whispered. "But I will do my best … to make you proud … to remember all that you taught me. I will honor your name and your throne. You tried to prepare me for this day, but … I don't know if I can do this without you. I … I'm not ready … I don't want to be king."

Almost an hour passed before Eochaid exited his father's tomb. Emotionally spent, with swollen eyes and slow, unsteady steps, he descended the hill. Collin was waiting below on his gray horse next to Eochaid's white stallion. The brothers remained silent as Eochaid mounted his horse.

"Let's take a long ride to the plains of Dunanglin," Eochaid said.

"I'll race you," Collin said.

His words were barely out of his mouth before Eochaid's horse sped past him. Eochaid pushed his horse hard. The faster he rode, he reasoned, the more distance he could put between himself and his father's grave. The brothers rode through the open grass fields of Lagore and across the rolling hills of Tulach, before Eochaid pulled up gently on the reins. He slowed his horse's pace as he neared the River Boyne, where he turned his horse around and waited for Collin.

"You took off before I finished speaking! That's not fair," Collin said. He slowed his horse as he rode up next to his brother.

"Ha. You're just not as fast as I am," Eochaid said. "Never were, never will be. If I had let you start off before I mounted my horse, we would have sped past you. Actually … if I'd let you start off before I got out of bed today, I would have arrived here before you!"

Collin rolled his eyes. "Very funny. At least you're still as competitive as you use to be."

"Maybe."

Eochaid dismounted his horse, then pulled gently on the stallion's reins as he led the large steed down to the river to drink. He stood silent for some time, just watching the water ripple over the smooth stones that lay at the bottom of the riverbed.

Collin walked over and stood next to Eochaid. "Are you alright?" he asked.

"Yeah, I'm alright. I was just thinking about Father. I wish I had been home in time to see him … to talk to him … before … he died."

"He was very sick toward the end. He wasn't doing any talking. I don't think he even knew who we were. It's been hard with you gone. Mother spent a lot of time in bed—until you arrived home. You were always her favorite."

Eochaid gave Collin's shoulder a little shove with his hand. "I'm not her favorite, just her firstborn. I know she missed me, but she's also worried about the throne—hers and the king's. Looks like she won't have to wait much longer for it to be filled."

"Do you want to be king?"

"Mm. Not really. I was happy with the way things were. Now everything's going to change. So let's just enjoy today."

Collin reached down and ran his hand back and forth through the water. "It's good to spend time with you. How long has it been since you and I have ridden together?"

"Over two years. You were only up to my shoulders when I left. Now you're almost as tall as me!" Eochaid said.

"Give me another year, big brother, and I'll be taller and stronger than you."

Collin walked away from the river and sat down on the grass. Eochaid turned and joined him. He lay back on the ground, folding his hands behind his head to watch snow-white clouds move across a blue sky. He relaxed while listening to Collin sum up what had taken place in Erin while they were apart.

"So that's what had happened," Collin said. "Now, from what you said, it sounded like you enjoyed your travels and your time away from here."

Eochaid propped himself up on his elbows and looked at his brother. "Most of the time I did. When I was little, when Father first took me out to sea, I use to get sick all the time. Spent most of the day hanging my head over the sides of his ships. But after a few months, I got over it. Then each time Father prepared to take to the sea, I would plead with him to take me with him … and you know that he usually did."

Collin nodded.

"Now," Eochaid said, "I find that I am most content when I'm at sea. I can't explain it. There is just something peaceful about moving over such a massive expanse of water. I feel small, yet so powerful at the same time. And at night, when the moon is full, the surface of the sea dances with light; on moonless nights, a canopy of brilliant stars flows down from the sky to the horizon. It's like sitting in the middle of a sparkling dome—a sight I never tire of. Even on stormy days, I'd rather be on the sea than on land." Eochaid sat up and crossed his legs. He plucked a tall blade of grass and spun it back and forth in his fingers. "Do you still get seasick?"

Collin smiled. "I did the last time I went out. That was several months ago."

"I'll take you out on a day when the seas are calm." Eochaid tossed the green shoot away. "We'll sail along the coast, not too far out. If you start to feel ill, we'll sail back in."

Collin pursed his lips. "I'll think about it."

"While you think about it, I'll race you back to the castle—not that it will be much of a race, of course."

The brothers got up and sprinted to their horses. Collin pushed his mount as hard as he could. But he could only squint his eyes and purse his lips as he watched his older brother pull away in front of him.

The first of February was set as the date the five kings of Erin would meet to vote for the man they would elect as their high-king. News of the vote spread over the prior weeks, and now the village of Cathair Crofinn, situated below Eochaid's castle, was crowded shoulder to shoulder with people from all over Erin, with everyone anxious to see who would be chosen as their supreme leader.

Eochaid, representing the Kingdom of Meath, sat at the head of the long table. He did not appear intimidated, even though he was much younger than the other four reigning kings.

"Let the vote begin," Eochaid said.

In succession, the kings of Ulster and Connacht voiced their support for Eochaid as the rightful heir to the throne. As Eochaid's immediate neighbors, they believed their own independence would be best secured by a friendship and an alliance with the largest and most successful war tribes in all of Erin. Together, the two kings had conspired and thought that if needed, they could demolish Muirdach's army and overthrow him as Leinster's king if he continued to threaten them.

Ugaine, the king of Munster, cast his vote for Muirdach. Munster's entire eastern border ran alongside the land of Leinster, and Ugaine felt threatened by its king. Muirdach, naturally, voted for himself.

Eochaid voted last. He didn't want to speak the words. He didn't want to be king. Reluctantly, Eochaid voted for the man his father would have wanted to have succeed him. With the final vote cast, the council of kings was divided, three to two. With the majority in Eochaid's favor, Muirdach stood and threw his chair back as he spat his words at Eochaid: "Don't expect me at your coronation!"

"Wait!" Ugaine called out as Leinster's king stormed out of the room. "Muirdach ... wait!"

The king of Munster continued to shout for Muirdach as he ran after the enraged king, who abruptly stopped and swung around to face the gathering.

"Ailill Finn's son will not reign over me!" Muirdach said. "I have been ruler and king since before the day he was born! I will not bow to that ... that boy! Lugaid and Cormac, you will pay for what you did today. I will not forget your betrayal."

Muirdach looked at Ugaine, standing next to him, but the king of Munster said nothing.

"We're leaving!" the king of Leinster shouted.

Then Muirdach threw open the door and gathered his soldiers, who were waiting outside. The throngs of people standing around the Great Hall were shoved aside as Leinster's king and soldiers pushed their way through the crowd toward their horses.

In the lead of the procession, Muirdach seethed. He lashed his horse hard as he sped out of the village.

Let him celebrate. Let him sit on the throne of the high-king ... for a little while. I will make certain that Eochaid's reign is brief ... and that his death is slow and painful. The poison worked well enough on his father. It will be more potent this time when it is slipped to the son!

Chapter 22

"In a few hours, you will be king. Oh, Eochaid … you look so much like a younger version of your father." Noirenn smiled, then sighed as she inspected her son's royal attire. "Wait. Where are your gold torques?"

For several seconds, the queen mother's words hung in the silence of her son's chambers.

Eochaid stared blankly at his mother as his memory jolted itself back to the shores of Egypt. From time to time, even with so much requiring his attention, he still thought about the beautiful princess. For a while, her memory had haunted him. But the many months at home had since dulled what had once been a vivid memory—and now seemed more like a pleasant dream.

"I only have one," Eochaid finally answered.

"And where's its twin?"

"On the arm of a Judean princess."

"This mysterious princess you met must have made quite an impression on you. Is this why you delay in selecting a bride?"

"No, that's not the reason." Eochaid's voice sounded weary. "A past memory does not cloud my thoughts of the present. I left the princess on the shores of Egypt. My life is now here, in Erin. But know, Mother, that *I* will decide when I will marry. I will guide my life by my own thoughts and will."

Eochaid searched his mother's face for a glimmer of understanding.

Noirenn responded with another smile. "Enough said on the subject for now. Today is not a day for us to bicker. It is a day of celebration. You have your coronation ceremony waiting."

A large circle of massive monoliths surrounded the temple in Cathair Crofinn. Embedded in the earth, the huge vertical stones enclosed a space over one hundred feet in diameter. Within the circle sat the sacrificial altar: a huge, flat granite boulder supported by six large, roughly hewn stones. The altar stood on a platform of raised earth in the center of the circle so that, on special feast days, the worshippers inside the stone enclosure could watch the ritual sacrifices.

At sunrise on the day of the king's coronation, the men, women, and children of Meath seated themselves on the soft grass that filled the interior of the temple. Over the surrounding valley, crowds of people strained to see inside the Druid temple. There, a dozen bards, each holding a small lyre, already stood in place in front of the altar. Standing before the bards was an aged man whose long white hair and flowing beard marked him out as the elder head of their order.

While the crowds awaited the arrival of the royal procession, the bards strummed their instruments and the chief bard sang songs about the nobility, bravery, and devotion of Eochaid to his kingdom. On each side of the bards stood a group of Druid priests, whose function during the ceremony would be to light sticks of fragrant incense, pray to the gods, and then crown the king.

The sound of joyful music brought the seated multitude to their feet all across the valley and inside the stone structure. Twenty-four musicians marching in pairs made their way slowly along the wide dirt path that wound its way across the grass-covered valley. They played a stirring melody on flutes, pipes, and fiddles as they passed by the crowds. The musicians changed their music to a softer tune when they entered the temple and then moved slowly up the center aisle before they separated and arranged themselves evenly on each side of the altar.

The music continued to fill the valley as the lords and ladies of Erin approached the temple in their best ceremonial attire. Fancy lace sleeves and collars adorned the women's dresses. Their jeweled necklaces sparkled in the morning sunlight as they were shown to a special area where they seated themselves on several stone benches near the front of the altar.

Eochaid's mother followed the noble men and women, escorted by Collin, who wore his royal green-and-gold robes over a white tunic. On his head, he wore the slim silver crown of a prince. Noirenn, meanwhile, wore the golden crown of the queen mother. Her elaborate white-and-golden-thread embroidered dress drew impressive gasps and sighs from the spectators, who rarely had the opportunity to be so close to members of the royal family.

Behind the queen mother came the kings of Ulster, Munster, and Connacht. They walked slowly up the path in royal red, green, and gold mantles, each of them followed by young men who carried their heavy polished armor. Ten young women followed behind them. Their long auburn hair flowed in waves over sleeveless, ankle-length green-and-gold tunics. The girls shook bells and tambourines in rhythm while they danced gracefully, prostrating themselves from time to time as one group before Eochaid, who came last in line.

Eochaid smiled at the adoring crowds, who bowed as he moved past them. He wore a tunic of white woolen cloth that reached to his knees. A wide band of braided gold wrapped around his waist. On his broad shoulders hung a long purple-and-gold robe secured by golden clasps, each shaped into the head of a lion. The heavy robe trailed behind him as he took slow steps with elaborately strapped sandals that wound from his feet, then up and around his bare legs.

Around Eochaid's neck hung heavy twisted bands of gold wire that flattened toward the bottom and rested collar-fashion on his upper chest. Wide hammered-gold bands gleamed on his muscular upper arms. One torque of gold with a lion's head at each end encircled his right wrist. Completing his regal attire were a huge gold signet ring on the forefinger of his left hand and a long sword, sheathed in a silver scabbard at his left side.

Three young men escorted Eochaid: one on each side, one following behind. The youth on his left wore a bronze helmet and bronze body armor. In his hands, he held a battle-axe. On Eochaid's right, the young man strode forward in silver breast, back, arm, and thigh armor. He carried at his side a long sword. These two youths represented the kingdoms of Connacht and Munster, both of whom had sworn their allegiance to support Eochaid in battle should they ever be called upon. The youth that followed behind Eochaid wore a plain white wool tunic, tied around the waist with a garland of mistletoe leaves. He represented the region of Ulster and the county of Meath, home to Erin's previous and now soon-to-be high-king. The trailing lad also represented the hope that there would be no battles to be fought and that peace would reign over the entire island nation.

As he entered the temple, Eochaid was thankful that the stacks of wood piled up behind the altar would not be used today. He would not have to witness what always both saddened and repulsed him. But like his father before him, he believed there would be times when he would have to yield to the demands of the Druid priesthood. He knew the stability of his throne depended on the priests' attitude toward him, and on their influence over the kingdoms' sometimes wild and illiterate people.

The chief Druid priest, with nine senior priests in tow, moved forward when Eochaid neared the altar. The Druids wore long, flowing linen robes without ornament of any kind. Their white and steel-gray beards covered their chests. Each held in his left hand a small branch of mistletoe and in his right a large stick of burning incense that sent snakes of smoke into the air.

As the pungent odor wafted over those assembled, the Druid high priest raised both of his hands above his head, then closed his eyes and led all who could hear him in prayer:

> *"Power of all gods and goddesses, we call on you.*
>
> *Cast your light on us that we may see. Honor us as we honor you.*
>
> *We bind you to ourselves and to our king today.*
>
> *Ancestors, ancient ones, old ones, hear our prayers and accept our offerings of devotion.*
>
> *We bind you to ourselves and to our king today.*
>
> *Earth spirits, fur and feather, leaf and stone, we meditate on your powers; sustain us, as we sustain you.*
>
> *We bind you to ourselves and to our king today.*
>
> *We call to all gods. We call to all ancestors. We call to all earth spirits. Come as we welcome you into this sacred place. Come as we anoint our king. Come and bestow your powers to him who will wear the ard-righ's crown."*

When the prayer ended, the chief bard sang a song about the many men who had worn the crown of the high-king in years gone by. Eochaid held his composure as the bard sang of his own father's many military victories and bravery on land and sea. The bard finished with tributes and praises for their soon-to-be-crowned high-king. Those present listened until the bard finished, and then they raised their voices and shouted, "Long live the ard-righ! Long live Heremon, Eochaid!"—using the familiar title from the House of Heremon as another name for their high-king, as was usually done.

As the people shouted, the chief priest stepped forward, holding in both hands the royal diadem: a two-inch-wide solid-gold crown. The front of the crown was shaped into a small peak, and in the peak was embedded a walnut-sized polished emerald.

The Druid priest motioned to Erin's three regional kings, who stood by the side of the altar, to come forward. He handed the high-king's crown to the king of Connacht, the elder of the three kings present. The priest then stood in front of Eochaid and pronounced a blessing on him, which would be followed by Eochaid's personal response:

> "Our Heremon, Eochaid Finn, I bestow on you the kingship of the ard-righ of Erin. May the power of the gods guide you, may the might of the gods uphold you, may the eyes of the gods watch over you, may the ears of the gods hear you, may the words of the gods give you speech, may the wisdom of the gods teach you, and may the power of the gods protect you always."

Eochaid swallowed hard, then began: "In the presence of our gods and all assembled here this day, I, Eochaid Finn, accept the crown of the ard-righ. I vow through the whole course of my life to serve the people of Erin to the utmost of my ability, to protect this land and its people, to rule with justice and mercy without exception to all, as I affirm by my solemn oath."

The three attending kings surrounded Eochaid, and each held a side of the king's crown with their right hand. They placed the circle of gold on Eochaid's head while swearing allegiance to him as ard-righ.

The ceremony concluded with repeated shouts from the crowd: "Long live the ard-righ! Long live Heremon, Eochaid!"

The procession immediately reformed, and the dancing maidens, musicians, bards, Druid priests, and kings exited the temple. Crowds lining the roads all the way back to the village cheered as Eochaid and his royal party now rode slowly by them on white horses decorated with flower wreaths around their necks. The members of royalty rode on the path that led up the hill to the Great Hall, where oxen, sheep, and cattle were roasting on large open pits in preparation for the coronation feast.

Countless pitchers of ale and mead were filled, as all the people in the village were this day guests of their newly appointed high-king. They spread their blankets across the grass and under the trees that dotted the hillside around the castle and hall, and they picnicked on food and drink provided by their new king.

Eochaid entertained his noble guests in the vast hall next to the castle of Cathair Crofinn. Massive amounts of boiled and roasted meats were placed on beautifully carved wooden boards in front of the guests. Seated near the back of the room, hungry soldiers stabbed at the food with sharp knifes that they pulled from their sheaths. Others grabbed from the platters with their bare hands, anxious to gnaw on the succulent meats. They ignored the polished cutlery lying on the table, which the refined aristocrats now held as they sat at the tables around the sides and front of the room.

Large loaves of bread formed into the shape of the king's crown encircled bowls of whipped sweet butter. Silver platters piled with colorful fruits and vegetables were set before the guests, and silver goblets were filled to the brim with wine, ale, and mead to satisfy thirst.

All the day and far into the night, the celebration continued. Various groups of singers and dancers performed in the center of the room for the king and his special guests, all of whom sat behind tables on a raised dais at the front of the hall.

Sitting next to Eochaid, Cormac, the king of Ulster, tilted his head back and poured the last of his sixth cup of wine into his mouth. He wiped his wet lips with the back of his hand and leered at the group of beautiful girls that danced before Eochaid and the other two kings who reclined near them.

After refilling his cup, Cormac leaned in close to Eochaid. "The young maidens dance in front of you and hope you will look at them, and when you do, they blush. You can have any maiden you want. With the celebration of your kingship coming to an end, and all these desirable women vying for your attention, would it not be the ideal time for you to consider selecting one of them for a wife?"

Eochaid turned toward the inebriated middle-aged king. "There is a time for all things. Right now, Erin is my beloved and its people are my wife. Why do you ask this of me?"

"We all know that you have powerful enemies. If you care about your position, and the people, wouldn't it be wise to have an heir? Your father wasted no time in choosing a queen and making sure he had an heir whom he wanted to sit on his throne. And so, here you are!"

Eochaid sighed, trying to contain his emotions but failing. "Not even the celebration of my coronation has passed, and again I am annoyed with the same tiring subject of selecting a queen. Do you speak your own words, or has the queen mother placed them in your mouth? There are other important matters for me to be concerned with. Soon, I will be moving out with my army to stop the skirmishes that continue on our border with Leinster over the rights to water and land."

Cormac pulled his head back, clearly surprised at the new king's outburst.

Eochaid rose up slowly, then leaned down toward Cormac. "While I am away, the queen mother will be sending out many of her trusted advisors to find the most beautiful and eligible maidens across our land. From this group, she will personally select the maidens she finds best suitable to be … what she is calling 'the king's bride and the queen mother's daughter.' When I am ready, I will meet the fair ladies, and then, if I find one that I desire, I will choose her as my bride. So set your mind to rest, and from this day forward, refrain from ever speaking to me another word on this subject. Have I made myself clear?"

Cormac cleared his throat. "Yes, very clear, Your Majesty."

Eochaid straightened up, then lifted his silver goblet into the air and tapped his knife against its side. When the music and buzzing of the conversations stopped, he addressed his assembled guests: "Noble men and women, soldiers, friends, and family, the night is drawing to a close. I want to thank you all for coming together today to witness and celebrate my coronation. I do not want you to leave before we have a toast to the health and prosperity of all who have honored me on this day with their presence.

"People of Meath, Ulster, Connacht, Munster, and Leinster, today we are one people, one in interest and one in thought. Some of us through the years have fought against each other, but we have also fought side by side. My desire as your high-king would be for us to strive to *live* side by side, in peace.

"To my trusted nobles and subjects, I give you my heartfelt thanks for your outpouring of love and support, in the past for my father, and to me now, as well as in the days to come. May the gods always protect our island home!"

With these last words, Eochaid drank off the contents of his goblet, while all those in the crowded room cheered and shouted, "Long live Eochaid! Long live the ard-righ!"

As the people continued to cheer, Eochaid moved past each table, thanking his guests for attending the festivities. As he approached the door of the Great Hall, one of Eochaid's officers rushed to his side.

"My lord, may I be of service to you?"

"No," Eochaid said. "I'm fine. After all the revelry today, I actually need some quiet and a little time to myself. I know you are not to let me out of your sight. But tonight, I ask that you keep some distance behind me."

"Yes, my lord."

A burst of cool night air hit Eochaid's face as the hall attendants pushed open the heavy wood doors. Eochaid strode outside and took in a deep breath before proceeding under the long wisteria-covered pergola that led from the Great Hall up toward the castle's main courtyard. He crossed through the side gatehouse, then into the castle just after midnight.

Eochaid moved through the long torch-lit corridor and excused the attendants waiting outside the door to his room. He didn't want to see or hear anyone after the long day of entertaining and endless conversation. He savored the quiet stillness as he rested his back against the door as it shut. After soaking in the silence, Eochaid walked across his room and opened the ornate double doors that separated his bedroom from its wide balcony. He could hear the distant sound of music and laughter coming from the celebrations that continued in the Great Hall and the many smaller parties taking place across all the villages in his land.

The new high-king moved across the balcony and leaned against the stone railing. Thanks to the light of a full moon overhead, he gazed at the great expanse of land that spread out below him. His castle stood on the highest hill in all of Erin. He knew that everything, below and beyond to the far reaches of the sea, now belonged to him—his kingdom. So why on this night, he wondered, did he not feel elated or at least satisfied? Why instead did he feel restless and empty? What was missing?

He knew his father's absence accounted for a part of what he was feeling, but yet … something else stirred inside him. Eochaid looked up into the sky and wondered what could he possibly want that he did not already have, or could not at his asking possess.

The young king walked slowly back into his room and stood in front of his dressing table. He lifted the heavy gold neck chain over his head that had belonged to his father, and placed it down on the table. He stared at the high-king's signet ring as he slid it off his finger, then loosened and removed the wide woven band of gold from around his waist. Finally, he gazed at the gold torque on his right wrist.

Princess of Judah … where are you now? Are you dancing in the waters of the Nile and singing in Pharaoh's palace? Have you grown more beautiful? Eochaid's thoughts wandered further afield as he removed the gold band and set it down. *Maybe sailing the seas back to you would satisfy my discontent … or perhaps the time has simply come for me to select my bride from here among my people.*

Eochaid removed his formal attire and lay down on his bed. From his position, he could see out across his balcony and into the night sky. The last thing his mind registered before sleep embraced him was how big and bright the moon looked.

CHAPTER 23

Jeremiah stood in his room and stared out the window, not really looking at anything. For the past few days, he had felt anxious, as if something significant was about to happen. Now, though, he felt at ease as he glanced up at the full moon and recited one of King David's psalms: "'The heavens declare the glory of God; the skies proclaim the work of his hands. Day after day they pour forth speech; night after night they display knowledge. There is no speech or language where their voice is not heard. Their voice goes out into all the earth, their words to the ends of the world.'"

"Mmm … yes. It is time … time to reinstate the feast days that we were commanded to observe," Jeremiah whispered to himself. He moved away from the window toward his bed. "Perhaps it might unify our people and strengthen their faith. I pray that it will lead them back to Yahweh and away from the multitude of gods in this land."

Early the next morning, Jeremiah summoned Baruch and Ebed to his room.

"I need to tell you that Yahweh has put upon my heart the need for our people to observe his ordained feast days. The Lord God would not have commanded the observance of the seven feasts if there was not a profound meaning for them. When I visited the temple last month on the island of Elephantine, I met many of our people—descendants of those who fled almost two hundred years ago during the time of the Assyrian siege. In Elephantine, each generation has followed the laws and special feast days Yahweh ordained since the time of Moses."

"But we have no temple here," Baruch said, "and even if we did, we are commanded to only offer sacrifice-slain animals in the temple in Jerusalem, which no longer stands."

Jeremiah held his hand up. "When I returned from Elephantine, I inquired in the villages all around Tahpanhes and found that most of the Hebrews who moved here long before we arrived, they no longer celebrate or even take notice of any of our feast days. Maybe that is why they have been so easily influenced to worship Egyptian gods.

"The least I will do while we live here will be to observe our day of deliverance! Next month, on the morning on the eighth day of Nisan—six days before Pesach—I would like to gather our people together to pray to Yahweh as one unified nation. Our people need to be reminded of the power of God, when through Moses, our ancestors were liberated after four hundred years of slavery in this very land! None should ever forget how our firstborn escaped death when the blood of a lamb caused the spirit of death to pass over their homes. Saved by the blood, they walked out of Egypt no longer in bondage, but a free people.

"I also plan to institute the annual observance of Shavuot. I will not stand by and see our people ignore the Lord God's giving of the Torah. The observance of Moses receiving Yahweh's teachings must not be overlooked. His word is what sustains us! As it was written: 'He humbled you, causing you to hunger and then feeding you with manna, which neither you nor your fathers had known, to teach you that man does not live on bread alone but on every word that comes from the mouth of the Lord.'"

Jeremiah sought and received Pharaoh's permission to erect a large tent in an empty brickfield adjoining one of the Hebrew villages. From the early hours of the morning, the Jews began to assemble under the tent. By ten o'clock, hundreds of Jewish men and women stood in the still warm air of an Egyptian spring day. A number of Egyptian priests of Osiris and Isis were also present, curious to hear what would be said at the foreign gathering.

After getting Jeremiah's permission to meet with a dozen or so of their friends, Teia and Hannah walked into the tent, then down the side toward the back, where they spotted Miriam, Tirzah, and the rest of their friends.

"Look at who they let out," Elan said when Teia and Hannah joined the group. "So what's Jeremiah going to yell at us about today?"

"He just wants to talk to everyone about observing our feast days," Teia said. "He wants us to celebrate Pesach next week."

Elan made a sour face. "What good will that do? Momma and Abba always celebrated the feast days, always obeyed Yahweh. It didn't help them! My brothers disappeared, probably dead … our friends, our neighbors in Judah, they're dead! They celebrated the feast days. What did Yahweh do for them? What has Yahweh ever done for any of us? Jeremiah shouts the same message from Yahweh—'Obey me or else!' The same old message, over and over. I'm tired of hearing it. If he starts with another one of his rants, I'm leaving."

"Shut up, Elan," said Benjamin, one of the older boys. "You're always complaining about something. Let's wait to hear what the prophet has to say."

Elan huffed, then said, "You're always sticking up for that old man. Is it because your father was a temple priest?"

Benjamin shook his head. "I don't know why I bother to try to talk any sense into you."

"I agree with Elan," another boy said. "Look at how many gods are here in Egypt … one for everything you want. You give them an offering: flowers, bread, oil—whatever. You just ask them to give you what you want. They don't demand anything from us!"

Elan nodded his head. "I like that a lot better than always being told what to do, or what not to do! And I'm not the only one. A lot of the people in my village are starting to feel the same. They seem a lot happier since we came here."

The girls in the group remained quiet and passed glances back and forth to each other as the boys continued to argue, until finally a hush fell over the murmuring mass of people. Teia turned and saw Jeremiah walking toward the front of the crowd. He was followed by a small group of his most loyal supporters, including Baruch and Ebed.

The prophet's flowing beard covered the front of his robe, which swayed from side to side as he approached the three-tiered brick staircase. Suddenly, he fell to his knees. The prophet buried his face in his hands and began to weep. The crowd stood around in stunned silence, which was only broken by the loud sobs of God's prophet who was frozen in place.

After several minutes, Jeremiah slowly rose to his feet. He walked up the stairs to the wooden platform and turned to face the crowd. With his face wet from tears, he raised his hands and addressed those assembled. His words flew like swift arrows that found their mark.

"Thus says the Lord of Hosts, the God of Israel: 'And I will take the remnant of Judah, that have set their faces to go into the land of Egypt to sojourn there, and they shall all be consumed, and fall in the land of Egypt; they shall even be consumed by the sword and by the famine: and they shall be an execration, and an astonishment, and a curse, and a reproach. For I will punish them that dwell in the land of Egypt, as I have punished

Jerusalem, by the sword, by the famine, and by the pestilence: So that none of the remnant of Judah, which are gone into the land of Egypt to sojourn there, shall escape or remain, that they should return into the land of Judah, to the which they have a desire to return to dwell there: for none shall return but such as shall escape.'"

The crowd remained in silence for a few moments, then a flurry of whispers and murmurs echoed throughout the tent.

"That's it! I'm outta here," Elan said.

He turned and pushed through his circle of friends, then moved through the standing crowd and out of the tent. Some of the adults also left. At the same time, many of the men and women who remained began yelling at the prophet:

"No harm has come to us as we have offered incense and poured out drink offerings to the queen of heaven. We have been well. Our families are fed. No evil has come upon us. Our lives are better now than when we lived in the cities of Judah! We're tired of your warnings! We will not listen to you!"

Jeremiah raised his voice above the shouts and jeers: "Hear the word of the Lord, all of Judah that resides in the land of Egypt. The Lord of Hosts says, 'This will be the sign to you that I will punish you in this place,' declares the Lord, 'so that you will know that my threats of harm against you will surely stand.' This is what the Lord says: 'I am going to hand Pharaoh Hophra king of Egypt over to his enemies who seek his life, just as I handed Zedekiah king of Judah over to Nebuchadnezzar king of Babylon, the enemy who was seeking his life.'"

At these words, the majority of those assembled began shouting at Jeremiah and cursing him. While the prophet continued to warn and condemn those before him, the crowd became further agitated, shifting positions and clenching their fists. Only a small number nodded their heads and wept. Most continued to shout back insults and threats. They condemned the prophet, denouncing him as a madman whose foolish words should not be taken seriously.

"Treason!" the Egyptians priests shouted. "He speaks treason against Pharaoh! Take him away that he may be judged, then put to death!"

Jeremiah was led quickly down from the platform and out of the tent by a few of his followers. They ran with the prophet back to his residence in the palace. The prophet struggled to catch his breath as he thanked everyone for their protection. He then politely asked all but Baruch and Ebed to leave his room.

"What happened … was not … not what I had planned … or had hoped for. But the Spirit of the Lord came upon me."

Baruch pulled over a chair and beckoned Jeremiah to sit. The prophet eased himself down.

"Why? Why do they never learn?" Jeremiah took a few deep breaths and waited a moment before he continued. "Sadly, this is not the first time in the history of our race that Yahweh's chosen people … have lost their way. How easily they forget that it was for this reason destruction came by the hand of the Assyrians against the House of Israel … and then devastation and captivity again by the hands of the Babylonians against the House of Judah."

He glanced from Baruch to Ebed. "Do you two realize that it has taken less than a year for most of our people to forget Yahweh and embrace the Egyptian gods?"

Ebed and Baruch both nodded, but remained quiet as the prophet went on.

"We can't stay here much longer. I have visited all the Hebrew villages and few if any have listened to my warnings. They call me a madman! Just like today. Many even told me that they have no use for Yahweh." Jeremiah closed his eyes. "Instead, they burn incense to the Egyptian queen of heaven, who they tell me has watered their soil and filled their bellies."

Jeremiah looked up at his companions again. "Our time here will soon end. It was not by our choice that we entered this land. Yahweh gave me the words that I have spoken. It will be he who protects us, for my mission is not yet complete. The Lord God has used my mouth for his words to root out and pull down, to destroy and throw down. Soon, he will use me to plant and to build … but not here. I will plead with our people, and if they still harden their hearts, and refuse to be rebuilt and planted in a new land, then they will perish in Egypt as the Lord God has proclaimed. When possible, we must leave this place."

"What are your plans?" Baruch asked.

"The man I met in Elephantine, his name is Nadav. He told me that one of his ships is soon to arrive in the port of Pelusium. We traveled together from Elephantine to Tahpanhes. He is staying here until the end of next week, then he leaves for the coast to meet his ship. Nadav told me he would offer us passage with him. He said his ship will sail from Egypt to Judah's port in Ashkelon and then on to Joppa. From Joppa, he sails south and then west along the African coast to a place called Rusaddir. He then plans to return to Judah before the winter months set in. I believe this is the man Yahweh has provided for our escape from Egypt."

"When will you tell the princesses?" Ebed asked.

Jeremiah thought for a minute, then answered, "I will tell them tomorrow. I will need to call upon both of you to help all of us prepare for our departure. Pharaoh Hophra was kind to offer us all a home in his palace, but over time he has tired of me. Not long ago, he warned me to stop causing unrest in the villages by condemning our people for worshipping his gods. He told me to cease, or he will have me silenced. What I spoke today was considered blasphemy against Pharaoh, for which the penalty is death.

"Pharaoh has recently also taken interest in Princess Teia, for her to be betrothed to one of his sons." Jeremiah shook his head. "I cannot allow that to happen. Johanan brought us to this land by force, and the Lord has now made it clear that we must leave. Yahweh's wrath will come down on this land, and the Jewish people who reside here will be destroyed. My heart breaks for them at his words: 'To this day they have not humbled themselves or shown reverence, nor have they followed my law and the decrees I set before you and your fathers. Therefore, this is what the Lord Almighty, the God of Israel, says: I am determined to bring disaster on you and to destroy all Judah.'"

———

Throughout the afternoon and evening, several men secretly came from their villages to the palace to meet with Jeremiah. They pleaded with him to lead their families out of Egypt. They believed the prophet. They believed what he said to be the true word of the living God. They feared for their lives because pressure was being put upon them to worship the numerous gods of Egypt. They were outcasts among their own people, with their neighbors willingly adopting and assimilating into the Egyptian culture.

Jeremiah listened to their pleas, then said, "I can't tell you where or when we will go, other than it will be soon. When the time comes, you will be given no notice, because we will most likely depart in secret. A knock will come to your door, and you will only have time to take what you can carry in your hands and leave all else that you have behind. So prepare now."

Chapter 24

Jeremiah sat across the table from the princesses as they ate their light breakfast of assorted fruit and a slice of barley bread, which he had asked to be served in their room. "Princess Teia, Princess Hannah, speak to no one of what I now tell you. On the day that follows the first Sabbath after Pesach, we will leave Tahpanhes and travel to the city of Migdol. We will gather together with some of our people there in a ceremonial tent to celebrate the spring harvest and the Feast of Unleavened Bread. When the feast day ends at sundown, we will be leaving Egypt. Ebed will help you with what you should pack or leave behind. We will have a two days' journey to Egypt's coast where we will sail for … for the place where the Lord leads us."

While hearing the prophet's news, Teia and Hannah had stopped eating. They remained silent while they listened to Jeremiah with looks of worry and fear on their faces.

"Yesterday, I was brought before Pharaoh," Jeremiah said. "He wanted to hear what I had to say regarding the allegations of treason that have been brought against me. I told him that the words I spoke were not mine, but Yahweh's. He let me go without any punishment other than being silenced. I am forbidden to speak to our people about Yahweh or the Egyptian gods. I think Pharaoh was merciful with me because he has also started to think that I am a madman and not of a sound mind. Pharaoh Hophra has been most hospitable to us, and I am grieved that, through me, the Lord has pronounced judgment against him."

The princesses said nothing, so Jeremiah continued. "When we travel to Migdol, you will change into the clothes that Baruch will give you. We will all wear clothing that will help to disguise us as local villagers."

Teia cleared her throat. "Where will we go after that?" she asked. "Would it not be wise to return to Judah where Yahweh told us to stay, and seek the protection that King Nebuchadnezzar promised you?"

"Nebuchadnezzar did promise *me* safety, but that was a long time ago—and I have yet to tell you that I found out, soon after we arrived in Egypt, that the Babylonian king imprisoned your father and had all of your brothers killed. They were murdered to ensure that no heir remained alive to claim the rightful throne of Judah." Jeremiah reached out and touched Teia's hand. "I am sorry, Princess, but you will never return to Jerusalem."

In that moment, Teia felt like she was no longer present in the room. Jeremiah's mouth continued to move, but to Teia, his words were incoherent. She didn't hear any more about the plans for the upcoming journey. She heard nothing but the last few words Jeremiah had spoken to her.

The Fourteenth of Nisan, 585 BC

By sundown, the attendants of Pharaoh's household had provided the meal as instructed by Jeremiah. After covering the table in Jeremiah's sitting room with food and drink, they quickly retreated. A large platter sat in the middle of the table, on which sat a whole roasted lamb, with the accompaniments of bitter herbs, unleavened bread, and wine.

Baruch, Ebed, Teia, and Hannah stood around the candlelit table as Jeremiah spoke. "We come together tonight to celebrate our deliverance, as we are commanded to remember what took place when the Lord God Almighty freed our people. Long ago, at this season, on such a night as this, a people—our people—set out on a journey from this land. All but crushed by their enslavement, they still held on to a distant memory of a time when they had heard the voice of their God, bidding them to summon up the courage to be free. With their faith in Yahweh, led by Moses, they left Egypt, crossed the sea, and moved through the desert toward his Promised Land.

"What our people experienced so long ago, they remembered, and told to their children, and to their grandchildren. From generation to generation, the story was retold. We now gather together on this night to tell it again as we give thanks for the deliverance of Israel—God's chosen people."

Jeremiah pulled his shawl over his head and prayed a blessing upon the feast. "Let God's children who gather at this table drink from the first glass of wine and remember their sanctification, as the Lord God separated his chosen people and said, 'I am the Lord your God, who brought you out of Egypt, out of the land of slavery.' Let us drink from the second glass of wine and remember our deliverance, as the Lord God said, 'I will bring you out from under the yoke of the Egyptians.' As we drink from the third cup, we will remember our redemption, as the Lord God said, 'I will redeem you with an outstretched arm and with mighty acts of judgment.' When we put our lips to the last cup, we will thank the Lord God Almighty, as we remember his words, 'I will take you as my own people, and I will be your God.'"

The prophet paused, then lifted his face toward the ceiling. "Since this feast was established by you, O Lord our God, through your servant Moses, as an ordinance forever to celebrate the miraculous deliverance of your people from bondage in the land of Egypt, bless now, we ask you, your children assembled this night who are also in need of deliverance from this land of sin and idolatry. Bring us in safety to a haven of rest that you have prepared for us in a place of your choosing, so that we may plant the seeds from the vine of David to build your everlasting kingdom.

"We rejoice, O Lord our God, this night in not merely the wine and the bread of life that the earth yields to us, but rather, we ask you to let earth and heaven be joined: the bounty of this night is of the earth, the holiness of the occasion is of heaven. As the Lord our God brings blessings to us, let us raise our hearts and minds toward him. Amen."

When the prayers, songs, and eating of the Pesach meal ended, Jeremiah nodded to Baruch and Ebed, who immediately rose and left for Jeremiah's bedroom. Jeremiah asked Teia and Hannah to collect all that was left of the meal and take it to a large brazier filled with glowing coals, which burned in the small outside courtyard. There, the prophet reverently laid the remnants of the feast on the brazier before he knelt down and engaged in silent prayer until all of the bits and pieces of the meal had been consumed. Afterward, he and the princesses returned to his room.

"In a few days, we will gather in a sacred assembly in Migdol," Jeremiah said. "We will meet with our people to celebrate the Feast of Unleavened Bread and First Fruits. We are required to present ourselves at the temple, but with its destruction and our exile, that will not be possible.

"Everyone in the village has been told to bring something from the fruit of their labor that will be burned as an offering to Yahweh. Knowing that I will not be speaking has met with the approval of our people, who now seem more likely to attend. Everyone will continue to meet under the tent until the end of the week. Assured that I will not speak, Pharaoh has approved our attendance at the weeklong ritual, so we will not be missed in the palace. By the time he expects us to return, we will already be far from here. The Lord has provided us with a favorable time of escape. According to my calendar, he will also be providing a full moon to guide us back to the sea.

"We will start our journey immediately after the first service, just before sundown. But, before our departure, I must tell you a story. Baruch, Ebed, would you remove the Bethel Stone from the chest and place it before me?"

Baruch unbuckled two leather lashes, then opened the top of the wooden chest that usually sat by the side of Jeremiah's bed. Both men reached down and lifted out the large pillow-shaped stone and set it down in front of the prophet.

"I am going to tell you this story," Jeremiah said. He looked over to Teia. "You will be familiar with the first part of the story … but now I will tell you the rest. Long ago, your great ancestor Jacob was on his way to Haran when darkness began to fall. He stopped his journey and planned to rest for the night in Luz. As he prepared to sleep on the ground under a tree, he looked around for something he could use as a pillow. He chose a large stone, placed his leather pouch over it, and lay down to sleep. That night, he dreamed a magnificent dream.

"As Jacob dreamt, he saw a ladder set up on the earth, and the top of it reached to heaven where the angels of God were ascending and descending on it. Yahweh stood above it, and said, 'I am the Lord, the God of your father Abraham and the God of Isaac. I will give you and your descendants the land on which you are lying. Your descendants will be like the dust of the earth, and you will spread out to the west and to the east, to the north and to the south. All peoples on earth will be blessed through you and your offspring.'

"Afterward," Jeremiah continued, "Jacob rose up early in the morning and took the stone that he had used for his pillow and set it up as a pillar and poured oil on the top of it. He called the name of that place 'Bethel' … which means 'House of God.' He returned to Bethel many years later and retrieved the stone. Jacob brought the stone with him when he traveled with his family from Hebron to Egypt. The stone left Egypt four hundred years later with the bones of Jacob's son Joseph and all his descendants when they followed Moses from here to the edge of the Promised Land."

Jeremiah pointed down at the large stone in front of him. "The stone was carried by wooden poles through the two iron rings embedded in it, through the forty years of their wanderings. It was placed in their midst when Yahweh gave Moses the Law. The stone entered the Promised Land with Joshua. It was present when David was crowned king, and when his son Solomon was crowned, and then through all successive generations. When it was not used for coronations, it was placed in a special chamber near God's holy temple.

"With the help of a few trusted companions, I removed the stone and other precious items from Yahweh's house through a secret underground tunnel and hid them in a mountain cave when the temple sacrifices ceased, when no priest entered the temple, long before I was imprisoned.

"I have taken my part in what has become the destiny of this precious stone. But you, Teia, as a descendant of Judah and the heir apparent to the throne of David, you will be the future guardian of this stone. You will be more than a princess, Teia. One day, you will be God's queen and your husband will be his king. As Nathan the prophet proclaimed the word of the Lord to King David, I also repeat his words to you: 'Your throne will be established forever.' I hope to be there on that day when Judah's sovereignty is restored."

Teia sat wide-eyed as she watched Jeremiah approach her and then softly kiss her on each cheek. Baruch and Ebed also came forward and gave Teia a tender kiss on her cheeks. Hannah waited behind them, then embraced her sister tightly even as Teia's thoughts whirled: *I will be the bride to a king of Judah? Then … that is a sign that we will return to Jerusalem! For it is only from there that the throne of Yahweh can reign. But … Jeremiah said I would never return. What has changed?*

Teia released her sister when she heard Jeremiah speak: "Soon, we will gather our belongings and begin a long journey. Now is the time for rest. Pray to the Lord our God before you sleep this one of only a few remaining nights for us in the land of Egypt. Pray that Yahweh will deliver *us* safely to a promised land that also flows with milk and honey."

CHAPTER 25

The crowds dispersed out of the large tent in several directions as the celebration of the spring harvest ended. As the sun began to set, no one took notice of Jeremiah's group as they moved away from the gathering and toward the banks of the Nile. Just before nightfall, they reached the wide, slow-moving water. By the time darkness fell, several other families had gathered at the river's edge, all of whom Jeremiah had agreed to take out of Egypt.

Waiting for the prophet on the river was Oporah, the old eunuch who had served Jeremiah and the princesses since the day they arrived at Pharaoh's palace. He and two of his most trusted friends each sat in one of the three large boats already laden with the baggage they had packed early that afternoon and transported to the river. The Judeans quickly climbed aboard and seated themselves on the barge-shaped vessels. They were told to remain quiet and try to sleep as the Egyptian men used one long oar to push their boats away from the riverbank and into the flowing water. In silence, they floated past the houses along the shore.

Teia looked into the sky as they moved with the current north toward the sea. A few stars peeked out from behind the wispy clouds.

I should have never doubted, Lord. I should have known that you would lead us back home.

An hour after midnight, the boats were beached under a bridge, where they were met by Joab—one of Nadav's sons—and several of their companions who would lead the Judeans to their ship in Pelusium's harbor. Before leaving, Jeremiah thanked Oporah and his friends for risking their lives in helping them make this journey.

On the road above the bridge, a few of Nadav's friends waited with camels that would be used for the refugees and their baggage. At Jeremiah's request, an oxen-led cart was also provided for some of the heavier items he'd brought with them. After all the items had been loaded and secured, the camels were brought forward and made to kneel so they could be mounted by their riders.

The road was fairly empty, and only a few small caravans passed by during their first hours of travel. Then, suddenly, from behind their group, shrill cries rose up from a large group of riders who converged around them.

"Toss us your weapons, coin pouches, your jewelry, and you will be spared!" shouted the man leading the group.

More than a dozen men rode up along the line of travelers waving their swords. As they passed by Jeremiah's cart, the prophet turned around to the princesses who sat behind him against a chest. "When I step off on the right side of the cart, you two get out on the other side, then cross the road and lie down."

Jeremiah stood next to the cart as the princesses followed his directions. As Teia pulled Hannah down next to her, Jeremiah poured all but a couple of the gold coins out of his pouch onto the ground just under the cart and used the edge of his sandals to scrape small mounds of the dirt over them.

"Where are your weapons? Your gold—your jewels?" the bandits asked.

They searched through everyone's baggage, taking what they wanted and leaving everything else strewn on the ground.

"We have nothing of value. We are simple farmers," one of the men of Judah replied.

"What's in there?" the leader of the thieves asked Jeremiah as he motioned to the cart.

"Nothing of value. This is all the money I have." Jeremiah held out the small leather pouch.

"Bring a torch!" the lead bandit shouted. He dismounted his horse and grabbed the pouch from Jeremiah's hand, then put the tip of his sword under Jeremiah's chin. "We'll see if you are lying, old man." He stepped up into the cart. "Shine some light over here," he ordered.

A man carrying a torch came around the other side of the cart. Teia and Hannah froze. The torcher's light splattered back and forth over the princesses and the road before it rested above the cart. Out of the corner of her eye, Teia could see the bandit's feet not more than a long pace away from her. She prayed that he did not step back.

"What's this?" the lead thief in the cart asked after he had tossed all the scrolls out of the chest.

Jeremiah moved a few steps closer to the side of the cart. "It is just a rock that we plan to use as the cornerstone for our new house."

"A rock! You value a rock? You are a pitifully poor group. At least we got some sellable jewelry and weapons from a few of you." The bandit dropped down from the cart, then mounted his horse. "We're finished here. Let's go!" he ordered.

The torchbearer lowered the flame and moved toward the back of the cart, away from the princesses, just as chilling screams erupted from the rear of their caravan.

"Nooooooo! Momma, help me! Momma, help meeeee!" a young teenage girl screamed as she was taken from the arms of her mother.

"Leave her—please!" the girl's father said.

The leader of the bandits rode up next to the screaming girl, whom one of his men was now holding. He smacked the man hard across the head with his sword. "I told you, no women this time! Let's go!" The robber shoved the girl to the ground, then moved toward his horse.

As the sound of galloping hoofs began to fade away, Teia heard the shuffling of footsteps approach.

"They're gone," Jeremiah said. He crouched down next to the princesses. "Let me help you up."

As Jeremiah led the princesses back into the cart, the rest of refugees picked up what was left of their belongings from the ground while Baruch and Ebed helped Jeremiah sift through the dirt for the gold coins. Leather satchels and most of the canvas bags had been taken. The bandits had left only a few woven baskets undamaged, which the refugees filled with the trampled-on clothes now scattered on the ground. The refugees tied the rest of their belongings in blankets that they held in their arms as they rode away, shaken and in fear of another attack.

For eight hours, they traveled with little or no conversation as all ears listened for the sound of approaching horses. The refugees picked up their pace, riding past sunrise, only stopping briefly in the late morning not too far from the road to rest in a small, shaded oasis. Several more hours of traveling unarmed and vulnerable lay ahead through the afternoon and another evening before they would reach what they hoped would be the safety of Pelusium's seaport.

Chapter 26

The harbor was crowded with ships when Jeremiah and his group arrived. The weary travelers slid off their kneeling camels as torchlights bobbed toward them in the dark. As the figures drew close, Jeremiah recognized the stocky man who approached.

"Jeremiah, it is good to see you again my friend."

"Thank you, Nadav, for offering your vessel and crew for our people. Thank you for leading us away from this land that will soon feel the wrath of God."

Nadav gave a short nod. "Jeremiah, my ship and its crew are ready and at your disposal. I am honored to be of service to Yahweh's prophet and to the members of the House of David. The Lord God has greatly blessed me. Offering all of you safe passage will be a way for me to thank him for all that he has given me. We sail at dawn."

Along with the princesses and their two attendants, twenty-three of Judah's refugees had sought and received Jeremiah's permission to travel with him from Egypt. They were to sail with Jeremiah's small group along with a crew of sixty-five that included the captain, his officers, cooks, cabin boys, and thirty oarsmen.

Almost a year had passed since Teia stood in this harbor. Vivid memories of the prince flooded back to her. She looked across the sea and recalled the morning she'd watched his ship sail away. *Where are you now, Prince Eochaid? Do you ever think of me? Do you still see me in your dreams?* Teia wrapped her fingers lightly around the gold band that always encircled her arm. *I'll never forget you ...*

In the light of a bright moon, Teia and her group held onto the thick ropes that rose up the sides of the wood plank as they climbed aboard the large wooden ship. The captain's crew had prepared one of the larger cabins for Jeremiah, Ebed, and Baruch, and a second smaller one for the princesses. Tired and sore, Teia and Hannah were relieved to lay their bodies down on the two cots in their room. They talked little as they listened to the scuffing noise of feet moving on the deck outside their door. Teia led Hannah in a short prayer of thanksgiving to Yahweh for their safe journey out of Egypt, and then they both fell asleep.

Although the crew tried to help, Baruch and Ebed insisted on carrying Jeremiah's chest aboard. Once it was safely inside the prophet's cabin, the crew finished loading the rest of the Judeans' supplies in the lower hold.

The refugees made themselves as comfortable as possible, spreading their mats and blankets next to each other near the stern of the ship, where the tall sides and back of the ship would give them some protection. Nadav's crew had erected a large sheet of heavy canvas to shield the Judeans from the sun, and from any rain they might encounter as they traveled. As crewmen and passengers settled down to rest, all was quiet except for the sound of the ocean lapping against the hull of the ship.

At the first light of morning, Teia dressed quietly, then stood outside her cabin. Careful to stay out of the crew's way, she watched a group of men shout in rhythm as they dragged a large anchor up and out of the muddy water. Then several crewmen near the bow of the ship pulled on thick ropes that raised a long square sail that stretched across almost one-third the length of the ship. The great single sail spread out before it finally turned and billowed as it caught a northeastern breeze that helped glide the ship out of the harbor. Oars creaked in the rowlocks as men on the lower deck maneuvered them down into the water. The long wooden paddles splashed down, then swept back in unison, like flapping wings.

Teia walked to the back of the ship and stared at the sand dunes above the harbor. She replayed her night with the prince over and over in her mind while she watched the long silhouette of land slowly shrink away. With her eyes fixed on Egypt's coast, she rested against the ship's rail until the sun had fully risen. Now several miles out to sea, all traces of land had vanished.

It took a few days for Teia to grow accustomed to the rocking motion of the ship and her new narrow surroundings. Hannah, though, was too sick to leave their cabin. While Teia sat on the open deck talking with the other refugees, Hannah stayed inside with a bucket, coming on deck only when the dark-blue surface of the sea was smooth.

"The day we leave this ship for good will be one of the best days of my life!" Hannah said while she and Teia rested inside their cabin. "And it will be the very last time I ever go out to sea! I am not as tough as I thought I was. This sickness has taken all the life out of me. I dread each day I wake up unless the sea is calm."

Teia lay on her stomach across her bed and stretched open one of Jeremiah's scrolls. "You'll be alright. Try to think about tomorrow, when we sail toward land. I heard someone say that we will stop at a port on the shores of Judah! We are finally going home!"

"But … Jeremiah said … he said we could never return home."

"I know what he said. But he also said that one day I will marry a king of Judah. Something must have changed. Maybe Yahweh spoke to him again. All I know is that I am happy and can't wait to go home!"

The following morning, just as they had finished dressing, Teia and Hannah heard a soft knock on their door.

"Teia? Hannah? It's Jeremiah. May I come in?"

Teia opened the door. Jeremiah looked at both girls as he entered, then leaned on the door after he closed it behind him. He paused for a moment, then spoke. "I wanted to talk with both of you alone, before … before we dock in Ashkelon. Daughters of Judah, I have fasted and prayed and have heard the word of the Lord. And I am sorry, but you will be staying on board this ship. You … We … will not be returning to the land of our fathers. It is still not safe for you. Yahweh has told me that one day soon you will call another place your home."

"What?" Hannah cried. "I can't stay on this ship! I'm sick all the time."

Teia remained silent as her sister began pleading with Jeremiah. As Hannah begged and whined, Teia's mind went blank, void of thought. She no longer heard what was being said until Jeremiah raised his voice: "There is nothing further to discuss! You know it is not a decision I make alone."

Jeremiah said nothing more before he turned and left their cabin.

Teia did her best to hold her emotions back as she comforted Hannah, who lay across her bed, crying. Teia ran her hand gently across her sister's back.

"It'll be okay. We'll get through this." A trail of tears ran down Teia's face. "It may be a long time before we can return home—maybe when we're older—so why don't we go out on deck and be with our friends when we sail to the coast. Let's at least go take a look at our homeland."

"No. You go ahead. I'm staying here. I don't want … I don't want our friends to see that I've been crying."

"Are you sure you'll be alright? Teia asked.

"Yeah, I'm okay ... You go ahead."

"Alright." Teia got up from the side of Hannah's bed. "I'll be back in a little while."

Teia's face rarely wore a frown. She seldom raised her voice and was never heard to speak an unkind word. She had been born to accept her lot and to smile at whatever her circumstances—until today. Anger mixed with sadness overwhelmed Teia as she gripped the rail of the ship. She yearned to place her feet on the shore below her. She envied the small group who walked slowly down the boarding plank. Two families, a total of nine Judeans, were leaving the ship. They would take their chances and return to Judah and live under Babylonian control. Teia's eyes flooded with tears as she watched the older men and women. She understood how they felt when she saw them kneel down and kiss the ground.

The ship sailed north from Ashkelon for two days, then stopped in the harbor of Joppa to trade some of their Egyptian goods with the locals, and to stock up on more provisions for the long journey ahead. From Joppa, the ship sailed south, and the captain informed all on board that soon they would travel west and sail much farther out to sea as they moved along the African coast. If the weather remained favorable, their next stop would be in a few weeks in the port of Cyrene.

Teia was with her sister and some of their friends when Jeremiah approached the group of girls sitting together in the afternoon sun near the stern of the ship.

"Teia, would you come here please?" Jeremiah asked.

Teia rose off the wood deck and listened to Jeremiah as they walked along the side of the ship: "Teia, it has been forty-five days since we celebrated the Feast of Pesach. In five days, I will gather our people together for a short ceremony as we remember the Feast of Shavuot, when we will thank Yahweh for giving us the Torah. Following Shavuot, either Baruch or I will spend some time with you over the next few weeks to teach you about the seven feast days that Yahweh set aside and marked as unique and holy. You will study the scrolls and learn all that we know, and then one day teach the significance of these days to your children and to your children's children."

Jeremiah put his arm around Teia's shoulder. "Teia, you are in the infancy of your studies; you've really barely scratched the surface. You have not yet discovered that there are several layers of meaning in our Lord's word. Every letter, every number, every jot and tittle has meaning. Even the blank spaces have their significance. The stories, the seven feasts … they are not only for the past and the present—they also reveal the future. They are shadows of things that may come in our lifetime or long after our lives have ended."

Teia stopped and looked at the prophet. "Please … teach me. I want to learn everything."

Jeremiah chuckled. "Yes, that is also my desire. But it does not come so easy. Our Lord has revealed much to me. But much is still hidden, even from my understanding. I'm not sure if even a lifetime would be long enough to learn all that exists within the tablets and scrolls."

When the ship docked weeks later in the harbor in Cyrene, other than taking whatever time was needed for her eyes to scan over all the ships in port, Teia stayed in her cabin while most of the Judeans eagerly left the ship and walked around the seaside village. Teia had lost interest in spending time with her friends and rarely spent time during the day with Hannah. She began to withdraw a little more as each day passed. Studying Jeremiah's scrolls kept her mind occupied. She didn't want to think about her former life in Jerusalem—or Egypt. Teia tried to bury every painful memory and her unending yearnings for Eochaid deep inside—out of reach.

Chapter 27

The excitement and newness of sailing for the refugees began to disappear, as did the calm seas. The farther they sailed along the African coast, the rougher the ocean became. Under a hot sun, strong winds pushed their ship south off their plotted course across the Gulf of Sidra, forcing their vessel to look for a place to set anchor and stock up on food and other supplies before their next scheduled stop in Carthage.

Nadav's crew struggled in the high winds that whipped up the oceans waves as they guided their ship closer to the coast. "I'm not sure what village we're approaching," the captain informed Jeremiah when the two men met in the prophet's cabin. "I've always sailed directly from Cyrene to Carthage. I know Carthage is north of us. Maybe we can purchase some food and some sailcloth here. Then we can bypass Carthage and sail directly to Cartenna and then to Rusaddir. We will spend a couple of weeks there before we sail back along the coast to the port of Joppa, where we should arrive sometime late in the month of Tishri or early Heshvan. That's if we don't have to make other stops or run into bad weather."

"Very well," Jeremiah said.

"While the crew is making repairs, I'll go on shore with a couple of my men and see what goods are available. Until I know where we are, it would be best to keep our passengers out of sight in the lower deck until I see if it is safe. I have heard stories from other ship captains of small villages along this coast that would be best to stay away from. My crew will help move your people while we are still a little ways out from shore."

The small village appeared to be busy. The docks were crowded with ships, manned mostly by rough, hard-looking men. Two such men, armed with drawn swords, came forward as Nadav and a pair of his officers walked down the dock toward the shore, which was lined with crudely constructed stone buildings and wood shacks.

"What brings your ship here?" one of the men asked Nadav. "Where do you sail from and who's on board?"

"We sail from Alexandria," Nadav said. "The winds blew us off our plotted course. We stopped here for supplies. I have an armed crew of over fifty men. We stopped to repair our ship's sail and replenish some of our food supplies. When we return to our ship, we sail to Carthage. Now … here is something for you from Pharaoh Hophra, for letting us stop in your village."

Nadav motioned to one of his men, who opened the palm of his right hand to reveal a mound of gold coins.

"Could you tell us where we can find sailcloth?" Nadav asked. "When we return this way again with our goods, we will have another handful of coins for you." He motioned to his officer to hand the coins over to the men.

The man asking the questions held out his hand, then looked at his partner, who eyed the strangers before he gave a quick nod of approval. "Alright. You can go," he said. "Food and supplies for your ship can be found down on the side streets, on your left. Don't wander any farther. This is a private village."

"I understand," Nadav responded.

He and his officers walked past the men, off the dock, and up the narrow dirt street. Along the way, they passed several open doors, from which poured forth the sounds of music and revelry. The deeper they moved into the town, the more drinking shacks and houses of prostitution they passed. Women in various stages of undress leaned out of the windows or stood outside, trying to attract customers.

The village was dirty. Mounds of garbage lined most of the twisting labyrinth of streets, at times almost too narrow to maneuver through. They passed men working inside small shops, hammering glowing strips of metal into swords or axe blades. They moved farther up the street looking for shops that might sell supplies for their ship, when the street turned into a back alley that led into a large open area. Nadav and his men gazed across the marketplace at the countless numbers of large wooden crates. The contents of the crates brought a look of alarm to their faces. Rank air wafted by the three men from the odor of hundreds of caged bodies sweating in the hot sun.

A slave auction was taking place at the far end of the square. Crowds of male merchants and pirates stood gathered in front of an open stage. A young girl with dark skin, likely snatched off the African coast, was dragged onto the stage by the slave traders. They tore off the ragged remains of her dress, leaving her standing bare. The terrified and humiliated girl, with her wrists tied behind her back, could do nothing to cover herself before the bidding began.

In less than a minute, the auctioneer pronounced the weeping girl "Sold!" The sobbing slave was led off to meet her new owner while another girl struggled and fought before she was struck hard across the face and dragged out of her cage.

"Let's go!" Nadav ordered. "We've got to get back to our ship." He turned and headed back down the alley. "We'll get our supplies from somewhere else. I hope our passengers did what I asked and have remained off the deck and out of sight."

The three men looked straight ahead to avoid any encounter as they pushed through the throngs of men that moved up and down the narrow streets of the pirate village.

"We've got to come back with something. See if you can spot anything we can buy for our ship," Nadav said.

When they reached the main street that led back to the harbor, Nadav could see the small figures of the two men still guarding the end of the dock.

"Over here," one of Nadav's men called out when he spotted a small shop wedged in between a couple of drinking rooms. A few oars leaned against the outside wall. The three men moved inside and grabbed a small open bucket of nails.

Nadav approached the blurry-eyed merchant who sat in a chair toward the back of the room. "Sailcloth? Do you have canvas, linen sheets?" the captain asked.

"Two doors down," the man answered.

"Ruben!" Nadav said. "Pay this man, then get a couple of handfuls of coins ready. We'll get some linen cloth, then get back to our ship. While you and Caleb pay off the two villains who are still standing guard, I'll continue down the dock and get on board to give the order to have our ship made ready to sail as soon as your feet touch the deck."

When Nadav and his men reached the waterfront, the guards at the dock blocked the way.

"We found what we needed," Nadav said.

He pushed past the men toward his ship as his officers dropped more gold coins into each of the men's hands. As soon as the captain boarded his ship, he started shouting orders: "Prepare the ship to sail! Bring the Judean men back on deck. Keep all females below, then close the door to the lower hold. When Caleb and Ruben step back aboard, I want this vessel moving out to sea."

Soon, though, Nadav stood in shock at what he saw. With their hands tied behind their backs and a knife held to their throats, Nadav's officers struggled up the boarding plank.

"They want more gold!" Ruben shouted.

Ruben and Caleb fell forward onto the deck, with the two pirates right behind them.

"Move us out to sea—NOW!" Nadav ordered.

Teia and her sister crowded in with the other females at the front of the lower deck. They watched as the men seated on low benches now grabbed their oars and followed the orders of the crewman sitting in front of them. The lead crewman looked through an opening in the side of the ship and shouted commands that told the oarsmen which direction to push their paddles through the water.

Some of the women lost their balance and fell as the ship lurched forward. The younger girls helped them up and held onto each other as the ship rocked side to side while making its way out of the harbor.

"I think I'm going to be sick," Hannah whispered to Teia.

"Here, hold my hand. Take some deep breaths," Teia said.

While Hannah struggled with nausea, the oarsmen in front of her labored to steady the ship. They pushed their wood blades deep into the swells of water that surged toward shore.

The two pirates lost their balance, staggering on deck as the ship swayed back and forth. Within seconds of their knives pulling away from the necks of Caleb and Ruben, both pirates fell dead from the blades of Nadav's crewmen. Trained as soldiers first, every crewman on board the ship would fight to the death to defend the ship, and its crew and passengers.

The door to the lower deck opened, sending a blast of fresh air over the huddled females. Captain Nadav walked down the first two steps, then shouted, "As soon as we get farther away from land, you can come back on deck. But stay seated when you're topside, until we make our next stop in Carthage. It should only take us a couple of hours to reach their port. When I open this door again, you can come out. Just remember to stay seated and be ready to return to the lower deck if I give the command."

Teia held her sister's hand as Hannah crouched in the corner and heaved up everything she had consumed earlier that day. Tears streamed from her eyes as her body continued to convulse and expel only the sour bile that remained in her empty stomach. Exhausted, Hannah fell on her side and lay across the ship's dirty floor. Teia used her sleeves to wipe Hannah's mouth as she lifted her head and cradled it in her arms. She dabbed the beads of sweat and tears from Hannah's ashen face and then she whispered, "We'll be out of here soon. We'll be out of here soon."

The door to the lower deck was thrown open. "Oarsmen to full speed! Oarsmen to full speed!" the first officer shouted. "We're being pursued!"

A line of men ran down the stairs next to the officer and joined each man already on a bench. A pair of men now drove each of the oak paddles down into the water, propelling the ship faster through the sea. The galley rowers tightened their grips on the wood and followed their orders, pulling the blades with all their strength in hopes of evading their pursuers before their arms gave out.

Captain Nadav rubbed the stubble on his chin as he watched the two ships that followed close behind. He could hear the commands shouted to his oarsmen echoing off the wooden bulkheads under his feet. At the same time, another chorus of male voices rose up from the side of the deck, where Jeremiah led ten men in a minyan—a communal worship quorum—and prayers were lifted into the sky as they petitioned Yahweh for everyone's safety.

Chapter 28

The captain gazed with concern as he watched the two vessels closing in on his ship. He turned and looked up at the full sail. If the twin pirate ships drew any closer, he would ready and arm his men along the open deck and any spare galley crewmen with knives, swords, and bows and arrows. He had learned long ago to staff his vessel with not only able seamen, but with men who were also hardened and experienced warriors.

As Captain Nadav kept his eyes fixed on his pursuers, he assessed their ships to also be oar- and sail-driven vessels, roughly half the size of his hundred-foot ship. But each pirate vessel carried twin sales, which accounted for the speed of their pursuit—as they were now within close range of his ship.

"Cut the ropes! Cut the ropes!" Nadav shouted.

His men scurried forward as a rain of grappling hooks flew through the air from the decks of the pirate ships. The two attacking ships were now lashed to Nadav's vessel. Swords, axes, and knives wielded by Nadav's crewmen cut through the taut lines to free their vessel while his other soldiers shot arrows from their bows into the men on the pirate ships.

Nadav turned and shouted orders to his first officer: "Turn north! Have the men steer us directly north! If we can take the wind out of their sails, then we should be able to outrun the pirates with our oars!"

Under the shouts of the commands, only the creaking of the oars and heavy breathing of the men could be heard. Teia, Hannah, and the other females sat on the floor, pressed back as far from the rowers as possible. The air felt stifling. Sweat poured down the faces and bare chests of the men as they exhausted themselves.

Teia's clothes stuck to her skin. Her scalp tingled as beads of moisture trickled from her head, down her neck and forehead. Like everyone else's around her, Teia's face was flushed red in the suffocating heat. The only movement of air was felt by the women who sat nearest the rowers as they whipped their oars back and forth.

For nearly twenty minutes, Nadav's ship held its distance from the pursuing vessels until finally they began to move ahead. Soon, the pirate ships became nothing more than a pair of distant gray dots.

When the door to the lower deck opened, two of the older women helped Teia carry Hannah up the stairs to the top deck. They laid her down on her bed, where she stayed motionless until the ship stopped when it was anchored a few hours later in Carthage's harbor.

Teia stayed with her sister while most of the passengers watched several of the crew members carry two Judean men off the ship—men who had been injured with deep wounds inflicted by a few of the pirates' grappling hooks. The sharp talons had pierced their bodies when the men were dragged across the deck.

After a short stay in Carthage, the Judeans' ship continued sailing west for another month without incident to the port of Cartenna, where they stayed for several days before setting a course to Rusaddir. There, the ship planned to stay in port for a few weeks, and then they would sail east and retrace their route all the way back to the shores of Judah. A week of calm seas passed as they moved closer to Rusaddir before the size and shapes of the waves began to increase.

"We have a storm moving in from the southeast," the captain told Jeremiah. The two men finished the last of their lunch as the ship rode up and over large swells. "It would be best for you and your companions to stay secured in your cabins today."

The ship struggled forward throughout the afternoon, listing to one side as gale winds began to sweep in and whistle across the deck through the ropes holding down the now-tattered sail. Teia and her sister stayed in their small cabin as the ship rocked and rain pounded down on their roof.

As each hour passed, darkness grew as waves from the storm continued to build. Soon, small waterfalls cascaded across the deck. Oars slapped against the sides of the ship as the men tried to row and hold them steady while they fought to move their ship forward through the storm.

BANG!

A sudden, loud explosion obscured the subsequent subtler sounds of shattering wood and an in-rush of sea. Teia and Hannah jumped off their cots as water poured into their cabin through a large hole in their roof.

The sisters opened their door and ducked under a large piece of the mast that rested on top of their cabin. A river of water now washed across their bare feet as they stumbled out onto the deck. They clung to each other as the nose of the ship rode straight up the face of a large wave, then slammed down the other side. The sisters fell back against their cabin as pieces of wood slid toward them from the broken mast. Its torn and crumpled sail now lay limp on deck in the center of the ship.

Teia's eyes stung from the spray of saltwater blowing off of foaming whitecaps that whirled their way toward the ship. Shivering from fright and cold, Teia held Hannah as she looked toward the back of the ship for their friends and the rest of the Judeans who traveled with them. Her search stopped when she saw the mass of bodies huddled together against the side of the ship as rain and waves poured down on them. Their canvas covering was gone. Through the rain, Teia could see them clinging to each other, to ropes, and to parts of the broken mast and sail in hopes of keeping their bodies anchored down.

Teia noticed someone struggling to move across the deck toward her, just as a huge wave crashed over the ship.

"Miriaaaaam!" But Teia's cry was lost in the noise of the storm.

She watched in horror as her friend was swept back across the deck, then over the side of the leaning ship and into the sea. Teia froze in place just as a huge wave lifted the bow of their ship before it fell downward again. The force of the drop swept a few more of the now-floundering passengers across the deck, then down into the raging sea.

The ship's crewmen grabbed ropes off the deck, tied them around their waists, then flung the ends into the ocean toward Miriam and the others who fought to keep afloat. The howling wind whipped the ropes back toward the ship as the individuals struggling in the water were carried away by the mountainous waves.

Jeremiah and Baruch appeared out of the storm and pushed Teia and Hannah back inside their cabin. A foot of water sloshed around their room. Water continued to pour in from the damaged roof as the men pulled blankets and any dry clothing they could find out of the girls' trunks before wrapping them around the princesses and themselves.

"You are safer in here than outside!" Jeremiah shouted above the storm.

"We are going to die!" Hannah cried out. "The sea will take us! Just like Miriam!"

Teia grabbed her sister and pulled her close as tears, rain, and seawater dripped down her face.

"Close your eyes! Close your eyes tight!" Jeremiah shouted to the girls before he began to pray. "Lord God, you would not have saved us from Babylon to have us now perish. You led us safely out of Egypt. You preserved our lives in the past so that we may fulfill your purpose in the future. Guide us through this storm, O Lord, as you guided the people of your kingdom who came before us—as you brought Moses and your children through the desert, as you brought Joshua and your chosen people into the Promised Land. In faith, we trust that you, O Lord our God, will deliver us to a place where your word will be planted, where the remnant of your everlasting kingdom will be built. Let us fulfill your promise to Abraham, Isaac, and Jacob, that your people will live and multiply as the stars in the heavens, as the sands of the sea, as they scatter to the north, to the south, to the east, and to the west. Preserve us, and fulfill your promise in us, O Lord, we pray. Lord God Almighty, Father in heaven, we pray that you will hold close your children who lost their lives tonight as their souls return home to you."

Teia sobbed quietly as their ship rode up and down the waves throughout the night. For two days, they drifted under stormy skies. Finally, on the morning of the third day, the black of night yielded to gray, and pale colors streaked across the sky as the sun broke from behind the clouds. The ship now floated over small swells from a steady breeze that pushed the battered vessel forward.

"Land ahead! Land ahead!" the captain shouted.

Through a thin veil of morning fog, Nadav had spotted a lush green mountain jutting out of the sea. At the sounds of the captain's cries, Jeremiah pushed open the cabin door and stepped out on deck, followed by Baruch and the princesses. Weak from lack of food and little sleep, they shuffled across the deck toward the side of the ship and peered through the misty air to see the tall cliffs that loomed ahead.

After endless days on the ship with only the smell of saltwater, Teia found the scent that blew off the land, fresh and sweet. But inside she felt sad, bitter, and afraid. Teia wondered what other horrors lay ahead, what pain and heartache she would suffer next. Teia closed her eyes and said a prayer for her friend Miriam. When her prayer ended, she lifted her eyes to the cry of seabirds that glided in wide circles above her.

I wish I had such a simple life.... I wish sometimes ... that I had never been born.

Soon, all on board clung to the ship's rail and gazed at the cliffs whose slopes met a rocky shoreline at their base. They cheered as they drew close to land. Small boats soon surrounded their vessel and helped direct them into the harbor. Hugs, laughter, and shouts of joy rose from the wet, weak, and weary travelers.

"Land! Praise Yahweh. Land!" they cried.

Along with several crew members, the captain's first officer went ashore to find out where they had landed and if it would be safe for their passengers to disembark. They found a local lad who agreed to come aboard their ship so that Captain Nadav's son, Joab, who spoke many languages, could ask him the name of this place.

"You are in Caer Melcarth in the land of Eber, which some call 'Gibraltar,'" the youth said. "We are at the gateway to the wide ocean."

Captain Nadav asked his son to have the young man show him on his map where they were. The youth listened to Joab's question, then pointed to a spot on the map next to the Pillars of Hercules, which opened to a vast ocean and two large landmasses in the northwest.

"Now ask him who governs their land," Nadav said.

Joab relayed the question and the youth responded, "Elier bar Ziza is our great ruler."

Nadav nodded. "Then tell this lad I must ask Elier bar Ziza for his permission for all who travel with us to come ashore. Some on board are injured, and all need nourishment and rest while our ship is repaired. Tell him that we sailed through a brutal storm and lost some of our crew and also a few companions several nights ago. Most of our food is damaged or was washed away."

After word reached Captain Nadav that Elier had given his permission for the refugees to enter his land, Teia was one of the first to walk down the wood plank that led off the ship. She felt unsteady on her feet as she descended the wide board. It actually took a couple of days before she didn't feel the rolling motion of the sea even when she sat or stood still.

The Judean travelers found that many of the people living in the seaside village claimed to be descendants of the Israelite tribe of Gad, and they welcomed the refugees as family into their homes. As the days and weeks passed, the sounds of laughter and song soon returned to the weary seafarers.

While most of the Judeans easily assimilated, Teia withdrew further from those around her. She could not wipe away the memory of seeing her friend being taken by the sea. Nothing made sense to her anymore. Nothing seemed to matter. She stopped praying. She stopped believing. The lines she read on the scrolls became meaningless to her. They were now just worthless old words.

CHAPTER 29

Eochaid grew restless as the end of October drew near. He abhorred the annual Samhain festival. Even as a child, he rarely went along with his friends each year when they put on strange disguises and roamed about the countryside while pretending to be spirits from the underworld and playing tricks on their elders.

The three-day festival marked summer's end and the beginning of the Druid New Year. The Druid priests and most of Eochaid's Celtic kingdom believed that when darkness fell on October 31, the thin veil between mortal and spiritual worlds would open. To protect their homes during the night, families carved faces onto large, hollowed-out turnips and gourds. After placing a lit candle inside their vegetables, they set the lanterns outside their front door to keep out any unwelcome roaming spirits.

Even though they feared an encounter with ghouls from the underworld, the villagers also found the festival to be a great time of celebration. As always, they gathered around a large bonfire in the center of the village and feasted on succulent roasted beef. Their Samhain meal always ended with baked apples, because the villagers believed the apple to be a sacred fruit that the dead ate this very night to ensure a happy eternal life.

The children sat with their siblings and friends, drinking cups of sweet apple cider, while the adults washed down their food with large pitchers of ale and mead. Soon, the elders in the village danced around the bonfires drunk, casting their gnawed cattle bones into the flames.

While the elders danced, the teenage maidens passed around a bag filled with hazelnuts. Each girl took out the number of nuts corresponding to how many suitors she had, and then each maiden placed a nut near the edge of the fire. The girls then held hands and swayed in a circle around the fire as they chanted, "If you love me, pop and fly. If you don't, then burn and die."

Meanwhile, younger children giggled and shouted as they gathered together around water-filled barrels and waited their turn to hold their breath and bob for apples.

Everywhere, laughter filled the night as the huge fire crackled and lit the faces of the villagers who celebrated their New Year's Eve.

Two hours before midnight, the revelry fell silent when the Druid ritual of darkness began. A parade of priests, priestesses, and bards walked into the center of the village. The small flames of lit candles and lanterns they carried cast an eerie light on their somber faces. The crowds fell in line behind them after they costumed themselves in various animal heads and skins.

Musicians played a solemn march as the procession passed through the village, then over grass fields toward the forest. The people chanted and sang while moving along the tall ash trees and gathering bundles of dried sticks and branches off the ground. Their voices could be heard as they entered the valley of Murthemni, where they dispersed into smaller groups and selected the site they would use to continue the evening's celebration. Small bonfires soon dotted the rolling hills, and animal-shaped figures began dancing around the flames.

Eochaid stood on his balcony. He watched the little flickers of light that twinkled across the land. His stomach clenched when he heard the faint drumbeats that started at midnight and called out to his people, who quickly moved with their lanterns across the fields and up the hill to the stone temple. There, the most important function of the year would take place. Eochaid watched the river of light move across the dark landscape as the pounding drumbeat intensified.

Twenty young Druid priests, wearing nothing but loincloths, danced in pairs toward the temple. Each priest was armed with a knife. Like crazed men, they scratched and punctured their chests and limbs from time to time with their blades, until they arrived at the temple's altar, covered in blood.

The elder Druid priests, dressed in black hooded robes, followed the young dancers up the center aisle toward the huge stone altar. Behind them walked four priestesses, who led two milk-white bulls pulling a cart. Inside the cart, huddled together, sat three women. Like caged animals, their eyes darted side to side. Their bodies trembled—for they knew what awaited them.

When the priestesses reached the altar, they pulled the blood-red hoods of their robes over their heads and began to chant:

> "Dark one, ruler of the night, god of death,
> we gather before you and ask for a sacred sign for all who worship here.
> Lift, now, the veil between spirit and mortal worlds,
> that we may unite with our dead ancestors, and those who dwell with you.
> Dark one, ruler of the night, god of death, lift your veil.
> Dark one, ruler of the night, god of death, lift your veil...."

The drumbeats quickened and chants grew louder as the villagers joined in summoning spirits of the underworld. A swirling wind of hisses, humming, and screeches blew over and around the worshippers, who offered themselves into the night that now released thousands of demons and ghosts of the dead over the earth. The wind whistled through the temple's stone columns, then down the hill and across the fields toward Eochaid's castle. Fallen leaves rustled and blew around Eochaid's feet before they swirled across his balcony and then up into the air.

As the ceremony's music intensified, the three women were taken from the cart to the stone altar and there were tied down. Their anguished cries were lost in the deafening chants of the people as the chief Druid priest slit each of their throats before he then dragged his dagger through each of their chests. With their bodies split open, the priests and priestesses gathered around the altar with blazing torches to see the future and predict coming events by examining the quivering flesh and exposed organs of the butchered bodies.

When all signs of life in the women were gone, the clerics stepped back and used their torches to ignite large bundles of tinder stacked up around the altar. The chief priest moved in front of the soaring flames and raised his arms as a signal for the music and the chanting to cease. After a lone drumbeat, he declared to the crowd:

"The god Baal declares that the coming year will be prosperous for the herdsmen, but not so for the cultivators of the soil.

"The god Baal declares that a new influence will soon be present in the land, which might mean danger to the kingdom. Our ancient rituals of worship handed down by our fathers will be challenged, but will not be overcome.

"The god Baal declares that our kings will return successful from warfare.

"The god Baal declares that our children will grow and prosper as long as they continue in the ways of our Druid traditions."

The priest lowered his arms to signal that he had finished. The musicians took hold of their instruments once more and began to play. More wood was thrown over the burning sacrifice as the villagers cheered and danced in place until they exhausted themselves.

As orange embers sank inside the cavities of the grotesque charred bodies, Eochaid stared at the glowing point of light that shone on the distant hilltop. He always found the culmination of the Samhain holiday sickening. What started with joyful singing and dancing always ended with death.

"Take leave of the temples of Baal. You will come to no good worshipping at the foot of evil!" Eochaid turned away from the view as he recalled Jeremiah's words of rebuke from long ago.

"The worst is over," Eochaid mumbled.

He turned and walked slowly back into his room. *Now only the Druid winter solstice festival remains. No sacrifices, thankfully ... just mistletoe branches and ritual prayers to the sun god.*

The thoughts in Eochaid's head fell silent as he passed by his dressing table—upon which lay his golden torque. He lingered a few moments as he thought about how he hadn't worn the band for many months, not since the night of his coronation. Was it a coincidence, he wondered, when he realized he also hadn't dreamt of the princess since then?

It's all for the best, he thought as he lay down in bed and closed his eyes. *What are the chances that I'll ever sail back to Egypt? She's probably already wed, just as I, too, shall be ...*

Chapter 30

Golden light from the wicks of the oil lamps lining the center of the large mahogany table lit up the two men's faces. Elier looked across the table at the prophet. "Jeremiah, I have been honored to have you in my home. The Lord God has truly blessed me and my people since the day his hand guided you to our land. We receive word often of our homeland from ships that have traveled from the coast of Judah. We heard for many years of Jeremiah, Yahweh's prophet."

"Yes, it seems it was God's will that we arrived here," Jeremiah said. "It was also by his mercy that we were allowed to flee from the destruction of Jerusalem."

Elier nodded his head. "Our people mourned for days when we received word of the destruction that fell upon Jerusalem and its holy temple. We recently received word that most of God's people are still held as captives in Babylon."

"And there they will remain for seventy years. That is what I prophesied. That is what the Lord gave me in his words regarding our captured people."

"How many fled with you to Egypt?" Elier asked.

"A group of almost two hundred. But I am grieved to say that most will die in that heathen place. Yahweh warned us not to go into Egypt. All who chose to stay there will soon be dead. This small group that sailed with me and two families that already returned to Judah are all that his word proclaimed: 'for none shall return but such as shall escape.'"

Jeremiah sat back and fixed his eyes on the ceiling. "His full and exact prophecy to me was: 'For I will punish them that dwell in the land of Egypt, as I have punished Jerusalem, by the sword, by the famine, and by the pestilence: So that none of the remnant of Judah, which are gone into the land of Egypt to sojourn there, shall escape or remain, that they should return into the land of Judah, to the which they have a desire to return to dwell there: for none shall return but such as shall escape.'"

For a few moments, silence filled the room, then Jeremiah looked back across the table.

"Elier, I thank you for all you have done for me and our people since the moment we landed on your shores. Most have healed physically and spiritually. They are now content to stay and make their homes here. But I and a few others will be leaving soon. The word of the Lord has come upon me once again. I have been told to take what the Lord wants planted to another land." Jeremiah leaned forward and clasped his hands together over the table. "After all the kindness and hospitality you have shown me and my companions over the past months, I am now required to ask more of you. As you know, the ship we arrived in was severely damaged. All repairs have been made, and now that the worst of winter's weather has passed, Captain Nadav is anxious to return to Judah.

"A couple of my companions and I will also be leaving … but not with the captain. So here is what I must ask of you. I studied the maps you gave me. It is clear that I will need a small ship with a crew and then a guide to lead us through the Pillars of Hercules and then to the land where Yahweh leads us."

Elier nodded and opened his hands toward the prophet. "Ask for whatever you need, Jeremiah, and it will be provided."

The following morning, Jeremiah called on Teia to join him for their morning meal. After they finished eating, he reached his arms across the table, opened his palms, and asked for Teia's hands. He held them gently as he spoke. "Teia, I have met with all those who traveled with us from Egypt. They want to stay here. They are weary of the sea. They suffered for months living on the deck of the ship, baking in the heat of the day and chilled to the bone at night. They have settled in and desire to make this land their home. Yahweh has blessed them, and has also revealed to me that only a few of us will leave this place. The journey for you and me is not yet over."

Teia gave a small nod. "I know that the many months at sea were difficult for our people," she said. "I realize that they didn't have a cabin to give them shelter like Hannah and I. After that last storm, I understand their wish to remain here. But only a few want to return with us to Judah?"

Jeremiah eyed her for a moment, then said, "We are not sailing east; we are sailing west. We are not sailing back to Judah."

Teia furrowed her eyebrows. "I don't understand. If we are not returning to Judah, then how … how can Yahweh's throne be restored?"

"Teia, Yahweh's throne will be restored, but it will be in another place—at least for now."

"But … No. If we are not going to Judah, then let's stay here! You can build Yahweh's kingdom here. Why do we have to leave? Nothing good has happened to us since we left Judah." Teia yanked her hands free of Jeremiah's. "If I can't go home, then I don't want to go anywhere!" Teia's voice began to rise as she felt hurt and anger resurface within her.

But then a look of alarm crossed Teia's face. "Wait. Why am I the only one here with you? Who's going with us?"

"Just you, Baruch, and I will be leaving."

"What about Hannah? You didn't mention Hannah."

Jeremiah shook his head. "Hannah is staying here. I have already spoken with her. You know better than all of us that she does not want to sail again. And Yahweh has not called her to leave. Ebed will also stay behind. He is needed to teach the word and Law of Yahweh to our people. Those who traveled with us, and those who live here, have lost over many years much of what their ancestors once knew."

"No! I'm not leaving!" Teia shouted. "Everything and everyone that has meant anything to me has been taken away. And now you tell me to leave my sister!" Teia shook her heard. "No! I'm not leaving Hannah. I can't!" Tears flowed down Teia's face as she pleaded with Jeremiah. "Please! Please don't make me. I can't do this anymore! I don't want to leave. I don't want to be Yahweh's queen! I won't leave with you! Don't ask this of me …"

"I am not the one asking."

Teia fell forward and buried her head in her arms on the table. Her shoulders shook as she sobbed. Jeremiah reached out and stroked her hair.

"Sometimes Yahweh calls on us to do things that are not easy. What might your future have been if your father would have listened to Yahweh? There would have been no siege, no death from starvation … none of our people killed or bound as a slaves and taken to Babylon … and no destruction of God's holy temple. Because your father chose not to obey, you and I, and so many others, now suffer the consequences. Your father turned away from what would have been difficult, and instead did what *he* wanted. Consider the results of his decision before you make yours." Jeremiah paused and took a deep breath. "Our ship sails in less than a month. But … I won't force you to leave."

Teia raised her head and looked at him with a glimmer of hope on her tear-stained face. The prophet placed his hands on the table and stood up.

"Pray to the Lord for guidance, Teia. Through the pain, listen for his voice and he will answer you. He will help you."

"Hannah!" Teia said. "I have been looking all over for you. Where have you been?"

"I was with Benjamin and his family. Oh, Teia! The past month has been wonderful. I … I have something to tell you."

"What? What is it?"

Hannah swallowed, then softly replied, "I have fallen in love."

Teia's eyes went wide. "In love? With whom?"

"With Benjamin."

A few seconds passed as Teia stared open mouthed at her sister. "I knew you spent time with him and his sisters in Egypt … and on the ship. But you never said anything about having feelings for him. When did this come about?"

Hannah shrugged. "Everything happened so fast after we got here. While you've been busy with your studies, I spent most of my time with Benjamin and his sisters. I know you thought I was just friends with Leah and Sarah. I didn't want to say anything to you until I was sure. And I remembered what you said. I remembered what you said it felt like when you met the prince from Erin. I didn't understand how you felt then … but I do now. It must have been hard for you to see him leave."

Teia looked away at the unintended sting of Hannah's words. An old wound tore open deep within Teia. She struggled to conceal her reaction—struggled to speak. She drew in a long breath, then her words came out slow, measured: "I'm … I'm sorry that I haven't spent much time with you since we came here. Jeremiah and Baruch set up a strict schedule for me to follow with my studies. I didn't realize until now how much time has passed and how little we spent together. If I only knew then …"

"It's alright. Don't feel bad," Hannah said. "I've been fine. I actually came here to tell you some exciting news. Tomorrow, Benjamin is going to ask Jeremiah—since he is our guardian—Benjamin is going to ask for Jeremiah's blessing. Benjamin wants me to be his betrothed! I feel certain Jeremiah will be pleased. Then we will marry as is customary in about a year. I'll be almost fourteen by then."

Teia reached out and gently tucked a long strand of hair behind her sister's ear. "You just turned eleven when we left Judah. How much we both have grown over the past few years. I'm glad that you've found someone to love and now have a chance for happiness after all you've been through." Tears welled in Teia's eyes. "We will have a big celebration when Jeremiah announces your betrothal."

The smile suddenly dropped from Hannah's face. "Teia, I know that you are leaving. Jeremiah told me yesterday. I cried so hard. But then, he said that Yahweh has great plans for you, that one day Yahweh would grant you the desires of your heart. He said that if you stayed here, you would be disobeying Yahweh and the good things intended for you would never come. Jeremiah reminded me that no matter what you or I would want or think is best for you, your life belongs to Yahweh and what he chooses for you will be better than anything we could ever imagine."

Teia sniffled to slow her runny nose and then wiped the moisture from under her eyes. "You sound so wise and grown up. You sound like the big sister. What you say might be true, but … I haven't decided if I will leave. I don't want to. I hoped that someday … I thought that maybe … I guess it doesn't matter what I hoped for." Teia reached for Hannah and held her in her arms. "I love you, Hannah."

The desires of my heart … I don't even know what they are anymore.

At the celebration following the betrothal announcement, Teia didn't noticed Elan making his way through the throng of guests toward her.

"So … your little sister is betrothed. How does that make you feel?" he asked.

Teia turned toward him. "I am happy for my sister."

"Yeah, sure you are. I don't believe you. I watched your face during the ceremony. I saw some envy, or at least sadness, in your face. Am I right?"

"No, Elan, you are never right about anything."

"Oh, is that so? I'm not right about you being scared to leave your sister and this place with old Jeremiah and Baruch? I bet I'm right about that!"

"I don't know if I am leaving. I'm not sure what I'm going to do. I still have a few more days to think about it."

"What's there to think about? What good's come from all that studying you've done of Jeremiah's ragged scrolls? What has Yahweh given you? Nothing!"

Teia listened quietly to Elan as the painful events of the last few years played out one by one in her mind.

Elan leaned closer. "Why would you even think about leaving here, leaving your only friends … leaving Hannah? She's all the family you have left. You could have a good life here. You don't know what will happen when you sail away. What are you gonna do if the next storm takes Baruch and Jeremiah, like the last one took Miriam and the others? Are you going to wander around the seas by yourself?"

A twinge of fear gripped Teia, quickening her pulse. She glanced over at Jeremiah, who stood on the other side of the room. She noticed his bent posture. Then his beard; once short and gray, it now grew long and white. Even at this distance, she could see the lines and creases on his face.

"I'm glad we're here," Elan continued. "I've got it all planned out. Through the winter, I'm going to offer my help to anyone in the village that needs it, to do anything—for a price. Then when spring comes, I'll take the money I've saved and head out on my own. Tirzah's got plenty of friends here. She doesn't need me anymore, so I'll finally be free to go and do whatever I want. Not what Abba or some invisible god tells me to do!"

Chapter 31

A group of young male servants crowded together along the castle's second-floor railing. Their eyes remained fixed below on the group of attractive girls as the maidens gathered just inside the first floor's main entrance. The girls had been selected from across the regions of Erin, and this was the only chance they'd get to see them all together. But the youths fled for cover behind a few thick pillars when the queen mother's head mistress, Brina, appeared below and led the girls into the reception room adjacent to the expansive foyer.

"Find a place to sit," Brina said.

She waved her hand toward the couches and overstuffed chairs scattered around the opulently furnished room. High-pitched giggling and whispers continued as the girls settled in—until Brina clapped her hands to get their attention.

"You all look lovely," said the tall, thin head mistress to the twenty-four maidens sitting around the room.

At the sound of her voice, the nervous girls straightened and beamed with their broadest smiles.

"Queen Noirenn will arrive shortly to tell you what will be expected of you should you be chosen to meet the king. If anyone knows and understands the role one of you will fill, it's our queen mother." The middle-aged Brina walked by each girl and gave them a tight smile. "Should you have any questions regarding the selection process when you are not in the presence of the queen, you are to direct your questions to no one other than me. I will inform Her Majesty of any concerns you may have. Our queen mother is gracious in her desire to help you. Show your gratitude."

Then Brina turned and walked toward the door.

Nervous murmuring rose until the mistress turned back and shushed the girls before she finally opened the door. Light footsteps could be heard approaching, and then the sound of rustling fabric filled the reception hall when the twenty-four girls rose from their seats to pay respects to Eochaid's mother as she entered the room. Noirenn walked slowly toward the center of the hall, smiled, then addressed the assembled maidens.

"Beautiful young women are plentiful in our land. But each of you was singled out from the many. Beyond your looks, you all possess something special. Most of you come from a royal line and from families of respect, significance, and stature. You have been taught to act like proper ladies. Most of you are well read and educated. Some of you have been taught in the fine arts. Thanks to your heritage and various talents, you have been chosen to stand in front of me now—because I am told that you are superior to other ladies in our land. I sent my brightest and most trusted emissaries into all of our villages, and you are the ones they chose. So … now here you are."

Noirenn walked forward, then slowly by each girl. Without a smile, she looked into their eyes after they bowed, then lifted their heads.

"One of you will be queen," Noirenn said. "Immense responsibility will come to whomever stands next to my son. Some of you think that becoming queen will give you power, and to an extent that is true—the power to provide an heir. I was fortunate to be married to a great king who was also a great man and husband. Whomever my son chooses will also be privileged to have a man of the same character by her side.

"In a few months, the king will select one of you as his queen. As each day passes, some of you will be dismissed. In a few weeks, only half of you standing here now will remain. The maidens who do remain will meet the king." Noirenn stopped and looked up and down the line of girls. "Then it will be up to the king to choose whom he desires to spend time with, until finally, he selects one of you as his bride.

"Starting today and finishing tomorrow, you will be called individually into the adjoining room. Once I have become acquainted with each of you, I may ask for a second or even a third meeting before I select the final group who will be introduced to the king. I will speak at length to each of you. You and I will get to know each other. If you have questions, I will answer them."

Noirenn walked back to the center of the room. "Besides thinking about how you will impress my son, it would be wise for you first to think about how you will impress me! So let us begin."

Noirenn started to leave, but then turned back. "My first piece of advice to all of you is to know that my son is a wise and fair man, but he is short on patience with those who gossip, boast, complain, or are ill mannered or ill tempered. The king will not tolerate even the slightest hint of deceit. My son is just like his mother—so be mindful of that!"

"Who did you say your father was?" Noirenn asked.

The queen mother's question interrupted the girl sitting in front of her. The maiden had spent the past five minutes chattering on nonstop about herself and her special qualities.

"Angus Calvag," the girl said. "My father is the cousin of the late King Ailill, your dead husband." Without a trace of emotion, she continued. "With the blood of royalty in my veins, I have been brought up with the expectation of being a queen. So you see, I am prepared and ready to sit on your … ah … I mean, on the new queen's throne. My mother told me when I was little that someday I would marry one of your sons."

Noirenn tilted her head. "Is that so? Well then, as a daughter of royalty, you are already familiar with life in the castle. So I won't take any more of your time. I don't want to bore you with what you already know. Our time is over for today."

"But I have yet to tell you of my education, my paintings, and—"

"You are excused," Noirenn said, offering a tight smile.

The young lady hesitated, then slowly pushed her chair back to give herself room to stand and make a small curtsy. "I thank the queen mother for her time." The girl's face contorted into a phony sweet smile before she turned and left the room.

For two days, each girl did her best to persuade the queen mother that she was unique and most qualified to be her son's bride. Some were sweet and humble about their accomplishments. Others who had been coddled and praised all their lives found it difficult not to boast. They were the first to be dismissed and sent home.

"Are they ready?" Noirenn asked.

"Yes, my lady," Brina said. "The last twelve girls arrived on time and are waiting for you."

"Good. I am glad that the time it has taken me over the last few weeks to select the final group of girls for my son to meet is over. Thankfully, I only found a few of the maidens unsuited to meet the king. Those that remain are all poised, well mannered, and are all-around delightful. I am pleased and look forward to soon calling one of them my daughter. But now it will be up to the king to choose which maiden will be his queen. I have a few favorites. I am curious to see if they will be the same as my son's. Well, I think I have left the girls waiting long enough. Shall we go?"

"Yes, my lady."

Brina turned and walked across the foyer behind the queen mother until they reached the reception hall. Noirenn stood aside until Brina opened the door. The line of girls stood still and silent when the queen mother entered. Only the patter of her footsteps could be heard as she crossed over the smooth stone floor before she stopped in the center of the room.

"A few weeks have passed since we first met," Noirenn said. "We've gotten to know each other, and now you who stand in front of me are the final group of maidens who will meet the king. Look around and see who else vies for the favor of my son's hand in marriage. Some of you know each other. You may think you know why you or those standing next to you are still here. Your assumptions may be wrong. Only I know why you now stand here."

The queen mother paused as the girls took quick glances around at one another.

"You will all meet the king today," Noirenn said.

Now all of the girls snapped their eyes to the queen mother. Noirenn saw a variety of expressions staring back at her: surprise, excitement, fear.

"You will not be alone with him, but will meet him as a group. You will follow me into the throne room, where you will walk before the king, introduce yourself, and then leave. The king will decide which of you he is interested in meeting with privately. If you are selected, you will each have no more than one hour with him … unless he requests for you to stay longer. You are all beautiful, so I advise you to find a way to impress him with something other than your looks if you want to stand out from each other."

Eochaid entered the vast throne room, where he would soon meet the group of eligible maidens. He looked at the large throne that sat on the dais. He recalled the times he had stood next to his father when he held meetings or heard the petitions of his people. Eochaid walked across the large rectangular room. Its walls, built of toughened clay and rock, rose up over thirty feet above him. Thick wood rafters tied in spiral crossbeams held up the domed-shaped ceiling, where a few pieces of slanted lumber allowed the smoke from the room's burning torches to drift skyward.

The king approached the dais that ran the width of the room: four feet high and ten feet deep, and upon which lay a coarse red-and-gold rug. In the center stood his throne, upholstered in crimson cloth and sitting beneath a canopy of the same material that was suspended from a gable-shaped wall. A second, but smaller, identical throne sat next to the king's. In between the two thrones, lying on a polished wood stand, was a small, ancient-looking harp.

The flag of Ulster and Meath with the scarlet hand encircled by a red cord, stood alone on the left side of the dais. The flag of the ard-righ stood on the right. Depicted on its flag in four separate squares were: a harp, signifying the flag of Leinster; the scarlet hand, for the flag of Ulster; three crowns, for Munster. In the final square were two symbols: one of an arm bearing a sword, next to an eagle, which signified the flag of Connacht.

A half-dozen suits of armor hung on the walls, along with swords, shields, and spears. The polished armor gleamed from the constant attention given to it by the king's attendants. Torches lined the side walls of the windowless room. Their flames cast a warm yellow light over everything and everyone who entered.

Eochaid stopped midstride when he heard the wood door creak open. The queen mother was first to enter. Twelve stunning and beautifully dressed maidens followed in line behind her. Eochaid turned and moved up the eight gently ascending stairs. As he sat down on the throne, his eyes glanced over the girls who drew near.

"Wait here," the queen mother said to the first girl, who now stood at the base of the stairs, directly in front of Eochaid.

"Are they not all beautiful?" Eochaid's mother said. She walked up the stairs, then moved past Eochaid and sat down on her throne.

"They are indeed lovely," Eochaid responded. He looked at each girl and made a mental note of which ones he found the most attractive.

"Then let us begin." The queen mother folded her bejeweled hands in her lap, then nodded to the first girl in line.

"Your Majesty, I am most honored to meet you. I am Shauna, from the family of MacClain, daughter of Liam, master of the village of Gailinga in Connacht." The young lady curtsied, then stood straight and smiled at the king.

"I am pleased to meet you, Shauna," Eochaid said. He watched the blushing girl as she turned and quickly left the room.

Each girl moved forward and introduced herself to Eochaid. His mother had done quite well in selecting girls of varying beauty. Striking blonde, brunette, and redheaded maidens greeted the king in turn. Eochaid noticed not only their beauty, but also their manner of dress. Most wore impressive jewelry and elaborate gowns with embroidered puffed sleeves and wide, ballooning skirts—all but one. Eochaid noticed that the dark-haired beauty wore a simple, low-cut gown of emerald green, which accentuated her slender but shapely figure. Her long hair was unadorned and flowed straight over her shoulders to her waist. She wore only a single piece of jewelry: a half-inch-wide, woven silver necklace hung down and came to rest in the crease at the top of her breasts.

"My name is Gweniss. I am from the family of O'Breislein. My father is Conall, first captain in the army of Ulster. I am honored to meet you, Your Majesty."

"The pleasure is mine," Eochaid said. He looked into the greenish-brown eyes of the maiden. As the young woman walked away, he thought how similar they were … but not quite the same as those he remembered from his past.

Two more girls followed in line after Gweniss. After politely introducing themselves to the king and exiting the room, Noirenn turned toward her son.

"Well, that should have been quite pleasant for you. Which girls do favor? Which ones would you like to meet with privately?"

Eochaid rested his head against the back of his throne as he drummed his fingers on its polished wood arms. He stared up into the ceiling before he answered. "What a strange way to select my queen." He blew out a long breath, then sat up and looked at his mother. "Yes. I will meet with Cairenn, Kaitlin, and Gweniss."

"What about the others? Should I have them wait until you meet with these three girls before I let them go?" Noirenn asked.

"I have no interest in the second or the fifth girl. The others … I'm not sure."

Chapter 32

While their ship was being made ready, Jeremiah paid several local craftsmen to paint a large golden lion on the sail. He also instructed them to build a flag post at the rear of the ship, where the same image of a lion would float on a banner, with the name: *The Lion of Judah*.

Elier commissioned the forty-five-foot ship from one of his seaside villages to be made ready for a long voyage. Elier also appointed his son Simon and another twenty of his best seamen to take the small group from Gibraltar and sail to whatever land the prophet instructed them.

Jeremiah's two and a half months in Gibraltar came to an end on a cold January morning. The air felt damp. Gray clouds hung low in the sky.

"It appears that she is not leaving with us," Jeremiah said. He stood next to Hannah and looked up toward the street that led down to the harbor.

"I don't know what to say," Hannah said. "It is not like Teia to do something like this."

Jeremiah gave Hannah a little smile, then placed a soft kiss on each of her cheeks. He embraced her warmly, then turned to Benjamin. "Take good care of her."

"I will," Benjamin said. He looked down at Hannah with a broad smile that spread across his dimpled face.

Jeremiah embraced Ebed. "I will miss you, my friend." A sparkle of a tear filled the corners of the prophet's eyes.

Ebed struggled to maintain his own composure. "Perhaps the Lord will bring us together again someday."

"That will be something to hope for. May the Lord God Almighty be with you until then," Jeremiah said.

He turned and walked slowly down the rocky path that led across to the harbor where the *Lion of Judah* was moored.

Baruch held the boarding plank steady as Jeremiah climbed aboard. The prophet and his friend found a place to stand out of the way of the crew as they pulled on the ropes that hoisted the sail up its mast. As the twelve crewmen on the lower deck maneuvered their oars through the water, the ship began to drift out of the harbor toward the open sea.

"Wait! Wait!" came a small cry from land.

Jeremiah turned to see Teia on shore, embracing her sister. They hugged, then kissed each other before Teia turned and ran toward the water.

"Wait!" Teia cried, waving her arms in the air until she saw Jeremiah's ship turn back toward the harbor.

No words were exchanged between Teia and Jeremiah when she climbed aboard. The two looked at each other, and then Teia dropped her tear-stained face and asked, "Is there a room, or someplace for me on this ship?"

"Yes, there is a cabin for you. Baruch will show you where it is."

As the ship sailed over choppy waters across the Bay of Algeciras and through the Pillars of Hercules, Teia stayed in her cabin. The weather outside felt bitter cold, so she was content to stay rolled up in a blanket on her cot. The hours and days of weeping and calling out her sister's name drifted by. The only prayer she spoke over and over was to say, "Why God?"

Teia's longing for her sister only grew as she sailed farther away from her. When not crying, Teia slept away most of her days. All she wanted was to escape her life into a dream world or into silent darkness. She only emerged from her cabin briefly to sit silently with Jeremiah and Baruch as they all ate their morning and evening meals. She didn't join their conversations and only gave a shrug of her shoulders when or if they addressed her.

As the weeks passed, the ship moved farther north along the coast of Iberia. Soon, the air temperature began to rise. Teia opened the door to her cabin late one morning and welcomed in the fresh air. She stood in her doorway and lifted her face to the warm touch of the sun.

"Good morning, Teia."

Teia turned toward the familiar voice and saw Baruch sitting on deck with his back resting against his cabin, a stack of parchments and a basket of tablets at his side.

"Good morning," Teia responded

"It's a beautiful day, isn't it? Here, have a seat." Baruch slid over and patted a spot on the deck.

Teia hesitated, then sat down and crossed her legs. She watched as Baruch pored over a long piece of parchment.

"That's a big scroll. Is it one of Jeremiah's?" she asked.

"Most of the scrolls I read are Jeremiah's, but this one has been handed down in my family for almost two hundred years. I am thankful that it was not damaged in the storm. I stored it in one of Jeremiah's leather pouches inside the chest, which kept the seawater out. I treasure all scrolls and tablets that contain God's words and his story."

Teia picked up an irregular four-inch piece of terra cotta from the basket. She ran her fingers over the small inscribed letters. "When I was little, I use to think the stories were made up for me. I always loved to hear the stories of Rebekah and Isaac, Rachel and Jacob, and Ruth and Boaz."

Baruch chuckled. "You seem to like the love stories."

A wave a red flushed through Teia's cheeks. She put the tablet down and changed the subject: "Now that we've left Gibraltar, do you know where we are going?"

Baruch's lips curled into a smile before he answered. "We sail to a place called Fisterra, on the west coast of Iberia. Before we left Gibraltar, Elier sent word of our route to the ruler of that land with our estimated arrival date. We should be expected and welcomed when we arrive."

"Oh. Is that where we will live? Has Jeremiah said anything about that to you?"

"No, not a word. I'm sure Jeremiah will let us know when he knows. It is not Jeremiah who determines where we stay or where we go. It will be Yahweh's voice that directs our route."

Teia rolled her eyes while Baruch kept his gaze focused on the scroll in his lap.

"Are you ready to resume your studies?" he asked.

A few moments of silence passed before Teia answered, "I don't know. I don't know anything anymore." She shrugged. "I don't know and … I'm not sure I really care. I just feel kind of … dead inside. I try, but I can't make sense of anything anymore. I wonder why I just didn't die under the temple."

"Ah. So that's what you have been thinking about. Welcome to life, Teia. It is a sign of your maturing that you now question your existence—your purpose. Yours has not been an easy road so far. It may not be an easy road ahead. But you, just as everyone else, have a reason for being here. That is why you were born. *That* is why you lived."

She sighed and shook her head. "What can Yahweh want or do with a sixteen-year-old girl? He uses boys and men, not girls, for his purpose."

"Yahweh calls upon both. Do I need to remind you of Ruth, who remained faithful to her mother-in-law Naomi and became an ancestor of King David? Or Deborah, who was a judge over Israel and ruled men? She rose in battle to defeat the Canaanites who had oppressed our people for twenty years! Miriam, who was Moses's sister … Rebekah and Rachel, whom you just mentioned."

"Hmm … I guess you're right," Teia said. "I never really thought much about all the girls and women I've read about."

"The list is endless, Teia Tamar. Even your name, 'Tamar,' is the same as the girl who by giving birth to the twins Perez and Zerah may have saved Judah's lineage from becoming extinct! Tragedy marred Tamar's life. She was a widow at a young age and it seemed she would remain childless, but Yahweh in his wisdom turned her fate to his own design. The Lord's steady, though not always readily visible, guiding hand never forgets his people and their destiny. Teia, do you ever wonder why you were born the daughter of the last king to rule in Jerusalem? Jeremiah said your father will be the last king to rule in God's city, until his Anointed One, blessed be he, takes his seat in Jerusalem as King of kings and Lord of lords over all kingdoms and people on the earth."

"I've wondered a little … but I really don't understand the reason. And it seems that each time I feel good about who I am, each time I have hope, something bad happens."

"What may seem bad to you is just a part of your journey. You will have good and bad, joy and sorrow, throughout your life, no matter how short or long it may be. But if you trust in Yahweh, he will not lay on your shoulders more than you can bear with his strength upholding you. Love him, and you will feel his love. When you find this truth, you can go to him and he will help you through the difficult times. He will become your refuge and your strength."

Teia looked down at the deck.

"Teia … look at me." When their eyes met, Baruch continued. "Yahweh is your creator. He knows everything that has happened to you, and everything that is still to come in your life. He knows your every thought.

He even knows the number of hairs on your head. He knows you better than you know yourself. Just remember to call on him in your time of need."

Baruch lifted up a scroll sitting on the deck and handed it to Teia. "Read his word, Teia. Truly seek him, and then be prepared to see your life change. I wish I could give you what I know to be true. But I can't." Baruch's eyes filled with tears. "The immeasurable love, joy, and peace that can be found in this life is a free gift offered to you. You will receive it when you put Yahweh first." Baruch turned back to the manuscript on his lap. "When you are ready to return to your studies, let me know."

Now Teia breathed a heavy sigh. She rubbed her fingers back and forth across the scroll's rough parchment. *I once felt your presence, Lord. But now … you feel far away. Why have I suffered so much pain? I'm afraid of what will happen next … What else might be taken away from me?*

Chapter 33

Twenty-six days after sailing from Gibraltar, Simon dropped the ship's anchor in Fisterra's harbor, where Menahem, the Iberian ruler, had a welcome party waiting to greet their ship. The following afternoon, the three Judeans rode in a horse-drawn coach six miles inland to the small castle in Breogan, where Menahem resided. After greeting Jeremiah, Teia, and Baruch, the gracious nobleman led his guests into a huge dining room.

More food covered the table than they had seen even while residing in Pharaoh's palace. Menahem noticed the wide eyes of his guests. "Please sit down and help yourselves." He pointed to several round loaves. "This bread is baked by my cooks with a dark gooey liquid they call 'molasses.' The sweet-tasting bread is my favorite. We have bowls of chickpeas and raisins mixed with a saffron-flavored rice. Some chopped vegetables from the palace garden, cod fish, beef sausages, and dishes filled with black and green olives. But don't fill up on this food," Menahem said. He rubbed his chubby hand on his protruding belly. "Save some room for the sweets that will follow."

Jeremiah, Teia, and Baruch could only smile at the seemingly guileless ruler.

Menahem grinned back at them. "You can probably see by my size that I like to eat. My staff jokes that if one of them can't find me in or outside the castle, to look for me in the kitchen." Menahem's cheeks rolled up into balls the color and shape of small peaches as he laughed. "If there is anything you prefer, I will make sure it is served to you while you are here. If anything displeases you, I will have it removed from the table. So go ahead. Please help yourselves!"

The three Judeans nodded and began taking from the many platters in front of them.

"When you finish your meal," Menahem said, "I have an extraordinary drink for you to taste. It is made from a bean 'cacao.' About a year ago, some traders brought the beans to me from a land far south from here. One of my ships is heading there now. When it returns, its cargo hold will be filled with bags of these delicious beans. For now, though, if you would like something to drink with your meal, the pitchers in front of you are filled with almond-water. And the large jug contains a nice rose-colored wine—one of my favorites that comes from the grapes grown here on the hillsides in Jerez, a small southern village of ours."

As the Judeans began to eat, Menahem filled his plate for a second time and then he listened to Jeremiah summarize the story of the Babylonian siege, the destruction of Jerusalem, their time in Egypt, and the storm at sea that brought their ship to the shores of Gibraltar. The prophet also told Menahem of his mission to carry out Yahweh's promise of a perpetual kingdom.

"Hmmm ... but, Jeremiah," the Iberian monarch said, "Jeremiah, I beg you! Please consider making your home here in Breogan. We know our ancient heritage. Many of our people still follow the laws given to Moses. We will make Teia *our* queen. We will build a grand palace for her and—Oh! Here it is!"

Menahem's attention shifted from the conversation to his staff as they served his guests a warm brown drink.

"What do you think?" Menahem raised his eyebrows up and down. "My cooks add a little sugar to the brew just before it is served."

"Mmm ... it's wonderful!" Teia said.

Jeremiah and Baruch gave Menahem nods of approval as they sipped the rich beverage from their cups.

"Good, good! I knew you would like it," Menahem said. He smiled with a dark stain of the drink glistening across his top lip.

"Menahem," Jeremiah said, "it would be with a glad heart that we would stay here with you on this beautiful coastland. But it is not up to me where I build and plant. Yahweh gave me a commission long ago. His words to me were, 'See, today I appoint you over nations and kingdoms to uproot and tear down, to destroy and overthrow, to build and to plant.'" The prophet paused, then said, "I completed the first part of my mission. The last part is yet to be fulfilled."

Two days after arriving in Breogan, Jeremiah announced that it was time for his group to return to the *Lion of Judah*. Menahem ordered his staff to fill several chests and baskets with clothes, food, weapons, and other goods that would be transported to the coast and loaded onto Jeremiah's ship.

Jeremiah, Teia, and Baruch said their good-byes and thanked Menahem for his gracious hospitality, then boarded a coach that took them from the castle and down the steep hill back to Fisterra's harbor.

After sailing past the coast of Iberia, the *Lion of Judah* crossed over deep oceans many miles from land. There, the ship was caught in a storm that lasted seven days. Their sails were torn, and most oars were broken, along with the rudder of their ship. They could no longer control the direction they sailed. After being blown north for many days, the crew sighted land in the late afternoon as winds from the receding storm pushed their damaged vessel into the shores of a small bay. Local fishermen cleaning nets and tending their boats stopped their work and helped Simon's crew secure ropes from their battered ship to one of several large pylons that jutted out from shore.

Other than sending a few of his crew ashore to get the needed supplies to repair their ship, Simon suggested that Teia stay on board and out of sight during the day. He assured Jeremiah that he would keep his crew working day and night to complete the necessary repairs as soon as possible.

"Do you mind if I take another look at your maps?" Jeremiah asked as he stood in the doorway of Simon's cabin.

"Please, come in. The map I'm using is right here." He gestured to the table next to him.

"Where would you place us?" Jeremiah asked. He looked down and studied the large unrolled piece of parchment.

"The storm brought us across the Bay of Biscay. I was told we are now in the village of Crazan. If I am right, we are here." Simon tapped his finger on the map.

"What is this land called over here?" Jeremiah asked. His finger rested on a large, oval-shaped landmass a little northwest of their current position.

"That is Britannia. Is that where you want to go?"

"What is it like there?"

"It's beautiful, with a lot of rain this time of year. I've sailed there less than a dozen times, so I am no expert about the land or its people. But I have always found those who dwell there to be friendly, and I have never encountered problems in any of their ports."

"I will pray for God's guidance. Then I'll let you know if that is where we are to go."

Chapter 34

A large oak table and matching chair stood off to the side of the first floor's barrel-shaped, vaulted room, which sat beneath one of the castle's four towers. A red-green-and-gold wool rug lay over the center of the stone floor, where Eochaid now paced back and forth. After wearing the king's crown for over a year, Eochaid felt trapped in his position, but he also felt a strong, even stern sense of duty toward fulfilling the once-held expectations of his deceased father. Even though it was never his desire to attain the position of ard-righ, he now aspired to improve the conditions for his people and bring honor to the crown he wore. But today, other matters weighed on his mind as he moved back to the table scattered with maps—just as his mother entered the room.

"The last two girls you wanted to meet are ready. I have met with these girls many times. Either one of them would seem to make an excellent queen."

"Yes, Mother, they are beautiful, but I won't be able to meet with them today." Eochaid moved behind his desk and sat down. "I am not in the mood for idle conversation. I have more pressing matters."

"Very well. I will send them home. But you don't have a lot of time left to make your final decision."

Eochaid closed his eyes and rubbed a hand across his forehead. He blew out a long, exasperated breath, then looked up. "Don't hold me to a specific date. I will try to make my decision by the spring festival. If I don't, then my announcement will just have to wait! I'm preparing for battle. As we speak, our army gathers to settle the feuds that have been threatening the peace of Ulster between the clans of Lurgan and Antrim. Their continued fighting has killed many over their struggle to control the rights to the waters of Lough Neagh."

"Very well. I understand. I'll leave you alone, and we will talk of this later." Noreen turned toward the door.

"Wait … before you go, I have a question for you. Do you not find our heritage important in selecting a queen?" Eochaid asked. "You said we are descendants of Jacob-Israel. Are these maidens you selected also descendants of this tribe?"

Noirenn paused, then shook her head. "I never thought about selecting maidens for you based on their earliest heritage. Most of those who live in Erin are descendants of the Danites or the tribe of Judah, and some say they are descendants from the tribe of Simeon. Most people, though, don't care about their ancient heritage. Why is it so important to you? And why didn't you mention this before? Is this something that you truly care about, or is it just another excuse to delay your wedding?"

Eochaid cursed under his breath. "Forget I asked! I just … I just remember what that prophet told me. He said I would marry someone from the branch, the lineage of King David. The prophet appeared to be a wise man who spoke the truth!"

"Eochaid, that was a long time ago." Noirenn walked slowly back into the room. "You only spent a few hours with that man. You don't know if he was a prophet or a fraud who purposely misled you. Regardless, I will see what I can find out about the heritage of the remaining girls. Will that satisfy you?"

"Being free and back out on the sea would satisfy me!" Eochaid snapped, his temper continuing to rise. "Like any man, I enjoy the companionship of a beautiful maiden. But I tire of the pressure of this ordeal. It feels like I am selecting the victor in some game instead of choosing someone that I desire to always have by my side! But don't worry, Mother: I will pick one of these girls for my bride."

"Good! Then this 'ordeal,' as you call it, will be over and you can run off to your ships and sail the seas—after you spend some time in your wedding bed and provide your kingdom with an heir!" Noirenn strode toward the door, then stopped and turned around. "Do I dare ask if you still plan to see Gweniss later today, or should I tell her to leave when she arrives?"

Eochaid kept his eyes down on his desk. "Yes. I am planning on seeing her before I leave."

"She is one of the most beautiful of all the girls you have met," Noirenn said. She watched her son closely as he appeared to mindlessly shuffle the parchments on his desk and then she left the room.

Gweniss walked slowly toward Eochaid when he entered the ivy-covered gazebo that concealed the couple from anyone outside. Long silver cords dangled down into the folds in the front of the ruby-red gown that was cinched around her small waist. Eochaid's eyes moved up from her slender hips to the top of her breasts, which bulged slightly out of the low neckline of the snug-fitting velvet fabric. Gweniss curtsied to the king, then stood and pulled Eochaid's face down. She kissed him with hunger and passion before she released him.

Eochaid leaned forward for another kiss just as Gweniss turned her head. The king buried his face into her soft perfumed hair. His pulse quickened as he felt her fingers dig into his back. With his hand, he gently pulled back her hair and kissed her neck. Slowly, he moved his lips up toward her face.

Gweniss pushed Eochaid away. "Not yet, my King. You have had just a taste of me. If I am the one you choose as your betrothed, you will have all of me—whenever you wish." She smiled, then slipped out from under Eochaid's arms.

"You dare tempt the king?" Eochaid smiled back. He grabbed Gweniss and pulled her close to him again. "Soon, I will announce whom I have chosen as my beautiful bride, and then, *if* I call your name, I will have my pleasure in taking all of you."

Eochaid kissed the eighteen-year-old girl with unrestrained fervor, leaving them both breathless when he pulled away.

Gweniss drew her teeth across her lower lip. Every nerve in her body tingled as she became aroused. "Why should we wait? We are here alone. No one need know. Take me now."

"A minute ago, you pushed me away, and now you plead with me? Would you—Quiet!" Eochaid whispered. He turned away from Gweniss and listened. "Someone's coming."

The snapping sound of twigs grew louder, along with the jingle of a harnesses and clopping of horse's hoofs against the ground. Eochaid pushed Gweniss gently behind him. He pulled out his sword and approached the open doorway.

A soldier emerged from the forest and rode up the small hill and dismounted his horse. "My King, I am sorry to disturb you, but you asked me to inform you as soon as we knew the exact location of … of the enemies' troops."

"You've received word of their present location?"

"Yes, my lord."

"Good. Then gather the commanders of my mounted troops, and foot soldiers. I want them in the throne room as soon as possible. I'll be there shortly."

"Yes, my lord." The soldier turned, mounted his horse, then galloped back down the hill.

Eochaid walked back into the shade of the gazebo. "I have to get back to the castle."

"No … not now.

"I'm sorry, but I have to go."

"When will I see you again?" Gweniss asked.

"I'm not sure. I'll be gone for a while. I have some matters to attend to far from here."

"You have to be back before the spring festival."

Eochaid's pursed lips turned up into a smile. "Yes, I'll be back by then so I can announce to the entire kingdom whom I have selected as their queen. Do you have one last kiss for your king before he leaves?"

"Yes, I will give you something to remember that will leave you wanting more."

Gweniss pressed her body into Eochaid's and they kissed.

CHAPTER 35

In less than a week after arriving in Crazan, all repairs to the *Lion of Judah* had been completed. The new oars pushed through the water as the repaired rudder guided the ship back out to sea. Teia was glad to be able to walk freely across the deck during the day after staying inside her cabin while they were moored next to the little fishing village.

The sea was calm and still as they sailed away from land. For three days, only the strength of the oarsmen moved the ship farther north. Moderate winds finally arrived on the fourth morning. The gusts swept across the ocean and filled and stretched the ship's canvas sail, pushing the vessel forward. Only a week later, the crew spotted land.

Not recognizing the coastal village where they landed, the captain went ashore with a few of his men to speak with the locals. Several men gathered around Simon and were telling him that his ship had sailed into Mont's Bay. Just then, two muscular men dressed in lightly armored uniforms pushed their way into the group.

"We are soldiers who serve King Elatha," the taller man said. "What's going on here?" Looking at Simon and his men, he asked, "Who are you?"

Simon introduced himself, then brought out two small scrolls from his pocket. "These letters I carry are from the rulers of Iberia and Gibraltar."

The soldier stuck out his hand to take the scrolls, then glanced at the wax seals before he unrolled each one and glanced over its contents. "These documents look authentic. Where are the people mentioned in these letters?"

"They are still on my ship." Simon pointed toward the bay. "The ship over there, the one with the lion on its flag."

"Gather your companions together. We will wait for you here and then lead all of you to King Elatha's castle."

When the captain returned to the ship, he gathered Jeremiah, Baruch, and Teia together. "I was told that we've sailed into Mont's Bay and have landed in a village called Mara-Zion, on the Island of Britannia. We will be escorted by two soldiers to their king's castle. If you look up there …" Simon pointed up over the cluster of shops and homes in the village. "… you can see the top of the castle. I suggest that we all clean up a bit and put on a fresh set of clothes before we meet with the king."

Moments later, Teia pulled out a dress from one of the chests that Menahem had given her. The dark-green gown looked modest enough, being ankle length with long sleeves and a slightly fitted flower-embroidered bodice. A three-inch band of golden cords wrapped around the waist of the dress. Teia pulled the gown down over her head, tightened and knotted the waist band, then quickly brushed out her hair. Finally, she gathered her tresses at the back of her head and cinched them together with a wide gold-wire clip.

While Teia dressed, Jeremiah met with Simon privately and asked him to please keep his cabin closed up while he was gone, as he had many old parchments inside that could be easily damaged. Simon said he would nail a board across the door to ensure that no one would enter the cabin until the prophet returned to the ship.

The soldiers led the group from the wharf along the main road and through the town, past tanneries, woodworking establishments, and clean little candle- and soap-making shops. Then they walked along the winding roads that stretched between the small hut-like homes of the local villagers scattered over the countryside. When they reached the end of the road, they approached a massive wood door embedded in a rock wall. The wall rose over ten feet and stretched as far as they could see to their right and left. Two guards stood in front of the door.

The soldier carrying Simon's scrolls addressed the guards: "These foreigners just arrived and bring with them letters from the rulers of two neighboring kingdoms."

One of the guards held out his hand. After reading the scrolls' contents and then looking over the four foreigners, he nodded to the other guard, who lifted the hilt of his sword and banged it against the door. A concealed one-foot-square block of wood in the door immediately swung open.

"We have visitors for the king," the first guard said. "They carry documents signed by Lord Menahem and by the ruler of the land of Eber." The soldier held one unfurled scroll up to the opening in the door.

The small window shut and the loud clanking of chains was heard before the door was opened. “This way,” one of the guards said, then motioned as the four visitors proceeded on a wide dirt path that stretched up a gently rising hill at least a half-mile in front of them.

Teia caught her breath at the sight of the beautiful landscape just as a light drizzle began to fall. The scent of earth rose up from the damp ground, and Teia took in the rolling green fields dotted with trees and lush blooming foliage that stretched endlessly on both sides of the road. White, yellow, and lavender flowers bloomed in patches near several large ponds, where flocks of mallard ducks and white geese swam. A variety of small birds flew across the landscape or wandered near the water as they pecked for food in the soft green blanket of grass.

When they reached the end of the road, the group stood in front of a wide moat that encircled the sprawling castle. The castle’s tall, round towers reflected in the mirror of water. Teia tightened the shawl around her shoulders as her eyes scanned over the enormous castle. She watched the small dark shapes of a dozen or so soldiers move across the rampart high above her. Her eyes followed their slow back-and-forth movements. Her thoughts flashed back to the rampart she had walked along on her last day in Jerusalem’s palace. The sound of loud clanking drew Teia’s eyes downward and her thoughts back to the present.

Heavy chains attached to the drawbridge dropped slowly through holes in the castle’s rock wall. When the wood bridge rested on land, the soldiers led the captain and his companions across the bridge. The two scrolls were handed to the guard stationed in front of the entrance into a short tunnel.

Once permission was granted, the soldiers led the small group through the tunnel until they stopped in front of an iron gate that was slowly drawn up. Then they walked into an expansive courtyard and finally into the castle’s portico, where they were told to wait.

It took only a few minutes before Elatha, the king of the grand castle, personally came to welcome the foreign travelers. He was a tall, large man, a little advanced in age. His face was etched with thin wrinkles around his short brown beard, which was streaked with gray, as was his shoulder-length hair. The soft-spoken king told them that he was a kinsman of Menahem of Breogan and also an ally of Elier bar Ziza of Gibraltar. With two armed soldiers at his side, Elatha looked over the small group as Simon introduced himself and gave a quick summary of the journey that had brought them from Gibraltar to Britannia. The king listened to the captain until he finished, then Jeremiah stepped forward.

"I am Jeremiah, known as the prophet of Yahweh, the God of Israel. I come from the land of Judah, which lies far to the east of here.

"Welcome, Prophet of God, to Dumnonia and to my castle. I am honored to meet you. There are many legends in our land of our ancient ancestors coming from a place in the East where the God of all creation dwelled. I would be grateful if, during your visit, you would tell me more of a people I have rarely heard of other than in fables."

Jeremiah nodded. "Of course, Your Majesty."

"And who is this beautiful maiden?" the king asked.

Teia stepped forward. "I am Princess Teia Tamar, daughter of King Zedekiah, the king of Judah."

King Elatha stepped closer and bowed his head. "I am honored to meet you, Princess Teia Tamar from the land of Judah. I welcome you to my land and to my home."

Teia smiled, bowed her head, then made a small curtsy before replying, "Thank you, King Elatha, for graciously receiving us. Your castle is impressive and the land that surrounds it is so beautiful. I could have never imagined anything as wonderful as this place."

"Well … thank you. I hope to have the time to show you around the castle and its grounds before I leave. Unfortunately, I will only be here for a few days before I depart again for Silures, a land that lies to the north of my kingdom."

As Teia stepped back, Jeremiah motioned his arm toward Baruch. "This man at my side is Baruch. He is also a servant of the Most High God. He is a scholar and teacher of Yahweh's word. He is also my scribe and my most dear friend."

The king smiled and shook his head. "My, I am so fortunate this day as my eyes behold a prophet, a princess, a man of knowledge, and a skillful sea captain. Ask what you wish of me."

The captain said, "The immediate needs would be for us to find a place for my eminent and regal companions to rest and have a meal off our ship, while my crew and I find the supplies we need in one of your villages to take care of some routine maintenance on our ship and to restock food and drink for our crew."

"Of course. You are all welcome to stay here for as long as you wish. I have a large staff that can attend to whatever needs you may have. Captain Simon, I hope you would also consider staying here, as well as any of your officers that you wish to have with you. Or, if you prefer, I will have my soldiers accompany you back to your ship. They will get others to assist you, or whomever you place in command, in supplying your ship with whatever you need."

Simon bowed his head. "Thank you, King Elatha, for your gracious offer, but I will leave my companions with you and return with your soldiers to my ship."

"Well, then, if the three of you would follow me." The king gestured toward the open door.

"King Elatha, you said this land is called Dumnonia, yet we were told that we had landed in Britannia," Jeremiah said.

"You have," the king said. He turned his face toward Jeremiah as he led the group through a long entrance hall. "Our large island and the smaller one to the west of us are *together* called 'Britannia.' The portion of land that I rule on this island, the lower southwest end, is what is called 'Dumnonia.'" Elatha put his hand in the air and waved it back and forth. "I know, it all gets a bit confusing. Some even call our land 'Albion,' because of the white cliffs east of us that rise up from the sea. If you think of this entire landmass as Britannia, you are correct."

"Ah. Thank you for clearing up my confusion," Jeremiah said.

"Wait here for a moment please." The king moved across a vast room, its high stone walls covered with muted colored tapestries.

Teia looked around and thought about the stark contrast between the beautiful colored landscapes on the outside of the grand castle, compared to the dreary darkness on the inside.

The king returned a few moments later with a thin man dressed in brown pants and a matching jacket. "This is my steward, Elwin. He will have his staff show you to your rooms and will also inform the cooks to prepare a meal for you. How much time would you like before you sit down to eat?"

The prophet looked to Teia and Baruch, then answered, "Just enough time to wash and refresh ourselves."

"Elwin will let the kitchen staff know that you will be down shortly. You will find the dining hall through that door." Elatha pointed to his left. "You will follow Elwin to your rooms up those stairs." The king then gestured to his right. "Then, when you are ready, come down and enjoy your meal. I'll join you a little later for some tea."

Soon enough, Jeremiah, Teia, and Baruch seated themselves in three of the twenty-two chairs that sat along the wood table. Elatha's staff then filled ceramic bowls with a vegetable-beef stew served with slices of hearty oat bread and tubs of creamy butter. Having only eaten dried fish and raisins for the past week, the Judeans enjoyed the hot nourishing meal, followed by a sweet dessert of juicy sliced pears and soft cheese drizzled with honey.

After the meal was finished and the table cleared, the king entered and joined his guests. He sat at the head of the table and instructed his staff to bring out four spouted iron pots. Fragrant steam of steeped chamomile and lemon balm leaves wafted around the table as Elatha's kitchen staff poured the warm, light-colored liquid into their cups.

As they sipped their tea, Jeremiah gave the king a brief history of the people of Israel, then told him what had led to the fall of Jerusalem and of the subsequent journey that had brought him and his companions to his island.

Later on, long after Teia and Baruch had retreated to their rooms, Elatha continued with more questions for Jeremiah as his staff continued to refill their cups with tea. Finally, the king waved his servants off, signaling that they'd had enough.

"You have brought interesting conversation to me, Jeremiah. I am thankful for our visit this evening."

"If you have no further questions tonight …" Jeremiah slowly raised himself off his chair. "This weary and aged man requires some rest."

Elatha apologized for keeping the prophet late into the night. Before Jeremiah retreated to his room, he asked the king if he would have his staff not disturb him in his room, as he needed to be alone to fast and pray. For two days, Jeremiah remained in seclusion before he finally opened his door early in the morning and went downstairs to find someone who could relay his request to meet with the king.

When they met later that morning, Jeremiah told the king that in a few days, his group would leave and return to the sea, where they would travel to the land that lay farther west. At Jeremiah's request, Elatha immediately sent a messenger on one of his ships with a letter dictated by the prophet. Elatha addressed it to the king of the neighboring island.

King Elatha then graciously offered his castle and his staff to his guests for the remainder of their stay after he said his good-byes to each of them, and then he prepared to leave for his own trip.

With the *Lion of Judah* fully stocked with supplies, Captain Simon returned to the castle with a few of the king's soldiers riding on horses that would be used to take the Judeans back to the coast.

Once everyone was back aboard, they sailed away from the village of Mara-Zion, then west along the cost of Britannia before they turned their ship north. They sailed throughout the coming days over small swells, only anchoring off the coast at night when the crew would rest. Simon followed the route given to him by King Elatha's ship captains, who had told him about a landmark to watch for—where he would turn his ship west across the narrowest part of the sea, keeping to Simon's plotted course that would bring his vessel to the shores of the neighboring island.

For twenty-one days they sailed, until late in the afternoon on the nineteenth of Nisan, 584 BC, they dropped anchor in Dun Laoghaire Bay.

Chapter 36

The long line of horses and riders emerged from the forest. Behind them, moving across the open land, came the foot soldiers. Dawn's first light gleamed down on their polished shields. A lone hawk circled overhead and eyed the armored men who marched into the field of tall grass. Ahead of the army, Eochaid and Aric rode their mounts slowly to the top of the nearest hill. They held their swords out in fighting position.

Eochaid looked down the hill into the valley where the enemy's camp appeared large and intimidating. He could see no movement. Except for the heavy breathing of the horses, and the shrill cries of the hawk, there was the silence. Eochaid could feel the eyes of all on him as their commander and king. He held the reins of his horse tight and took a deep breath, aware that soon he would begin the battle.

The young king had heard enough of the small raids that Muirdach led against the people of Meath. But it was the recent death of one of his palace attendants that made Eochaid burn with hatred. It didn't take long for his spies to find out who had brought the poisoned wine into the palace and from whom the spy had taken his orders. Eochaid knew the poison had been meant for him. He still couldn't shake the vivid memory of watching his loyal cupbearer suffer through a slow and painful death. He sought revenge for the servant's death—even before he'd found out that it was the same enemy who might have provided the poison responsible for killing his father.

Eochaid's troops had traveled for two days. They moved at a steady pace along untraveled back roads or under the cover of the dense forests during most daylight hours until they finally reached the low hillsides of Laragh, which sat just above the valley where Leinster's army now camped.

With Aric's input, Eochaid had planned the attack for months. Several of Eochaid's men had infiltrated Muirdach's regiment and befriended the cooks by providing large amounts of food and drink—especially drink. It didn't take long for Muirdach's troops to become sluggish and usually drunk at night, with ill aftereffects in the morning.

Eochaid's troops formed into a battle line. Two hundred warriors on horseback and one thousand infantry marched behind him. With one swift downward motion of his sword, Eochaid gave the signal for his men to charge down the hill and into the enemy's camp.

At the thundering sound of the stampeding horses, Leinster's soldiers fled out of their tents. Many plunged into the nearby river as Eochaid's soldiers charged through their camp. Groups of hungover men stood frozen in place, dazed as Eochaid's troops bared down upon them. Dozens jumped onto their mounts and fled across the river into the forest even as Eochaid's men continued to pour down the hill. Ulster's soldiers struck every Leinster man they encountered, slicing through their flesh with their swords, or plunging them into their bellies. Blood spattered across the clothes and skin of Eochaid's men as they continued to move forward and kill.

Eochaid himself fought as he had been trained. He kept his eyes open, constantly checking his sides and then his back as he waded into the battle. Just as he turned to look behind him, two men grabbed him and pulled him off his horse. The young king hit the ground, hearing the whoosh of a sword cutting through the air before it slammed into the side of his head, glancing off his helmet but catching his forehead. Eochaid's hand still clutched his sword, though. He came up fast to his knees, swinging hard in a circle and catching one attacker across the face. Eochaid jumped to his feet and slashed down on one man's sword arm and then the other's, severing them with their fingers still gripping their weapons. Whirling around with the momentum of his last blow, Eochaid struck each one in turn across the neck, and then in the chest with a final death blow.

As the battle went on, Eochaid fought off and killed several more of Muirdach's soldiers before a last anguished cry led to silence in the camp. The fight ended with small remnants of Leinster's wounded soldiers trying to escape across the river. Most, though, drowned before they reached the other side.

Drenched with sweat, Eochaid stumbled toward his horse. His ribs, he knew, were badly bruised. Blood ran from the gash on his head. He whistled for his horse, and it came to him. He slowly mounted the steed, then rode to the center of the enemy's camp. There, he saw Leinster's dead king. Eochaid looked down on Muirdach's body, which now sat propped up against the side of his tent—the blade of an axe still buried in the center of his head. Ulster's young king raised his sword high in the air and a cheer rang out from his men.

Eochaid ordered those who were not wounded to search the camp and countryside for any of their own dead or injured soldiers. With care, they wrapped the fallen men in their enemy's blankets before placing them in a few of the carts scattered around the camp.

Fatalities, thankfully, were light, but serious wounds were plentiful. The river soon ran pink as Eochaid and his troops rinsed their bodies and blood-soaked clothes in the cool flowing water. After the men cleaned and bound their wounds, they gathered all the weapons they could find on the battlefield before finally resting for the night. In the morning, they would begin their fifty-six-mile journey back home.

The young king's outward demeanor of confidence and strength hid his inner thoughts as he adjusted the bloodstained cloth wrapped around his head. *Is this my fate: to kill or be killed? Is this what it means to be king? At sea, those who sought to harm me were strangers—bandits, pirates. Here, it is my own countrymen who seek to destroy me. Will I always have to fear what I drink … what I eat? If I would have known this to be my fate, I would have stayed at sea … or in some far-off land.*

Eochaid's thoughts continued to wander as he looked down at his hands that held his horse's reins. The bands of light skin he'd once had on his wrists, long hidden from the sun by bands of gold, were now tanned like the rest of his arms.

Does she still wear my torque? He wondered. *Bah … What does it matter anymore? In a few weeks, Gweniss will be my bride.*

Dark skies gathered as Eochaid and his troops crossed the border into Meath. Rain soon splashed onto Eochaid's head and off his shoulders as he rode on the muddy roads that led into the village of Cathair Crofinn. Eochaid turned and lifted a hand that spoke good-bye to Aric, who had ridden over the long miles silently behind him.

The young king was too exhausted to speak with anyone when he finally reached the castle. He acknowledged but dismissed his servants as he walked through the halls directly to his room, where he peeled off his wet clothes and fell into bed. Eochaid's mind was blank as he listened to the patter of rain on the roof. In less than a minute, he drifted off to sleep.

Eochaid awoke the following morning, still worn from the battle and journey home. His ribs ached, as did the gash on his head. He swung his legs slowly out of bed and moved to the fresh basin of warm water that had been brought into his room as he slept. He felt and heard the rumble of hunger in his stomach as he washed and dressed.

After the castle's physician redressed his head wound, Eochaid made his way to the table in the dining hall, where he poured streams of milk and honey over a large bowl of porridge. In between each spoonful of oats, he munched on warm slices of his favorite bread, smothered in butter and piled thick with strips of salted meat.

Feeling full and a little stronger, Eochaid walked from the dining hall to the room of maps and records. He entered the musty library and yanked the thick curtains back from two large windows. Shafts of light brightened the space as Eochaid's eyes scanned over the floor-to-ceiling shelves of rolled maps and manuscripts.

"Hmm … They should be right around here."

Eochaid's fingers traced over one section of ancient documents. He unrolled several scrolls until he found the ancient Hebrew letters he recognized. He grabbed all the scrolls he could hold, then carried them across the room and set them down on the table sitting in front of the windows.

As Eochaid recuperated from his injuries, he returned each day after his morning meal to the study the Hebrew scrolls and parchments, now actually finding himself thankful that his father had insisted he not only learn to speak the languages of foreign nations, but also to read them. He sat alone for hours, reading through the ancient manuscripts. Many nights after closing the scrolls, his sleep was interrupted by the same reoccurring dream, in which blood flowed across everything, even as slashed faces, body parts, and severed heads lay in mounds around him. Blood dripped from his hands and covered the sword he held at his side.

In those dreams, Eochaid found himself always returning to the scene of his last battle, where he would stand alone among the dead, his body and mind drained. Falling to his knees, he looked to the heavens and asked, "Are you there? Can you hear my voice? If you are there, do you care about the desires and fate of this king?" The heavens, though, were always silent as Eochaid drifted from the battlefield into dreamless sleep.

Several days after his victory over Leinster's army, Eochaid's usual time in the library was interrupted when a courier arrived at his castle—with a letter from a neighboring kingdom. The guard on duty immediately brought the wax-sealed scroll to the king.

"Wait here," Eochaid said.

The guard obeyed and stood at attention as Eochaid unrolled the parchment and read the words written by Dumnonia's king, Elatha.

"Would you locate the queen mother and request that she join me here?" Eochaid asked.

When Noirenn came through the door several minutes later, she asked, "What is it?"

Eochaid handed the letter to his mother. "Here, read this. Will you or one of your staff take care of this for me? Send a small party with some gifts to greet these foreigners when they arrive. I suppose we should have some kind of welcoming ceremony. Forming an alliance and extending goodwill to those who could become our local trading partners would be wise."

"Mm. It is an odd letter," Noirenn said. "No specifics … and no names are given. Just notice to us that a small party is traveling with a member of royalty from Gibraltar and will soon be arriving in Erin."

"Perhaps their kingdom is somewhere in Iberia … some small settlement," Eochaid said.

"If they arrive before our spring festival celebration, we could invite them to sit with us in the royal pavilion, where you can officially welcome them to Erin." Noirenn handed the scroll back to Eochaid. "The entire village will be there, as well as many people from our neighboring kingdoms—all of whom will be anxious to see whom you will be introducing as your betrothed and future queen. It will be one of the most celebrated days in all of Erin. A day that will surely impress our royal visitors!"

CHAPTER 37

The captain and a few members of his crew left the *Lion of Judah* and went into the village to find the local ruler. Jeremiah instructed Simon to take with him the last of his gold Babylonian coins as a gift for the leader or monarch, in order to negotiate permission for their party to come ashore.

The chief nobleman, Lord Aidan, was gratified at the rich gift he received. He promptly made arrangements to travel to the coast in order to offer his respects and to welcome the distinguished travelers. Once they met, Lord Aidan graciously offered three adjoining rooms for Jeremiah, Teia, and Baruch in his country manor.

Teary good-byes and words of appreciation were offered to Simon and his crew when the three Judeans said their farewells. Once everyone was ashore, Baruch and two of the captain's men carried all the belongings of the prophet and the princess to land. Baruch made sure that the heavy chest that had traveled with them for almost two years was first to be unloaded and set ashore with Jeremiah.

The prophet soon discovered that many of the local inhabitants belonged to the same clan as some of the crewmen who had sailed their ship from Gibraltar. The Tuatha de Danann's language, though different from pure Hebrew, sounded similar, so it took little time for the Judeans to converse easily with the coastal residents.

After the three Judeans had settled into their rooms and had some time to rest, the lady of the manor sent her staff to ask the guests to join her and her husband in the main house. Over a simple meal, Aidan and his wife, Maire, talked to their guests about their homeland and their many months of sea travel.

"I would keep you up all night in my desire to hear more," Aidan said, "but I can see that you are all tired. There will be time for us to talk again tomorrow."

Jeremiah, Teia, and Baruch thanked the lord and lady, then retired to their rooms. Teia and Baruch fell quickly to sleep, but not before Jeremiah had given both of them instructions that he should be left alone in his room. No one was to disturb him no matter how long he remained secluded.

After four days, Jeremiah opened his door to find a bowl of freshly picked apples. After eating two of the sweet fruits, he asked a servant if he could see Lord Aidan.

"I have a request," Jeremiah said to Aidan in one of the manor's sitting rooms. "I would like to meet with the king of this land. Can that be arranged for me?"

"We have several kings—one for each region in our land. You are now in the region of Leinster, in the village of Wicklow. Our king was recently killed in battle. His successor has not been chosen."

"Is one of your kings greatest among them all?"

Aidan nodded. "Our high-king—our Heremon. But I believe he is away from his castle. I have recently received word that he is traveling somewhere in the northern part of Ulster."

"And where is his home?"

"His castle sits high on a hill above the village of Cathair Crofinn. It's in the kingdom of Ulster, in the county of Meath."

"Then it is to Cathair Crofinn that I must go. Is it far—and can you secure accommodations for me and my companions? Or must we first receive permission from your high-king?"

"It is about a three or four days' journey. I can send word to the king's castle that you have arrived in Wicklow. I am sure someone there could secure lodging for all of you in their village. Since you have a member of royalty traveling with you, perhaps the queen mother would even provide rooms for all of you within the castle's fortress."

"Our arrival should be expected," Jeremiah said. "The castle should have already received word from a neighboring king in Britannia of our impending visit."

"Then I'll have a messenger sent off today to the castle to let the queen mother know that you have arrived. I will notify you when I receive word back from the king or his staff that a place to stay has been made ready for you. When it has been arranged, I can provide you with horses, carts, carriages … whatever you might need to transport your party and your possessions to Cathair Crofinn."

Teia awoke in her room, feeling more rested and refreshed than she had in some time. Light shone through the single window, brightening the dull stone walls. She pulled the wool blanket aside and lowered her feet to the smooth clay floor. Her room smelled fresh from the large bouquet of dried herbs tied with a white silk ribbon that sat on the small table under the window.

Teia smiled. How nice it was to place her feet day after day on solid ground. She bent down next to her bed and opened the wood chest that held her clothes. After rifling through its contents, she pulled out a long-sleeved cream-colored dress. She was shaking the wrinkles out of the soft fabric when she heard a knock at her door.

"Teia, are you awake?" Jeremiah asked. He knocked again before he cracked open the door.

"Good morning, Jeremiah. I was just starting to dress. Please come in," Teia said. She held the dress against her chest and moved toward the door.

"I'm glad you are up. I needed to tell you that I have to leave the village for a short while. I should be back before sundown."

"Oh. I was hoping we could look around the village today. I know we have been here only a few days. The manor and its gardens are beautiful, but I am curious to see the village and meet some of the people who live here."

"You can do that. Just make sure to let the lord or lady of the manor know where you plan to go—and take Baruch with you."

"Very well."

"And I think it would be best if you didn't wander too far. We are still strangers in a strange land. Stay within the boundaries of the village. And … I would advise that you keep that gold band hidden."

Teia froze. Her eyes glanced down at her uncovered left arm that held the dress. Then she looked up at Jeremiah.

"Teia, I have known that you wore that band since the day we left the coast of Egypt for Tahpanhes. I noticed the bands on the prince when I first met him in the harbor. I noticed it on your arm the morning I came up behind you as you watched the prince's ship sail away. You always kept it well hidden … until today."

Teia stood silent before finally responding, "I … I don't know what to say."

"Teia, do you know where we are?"

"The captain told me that we landed in the village of Wicklow, in the country of Leinster."

"Yes. The village of Wicklow, in the *county* of Leinster … on the Isle of Erin."

Teia burst into tears. She felt both surprised and embarrassed by her sudden reaction, as her feelings now flowed freely after being hidden and held inside for so long. She struggled to gain her composure, then wiped the tears from her face.

"I'm … I'm sorry … I don't know why that happened … I'm sorry, Jeremiah."

He took hold of her right hand and held it gently in both of his. "There is nothing to be sorry about. I have known that you held the prince in your heart for a long time. I thought it best not to speak of him to you. Before you ask, I will tell you that I do not know if he is here. I have not asked. In time, we will both know."

Sunlight reflected off the stone cottages as smoke from the early morning fires drifted skyward; some came out of crude rock chimneys, but most escaped from holes in thick thatched roofs.

Teia and Baruch walked past a cluster of homes, then stopped to watch sheep graze in a small meadow. Teia took a deep breath of fresh air as they crossed over a bridge that spanned a narrow river. At the end of the bridge, she stopped and looked across the rolling fields of green that stretched to the distant forest. Flocks of sheep wandered the emerald pastures, and their bleating cries broke the silence of the crisp morning air.

Teia rested against the side of the bridge and took in the colorful landscape. *I wonder if Prince Eochaid still lives here. Did he sail safely home when he left Egypt? Is he sailing now, somewhere far away? Did he ever marry? Is he still alive?*

"You're not planning on going any farther, are you?"

Teia turned from her thoughts to Baruch. "No … I was just looking at how beautiful everything is; how different it is from Egypt or the many other places where we've traveled. I'm glad to be here after sailing on all the endless blue water that seemed to forever surround us."

"Yes, it is impressive to view this lush land after being at sea for so long."

Teia let out a long sigh. "I'm so glad that our travels are over. I hope the king of this land will give his consent for us to stay, since Jeremiah said he had no plans at this time for us to leave. Do you know where Jeremiah was going today?"

"He is meeting with some men who are preparing more permanent lodgings for us, a few days' journey from here in a place called 'Cathair Crofinn.' We will travel there soon, and you will be officially welcomed by Meath's king. It seems that a message was just received today that says we have been expected and that we have also been invited to this king's upcoming wedding celebration, which will take place soon after our arrival in his village."

Teia unconsciously brushed her hand back and forth over the gold band under her sleeve. She swallowed hard, then asked, "Do you know the name of the king?"

"Yes. I have heard that he is called 'Heremon.'"

Teia's hand dropped to her side. "King Heremon. I will have to remember that when I meet him."

Chapter 38

Eochaid and Collin rode for miles under the cool shade of the forest and over soft, leaf-covered paths before they moved out under the warm afternoon's sun. There, they ran their horses down the sloping hills of Slane. Eochaid rode next to his brother as they splashed across narrow stream beds where the last of winter's rains still flowed down from the saturated hills before winding its way through the bogs and then across the flat peat fields.

"It's good to ride with you again, brother," Eochaid said. "I'm glad we could spend some time together before I become a married man."

"Do you think being married will change you?"

"I don't know. I don't think so. But becoming a father surely will."

Eochaid and his brother continued to talk while riding up the side of a steep hill. When they reached its crest, they stopped their horses. All conversation ended as their attention was drawn down to the sound of laughter and song. Gathered around the oval-shaped lake that lay far below the hill was a large group of young women. Some swam in the sparkling blue water, while others sang songs as they reclined on the grass. Waist- or knee-length red or brunette hair was all that covered the maiden's shapely bodies.

Eochaid and his brother remained silent as they smiled and feasted their eyes on the girls. The smile soon left Eochaid's lips, though, when he realized where they were. Just as he was about to tell his brother that they had to leave, he stopped himself, for his eyes now followed one of the dark-haired girls walking out of the shallow water that lapped against the grassy shore. His eyes narrowed as he focused on her face while she moved across the grass and joined some of those who basked and warmed their bodies in the sun.

Eochaid swallowed hard as his mouth went dry. "Let's get out here." His fingers curled into a fist as he pulled on his horse's reins, turning the stallion around.

"Now?" Collin asked. "I kind of like the view from here!"

"We've trespassed into an area not even the king is allowed to enter. We are on the land that belongs to the Druid priests—and priestesses."

"They sure are beautiful … every one of them!" Collin said.

"Yes, they are chosen not only for their exquisite beauty, but also for their innate ability to learn the secret incantations and sorcery of the Druids, and then willingly participate in their sacred rituals … and orgies," Eochaid said.

As he spurred his mount forward, Eochaid wondered if his brother had recognized Gweniss from her many visits to their castle.

The brothers remained silent as they rode at a fast pace for almost an hour back to the castle. Only when they dismounted near the stables did they speak.

"Tell no one of our crossing today into the Druids' sacred land," Eochaid said.

"Alright. Although, I'm sure we were not the first ones to do so," Collin said. "I would bet that other men have pleaded ignorance of their location to get a glimpse of what we saw today!"

"You're probably right. But no one needs to think that the king and prince of Erin are either ignorant or lecherous spies. So keep what happened today to yourself! Swear to me that you will do so."

Collin smirked. "Yes, brother, I swear that what we saw will remain our secret."

CHAPTER 39

Jeremiah, Teia, and Baruch were soon escorted to Cathair Crofinn, where the king's country manor was prepared and staffed for them. One day after their arrival, they received a message that informed them that the queen mother was sending a few of the castle's select guards to them that afternoon with gifts of welcome from the king.

When the guards arrived, Jeremiah and Baruch stood on each side of Teia in one of the manor's formal greeting rooms to meet them. Two fully armored soldiers of the king were the first to walk in, followed by two younger men wearing green-and-gold tunics.

"Our king, our Heremon, sent us with gifts to welcome you," one of the armored soldiers said.

He waved the youths forward, and they unrolled beautiful wool rugs and blankets, then placed silver goblets and swords on the floor. They rose and bowed, then presented Teia with a beautiful gold-wire necklace.

When the young men retreated from the room, one of the soldiers stepped forward. "Our high-king and the queen mother send these gifts of welcome and friendship. They look forward to formally welcoming you to Erin. The king would like to extend an invitation for you to join him in five days in the royal pavilion. It will be there that he will introduce you to the people of Erin before our annual Eostre festivities begin. A carriage will be provided on that morning to take you to Brendan's Hill, where the festivities will start."

"We accept your king's gracious offer," Jeremiah said. "And we look forward to meeting the king and the queen mother, to thank them for all these wonderful gifts and for the use of the royal family's impressive country manor. Is there a chance that we could meet with the king before your annual festival?"

"I was told that he will not return until the afternoon before the Eostre celebration. I was also told to inform you that on the same day as your official welcoming ceremony, the king will announce from the royal pavilion whom he has selected as his queen. Several days of festivities are being planned throughout the kingdom in celebration of the king revealing whom he has selected as he bride. You will all be receiving an invitation to their royal wedding, which is to take place within a month after the king's announcement.

Teia smiled. "Then we look forward to meeting the king and also celebrating the joyful occasion of his marriage."

The following day, Jeremiah asked for a carriage to be available to take him, Teia, and Baruch from the country manor into the village of Cathair Crofinn. They left in the late morning and traveled along a hard-packed dirt road that wound through the rolling green landscape. As they drew closer to the village, they found that most of the homes and shops were spread out in an expanding circle below a wide hill. Atop the hill, Druid priests had placed a thirteen-foot, phallic pillar stone for use in their worship of Baal.

Jeremiah knew that worshipping anyone but Yahweh, and the making of graven images of false gods or anything else, was strictly prohibited by God and carried the penalty of death. He knew he could not remain silent as he soon stood on the hill and beheld the heathen pillar. That evening, the prophet asked for a meeting with the Druid priests.

The next day, three priests arrived at the country manor. Once they were shown inside, Teia and Baruch followed Jeremiah into the large reception room.

"I thank you for granting my request to meet with you. I am Jeremiah, prophet of Yahweh, the one and only Holy God of Israel, and the God of all creation." Jeremiah motioned toward Teia. "This is Princess Teia Tamar, daughter of the king of Judah. And this …" Jeremiah raised his hand. "This is Baruch, a sage and scribe."

The Druid priests bowed to them.

"I asked to meet with you," Jeremiah said, "because I have seen the obscene stone pillar that you worship. You pray to Baal and numerous other gods. I have been told that you even sacrifice your men and women. No good will come to you and your people if you continue in these depraved evil ways."

One of the priests scoffed at Jeremiah. "You may be a prophet of a god, but you have no authority over us. It is not for you to tell us how or who to worship. We, along with our high-king, have authority over you in this realm."

Another priest added, "If you choose to live here, you can worship whom you wish, but you will remain silent in telling us what we will do!"

The third priest who had remained silent now moved directly in front of the prophet. The Druid stood a good foot above Jeremiah. His flesh sagged on his facial bones around a long nose. The elderly priest left his arms crossed over his chest, hidden inside the wide cuffs of his robe as he addressed Jeremiah: "I am Serejin—the chief priest of this order. As my assistant has said, you have no authority here. It is our gods who rule this land. With the power of our gods, we have a recognized and valued authority, unified with and approved by all the kings in this land. You being here will not change that. By the power of Baal, we can tell your future, your prosperity, or your failures. Our gods even have the power to choose who among us will have your princess for his mate!"

With a cold glare, Jeremiah held Serejin's clearly arrogant gaze. The prophet's words came out slow and piercing: "It is clear that the tentacles of evil reach up from the bottomless pit and out of spiritual darkness to cover you and the people who live in this pristine land. Beware! None of the gods that you choose to call upon will have any power or influence over us. Only the one, true, and everlasting God of Israel has authority over his prophet and his future queen. He will be the one to choose her destiny!"

Serejin turned away from Jeremiah, appearing unimpressed. He took a step toward Teia. "Princess Teia Tamar, your prophet is mistaken. If you stay in Erin, it will be our traditions and laws that you will find just and true. You will find our gods are the ones to worship. If you doubt, let us show you our sorcery. Let us show you the power of our gods. In a few days, one hour before your formal welcoming ceremony, join us on the sacred hill and we will demonstrate our divining power."

"I will be present at the welcoming ceremony only because your king has graciously consented to our request to take refuge in his land," Teia said. "But know that the God of Israel will lead my life and select my betrothed. I submit only to his voice."

"We will be there," Jeremiah said. "With the pillow stone of Jacob—*our* pillar of witness."

"Bring whatever you wish." Serejin peered through narrowed eyes and sneered at the prophet. "In a few days, it will be revealed to all as to whose god has the greater power!"

"Teia," Jeremiah called on the morning of the welcoming ceremony. He knocked softly against her bedroom door. "Teia, I have something for you."

Teia opened the door and stared at the beautiful dress that Jeremiah held out in front of him. "Oh my! It's exquisite!" she said. "Where did you find something so beautiful?"

"I bought it when we were in Gibraltar. I used some of the gold coins I had to commission the making of this dress. King Elier also helped by assigning the best of his seamstresses to purchase the finest fabric, then design and create what would look like a royal gown. You were probably unaware that they watched you closely while we stayed in Elier's manor. Let us hope they had keen eyes in fashioning a dress that will fit you."

"Oh, it is … perfect!"

"I thought now would be a good time to give it to you, as you will represent the throne of Judah when you meet the king of Meath."

"So beautiful …" Teia said. Her fingers traced over the small pearls and crystal beads sewn around the neckline on the shimmering light-blue fabric.

"Coleen, one of the queen mother's attendants will be here soon to help you prepare and dress. Let her know if there will be anything else that you might need for today."

Teia took the dress from Jeremiah, then gave him a sad smile. "I only wish Hannah was here. It's seems like such a special day. I wish I could share it with her."

"I know, Princess. I miss her too. Now that we are settled here, we can send word to her. You can tell her everything that's happened since you were last together. After she reads your letter, she can write back to you. If it be the Lord's will, there may be a day when you could sail back to Gibraltar, or Hannah could travel here, maybe even live here. We can hope and pray for what the future might bring."

The dress fit perfectly: close over the curve of Teia's chest, flat and tight around her small waist and slender hips, where several layers of silvery-blue fabric billowed out and down around her feet. The silky fabric fit snugly over her upper arms, then opened into loose bell shapes from her elbows to her wrists. Little pearls and crystals attached around the edge of her sleeves gleamed and sparkled as she moved, as did the gemstones on the flattering heart-shaped neckline that was low, but still modest.

"Oh, Princess, you look beautiful," Coleen said. She lifted up Teia's sheer veil from where it lay on a nearby table.

"Thank you for all your help. You thought of everything." Teia slipped her feet into the soft-leather shoes. "And you did wonders with my hair. I've never had such soft, beautiful curls. And the perfume … the fragrance is lovely. What is it?"

"The scent is from wild jasmine and from roses in the palace garden. Their petals are picked every spring when most fragrant, then made into perfume. The queen mother has many fragrances: some from apple blossoms, others from honeysuckle. But this one she seldom wears, but I know it to be the king's favorite."

Coleen placed the thin veil on Teia's head, and it fell softly over her face.

Then came three knocks at Teia's door. "Are you ready, Teia?"

"Yes, Jeremiah," Teia said. "Please come in."

"Oh, Princess," the prophet said upon entering. "Breathtaking. You are absolutely breathtaking. What a beautiful princess Yahweh has in you … on the outside as well as on the inside."

"Thank you, Jeremiah."

"I have one more gift for you. Something I had fashioned when we were in Egypt. I have waited for this day to present it to you."

Jeremiah then unfolded the linen fabric he held in his hands and lifted up a slender gold tiara that widened in the front—into the shape of the Star of David. One large polished red jewel was embedded in the center: a ruby, the gem that symbolized the tribe of Judah. Eleven smaller, various colored stones were affixed around the front base of the crown, each representing another tribe of Israel.

"Jeremiah … it's … spectacular."

Jeremiah placed the crown securely on Teia's head. "Princess Teia, are you ready to meet the king?"

"I think so. I'm not sure why, but I am actually quite nervous."

"You will be fine. Ready?"

Teia hesitated. *Should I ask if he found out if Eochaid will be there? No … I'm not sure I want to know.*

Finally, Teia nodded. "Yes, I'm ready."

She followed Jeremiah toward the door. *If he's not there, I'll ask someone about him. Yes … I'll ask the king. Surely he will know …*

CHAPTER 40

The palace provided a large carriage and several horsemen to take Teia, Jeremiah, Baruch, and the sacred stone to the grounds where the spring festival was being held. Ten Druid priests and a large crowd were already waiting when Teia stepped out of the carriage. Whispers echoed through the crowd as the onlookers caught a glimpse of the lightly veiled foreign princess with her exquisite gown that trailed behind her over the grass as she ascended the gentle slope.

The Druid priests led Teia, Jeremiah, and Baruch—who carried Jacob's pillow stone—to the top of the low mound. They stopped not far from the Druids' pillar of Baal, which stood about eighty feet to the north of the royal pavilion. There, seven empty chairs sat under a covered platform.

When Serejin saw that a large crowd had gathered to watch the priests perform their sorcery, he approached Teia. "Princess of Judah, we will now demonstrate the power of our gods. Gather the bows and arrows!" he shouted. "We will fire the Bow of Baal into the sky, and whoever the arrow lands closest to, he will be the chosen one—the one who will have the princess as his bride."

Teia stood quietly as she watched the arrow fly from the black bow. The dark shaft shot into the sky, then veered off to the left and disappeared into a grove of trees behind the hill. The chief Druid priest motioned for a second arrow to be placed in the bow. It flew off to the right, far above the crowds and landed in a marshy bog. The mass of people now covering the top of the mound scattered each time the wild spinning arrows flew over their heads as a third, fourth, and then fifth arrow were released in turn—all with similar results.

With no success in their efforts, the Druid priests decided that they should instead use the Bow of Strength, which had belonged to one of their ancient ancestors. The huge bow had only three arrows that fit it. Before it could be used, though, they had to find someone strong enough to string it.

The largest man they could find in the crowd was Ronan, one of the king's soldiers. The tall, broad-chested man moved to the center of the mound. He sat on the ground and placed his feet to the bow as he fit the nock at the end of the arrow into the string. With all his strength, he pulled back the arrow as he leaned his body toward the ground and fired the first arrow. The gold-tipped shaft disappeared high into the sky, then came straight down with a ray of bright light and hit the sacred Bethel Stone that Jeremiah had placed near the Druid pillar.

Jeremiah raised his hands and proclaimed to all who could hear, "The arrow striking this stone, which represents the House of our God, makes known to all that our princess is first and foremost betrothed to the Lord Almighty and to his Law, humbly serving her people as the heir-apparent queen. It is not for man to decide whom our princess will marry! Yahweh mocks your priests! He uses them for his purpose as he also condemns the divining of issues by such use as your arrows."

The Druids ignored Jeremiah and instructed Ronan to use the second arrow, which was silver tipped. When Ronan let loose the string of the bow, the arrow shot straight up, then down through the fabric of the royal pavilion, where it landed in one of the seats in the center of the raised platform.

Because the chair was empty, and no one knew to whom it belonged, the Druid priests decided to have the soldier fire the last of the three arrows. As he released the lead-tipped shaft, it spun up the hill—stopping with a direct hit to the Baal pillar. The obscene sculpture exploded into the air. Small pieces of stone rained down and struck the Druid priests.

As Serejin watched what occurred, he remembered Jeremiah's words of warning. He wondered if perhaps the prophet had spoken the truth regarding the authority and ability of his foreign God—or if the prophet had used some kind of new powerful magic.

Along with everyone else gathered on the hill, Serejin found his attention suddenly drawn away from the Druid spectacle to the sound of cheers rising from the back of the crowd and then moving forward. The throng of people parted and bowed while opening a path for Eochaid, his brother, and the queen mother, who walked forward with guards all around them.

The royal family moved through the cheering crowds across the hill, then directly up the stairs of the raised platform. Eochaid glanced up at the torn canopy as he walked to his seat. He stopped in front of his chair, reached down, and lifted the silver-tipped arrow. Turning toward the multitude of people who were moving toward the pavilion, he asked, "Whose is this?"

The chief Druid priest pushed his way through the crowd. "Your Majesty, we have used the Bow of Strength and three arrows to divine whom the foreign princess will marry. That arrow … the one that landed in that seat—your seat, it seems—dictates that … that it is you, Your Majesty, whom our gods have chosen to wed the princess.

"Is that so?" Eochaid tossed the arrow to the ground in front of the priest. "No one will tell the king whom he is to marry! That is my decision, not yours or the gods! But before I make any announcements or start our spring celebration, I, along with the queen mother and prince of Erin, will first welcome our foreign visitors and member of royalty, who I am told are already here." Eochaid eyes scanned across the crowd.

"Yes, Your Majesty," the priest said, bowing.

———

"Yahweh walks with you, my Princess," Jeremiah whispered. He took hold of Teia's trembling right hand and guided her through the crowd toward the platform as Eochaid descended the stairs.

Teia's heart raced when she saw the faint image of Eochaid through the thin veil that covered her face. Teia and Jeremiah stopped several feet in front of the king as Teia lowered her head and made a deep curtsy. So caught up in this long-dreamed-of moment, she froze down on one knee, her pulse pounding and her body feeling almost faint.

"Please rise, Princess," Eochaid said. He leaned forward and held out his hand.

Teia placed her trembling left hand in the king's. His warm fingers wrapped gently around her palm. As he helped her up, the sleeve of her dress slid back and uncovered the gold torque. Jeremiah pulled back the hood on his embroidered cloak.

"King Eochaid, may I present Princess Teia Tamar, of the royal House of Judah."

Teia slowly withdrew her hand from Eochaid's and lifted her veil. With all her will, she raised her eyes to meet Eochaid's. She forgot to breathe as she searched his face.

Eochaid met Teia's gaze. He had never forgotten her hazel eyes or how Teia's lips curved into that sweet smile. She was even more beautiful now than when he had last seen her.

He finally broke the silence with no more than a whisper. "Welcome to Erin, Princess Teia."

Teia responded with a smile. She lowered her eyelids and pushed a few tears of joy onto her cheeks. His eyes told her: *He does remember.* In an instant, all the years apart melted away. It was as if they were once again alone on the seashore—once again falling in love.

"I … I can't believe you are here. How has this come to be?" Eochaid asked.

"The Lord God predestined this day, King of Erin," Jeremiah answered. "It was Yahweh who ordained this day, long before we ever met on the shores of Egypt. Do you not remember the words of my blessing to you?"

Eochaid nodded. "Yes … I remember them. But you said nothing about coming to Erin."

"My words to you of this day were: 'You shall hold a scepter, and will have a queen fair to see from the branch of David.' It seems Yahweh even used your Druid priests to proclaim what he long ago ordained."

As Eochaid began to respond, someone cleared their throat from behind them on the platform.

Eochaid turned around, then back to Teia. "It seems my brother and the queen mother are anxious to meet you. Princess Teia, may I escort you to your seat?"

She nodded and let Eochaid take her hand.

As Eochaid led Teia up the stairs, Jeremiah motioned toward Baruch, who had waited in the crowd to come forward and join them. The prophet approached Eochaid's mother first after ascending the stairs of the pavilion.

"Queen Noirenn," Jeremiah said, "by Yahweh's grace, we meet today. How you have been in my thoughts since the day the Lord revealed to me your son's heritage. Thank you for welcoming us to Erin. I am Jeremiah, servant of the Most High God, and this is Baruch, my trusted companion and a renowned scholar and scribe."

Jeremiah and Baruch both made a slight bow, then waited to be addressed by the queen.

Before she said anything, though, Eochaid moved toward his mother and said, "Mother! This is the prophet. The man I spoke of … the man I met in Egypt! And this is … I mean, may I introduce Princess Teia Tamar, from the land of Judah. Princess Teia, this is my mother, Noirenn, the queen mother of Erin."

Teia's dress billowed around her feet as she bowed low to Eochaid's mother. "I am honored to meet you, Queen Noirenn."

When the princess rose, Noirenn took Teia's hands in hers. And then Noirenn's breath caught when she saw the golden band on Teia's arm. "It is a pleasure to receive you, Princess Teia." Noirenn glanced from Teia to Eochaid and then to Jeremiah. "It is also an honor to meet you, Jeremiah, as my son has spoken highly of you. I also welcome you, Baruch. And this is my son, Collin, prince of Erin." Noirenn gestured with her hand toward Eochaid's brother, who sat beside her.

While watching the introductions, Eochaid forgot the huge crowd that stood on the hill and across the valley until his mother spoke again: "My King, will you do the honor, or would you like me to introduce our guests to the people?"

"Yes, of course, Mother. I will announce them." Eochaid walked to the edge of the platform. "People of Erin, we are honored this day to welcome to our land the great prophet Jeremiah, the scholar Baruch, and Princess Teia Tamar, of the royal House of Judah." Eochaid held out his hand and brought Teia forward. "They have traveled across the Great Sea from the kingdom of Judah, from their home is the city of Jerusalem. They are our kindred people.

"It is not by chance that they have arrived on our shores. Jeremiah is the prophet of Yahweh, the God of our ancestors, the God I have come to know from reading through the ancient scrolls ... the God I have come to believe to be the one and only true God."

Gasps came from behind Eochaid and from the huge crowd in front of him. Expressions of shock, then anger, crossed the faces of the Druid priests who stood just below the platform.

CHAPTER 41

Noirenn moved quickly out of her chair to Eochaid's side. "My son, I am surprised that you have found it necessary to express your new beliefs today!"

The queen mother turned away from Eochaid and lifted her hands to hush the restless crowd—and then she saw the expectant look on the face of Gweniss, who stood in a beautiful dress next to her parents near the stairs of the platform.

Noirenn moved close to Eochaid and whispered, "Due to the arrival of our distinguished guests, would the king want to delay his betrothal announcement today?"

"There was never going to be a betrothal announcement," Eochaid said. He raised his hands until the voices in the crowd finally subsided. "People of Meath, people of Ulster, people of Erin, hear me. There has been a change in our festivities today. Due to the arrival of our noble and royal guests, the announcement of my betrothal has been postponed."

Eochaid heard loud groans and jeers spread throughout the crowd.

"I will make my announcement soon!" Eochaid shouted. "When I do, we will throw a great party and will provide a grand feast for all who attend. All of you are invited when I promise you a celebration, greater than what we had planned today.

"Some of you watched our priests as they determined by the Bow of Strength whom I will marry. But it will not be the priests, but the king who will declare who will be your queen! For now, we will come together as we do each year on this day to celebrate our spring festival of Eostre. So let the parade and festivities begin." Eochaid motioned toward the musicians to start the music.

The king then waited to see the crowd begin to disperse before he turned back toward Teia and his mother. "Excuse me for a moment, Mother … Princess Teia." Eochaid gave a bow of his head, then moved with quick steps across the platform and down the stairs.

Teia watched Eochaid as he approached a beautiful girl at the front of the crowd. Soon, tears poured down the girl's face, and then she turned and ran through the crowd. Teia watched the young woman flee away from the king.

What did Eochaid say to her? Is she the girl Eochaid was going to announce as his queen?

Teia's eyes followed the dark-haired girl until she disappeared into the retreating crowd. Then Teia's attention was drawn back to the pavilion as Eochaid ascended the stairs with a red-haired man, who stopped and bowed to the queen mother before walking toward Teia.

"Princess Teia. I am pleased to see you again," the man said. He bowed his head, then looked up at her. "I am Aric, the king's first captain at sea and the commander of his army on land. I met you with the king … on the shores of Egypt."

"Oh … yes. I remember. Please forgive me for not being in a friendly mood that morning."

"No need for an apology, as I am sure we startled you and most likely caused some fear. Is your sister with you?"

"No. I wish she was. She is living in Eber, a land that you may know better as Gibraltar. I hope to sail back someday to see her."

"Well, it is a pleasure to see you again." Aric made another slight bow, then followed Eochaid across the platform to be introduced to Jeremiah and Baruch.

When the men's introductions continued with conversation, Teia turned to the queen mother. "May I ask what this celebration of Eostre signifies?"

"Eostre is our spring festival," Noirenn said. "There are many myths and legends of how it first began. Some tell of a fertility goddess named Ishtar. Others tell us of the goddess Eostre, who found an injured bird on the ground one winter. To save its life, she transformed it into a hare. But the transformation was not complete. The bird took on the appearance of a hare, but still retained the ability to lay eggs. So each spring, to honor the goddess who saved her life, the hare would decorate her eggs and leave them as gifts to the goddess." Noirenn turned in her chair to better face Teia. "Another legend says that the egg symbolizes Eostre's wholeness and her fertility. The golden yolk represents her lover, the sun god; its white shell is seen as the white goddess, who is known as our virgin goddess of spring.

This festival takes place on the day when the young sun god, Lugh, celebrates his sacred marriage with Eostre. Which is why … today was chosen for my son to announce whom he would select as his bride."

The queen mother turned away from Teia, then rose from her seat to walk forward and interrupt the men's discussion. "Would any of you gentlemen like to escort me to the spring festivities?"

Jeremiah was first to speak up: "I would be delighted. There is so much I wish to discuss with you. But first, if you would allow me, Baruch and I need to return our sacred stone to the chest that sits in the carriage we arrived in this morning."

"Collin, would you please come with us?" Noirenn asked. "Perhaps you will be needed to help Jeremiah and Baruch with this stone."

"Surely," Collin said. "I'll be glad to help—that is, if it is alright with the king. Will the king excuse me? Pleeeease, dear brother?"

Eochaid grinned. "We will talk later … *brother*."

"Will you also excuse me, Princess Teia?" Collin took one quick look back at his brother, smiled, and raised his eyebrows before he turned and followed Baruch down the stairs.

When the small group reached the top of the hill, they found the Druid priests assessing the damage done to Baal's pillar stone. The priests turned and watched Jeremiah, but said nothing in front of the queen mother as Baruch and Collin lifted opposite ends of the two poles fitted through the rings in the stone. Turning, they carried the stone down the hill.

When the foreigners and members of royalty were thought to be out of hearing range, one of the Druid priests picked up a piece of the shattered pillar from the ground.

"How could this happen?" he asked. "We have never seen a power that could defeat any of our gods."

His fellow priests remained silent, unable to answer.

Serejin knelt down and rubbed his hands over the stump of the stone, the only solid piece left standing in the ground. "I don't know—but I will find out. I will not allow anything or anyone to weaken the power of our sacred order!"

Eochaid sat quietly next to Teia on the platform. Only the soft rustle of the wind blowing through the trees broke the silence until Eochaid spoke: "I never thought I would see you again. Not here … not like this. Today, I was supposed to announce the maiden that I selected as my queen. She was to sit in that chair. And now … you sit in it next to me."

Teia nodded. "Before today, I was struggling with my faith," she said. "And then I saw you. It … doesn't seem real. I sit with you as if in a wonderful dream, and at the same time, I feel deeply ashamed that I didn't trust in my God."

Eochaid turned and looked at Teia. "It was a long time ago, when we met. I've grown and changed, as I suppose you have also. I had hoped, but I just … I just never thought I would see you again. I gave up on that possibility long ago."

"Indeed. I didn't know that I would ever come here … that I would ever see you again. I didn't know if you were dead or alive. It wasn't until days after we arrived that I heard the name of this land was Erin. And even then, we were told that the king's name, that your name, was 'Heremon.' It was only when I stood in the crowd today and heard your voice and saw your face … that I knew it was you. Why were we not given your real name?"

"'Heremon' is one of my names, but it's also my title. It declares my identity, my lineage. I come from what is known in our land as the 'House of Heremon,' a name given to all descendants of the son of Gallam Milesius, whose name was 'Heremon.' From him were descended, as far back as our legends and records tell, the first kings of Erin. My father was one of his descendants, as am I and my brother. The name 'Heremon' is frequently used by our people, substituted sometimes with my given name. They all know the name 'Heremon' refers only to me. I'm sorry that whoever gave you this name did not think that it would be misleading for you."

"Well … maybe it was better this way. Maybe it was better that I was surprised when I saw you."

A smile crossed Eochaid's lips. "You still wear my torque."

"You made me promise."

"Yes, I guess I did."

"I've …" Teia swallowed. She took a deep breath. "I have worn it every day since … since that night. There was a time, soon after you left, when I thought it best that I should take it off … but I never could."

"You never wed?" Eochaid asked.

"No. And you said you were not yet married?"

"No. I was supposed to wed my chosen queen soon after this festival." Eochaid paused before he continued. "I dreamt of you many times Teia, when I sailed from Egypt to Erin, and even long after I arrived home. But over time, the dreams stopped. And now here you are. I don't understand it. After all this time has passed, I still feel as if … as if it would be easy to start again where we left off."

Teia spoke just above a whisper: "I know. I feel the same. I don't understand it any more than you do. I don't understand how … how one night changed my life." Teia looked at Eochaid, who was now more man, more handsome, even more attractive to her then when they'd first met. She longed to feel his embrace. It took all her will to not reach over and touch him. She knitted her fingers tightly together in her lap.

"I have a trip planned in a few weeks," Eochaid said. "We are crowning a new king for our region of Leinster. I have to attend. But I'll have some time before I go. If you would like, we could spend some time together over the next couple of weeks or so. I would like to hear of your time in Egypt and how you arrived in Erin."

She nodded. "I would also like to hear of your travels home, becoming king. And even more, I would like you to tell me of how you came to know Yahweh as your God."

"Certainly," Eochaid said.

"May I ask …" Teia hesitated. "I met your mother. And you are now the king of the land. Is your … father not here, then?"

Eochaid looked out across the hill. "No, he is not here. He died before I returned home."

"I'm sorry. I shouldn't have asked. I just remember you speaking of him when I stood with Jeremiah in the harbor … when we were introduced."

"You remember what I said that long ago?"

"Yes." A blush rose on Teia's cheeks. "I think I can recall almost every word you spoke."

"I also remember quite a bit about when we first met … and the night when we last saw each other." Eochaid sat back and ran his fingers through his hair, pushing it back, away from his face. "Before we spend any time together, I will have to meet with the young lady you might have seen me speak to—the one that ran off crying."

"I understand," Teia said softly. "And, yes, I saw her." Teia looked away from Eochaid as she replayed the scene in her mind. "She's beautiful. I'm sorry if my arrival here today has caused a problem for you."

Eochaid shook his head. "No, you have nothing to be sorry about. You haven't caused any problems for me." Eochaid smiled. "I would have provided rooms in my castle if I would have known it was you and Jeremiah who had arrived in Erin. How strange that my name was hidden from you, and your name hidden from me." Eochaid stared off in the distance and was quiet for a moment. "Well, I think we should make an appearance at the spring festivities. It's actually my favorite festival of the year. May I escort you?" Eochaid stood and lowered his hand to Teia. "Just be ready for the whispers and stares that will soon come our way. Not only because you are a foreign princess, but because you will be the most beautiful young woman anyone in our village has ever seen."

As they moved through the crowds, Teia and Eochaid could hear some of the people gossiping about the king's declaration of new faith, his broken promise of announcing his queen, and the beautiful princess who walked by his side. But it didn't take long for most of the people's attention to return to their family and friends as they gathered around festively decorated booths that served their favorite foods and libations.

Teia and Eochaid talked for hours as they wandered around the fair grounds. They told each other some of the highlights of what had occurred in each of their lives since they had last seen each other. They stopped to see parents who smiled and laughed while watching their young children run with empty baskets, eager to fill them with the colored eggs hidden in the meadow.

It was near sundown when Eochaid and Teia gathered with Jeremiah, Baruch, Noirenn, and Collin, along with most of the people of Meath, below one of its tallest hills. There, they watched several men roll a huge wooden wheel to the top of the hill. As darkness began to fall, bright flames covered the wheel before it was released. The burning circle of light rolled down the hill into the empty field below, signifying that the day's festivities had officially come to an end. The villagers dispersed, believing the fire wheel would now bring the warmth and energy of the sun to their fields for the spring's first plowing and planting season.

———

While the people of Meath made their way back home to their villages, Serejin called the Druid priests together in their underground meeting chamber.

"You heard what he said! What he shouted to us and the entire kingdom! We will demand a meeting with Eochaid—and the queen mother. I want her there. King Ailill was no great friend to our order, but he never interfered, never rejected our rituals. He attended and even condoned our festivals. Eochaid is rarely present. Where was he on Samhain?" Serejin raised his clenched fists. "Where was he when we celebrated the winter solstice or Imbolc, Beltane, or Lughnasadh?

"I thought we had everything under our control. Nothing has gone our way since he became king! We need another sacrifice—a human sacrifice to make amends to our gods for the curse Eochaid has brought upon our land."

Chapter 42

Eochaid rehearsed what he would say as he guided his horse along the back roads, avoiding the main route as he urged his stallion forward into a fast pace. The king's wool tunic waved behind him, making a bright splash of purple and gold against the sea of green grass that surrounded the path he rode across.

Soon, Eochaid reined in his steed as he approached the village of Mullingar. He remained on the outskirts of the village and traveled at a slower pace behind the thatched-roof homes and village center as he led his horse closer to the manor of Ulster's army captain.

Before Eochaid even reached the bronze gate, it swung open, creaking on its metal posts as the king rode into the front courtyard.

"Welcome, Your Majesty," the gatekeeper said. "May I ask Your Majesty if it is the captain or his daughter whom I should inform of your most welcome visit?"

"You can let Gweniss know that I am here." Eochaid dismounted his horse and handed the man his horse's reins.

"Would Your Majesty like to see the maiden Gweniss inside the manor or here in the gardens?"

"Here will be fine."

A light breeze blew the curtains on the second-floor window. Gweniss stood behind them and watched Eochaid. She checked her face and hair in the hand mirror, then tugged down on her thin, low-cut gown before she left her room and hurried down the staircase.

"I am pleased to see you, Your Majesty," she said.

Eochaid turned toward the low, sensuous voice as Gweniss came across the front porch and down the stone path toward him. She stopped inches away, tilted her head slightly down, and peeked through her heavy dark lashes.

"I've missed you, Your Majesty."

For an instant, Eochaid thought he glimpsed something strange in Gweniss's face, a chill, wicked darkness behind her eyes. But it was only for an instant. He stared at Gweniss. She looked sultry and beautiful. The angry outburst Eochaid had planned now evaporated.

"We need to speak." Eochaid placed his hand gently on Gweniss's back and led her around the side of the manor. "Look, I want to explain what happened—or what didn't happen a few days ago. I've got a good reason for..."

Eochaid went silent and looked toward the second-floor widow, where he heard the sound of soft laughter. He noticed the curtains moving.

Gweniss followed his eyes, then put one finger to her lips as she took hold of Eochaid's hand.

"Let's talk over here," she said. "We'll have more privacy."

Gweniss led Eochaid through the garden, then under the shade of a large willow tree. Its branches hung low, concealing the stone bench beneath its leaves. As soon as they were hidden from view, Gweniss turned and embraced Eochaid. She made sure he could feel every curve of her tightly clinging body before she lifted her head and moved her lips toward his. Before Eochaid knew it, they were locked in a passionate kiss.

Gweniss was the first to pull away. A little out of breath, she asked the king, "What where you going to tell me?"

Eochaid stared at Gweniss and waited for his mind to clear. "I don't know what to do with you. I'm drawn to you like a bee to a flower." Eochaid ran his hands hard through his hair and steadied his breath. "You know that some flowers lure their prey by their nectar, their scent—their beauty. Then ... snap! They close their petals around their victim and suck the life out of them." Eochaid's voice began to rise. "Oh, they look beautiful, but beneath their appearance is something deceitful and evil. Is that you? Is that who you are, Gweniss?"

"What are you saying?"

"Is there anything that you have not told me?" Eochaid's eyes narrowed as he glared at Gweniss. "Would you dare to deceive your king?"

"What ... What do you mean?" Gweniss asked. Her face turned ashen. She swallowed hard, then sat down on the stone bench.

Eochaid moved directly in front of her. "I had planned to announce to the entire kingdom that you would be my bride—that was until I found out something about you that you have kept hidden from me. You know that I could have you killed for your lies!"

"I never lied to you." Gweniss lifted her hands under her hair and unclasped the silver chain she wore around her neck. As she drew the two ends together in front of her, she pulled the necklace up from the inside of her gown and revealed an amulet dangling on the end. Without looking up, she handed it to Eochaid.

The king lifted the oval charm in his hand and examined the carved figure of a bare woman wrapped around the phallic pillar symbol of Baal. His stomach twisted. "You're a Druid priestess." His words came out slow and thick, as if he had something sour in his mouth.

"Yes," Gweniss whispered. "I thought I would surprise you. I thought you would be proud. Young girls across this land hope all their lives to attain the role of priestess. You shouldn't be angry with me; you should be pleased." Gweniss raised her head a little. "Just think of the role I could play! Think of the loyal support you would have from the priests and priestesses. You know how valuable that can be. You know—"

Eochaid cut through her words: "You deceived me! Do you partake in all the Druid rituals? Where you involved in the Samhain festival? Tell me the truth of your participation in the annual Druid orgies!"

"I haven't … I mean … I didn't take part in the festival or any of the … the other rituals. I was waiting—waiting to see if you would choose me." Gweniss covered her face with her hands as she broke down. "I'm sorry … I'm … so … so sorry." Her face wet with tears, she looked up. "I love you, Eochaid … more than you could ever know. I thought I would surprise you. I thought … I truly thought you would be pleased. I'll leave … I'll leave the order. I'll do anything you want. Just don't … don't stop loving me."

Eochaid looked down at Gweniss. He watched her cry for a minute before his heart began to soften. Things had not gone as he had planned. Eochaid stood for several moments before he sat down and put his arm around Gweniss, who turned and clung to him.

"Alright, calm down … don't cry."

With Gweniss wrapped tightly around his chest, Eochaid looked into the sky and blew out a long breath.

"I'm going to need some time to think this through."

Chapter 43

A half-dozen wall torches provided a scant amount of light inside the large circular stone chamber. Nine Druid priests sat around the dimly lit room on rough-hewn sarsen benches. In silence, they watched their chief priest pace back and forth in front of them. Most of the priests whispered to each other as they shifted their weight occasionally from side to side while trying to find some comfort on the hard stone. Only the tongues of the torch flames continued to move when Serejin started to speak.

"We are seeing one of our New Year predictions come to pass. You all heard on Samhain when the god Baal declared that a new influence would soon be present in our land, which might mean danger to the kingdom; that our ancient rituals of worship handed down by our fathers would be challenged. Now not only do we have our king declaring his … his so-called faith to a new god, but we also have this prophet and princess who claim their god—Eochaid's god—is the only god! Word has reached me that this prophet plans to start spreading his beliefs among our people!"

Gamlair, one of the senior priests, stood. "Master Serejin, the priestess Gweniss, sent word to me that she met yesterday with the king and managed to sway him into not rejecting her—at least not yet. If the king still chooses her as his queen, then perhaps all will remain well and we can still carry out our plans."

"Let us hope so," Serejin said. "With our powers and potions, Gweniss can help us clear the king's head of this foreign god. Our sorcery brought her into the castle to seduce Eochaid. If he somehow rejects her, we will get rid of him and install the man we originally planned to have on the throne as king. The only other obstacle is the foreign prophet and princess. Our accomplice in the castle has sent word to me that this princess and the king have met before. That prophet must have worked some kind of powerful magic to make our arrow land in Eochaid's chair.

"Now … while we wait to see what happens between Eochaid and Gweniss, we will also prepare a plan to drive the three foreigners from our land. It won't be long before we will know what we will have to do. Since our last attempt to kill Eochaid failed, it is now up to our priestess to lure him into marrying her. If he doesn't, then we will have to find another way to get rid of the king."

The most recently initiated priest into the Druid order, Tarlach, now stood. "Master Serejin, is this really the best way for us to handle this … this problem? Is more death the only answer? We never had the meeting you first suggested with Eochaid. Perhaps he has no intention of doing anything to our order. So far he has done nothing to indicate that he will try to change our beliefs or rituals. I think we should—"

"Don't be foolish! Did you not hear what Baal predicted on Samhain?"

"Yes, I heard, but—"

"Well then, sit down!"

Serejin stared at the priest until he took his seat, and then he continued. "The king said he couldn't meet with us because he is preparing to travel to Leinster for the coronation of King Gilliam. That was quite handy for us when Eochaid disposed of Muirdach. Leinster's king was loyal to the way of our order, but he was too unpredictable. He would have been too hard to control as ard-righ. I should have seen that sooner." Serejin paused. "I think we now have the right man ready to take Eochaid's place. He is pliable, easy to mold into whatever we want him to be. One way or another, we will have a new king and our priestess as his queen."

The chief priest looked around at the others. "I will ask Gweniss to try and persuade Eochaid to see her once more before he leaves for Leinster. If she is not successful in securing her role as his queen, then we will have to move fast to put our man on the throne … and dispose of the three foreigners."

The wheat fields across the open plains of southern Ulster stood tall under the warmth of the midday sun. One narrow road thread its way through the waving stalks toward the small stone cottage that had been in Eochaid's family for centuries. Two horses riding some distance apart made their way along the rarely traveled path that led to the house.

"You're sure no one followed you?" Collin asked.

"I'm sure."

"You've played your part so well. My brother suspects nothing. Come here." Collin pulled Gweniss close and turned her around as he kicked the front door of the cottage closed behind them. "My little priestess. One way or another, you will be *my* queen." He lowered his head and ran his tongue up Gweniss's neck before roughly kissing her. "It's been killing me to stay away from you. And then knowing you were with *him*." Collin spoke the words through clenched teeth. "I thought everything was going to be easy when we received word that he was dead. I had the man that brought me that falsehood killed when my brother arrived home."

"Well, *you* didn't do so well with the poison wine," Gweniss said.

"Don't remind me. It was so easy when Muirdach and I planned everything. Father was already sick, so trying different potions was nothing unusual, to the point that he'd drink almost anything. I told him the wine had special healing herbs in it." Collin laughed. "I'm still not sure why Eochaid started to have his food and drink tasted. I don't know what made him suspect any danger to him."

"Maybe his new god warned him."

"Yeah, his Hebrew god. For weeks, he locked himself in that library reading parchments and scrolls. How likely is it for anyone to find a god in old goat skins?"

"Something changed him." Gweniss reached up and put her arms around Collin's neck. With her fingers, she played with the long locks of wavy brown hair that fell to his shoulders.

"Well, something is finally going to change for me," Collin said. He tightened his arms around Gweniss's waist. "No longer will I be invisible or left standing in Eochaid's shadow. Never again! When you become queen, it will be up to you to feed him the poison. Then with the help of the Druid masters, I will claim the throne as my own."

Gweniss put her finger to Collins lips. "No more talk of Eochaid. I am here with *you*."

Collin opened his mouth and bit down gently on Gweniss's finger. When she pulled it out, he swept Gweniss up in his arms and carried her down the hall and into the nearest bedroom.

"Well, what have you found out?" Serejin asked.

"Eochaid hasn't called on Gweniss or asked her to meet with him," Gamlair reported. "Collin told me that the king has been spending all his spare time with the foreign princess."

"So now we know what has to be done," Serejin said. "We will have to find a way to get the princess alone when Eochaid leaves for Leinster. We will use Collin to distract the prophet and his scribe. That prophet must have cast a spell on Eochaid. We will deal with the prophet later. First, we need to get rid of the princess."

Chapter 44

Elongated shadows moved across the stone walls and ceiling of the Druids' underground chamber as six of their most senior priests circled the fire pit, which was filled with burning mounds of juniper berries covered in pine tree sap. The gooey mixture sizzled in the flames and emitted a pungent scent throughout the dimly lit room.

Teia could hear her heart pound as she lay on the cold stone table. The priests and their servants had come and stolen her away in the night, then brought her here—wherever that might be. Now she felt sick, swallowing several times as she tried to hold down the contents of her stomach.

"What do you want with me?" she asked. "Your sorcery cannot harm me. It will only condemn you."

"Bravely spoken." Serejin's voice was almost a hiss. "It's your body and mind that we seek to destroy. It would be easy to just throw you over a cliff into the sea. But that's not our way. You might be surprised at what strong poisons can be made from such lovely flowers. Ragwort mixed with a little hemlock is all we will need."

Serejin held a small spray of yellow and white blossoms to Teia's nose. At the same time, the priests continued to move in a circle and chant softly while throwing small twigs and leaves into the fire. At various times, they sang and spoke incantations.

Strapped down and unable to move, Teia could only watch as the chief priest held her nose shut with one hand and then began to pour a crimson-colored liquid into her mouth, forcing her to swallow so she could take a breath. Teia choked down the liquid, then gasped. As air filled her lungs, her mind flowed with prayers for Eochaid, Jeremiah, Baruch, and for her sister and Benjamin and Ebed. She prayed to Yahweh to forgive her for turning away from him for so long even as she now felt his overwhelming presence and his peace. She listened to the words of the still, small voice that spoke within her: *"I am with you … Do not fear, for I am with you; do not be afraid, for I am your God. I will strengthen you; I will help you; I will hold on to you with My righteous right hand. I am with you … I am with you…"*

Teia couldn't tell how much time had passed, and then she felt like she was slipping into a dream. She struggled to keep afloat in a dark ocean, a numbing cold force dragging her under into deep, dark depths. With all her will, she tried to keep her eyes open, to stay awake, as if knowing that, once she slept, she would never wake up. When her eyelids finally closed, muffled sounds and distant voices swirled around her. They seemed far away, unfamiliar and incoherent.

As the poison worked its way through Teia's body, she couldn't see or hear Eochaid as he called to her.

"Teia! Teia!"

Eochaid cut the ropes around Teia and lifted her off the narrow stone slab. "Take a sample of what's in that caldron so we can find out what they gave her! Then gather the best physicians to the castle!" the king shouted.

Eochaid's soldiers continued to pour down the stairs into the underground chamber. Every member of the Druid order lay dead on the ground. The angry slashing force of Aric's sword left Serejin's robed, lifeless body crumpled on the ground several feet away from his head, which rested with eyes wide open against the wall.

For days, Teia's mind remained murky. She never could tell Eochaid or Jeremiah what had happened in the hours before she was rescued. Not that it was so painful to remember—she knew it hurt some, and was unpleasant, but no more than some sickness … But her memory of her kidnapping was still blurred from the ill effects of the poison. Teia made no effort to remember what she preferred to forget.

While Teia recovered, Eochaid brought the commanders of his army together.

"I want the rest of them out of Meath, out of Ulster!" Eochaid said. "Run them out or kill them! Destroy their temples, their pillar stones. I want nothing of the Druid order left standing!"

"Your Majesty, what should be done with … with the prisoners?" the chief guard asked.

Eochaid lowered his head and stared at the ground. "Where are you keeping my brother?"

"In the dungeon."

"It would destroy my mother if I have him killed. If anything would have happened to Teia, he would already be dead by my hands." Eochaid ran his fingers across his forehead as if to collect his thoughts, then looked up. "Banish him … and Gweniss. Let them have each other. Take them to one of the small islands off our west coast. They are never to be allowed back on our mainland. I don't want to see either one of them ever again!

"All I want to remember about my brother is the look of shock and fear that came across his face when he came running out of our old country home when I rode up with my troops. He didn't even try to run. Just stood there." Eochaid shook his head, then rose from the throne.

He walked down from the dais and over to the lone remaining Druid priest from the local order. "Tarlach, I don't know how to repay you for what you did. You are free to go or to stay in my castle, or in the country manor where you could spend some time with Jeremiah and Baruch. Ask whatever you wish, and I will grant it to you."

The Druid priest bowed his head. "My king … I thank you." He lifted his face and looked at Eochaid through watery eyes. "Yes, I would like to meet with the prophet Jeremiah. If there is room for me in the manor, that would be my choice of a place to stay, at least for a while, as it seems all that I knew will soon be gone. Yes, perhaps the foreign prophet could help explain what prompted me to betray my order." Tarlach shook his head "I am still at a loss for what compelled me to travel by coach to Leinster to warn you of Serejin's plans. There must be a power at work here that is far greater than the gods I have worshipped all my life."

Eochaid smiled. "There is, and you will find no one better than Jeremiah to tell you all about him."

Chapter 45

Teia stood under the white-rose-covered arch in a gown that shimmered from the array of small jewels embroidered onto the white fabric. A long, finely spun lace veil was held in place by her gold crown. Next to Teia stood Eochaid, wearing a long white-and-gold tunic with a matching wool mantle that just touched the ground around his feet. On his head, he wore the crown of the ard-righ. No other jewelry or adornment was worn by the bride and groom, except for each one wearing a single, matching band of gold around one of their wrists.

Jeremiah, as God's representative, stood in front of the couple and began the wedding ceremony. The prophet joined the hands of the prince and princess as they each placed one foot on the sacred stone that sat on the ground between them. With a shawl covering his head, Jeremiah closed his eyes, then raised his hands in prayer.

"You, O Lord our God, created everything for your glory. You, O Lord our God, the Sovereign of the world, created man in the image of your own likeness. Blessed are you, O Lord our God, who fashioned the woman out of man. I humbly ask this day for your blessings to fall upon this man, Eochaid, and this woman, Teia Tamar. May your blessings and love fill their hearts as they live together forever as beloved companions."

Jeremiah uncovered his head and turned toward Eochaid. "King of Erin, you were marked since birth for this day. From your mother's womb, you arrived into this world as a descendant of Jacob's son, Dan, and through the seed of your father, you are descended from Jacob's son, Judah, through the line of Zerah. Today, I join you in marriage to Princess Teia Tamar, descendant of Judah through the line of Perez. Through the two of you, the House of Judah and the House of Israel are now reunited. May the Lord our God pour out his blessings on your lives and on the everlasting throne of David that you have this day restored."

The young boys and maidens of Erin were clad in white wool raiment, walking with their parents who had arrived in their most elegant attire. The aroma of roses and jasmine filled the Great Hall, while soft flickering light from hundreds of honeycomb candlesticks provided a warm glow throughout the grand space.

The roads that led up the hill to the hall were lined with men and women who cheered as the king and queen appeared after the ceremony at the hall's entrance. With the queen mother standing beside them, Teia waved to the crowds as she leaned on her bridegroom's arm, showing an expression of queenly dignity mixed with an obvious tenderness and affection for the man she'd loved since first meeting him.

From that day forward, the marriage of Eochaid and Teia was forever symbolized on the new flag that Eochaid had commissioned to be flown across the land of Erin. The flag displayed the red hand of Zerah, fitted on the Star of David, under a single royal crown that symbolized to all the union of Yahweh's two-kingdom nation.

———

Tara's Hill, Erin: 577 BC

The children's laughter caught Teia's attention as she and Eochaid spread a blanket over the grass on one of the highest hills in Erin. Teia glanced up to see Hannah's daughter hold on to her mother's hand as Hannah led her little girl and Teia's two sons under Baruch and Ebed's human bridge of outstretched arms. Around and around they went, until they all fell laughing to the ground.

Teia's four-year-old son, Ailill, pleaded with his aunt, "Do it again … Do it again!"

Teia smiled as she watched the children play together before she sat down between Eochaid and Jeremiah. Once seated on the blanket, Teia reached over and placed her hand softly over the prophet's.

"Do you really have to leave tomorrow?" she asked.

"The time has come. I have already stayed too long. I am content knowing that the Bethel Stone rests safely in your throne room and will be used during the coronation ceremonies of Judah's descendants … your descendants. I have been blessed to witness the birth of your children and have seen Yahweh's teachings spread throughout this land." Jeremiah patted Teia's hand. "But there are places to the north and to the west that now call to me. They have not yet heard the word of our Lord. My mission from Yahweh, to build and plant, is almost over. But as long as these feeble legs will carry me, I will plant the word of the Lord in the hearts and minds of all who will listen."

"I can't bear to think of you being gone. I've dreaded this day." Tears glistened in Teia's eyes. "You will come back, won't you?"

"I will try. But while Baruch, Ebed, and I are away, it will be up to you and Eochaid to keep Yahweh's Law established here. As your little ones grow, they must learn, as you did, to love the one holy God of Israel. But before I leave, I must give you the word of the Lord that last came to me. These words should be passed down to your children and grandchildren, and they to their children, and so on and so on.

"One day, Almighty God will send his Anointed One. Know and teach your children that *this* son of David with be both the Son of Man and the Son of God. He will be the everlasting King who will reign from his throne in Zion. He will reunite the descendants of the twelve tribes of Israel, as they and all who live on the earth will know him as their Messiah—their Redeemer."

Teia nodded.

"God spoke through his prophet Micah when he wrote that one day a child will be born in the land of our fathers—in Bethlehem," Jeremiah said. "The Son of God will be given to all of creation. He will be the light and the spirit of truth that will dwell within the hearts and souls of his people. He will bring sight to the blind and hearing to the deaf; the lame will walk and the dumb will speak. He will be Immanuel—God with us.

"Many seasons, though, may pass before this occurs. But how blessed they will be, those who with their eyes will look upon him, and with their ears will hear his voice—at least, I pray it is so. Sadly, I have witnessed too many times how our people have rejected and turned their hearts and minds away from Yahweh, his word, and his prophets. I pray that they will recognize and not reject their Messiah when he comes."

Eochaid lay quietly on his side, facing Teia, as her conversation with Jeremiah continued. He reached over the edge of the blanket and plucked a dandelion stem from the ground. He twirled it in his fingers before holding it still. He focused his eyes on the tiny, feather-like seeds that formed the white circular ball. When he realized the voices next to him had become silent, he held out his hand.

"Teia. Here, this is for you. Make a wish."

Teia took the slender stem in her fingers, then paused as she looked around. She watched Hannah sitting in a circle with Baruch and Ebed as they played games with the three children. She glanced toward Jeremiah on her left, then back to Eochaid, who was watching her.

She leaned down to Eochaid. Her hair fell like a soft curtain around their faces as she gave him a tender kiss, then whispered, "Yahweh has given me everything I would wish for."

Teia smiled. Then, raising her hand in the air, she waved the dandelion back and forth and watched the fluffy seeds take flight and float away.

EPILOGUE

"I will establish your line forever
and make your throne firm through all generations."
–Psalm 89:4

United Kingdom: Present day

Paired lines of blue-and-yellow police motorcycles led the stone's procession away from St. Gil's Cathedral. They passed by a multitude of spectators who leaned against metal gate barricades that kept them from spilling off Edinburgh's sidewalks and into the path of the moving vehicles.

The waving hands and cheers continued to be seen and heard throughout the populated cities and towns, but disappeared as the motorcade sped onto the M8 Highway. The closely guarded convoy traveled throughout the day and night, arriving in the late morning in the rural town of Roxburgh. There, the stone's vehicle stopped in front of the Coldstream Bridge that spanned the River Tweed.

The river marked the border between Scotland and England, where sixty Coldstream Guards stood at attention along both sides of the bridge in their bright red coats, black trousers, and tall bearskin hats. An elaborate transfer ceremony soon began when Scotland's Secretary of State and Britain's Duke of York met at the middle of the bridge.

When the short speeches by both distinguish public figures ended, England formally took possession of the stone, which had been on loan to Scotland since 1996. His Majesty's Royal Marine Band played "Procession of the Nobles" while they marched behind the stone's vehicle when it crossed the bridge and entered England.

The king's cavalry regiment led the motorcade for several hours through the English countryside and after one overnight stop, moved south toward the heart of Britain's capital, where the stone's arrival at Westminster Abbey was broadcast around the globe.

The dean and members of the Chapter of Westminster met the procession at the east door of the abbey. The dark circles under the clergymen's eyes revealed their sleepless night as they waited for the ancient stone to arrive in London and safely back into their care.

In a few days, Dean John Hall would crown Charles Philip Arthur George as the next king of England. The dean knew that he could not conduct the sacred coronation ceremony without this same block of stone that had been present during the coronation of England's previous kings and queens, Scotland's kings, and before them, all the high-kings of ancient Ireland.

With King Edward's thirteenth-century coronation chair already in position facing the golden altar in the center of the Abbey's Sanctuary, the stone was carefully placed on the shelf beneath its seat. The dean let out a sigh of relief, then stepped up to a small podium to address the members of royalty, the clergymen, and the large group of local and international press who were present.

With a smile, he welcomed everyone to the abbey, along with those who were viewing the proceedings across the United Kingdom and around the world. He spoke briefly about the importance of the stone being returned to England and to the abbey for the upcoming ceremony.

"I will close my speech with a statement that I feel sums up the significance of the coronation stone," the dean said. He lifted a small piece of paper in his hand. "I will read for you a quote regarding the stone, taken from the book *Memorials of Westminster Abbey*, written by Dean Stanley, one of the stone's former custodians:

"'It is the one primeval monument which binds together the whole Empire. The iron rings, the battered surface, the crack which has all but rent its solid mass asunder, bear witness of the English monarchy—an element of poetic, patriarchal, heathen times, which, like Araunah's rocky threshing floor in the midst of the Temple of Solomon, carries back our thoughts to races and customs now almost extinct; a link which unites the Throne of England to the traditions of Tara and Iona."

Five days later, at precisely eight o'clock in the morning, a team of eight gray stallions pulled an ornate golden coach through the gates of Buckingham Palace under a clear blue sky. Along each side walked ten uniformed coachmen. Inside the carriage, King Charles sat in his full-dress naval uniform as his coach followed a royal procession to Westminster Abbey. At his side sat Camilla, dressed in an exquisite white satin gown with gold and silver embroidery. The royal couple waved to the multitude of spectators who lined the streets of London.

Charles heard camera shutters click in rapid succession as a roar rose up from the crowd when he stepped from his coach. Trailing from the shoulders of his elaborate gold-adorned uniform was the six-yard-long royal Robe of State. Four men of honor straightened the robe behind Charles as he entered the west door of the abbey.

Immediately, as tradition dictated, the king was welcomed with verses sung from Psalm 122 in the Bible:

"I was glad when they said unto me,
We will go into the house of the Lord.
Our feet shall stand in thy gates, O Jerusalem.
Jerusalem is built as a city that is at unity in itself.
O pray for the peace of Jerusalem:
They shall prosper that love thee.
Peace be within thy walls, and plenteousness within thy palaces."

The procession into the abbey began in front of Charles, with dukes, earls, and admirals leading the way. Dressed in heavy ceremonial robes, the men swayed from side to side as they walked up the abbey's center aisle. They carried silver swords, golden scepters, the sovereign's orb and coronation ring, and, on a velvet pillow, the solid-gold and bejeweled King Edward's Crown, used for centuries to crown British kings and queens.

The crown sparkled under the abbey's lights with its 444 precious stones. The largest of these were the twelve stones that encircled the crown's base. The number and the coloring of these stones were identical to those that God commanded Israel's high priest to wear on his breastplate, each signifying one of Israel's twelve tribes—and together representing God's kingdom-nation.

The king's coronation day was an occasion of elaborate pageantry and celebration, but once in the abbey, it became a reverent religious ceremony that culminated with the anointing of the king with consecrated oil.

As the anointing service began, Charles looked up at the mosaic picture of *The Last Supper,* which stretched behind the altar, and then he took his seat in King Edward's Chair. In silent prayer, he prepared himself for the most sacred part of the service, which would be concealed from all but those who participated in the ancient ritual. It would not be photographed, videotaped, streamed, or televised. To shield the king from public view, four Knights of the Garter came forward and held a canopy of golden silk above him.

The archbishop and dean of Westminster approached Charles with the fourteenth-century ampulla and the anointing spoon. The dean lifted the six-inch-tall golden vessel—in the shape of an eagle—and poured a small amount of oil out of its beak into the twelfth-century, silver-gilt spoon. With his right thumb, the archbishop dipped his finger into the oil, then anointed the king in the form of a cross on the palms of both hands, over his heart, and finally over his head as he prayed:

"Be thy head anointed with holy oil, as kings, priests, and prophets were anointed: And as Solomon was anointed king by Zadok the priest and Nathan the prophet, so be thou anointed, blessed and consecrated King over the peoples, whom the Lord thy God hath given thee to rule and govern."

The silk canopy was removed when the anointing service ended. Charles was then presented with the royal and sovereign's scepters. Once holding these symbols of kingship in each of his hands, all in attendance stood. The guests this day represented 130 nations and territories, in addition to British royalty, church leaders, commonwealth prime ministers, members of the royal house, and civil and military leaders. They all watched a ceremony that had been conducted essentially the same as it has been for over nine hundred years, as each king or queen was crowned sitting over the sacred Bethel Stone in King Edward's Chair.

With the abbey in complete silence, the archbishop stood in front of Charles with the coronation crown in his hands. He raised his arms in the air, then reverently placed it on the king's head as he prayed:

"O God, who crowns thy faithful Servant with mercy and loving kindness: look down upon this thy servant Charles, our king, who now in lowly devotion bows his head to thy Divine Majesty; and as thou does this day set a crown of pure gold upon his head, so enrich his royal heart with thy heavenly grace, and crown him with all princely virtues which may adorn the high station wherein thou hast placed him, through Jesus Christ our Lord, to whom be honor and glory forever."

The dean of the abbey walked forward and received the scepters from Charles, who then opened the palms of his empty hands. The archbishop placed a purple-velvet-bound Bible in the king's fingers, then prayed: "Our gracious King, we present you with this Book, the most valuable thing that this world affords. Here is wisdom. This is the royal law. These are the lively Oracles of God."

As the ceremony neared its completion, a final acknowledgement of Divine Providence was given by the choir, who sang out the words inspired by King David's twenty-first Psalm:

"The king shall rejoice in thy strength, O Lord. Exceedingly glad shall he be of thy salvation. For thou hast presented him with the blessings of goodness; Thou hast set a crown of pure gold upon his head."

This final historic moment was viewed simultaneously around the world. Church bells rang out across the United Kingdom as a twenty-one gun salute was fired from the Tower of London. Many stood in their homes, on the streets, and wherever else they watched the global broadcast. All joined together with those in the abbey with loud and repeated shouts: "God save the king! God save the king!"

The midday's sun illuminated the blue, red, and gold colors displayed in the twenty-four panels of stained glass that stood high above the western front door of the abbey, where every important procession always entered, and where all those who had witnessed the coronation ceremony now filed out.

Most didn't notice the window above them, though. They talked among themselves about the beautiful ceremony, the music, the hats, and the jewels that hung from the ears and necks of the female aristocrats. Some conversations could be heard discussing the attire worn by the royal family, William and Kate's children, or how handsome Prince Harry looked in his highly decorated military uniform.

Some exiting the abbey glanced up briefly and admired the colorful glass above them, but took no notice of the figures depicted there before lowering their eyes as they moved closer to the open door.

Among the crowd moving slowly down the abbey's center aisle, two portly, elderly men walked side by side with their eyes fixed on the glass window. One of the men pointed up to the window.

"There's the whole story, displayed in life-size for everyone to see."

"Yes, indeed, Timothy, there they are. Ah … yes. The standing figures on the top row: Abraham, Isaac, and Jacob. Below them, Jacob's sons: the leaders of the twelve tribes of Israel, shown in the order of their birth—Ruben, Simeon, Levi, Judah, Dan, Naphtali, Gad, Asher, Issachar, Zebulun, Joseph, and Benjamin. And look at who stands next to Benjamin ... Moses, holding the tablets of the Law, and Aaron, dressed in his priestly garments. It's just so beautiful."

"Yes, Jerome, it is splendid—especially at this time of day, the colors are so vivid. The bottom row is also magnificent, with the emblems of Moses and Aaron on each side of the three-paneled depiction of the Royal Coat of Arms of the British monarchy. You and I know that the window proclaims to all who enter and exit this grand house of worship, Britain's rightful place within this family. Yet, sadly, most don't notice or care to understand its meaning ... just like the meaning of the coronation stone itself." He shook his head, then looked down as they neared the door.

"Oh my, it's bright out here," Timothy said. He held one hand over his bushy gray eyebrows and squinted in the sun as the two men made their way down the abbey's front steps.

Jerome pulled his folded wool cap out of his side suit pocket and fitted it over his thinning gray hair. "What do you think about stopping for a cup of tea? The entrance to the abbey's café is just up ahead."

"Hmm ... yes, that sounds good. Let's hope they still have a few open seats."

The two men continued their conversation as they waited in line.

"What wonderful memories we will have of this trip," Jerome said. "Traveling from Ireland to Scotland to see the procession that brought the stone to St. Giles. And then to London to witness the coronation ceremony—"

"Gentlemen, we can seat you now if you don't mind sharing a table with someone else," the café's hostess interrupted. "Otherwise, it could be another twenty minutes or so before another table opens."

"I don't mind sharing a table," Jerome said. "What do you think, Timothy?"

"Considering how crowded it is, I think we should take any seats that are available."

"Very well, then if you gentlemen would please follow me." The hostess led the men to an oak table along the wall where two men were already seated.

"Thank you for sharing your table with us," Timothy said.

He smiled and tipped his head toward the men, both of whom appeared to be in their forties.

The man sitting on the aisle, where Jerome took a seat, moved a few plates over to make more room on the table.

"Please, by all means, join us," the man said. A friendly smile spread within the frame of his long mustache. "We're just finishing up the last of our lunch."

Jerome and Timothy reviewed the single-sheet menu, then placed their orders for the afternoon tea special. When their food and drinks arrived, Jerome laid his napkin across his lap before taking a sip of his earl grey tea, followed by a bite of an orange-flavored scone. He dabbed the corners of his mouth with his napkin, then resumed his conversation with Timothy as the other two men spoke to each other.

"Well, my friend, we have seen the last coronation to take place with Jacob's pillow stone in the abbey … unless something happens to Charles in the next few years, then William will be the last king to be crowned. That would be fitting, as everyone seems to love William and Kate."

"Yes, it would be good to have William on the throne when, as the Scriptures say, 'The scepter will not depart from Judah, nor the ruler's staff from between his feet, until he comes to whom it belongs and the obedience of the nations is his,'" Timothy quoted. "Do you realize how extraordinary it is that we are alive at this point in human history? We are truly favored."

The man sitting next to Jerome turned in his seat. "Excuse me," he said. "I'm sorry for the intrusion, but I couldn't help but to hear you say that the last coronation has taken place with the coronation stone in the abbey. Is something going to happen to the stone or the abbey?"

The elderly men exchanged a quick glance at each other before Jerome responded, "No, nothing that we know of will happen to either one of them. It is what is written in this book that reveals future events." Jerome slid his hand under his jacket and removed a small, tattered leather-bound Bible. He held it in his hands as he continued to speak. "It's all in here: the beginning, the story of mankind, the end of life on earth as we now know it, and all that comes in between. It's all in here." He set his Bible on the table and reached out his right hand. "My name is Jerome. I am a pastor for a church in Ireland, and this is Timothy, my friend and fellow pastor."

"It's a pleasure to meet you." The man returned a firm handshake. "My name is John, and this is my brother, David." He gestured across the table. After handshakes were exchanged, and everyone was settled back into their seats, John continued. "I'm a writer from the United States, doing some research over here on the British monarchy and the coronation ceremony, so your comments piqued my interest. So, if nothing is going to happen to the stone or the abbey, then may I ask again what you meant by today's coronation being the last one to take place there?"

"Many biblical scholars believe we will soon see what is called the 'end of days,'" Jerome said. "Some say the promised Messiah will come on what is known as a 'Jubilee year,' in the fall of 2033, after the blood moons appears during Rosh Hashanah."

"Well, it is not certain," Timothy interjected. "What I mean is, no one is certain of the time of the next Jubilee year. Some rabbis believe the Jubilee year is somewhere between the years 2029 and 2036."

"Well, we do know that the next series of blood moons will appear in the years 2032 and 2033," Jerome said. "All will see the red moon in the sky on the Feast of Passover, and then again during Rosh Hashanah, on the Feast of Tabernacles, in the year 2033."

"It sounds like you are talking about a tetrad," David said. "I've studied astronomy, so I'm familiar with the two-year string of four total lunar eclipses. A series of four together is rare. After the sixteenth century, none even occurred until the twentieth century. However, the frequency of these events has accelerated, especially since 1949."

"Yes, very good—once Israel again became a nation in 1948," Timothy said. "Israel has seen war come to their land during every tetrad that has occurred since then. The wars have been just shadows of the time of tribulation to come."

"Mmm. That's interesting," John said. "I've never heard about the cycles of the moon having a direct correlation with Jewish holidays and future biblical events."

"Well, if you would allow me," Jerome said. "I'll quote from the book of Joel, chapter two, verse thirty-one: 'The sun will be turned to darkness and the moon to blood before the coming of the great and dreadful day of the Lord.' In the book of Acts, chapter two, verse twenty, it reads: 'The sun will be turned to darkness and the moon to blood before the coming of the great and glorious day of the Lord.' And then in the book of Revelation, it is written in chapter six, verses twelve and thirteen: 'I watched as he opened the sixth seal. There was a great earthquake. The sun turned black like sackcloth made of goat hair, the whole moon turned blood red, and the stars in the sky fell to earth, as late figs drop from a fig tree when shaken by a strong wind.'

"There are other references about signs in the sky at the end of days in the books of Ezekiel, Isaiah, and others. Too many to quote for you now. You see, Almighty God set seven specific appointed times in all of man's history. Yeshua—Jesus—fulfilled the four spring feast days when he came as the Son of Man and the Son of God. He will fulfill the three fall feast days when he returns as the King of kings—exactly two thousand years from the time he was crucified!"

"Wow. Well, John and I are both Christians," David said. "So … if what you say is true, 2033 is not that far off, meaning we may all be alive to see Jesus return."

"Indeed! We may be," Jerome said.

"A lot of people who read the Bible take no notice of God's specific appointed times. It's rarely taught," Timothy said. "Messiah's birth is celebrated in December, although everything points to his birth as taking place in the fall, on Rosh Hashanah, the Jewish New Year—the birthday of the world. Most know Yeshua was sacrificed on Passover, yet seem to have no understanding of him being laid in the tomb on the Feast of Unleavened Bread, and then rising from the dead on the day known as Reshit Katzir, the Beginning of the Harvest of First Fruits. If I may quote Paul, from First Corinthians: 'But Christ has indeed been raised from the dead, the firstfruits of those who have fallen asleep. For since death came through a man, the resurrection of the dead comes also through a man. For as in Adam all die, so in Christ all will be made alive. But each in his own turn: Christ, the firstfruits; then, when he comes, those who belong to him.'"

"And you must be familiar with Pentecost?" Jerome said. "When, after Yeshua ascended into heaven, he sent the Ruach HaKodesh, the Holy Spirit, to dwell inside his followers. Pentecost to Christians is really the Feast of Shavuot that celebrates when mankind was given the Torah—God's words on tablets, and then on scrolls … until …" Jerome paused. "I love the way it is written in the first chapter of John: 'The Word became flesh and made his dwelling among us. We have seen his glory, the glory of the One and Only, who came from the Father, full of grace and truth.'

"The true light, which gives light to everyone, came into the world that had its being through him, and yet … the world did not know him."

Tears formed in the corners of Timothy's eyes as the four men sat quiet for a few moments.

"Are either of you very familiar with the book of Daniel and Ezekiel, or the Book of Revelation?" Jerome asked.

"Yes, but they are a bit obscure, easily misinterpreted," David said.

"Well, the times of trouble are ahead. There will be war in the Middle East—war with Israel—and then a period of peace when the temple will be rebuilt in Jerusalem. And then … for three and a half years, all will seem well and good. After that, an evil unlike no other will be unleashed on the earth, then soon after, most still alive will wish they were dead … until Messiah comes." Jerome stopped and looked down at his Bible. "There are over three hundred scriptural prophecies in this book that speak of the Messiah—his birth, his death, and his glorious day of return. I continue to marvel at the unending revelation of God's word. There's nothing on earth like it. Some rabbis say they are four layers of meaning in the Torah, but it wouldn't surprise me if there were even more."

"Well, I appreciate you taking the time to answer what I thought was a simple question—with all those scriptural references," John said. "You've given us a lot to think about." He took a last sip of tea. "I think it's time for David and me to surrender our seats to those still waiting in line." He put a £5 note on the table, then pushed his chair back and rose from his seat. "It was a pleasure meeting both of you."

John and David said their farewells, then left the café.

Timothy poured more tea into his cup, then sat back. "I wonder what will happen to the coronation stone. I know that some believe it will go to Jerusalem and be put into the new temple. But who knows what will happen to the stone, the coronation chair, the abbey, or even the temple itself in the last days? They may all be destroyed by events stemming from the fulfilled predictions of earthquakes, wars, famines, and all kinds of calamities that will fall upon the earth at the end of days."

Jerome nodded. "Well, it won't be too many years before we find out what happens to the stone. It won't be much longer until everyone on earth sees Yeshua coming on the clouds of the sky, with power and great glory. He will send forth his angels with a loud trumpet call, and they will gather his true followers from the farthest ends of the earth to the farthest ends of heaven. What a day that will be!" Jerome smiled as he lifted his Bible from the table and slid it back inside his coat pocket. "I love how the Good Book ends with Messiah's own words: 'Yes, I am coming soon.'"

"He will be great and will be called the Son of the Most High.
The Lord God will give him the throne of his father David,
and he will reign over the house of Jacob forever;
his kingdom will never end."

–Luke 1:32-33

A NOTE FROM THE AUTHOR

The fictional story of Teia and Jacob's pillow stone was inspired by ancient legends and myths that created a framework for the story of the stone's movement from Israel to ancient Ireland. Once it arrived there, it is believed the stone was used for over nine hundred years in the coronation of all Irish kings. A number of historical records follow the stone's movement from Ireland to Scotland in 575 AD, where it remained and was used during the coronation of all Scottish kings until 1296 AD, when England's King Edward I removed the stone from the abbey in Scone. Immediately afterward, he commissioned the makings of a chair that would hold the stone beneath its seat.

As of this writing, the stone resides only temporarily behind the glass case in Edinburgh Castle's Crown Room. The stone is not impressive; quite dull, in fact—a simple block of sandstone, roughly hewn, pockmarked, and cracked. But before the United Kingdom's next sovereign is crowned, this battered ancient stone will travel to London and will be set back into its designed resting place in King Edward's coronation chair in Westminster Abbey.

The tradition of the stone being the actual one that Jacob used at Bethel will never be proved; the details of its migrations from Israel through various countries to Ireland remain uncertain.

There are many legends: some similar to the one told in this book, but many quite different. Most, though, do tell of a princess and a prophet who long ago brought a special stone to the British Isles. One can dispute which myth is true and which is false. The fact will remain, for those who do their own research, that a stone, treated as sacred, did find its way to ancient Britannia.

For those with an interest in perusing additional background materials used in the writing of this book, visit www.judahsscepter.com, or www.dabrittain.com, where numerous resources are available.

At the end of this book, I have included three appendices for your convenience. The first consists of some brief information related to the Hebrew religious calendar, which is referred to throughout this novel. Second, is a list of the biblical references you will find in the running text throughout this story. This will allow you to more easily read for yourself the biblical material I used to help create and shape the characters and story world in *Judah's Scepter*. Finally, a selected bibliography that contains a very modest sampling of several thousand works that could be potentially accessed, but I have included these specific works because of the role they played in crafting this tale.

If your curiosity has been roused on any of the above subjects, then dig deep into the biblical text and ancient history. You may be surprised by what you find.

I leave you with a quote from one of the famous writers and thinkers of the past—Sir Francis Bacon, who wrote:

"Read not to contradict and confute,
Nor to believe and take for granted,
But to weigh and consider—
Histories make men wise."

APPENDIX 1: HEBREW RELIGIOUS CALENDAR

NISAN (March-April)

- 14th Pesach (Passover—Yeshua's Crucifixion and Burial)
- 15-22nd Chag HaMatzot (Feast of Unleavened Bread/Feast of First Fruits—Yeshua's body in tomb before sundown on the 14th-17th)
- 17th Reishit Katzir (First Fruits-Beginning of the Harvest—Yeshua's resurrection)

IYAR (April-May)

SIVAN (May-June)

- 6th Shavout (Pentecost/Feast of Weeks)—Giving of the Torah at Mt. Sinai and the giving of the Rauch HaKodesh (Holy Spirit) to the (Christian church) true followers of Yeshua

TAMMUZ (June-July)
AV (July-August)
ELUL (August-September)

TISHRI (September-October)

- 1st Yom Teru'ah (Feast of Trumpets)—Some believe this date to be the future rapture of the Kellat Mashiach (the Christian church, or the Bride of Messiah Yeshua)
- 1st Rosh Hashanah (New Year's Day/Day of Creation)
- 10th Yom Kippur (The Day of Atonement)
- 15-22nd Sukkot (Feast of Tabernacles—Yeshua returns)
- 22nd Shmini Atzeret (Last Great Day—Ushering in of the millennial kingdom)

HESHVAN (October-November)
KISLEV (November-December)
TEVET (December-January)
SHEVAT (January-February)
ADAR (February-March)

The biblical year begins in the spring (Exodus 12:2). The Jewish day begins at sundown and ends at sundown on the following day. Feast days begin at sundown on the dates specified above.

The moon and its phases in the night sky are what determine the period of time for each month. The seasons of the year are marked with festivals or appointed times. All years are numbered: every seventh year is a Sabbatical year (Leviticus 25:2-5), and after seven cycles of seven years, the Jubilee Year is observed (Leviticus 25:8-17). The Talmud (Sanhedrin, 97 a-b) states that the Messiah will return during a Jubilee Year.

According to Jewish sages, the history of the world may be understood as seven 1,000-year "days," corresponding to the seven days of creation. The Talmud (Avodah Aarah, 9a) states that this world will only exist for 6,000 years, while the seventh millennium will be an era of worldwide peace called "the world to come." For Christians, the millennial kingdom will be a time when Messiah Yeshua reigns as King on the earth (Revelation 20).

APPENDIX 2:
BIBLICAL REFERENCES

Acknowledgement Page

James 1:17-18 (NIV)

"Every good and perfect gift is from above, coming down from the Father of the heavenly lights, who does not change like shifting shadows. He chose to give us birth through the word of truth, that we might be a kind of firstfruits of all he created."

Epigraph Page

Psalm 89:34-37 (NIV)

"I will not violate my covenant or alter what my lips have uttered. Once for all, I have sworn by my holiness—and I will not lie to David—that his line will continue forever and his throne endure before me like the sun; it will be established forever like the moon, the faithful witness in the sky."

Prologue

Page 4-5

Genesis 28:10-22 (NIV)

Jacob left Beersheba and set out for Haran. When he reached a certain place, he stopped for the night because the sun had set. Taking one of the stones there, he put it under his head and lay down to sleep. He had a dream in which he saw a stairway resting on the earth, with its top reaching to heaven, and the angels of God were ascending and descending on it. There above it stood the Lord, and he said: "I am the Lord, the God of your father Abraham and the God of Isaac. I will give you and your descendants the land on which you are lying. Your descendants will be like the dust of the earth, and you will spread out to the west and to the east, to the north and to the south. All peoples on earth will be blessed through you and your offspring. I am with you and will watch over you wherever you go, and I will bring you back to this land. I will not leave you until I have done what I have promised you."

When Jacob awoke from his sleep, he thought, "Surely the Lord is in this place, and I was not aware of it.' He was afraid and said, "How awesome is this place! This is none other than the house of God; this is the gate of heaven."

Early the next morning Jacob took the stone he had placed under his head and set it up as a pillar and poured oil on top of it. He called that place Bethel, though the city used to be called Luz.

Then Jacob made a vow, saying, "If God will be with me and will watch over me on this journey I am taking and will give me food to eat and clothes to wear so that I return safely to my father's household, then the Lord will be my God and this stone that I have set up as a pillar will be God's house, and of all that you give me I will give you a tenth."

Chapter 2

Page 15-16

Jeremiah 11:2-8, 10-12 (NIV)

"Listen to the terms of this covenant and tell them to the people of Judah and to those who live in Jerusalem. Tell them that this is what the Lord, the God of Israel, says: 'Cursed is the man who does not obey the terms of this covenant—the terms I commanded your forefathers when I brought them out of Egypt, out of the iron-smelting furnace.' I said, 'Obey me and do everything I command you, and you will be my people and I will be your God. Then I will fulfill the oath I swore to your forefathers, to give them a land flowing with milk and honey'—the land you possess today.

"Proclaim all these words in the towns of Judah and in the streets of Jerusalem: I warned them again and again, saying, 'Obey me.' But they did not listen or pay attention; instead, they followed the stubbornness of their evil hearts.

"They have returned to the sins of their forefathers, who refused to listen to my words. They have followed other gods to serve them. Both the house of Israel and the house of Judah have broken the covenant I made with their forefathers.

"I will bring on them a disaster they cannot escape. Although they cry out to me, I will not listen to them. The towns of Judah and the people of Jerusalem will go and cry out to the gods to whom they burn incense, but they will not help them at all when disaster strikes."

Chapter 9

Page 59

Jeremiah 42:9-16 (NIV)

"This is what the Lord, the God of Israel, to whom you sent me to present your petition, says: 'If you stay in this land, I will build you up and not tear you down; I will plant you and not uproot you, for I am grieved over the disaster I have inflicted on you. Do not be afraid of the king of Babylon, whom you now fear … for I am with you and will save you and deliver you from his hands. I will show you compassion so that he will have compassion on you and restore you to your land.'

"However, if you say, 'We will not stay in this land,' and so disobey the Lord your God, and if you say, 'No, we will go and live in Egypt, where we will not see war or hear the trumpet or be hungry for bread,' then hear the word of the Lord, O remnant of Judah. This is what the Lord Almighty, the God of Israel, says: 'If you are determined to go to Egypt and you do go to settle there, then the sword you fear will overtake you there, and the famine you dread will follow you into Egypt, and there you will die.'"

Chapter 11

Page 76

Genesis 49:8-10 (NIV)

"Judah, your brothers will praise you; your hand will be on the neck of your enemies; your father's sons will bow down to you. You are a lion's cub, O Judah; you return from the prey, my son. Like a lion he crouches and lies down, like a lioness—who dares to rouse him? The scepter will not depart from Judah, nor the ruler's staff from between his feet, until he comes to whom it belongs and the obedience of the nations is his."

Page 77

Jeremiah 1:9-10 (NIV)

"I have put my words in your mouth. See, today I appoint you over nations and kingdoms to uproot and tear down, to destroy and overthrow, to build and to plant."

Page 78

Genesis 17:5-7 (NIV)

"Your name will be Abraham, for I have made you a father of many nations. I will make you very fruitful; I will make nations of you, and kings will come from you. I will establish my covenant as an everlasting covenant between me and you and your descendants after you for the generations to come."

Page 79

Proverbs 8:17 (NIV)

I love those who love me, and those who seek me find me.

Page 81

Psalm 89:3-4 (NIV)

"I have made a covenant with my chosen one, I have sworn to David my servant, I will establish your line forever and make your throne firm through all generations."

Page 81

2 Samuel 7:16 (NIV)

"Your throne will be established forever."

<u>Chapter 12</u>

Page 86

Psalm 23:1-3 (NIV)

The Lord is my shepherd, I shall not be in want. He makes me lie down in green pastures, he leads me beside quiet waters, he restores my soul....

<u>Chapter 16</u>

Page 111

Jeremiah 29:13 (NIV)

"You will seek me and find me when you seek me with all your heart."

Page 111-112

Isaiah 55:10-12 (NIV)

"As the rain and the snow come down from heaven, and do not return to it without watering the earth and making it bud and flourish, so that it yields seed for the sower and bread for the eater, so is my word that goes out from my mouth: It will not return to me empty, but will accomplish what I desire and achieve the purpose for which I sent it. You will go out in joy and be led forth in peace; the mountains and hills will burst into song before you, and all the trees of the field will clap their hands."

<u>Chapter 19</u>

Page 134

Jeremiah 44:11-12 (NIV)

"I am determined to bring disaster on you and to destroy all Judah. I will take away the remnant of Judah who were determined to go to Egypt to settle there. They will all perish in Egypt; they will fall by the sword or die from famine. From the least to the greatest, they will die by sword or famine."

Chapter 20

Page 142

Psalm 23:1-3 (NIV)

The Lord is my shepherd, I shall not be in want. He makes me lie down in green pastures, he leads me beside quiet waters, he restores my soul. He guides me in paths of righteousness for his name's sake....

Chapter 23

Page 167

Psalm 19:1-4 (NIV)

The heavens declare the glory of God; the skies proclaim the work of his hands. Day after day they pour forth speech; night after night they display knowledge. There is no speech or language where their voice is not heard. Their voice goes out into all the earth, their words to the ends of the world.

Page 168

Deuteronomy 8:3 (NIV)

He humbled you, causing you to hunger and then feeding you with manna, which neither you nor your fathers had known, to teach you that man does not live on bread alone but on every word that comes from the mouth of the Lord.

Page 170

Jeremiah 44:12-14 (KJV)

"And I will take the remnant of Judah, that have set their faces to go into the land of Egypt to sojourn there, and they shall all be consumed, and fall in the land of Egypt; they shall even be consumed by the sword and by the famine: and they shall be an execration, and an astonishment, and a curse, and a reproach. For I will punish them that dwell in the land of Egypt, as I have punished Jerusalem, by the sword, by the famine, and by the pestilence: So that none of the remnant of Judah, which are gone into the land of Egypt to sojourn there, shall escape or remain, that they should return into the land of Judah, to the which they have a desire to return to dwell there: for none shall return but such as shall escape."

Page 171

Jeremiah 44:29-30 (NIV)

"'This will be the sign to you that I will punish you in this place,' declares the Lord, 'so that you will know that my threats of harm against you will surely stand.' This is what the Lord says: 'I am going to hand Pharaoh Hophra king of Egypt over to his enemies who seek his life, just as I handed Zedekiah king of Judah over to Nebuchadnezzar king of Babylon, the enemy who was seeking his life.'"

Page 173-174

Jeremiah 44:10-11 (NIV)

"To this day they have not humbled themselves or shown reverence, nor have they followed my law and the decrees I set before you and your fathers. Therefore, this is what the Lord Almighty, the God of Israel, says: I am determined to bring disaster on you and to destroy all Judah."

Chapter 24

Page 177

Exodus 20:2 / Deuteronomy 5:6 (NIV)

"I am the Lord your God, who brought you out of Egypt, out of the land of slavery."

Page 177

Exodus 6:6 (NIV)

"I will bring you out from under the yoke of the Egyptians."

Page 177

Exodus 6:6 (NIV)

"I will redeem you with an outstretched arm and with mighty acts of judgment."

Page 177

Exodus 6:7 (NIV)

"I will take you as my own people, and I will be your God."

Page 179

Genesis 28:13-14 (NIV)

"I am the Lord, the God of your father Abraham and the God of Isaac. I will give you and your descendants the land on which you are lying. Your descendants will be like the dust of the earth, and you will spread out to the west and to the east, to the north and to the south. All peoples on earth will be blessed through you and your offspring."

Page 180

2 Samuel 7:16 (NIV)

"Your throne will be established forever."

<u>Chapter 30</u>

Page 211

Jeremiah 44:14 (KJV)

"… for none shall return but such as shall escape."

Page 212

Jeremiah 44:13-14 (KJV)

"For I will punish them that dwell in the land of Egypt, as I have punished Jerusalem, by the sword, by the famine, and by the pestilence: So that none of the remnant of Judah, which are gone into the land of Egypt to sojourn there, shall escape or remain, that they should return into the land of Judah, to the which they have a desire to return to dwell there: for none shall return but such as shall escape."

<u>Chapter 33</u>

Page 235

Jeremiah 1:10 (NIV)

"See, today I appoint you over nations and kingdoms to uproot and tear down, to destroy and overthrow, to build and to plant."

<u>Chapter 44</u>

Page 300

Paraphrase of Isaiah 41:10 (NIV)

"So do not fear, for I am with you; do not be dismayed, for I am your God. I will strengthen you and help you; I will uphold you with my righteous right hand."

<u>Epilogue</u>

Page 309

Psalm 89:4 (NIV)

"I will establish your line forever and make your throne firm through all generations."

Page 311

Song lyrics inspired by Psalm 122:1-3, 6-7 (KJV)

I was glad when they said unto me, Let us go into the house of the Lord. Our feet shall stand within thy gates, O Jerusalem. Jerusalem is builded as a city that is compact together: Whither the tribes go up, the tribes of the Lord, unto the testimony of Israel, to give thanks unto the name of the Lord. For there are set thrones of judgment, the thrones of the house of David.... Pray for the peace of Jerusalem: they shall prosper that love thee. Peace be within thy walls, and prosperity within thy palaces.

Page 314

Song lyrics inspired by Psalm 21:1, 3 (KJV)

The king shall joy in thy strength, O Lord; and in thy salvation how greatly shall he rejoice! ... For thou preventest him with the blessings of goodness: thou settest a crown of pure gold on his head.

Page 317

Genesis 49:10 (NIV)

"The scepter will not depart from Judah, nor the ruler's staff from between his feet, until he comes to whom it belongs and the obedience of the nations is his."

Page 318

Joel 2:21 (NIV)

"The sun will be turned to darkness and the moon to blood before the coming of the great and dreadful day of the Lord."

Page 318

Acts 2:20 (NIV)

"The sun will be turned to darkness and the moon to blood before the coming of the great and glorious day of the Lord."

Page 318-319

Revelation 6:12-13 (NIV)

I watched as he opened the sixth seal. There was a great earthquake. The sun turned black like sackcloth made of goat hair, the whole moon turned blood red, and the stars in the sky fell to earth, as late figs drop from a fig tree when shaken by a strong wind.

Page 319

1 Corinthians 15:20-23 (NIV)

But Christ has indeed been raised from the dead, the firstfruits of those who have fallen asleep. For since death came through a man, the resurrection of the dead comes also through a man. For as in Adam all die, so in Christ all will be made alive. But each in his own turn: Christ, the firstfruits; then, when he comes, those who belong to him.

Page 320

John 1:14 (NIV)

The Word became flesh and made his dwelling among us. We have seen his glory, the glory of the One and Only, who came from the Father, full of grace and truth.

Page 321

Mathew 24:30-31 (NIV)

"They will see the Son of Man coming on the clouds of the sky, with power and great glory. And he will send his angels with a loud trumpet call, and they will gather his elect from the four winds, from one end of the heavens to the other."

Page 321

Revelation 22:20 (NIV)

"Yes, I am coming soon."

Page 321

Luke 1:32-33 (NIV)

"He will be great and will be called the Son of the Most High. The Lord God will give him the throne of his father David, and he will reign over the house of Jacob forever; his kingdom will never end."

APPENDIX 3: SELECTED BIBLIOGRAPHY

Allen, Bishop J. H. *Judah's Sceptre and Joseph's Birthright.* (Massachusetts: Destiny Publishing, 1917).

Bennett, W. H. *Symbols of Our Celto-Saxon Heritage.* (Ontario: Canadian British Israel Association, 1976).

Benson, Reed. *The Anglo-Israel Thesis.* (Missouri: Watchman Outreach Ministries, 2013).

Breeze, David. *The Stone of Destiny, Symbol of Nationhood.* (Edinburgh: Historic Scotland, 1997).

Capt, E. Raymond. *Jacob's Pillar, A Biblical Historical Study.* (California: Artisan Sales, 1977).

Connon, Wallace F. *The Stone of Destiny.* (London: The Covenant Publishing Co. LTD., 1951).

Dickey, C. R. *One Man's Destiny.* (Massachusetts: Destiny Publishing, 1951).

Glover, F. R. A. *England, the remnant of Judah and the Israel of Ephraim.* (London: Rivingtons, 1881 / Digital reprint by University of Michigan Library, 2014)

Goodchild, J. A. *The Book of Tephi.* (London: Kegan Paul / London: Trench Trubner & Co. LTD, 1897 / Digital reprint by Cornell University Library, 2010).

Herodotus. "Herodotus Histories – Book II." Translated by G. C. Macaulay. *Classical Wisdom Weekly,* accessed July 8, 2015.
www.classicalwisdom.com/greek_books/herodotus-histories-book-ii/.

Hyde, Douglas. *A Literary History of Ireland: From Earliest Times to the Present Day.* (New York: Charles Scribner's Sons, 1901 / Digital reprint by Cornell University Library, 1999).

Kissick, Robert G. *The Irish Prince and the Hebrew Prophet.* (New York: Masonic Publishing Co., 1896).

Morris, Alfred. *Eochaid the Heremhon: Or, The Romance of the Lia Phail.* (London: Robert Banks & Son, 1900).

Totten, Charles A. L. *Our Race and its Origin and Destiny.* (Connecticut: Our Race Publishing Co., 1897 / Republished, London: Forgotten Books, 2012).

Totten, Charles A. L. *The Romance of History, Lost Israel Found.* (Connecticut: Our Race Publishing Co., 1891).

Totten, Charles A. L. "The Story of Ireland." (Massachusetts: Destiny, 1946). *The Kingdom of David,* accessed July 8, 2015. www.thehouseofwemyss.com/page/the-story-of-ireland-by-professor-totten.

Wilkinson, James. *The Coronation Chair and the Stone of Destiny.* (London: Tudsbury Press, 2006).

ABOUT THE AUTHOR

D. A. Brittain writes adventure-filled stories that illustrate biblical truth through compelling and realistic characters. In addition to being a passionate student of the Bible and ancient history, she has traveled throughout Europe and the Middle East, giving her the opportunity to research and explore the land, historic sites, and larger-than-life heroes and heroines appearing in Judah's Scepter and the Sacred Stone, the first in a series of historical novels.